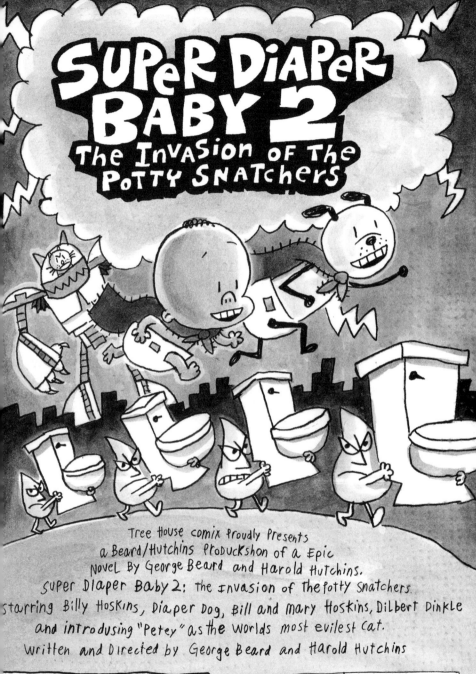

SUPER DIAPER BABY 2
The Invasion of the Potty Snatchers

Tree House comix proudly Presents
a Beard/Hutchins ProDUCKshon of a Epic
Novel By George Beard and Harold Hutchins.
SUPER DIAPER BABY 2: the Invasion of the Potty Snatchers.
starring Billy Hoskins, Diaper Dog, Bill and mary Hoskins, Dilbert Dinkle
and introdusing "Petey" as the Worlds most evilest cat.
Written and Directed by George Beard and Harold Hutchins

THE BLUE SKY PRESS
An Imprint of Scholastic Inc. • New York

this novel
has been
rated:

TA

TOTALLY AWESOME!!!
Some material may be too
Awesome for Boring old grown-ups

For Madison
Mancini

THE BLUE SKY PRESS

Be sure to check out
Dav Pilkey's Extra-Crunchy Web Site O' Fun at
www.pilkey.com.

Library of Congress Control Number: 2011922743
ISBN 978-0-545-17532-6
18 17 16 15 14 13 12   18 19/0
Printed in the United States of America   23
First printing, June 2011

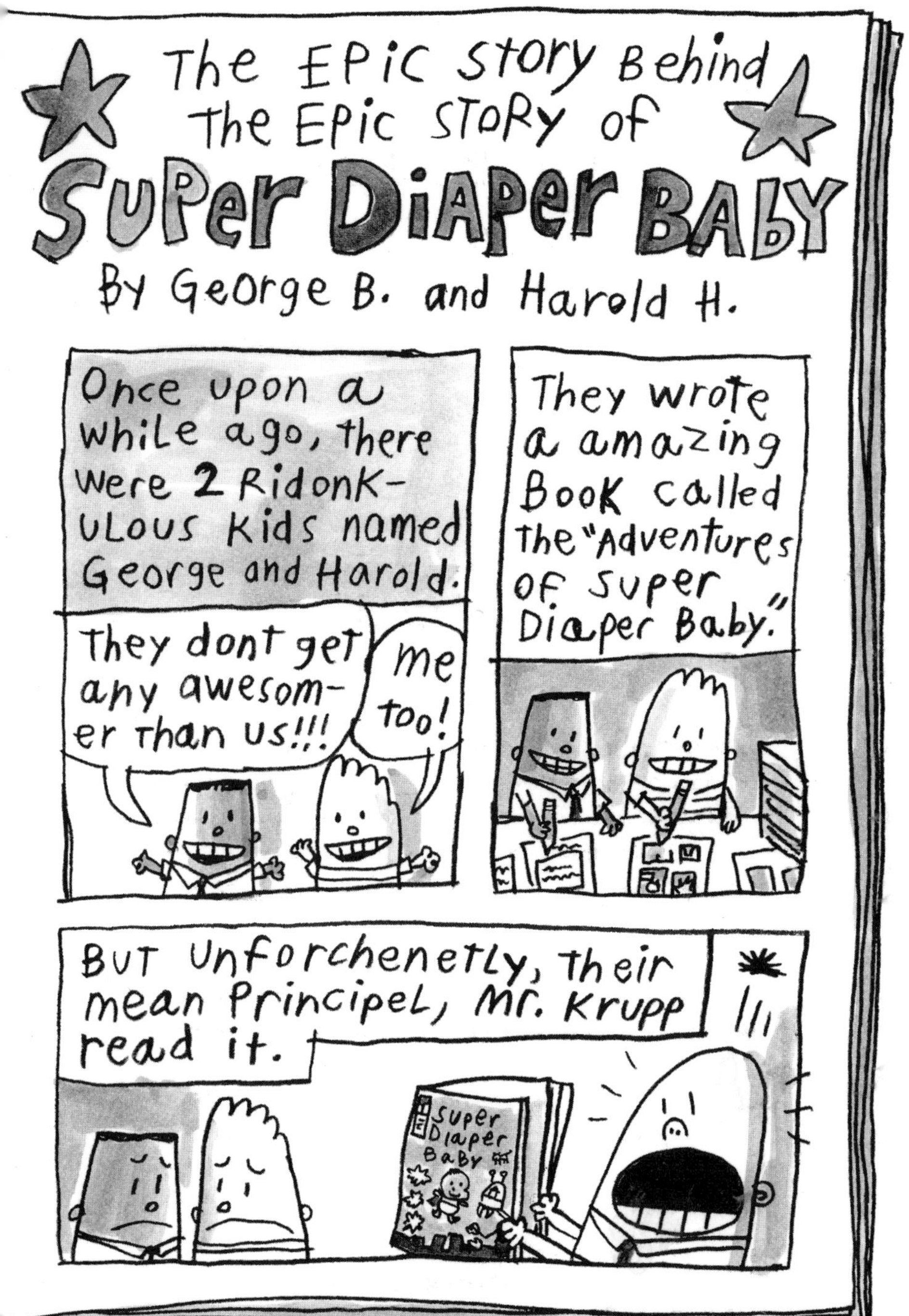
The Epic Story Behind the Epic Story of
Super Diaper Baby
By George B. and Harold H.
Once upon a while ago, there were 2 Ridonk-ulous kids named George and Harold.
They dont get any awesomer than us!!!
me too!
They wrote a amazing Book called the "Adventures of Super Diaper Baby."
BUT Unforchenetly, their mean Principel, Mr. Krupp read it.
Super Diaper Baby

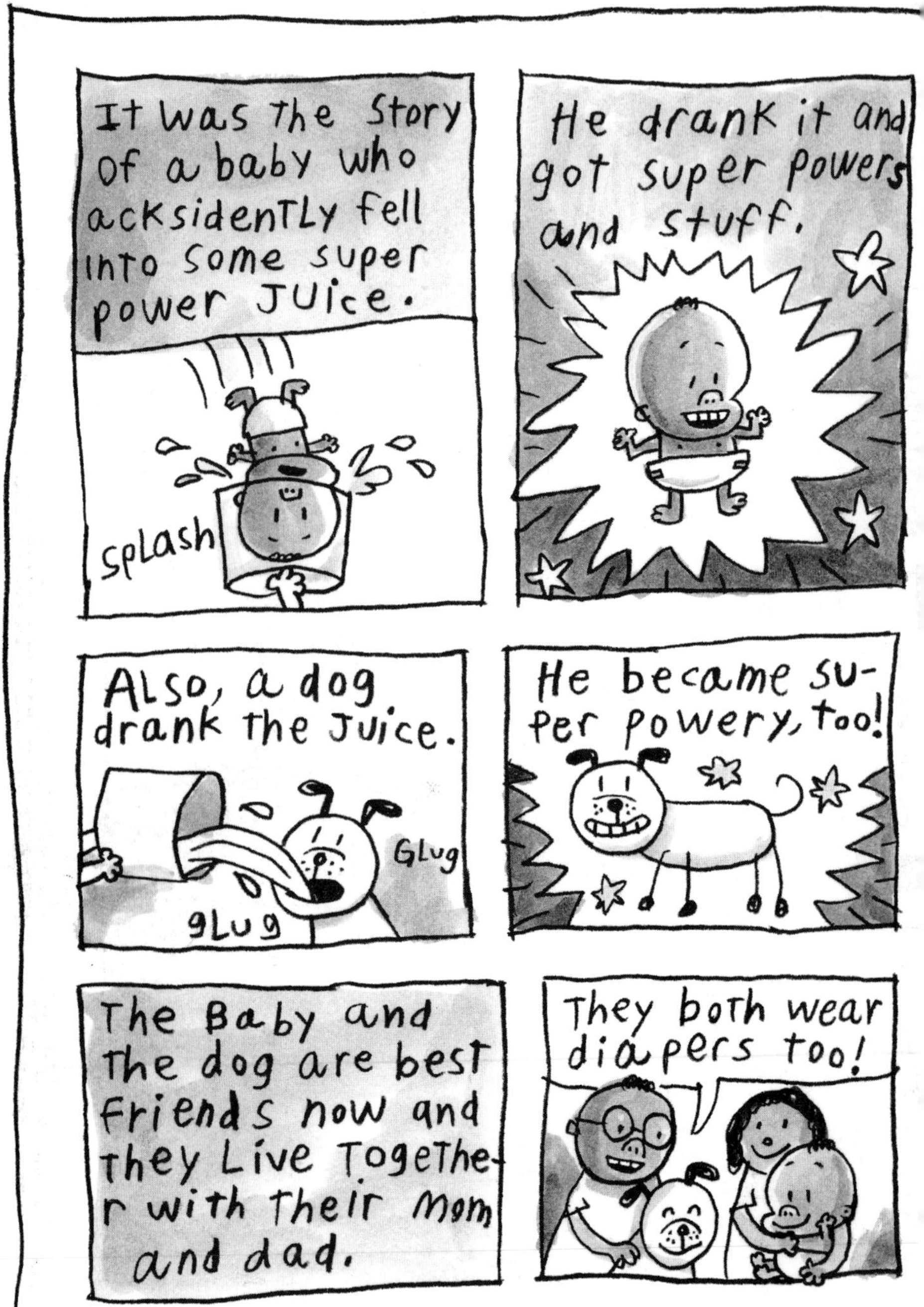
It was the story of a baby who acksidently fell into some super power Juice.
splash
He drank it and got super powers and stuff.
Also, a dog drank the Juice.
Glug
glug
He became super powery, too!
The Baby and the dog are best friends now and they Live Together with their mom and dad.
They both wear diapers too!

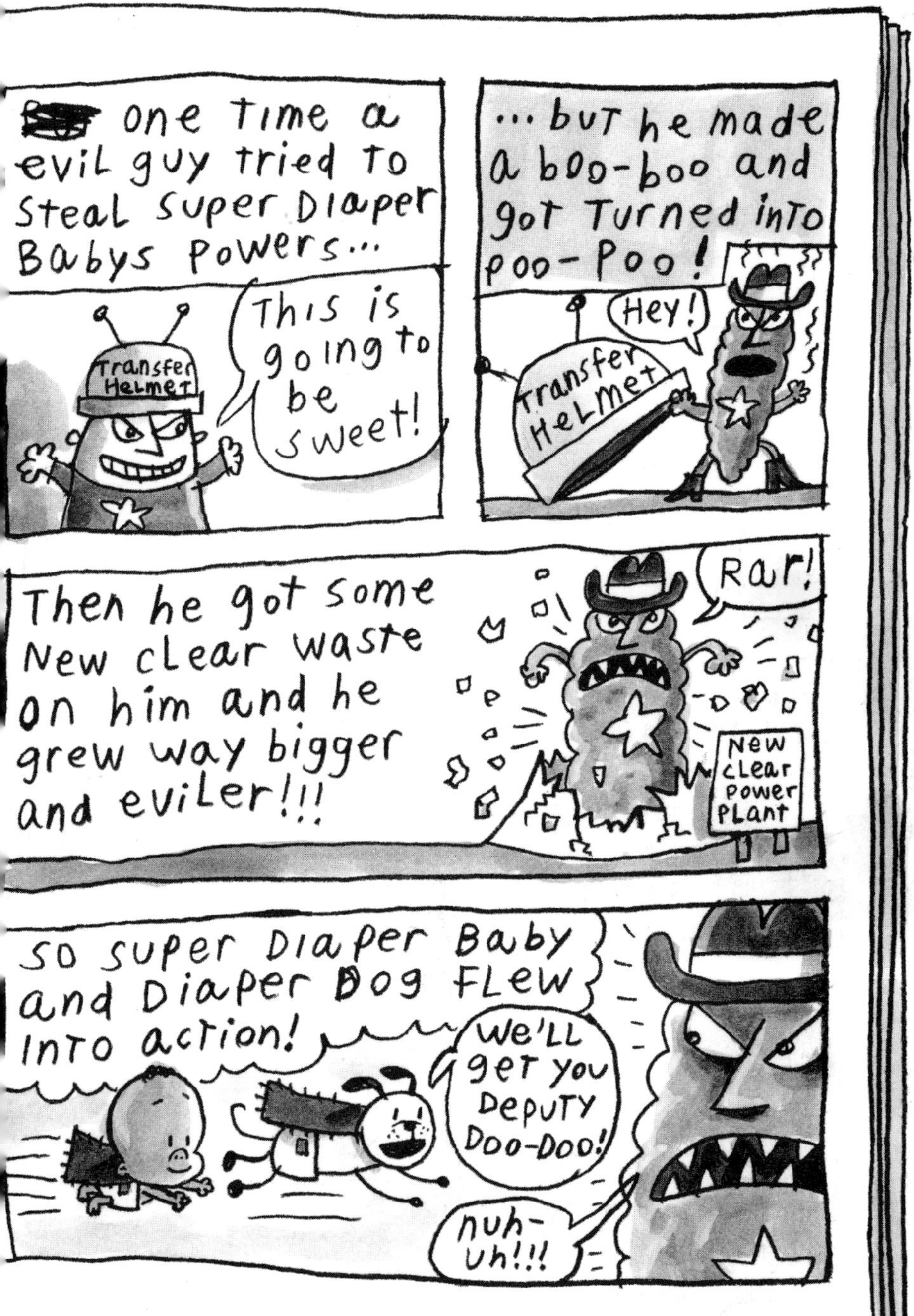
[redacted] one time a evil guy tried to steal Super Diaper Babys powers...
This is going to be sweet!
Transfer Helmet
...but he made a boo-boo and got turned into poo-poo!
Hey!
Transfer Helmet
Then he got some New clear waste on him and he grew way bigger and eviler!!!
Rar!
New clear power plant
So Super Diaper Baby and Diaper Dog flew into action!
We'll get you Deputy Doo-Doo!
nuh-uh!!!

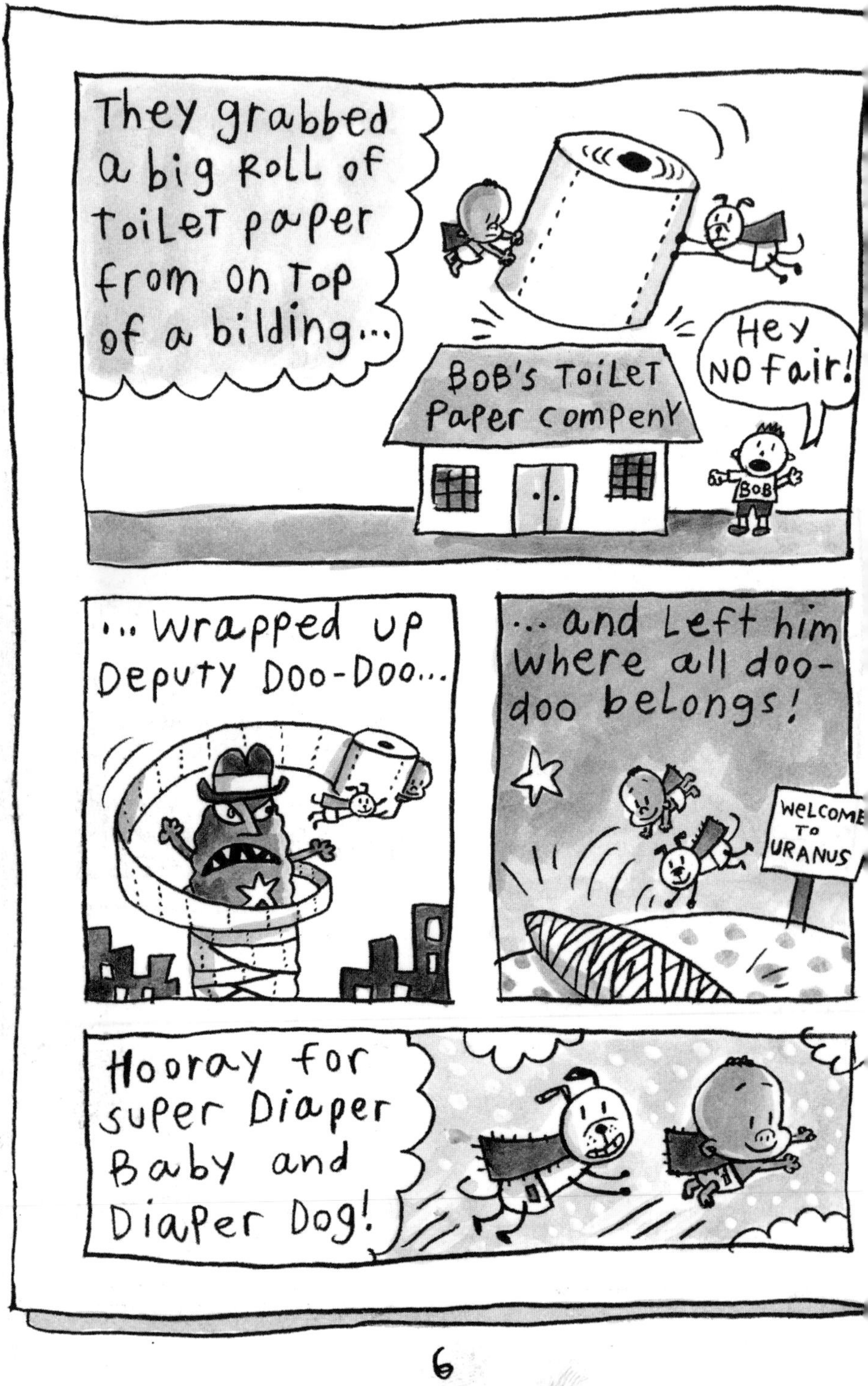
They grabbed a big Roll of toilet paper from on top of a bilding...
BOB'S TOILET Paper compenY
Hey NO fair!
BOB
...Wrapped up Deputy Doo-Doo...
...and Left him where all doo-doo belongs!
WELCOME TO URANUS
Hooray for super Diaper Baby and Diaper Dog!

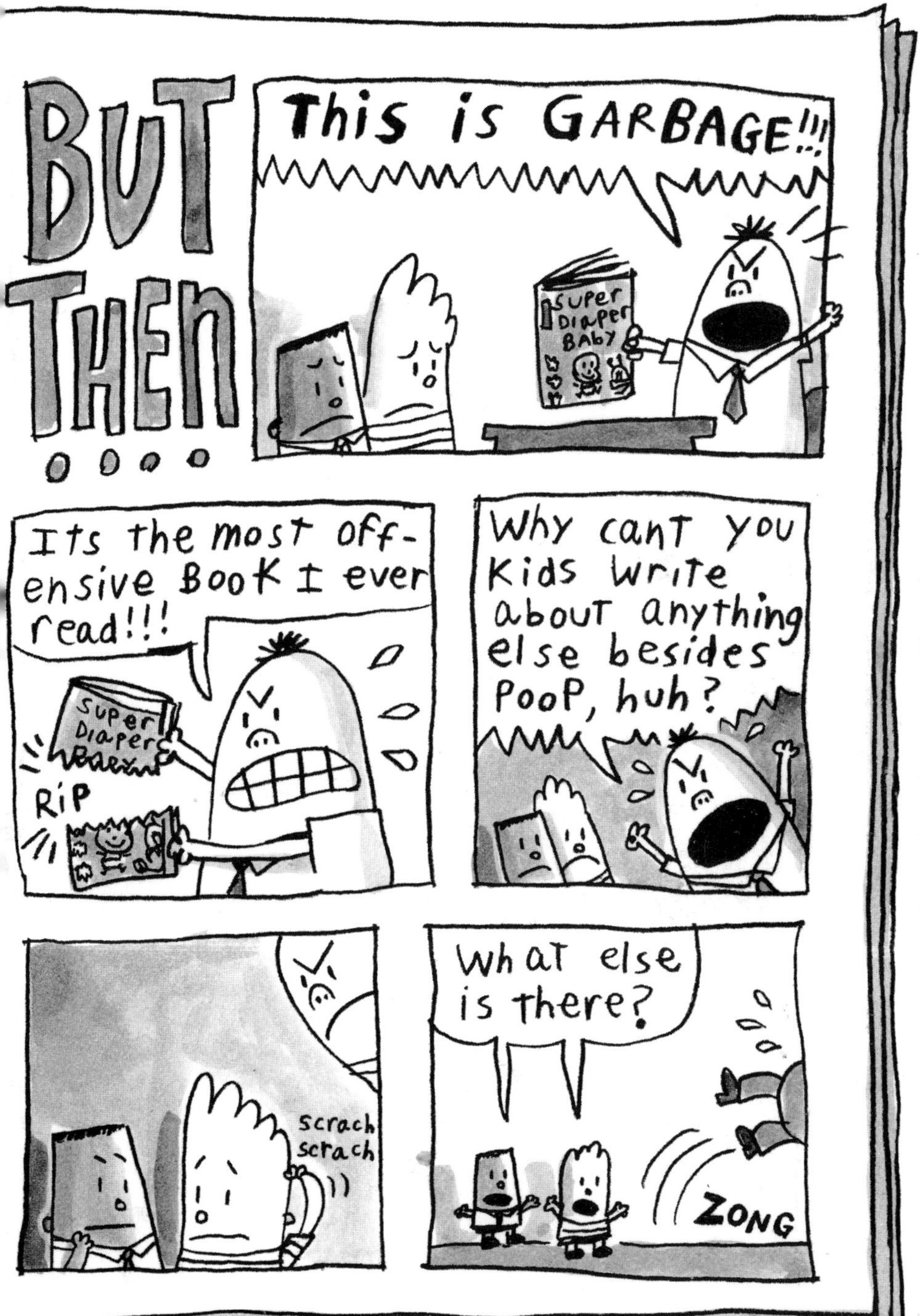
BUT THEN....
This is GARBAGE!!!
Super Diaper Baby
Its the most offensive Book I ever read!!!
Super Diaper Baby
RIP
Why cant you Kids write about anything else besides Poop, huh?
scrach scrach
What else is there?
ZONG

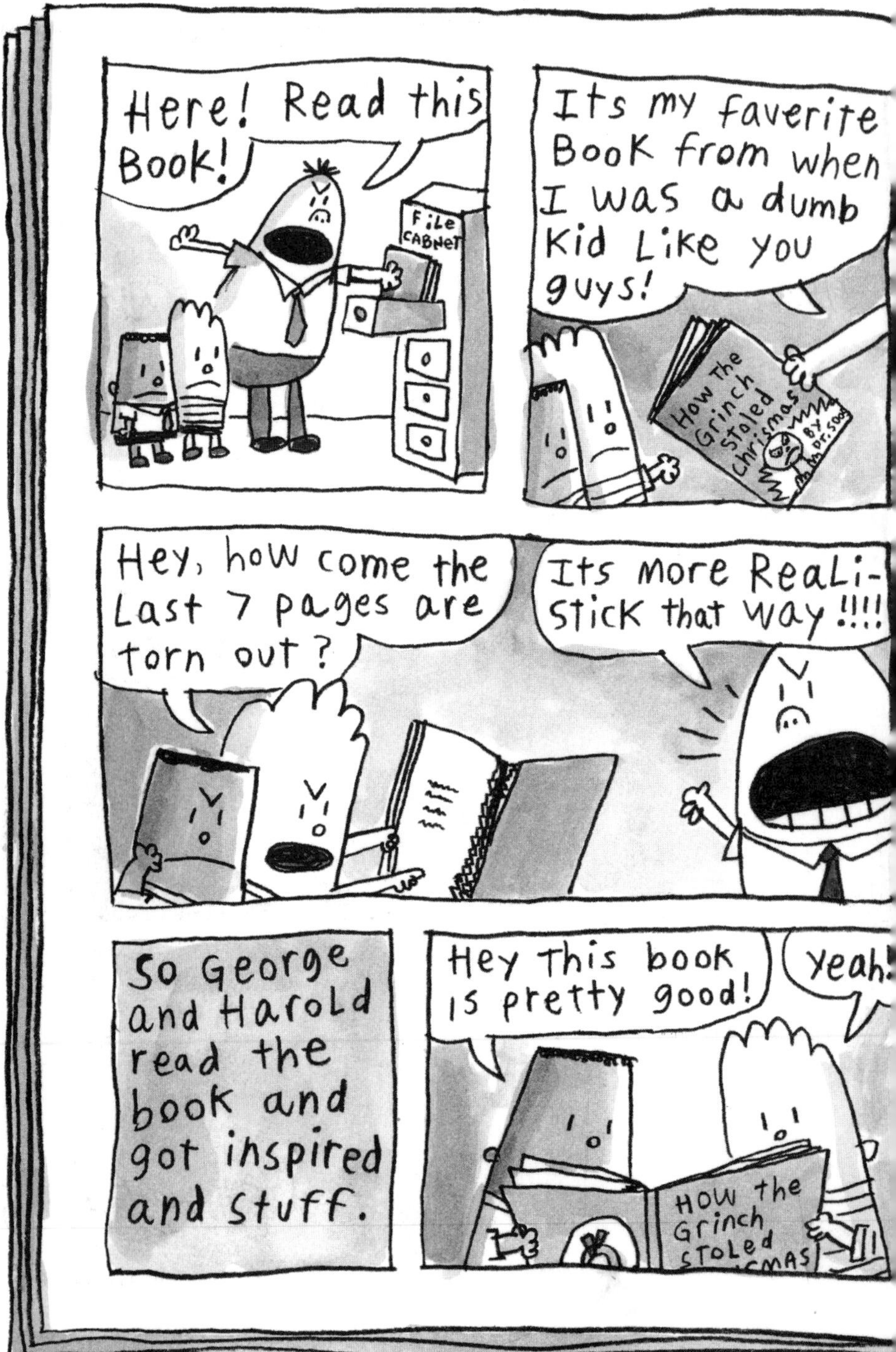
Here! Read this Book!
FiLe CABNET
Its my faverite Book from when I was a dumb Kid Like you guys!
How The Grinch Stoled chrismas
BY DR.
Hey, how come the Last 7 pages are torn out?
Its more ReaLi-Stick that way!!!!
So George and Harold read the book and got inspired and stuff.
Hey This book is pretty good!
Yeah!
HOW the Grinch STOLed

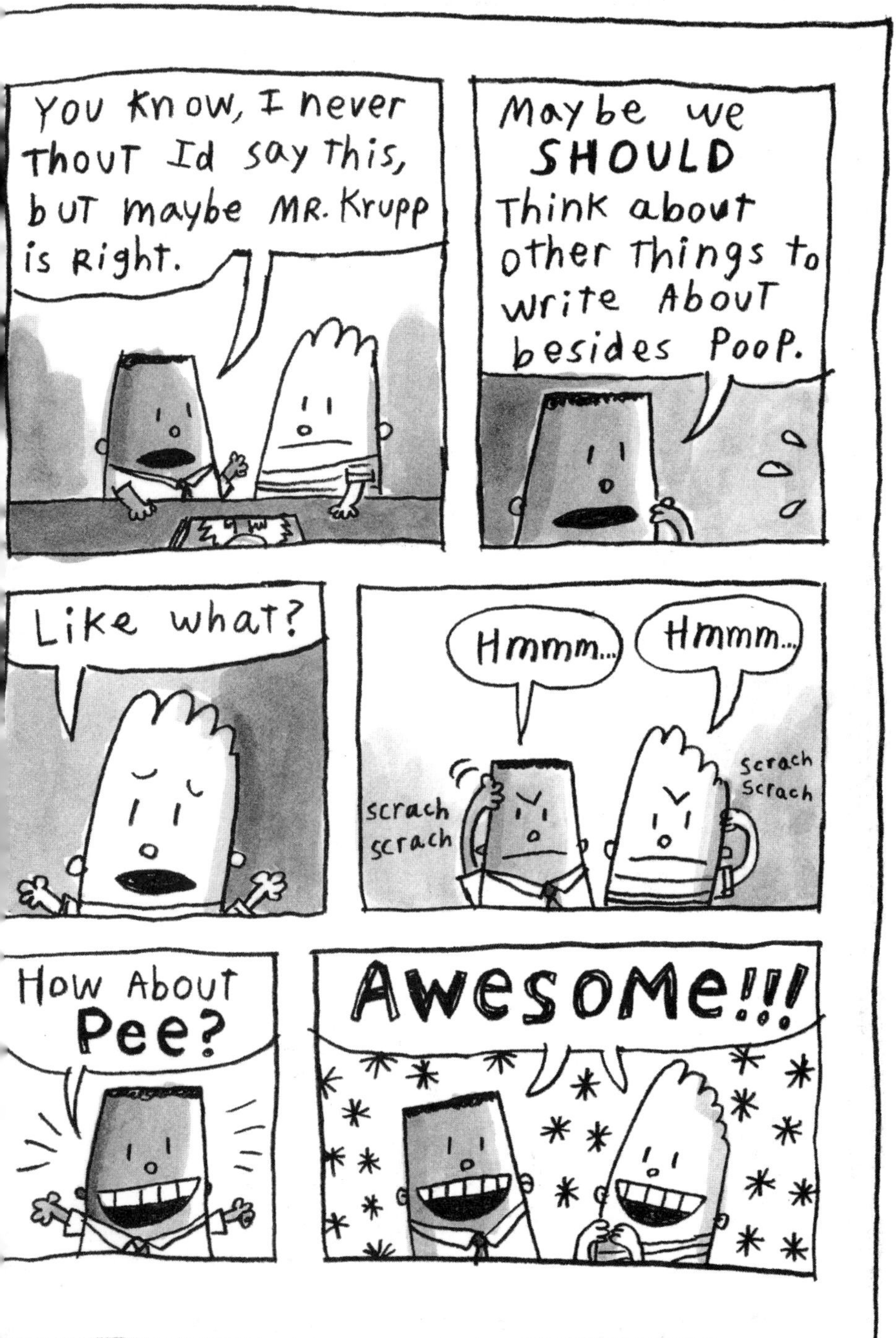
You know, I never thout Id say this, but maybe Mr. Krupp is right.
Maybe we SHOULD think about other things to write About besides Poop.
Like what?
Hmmm...
Hmmm...
scrach scrach
scrach scrach
How About Pee?
AWESOME!!!

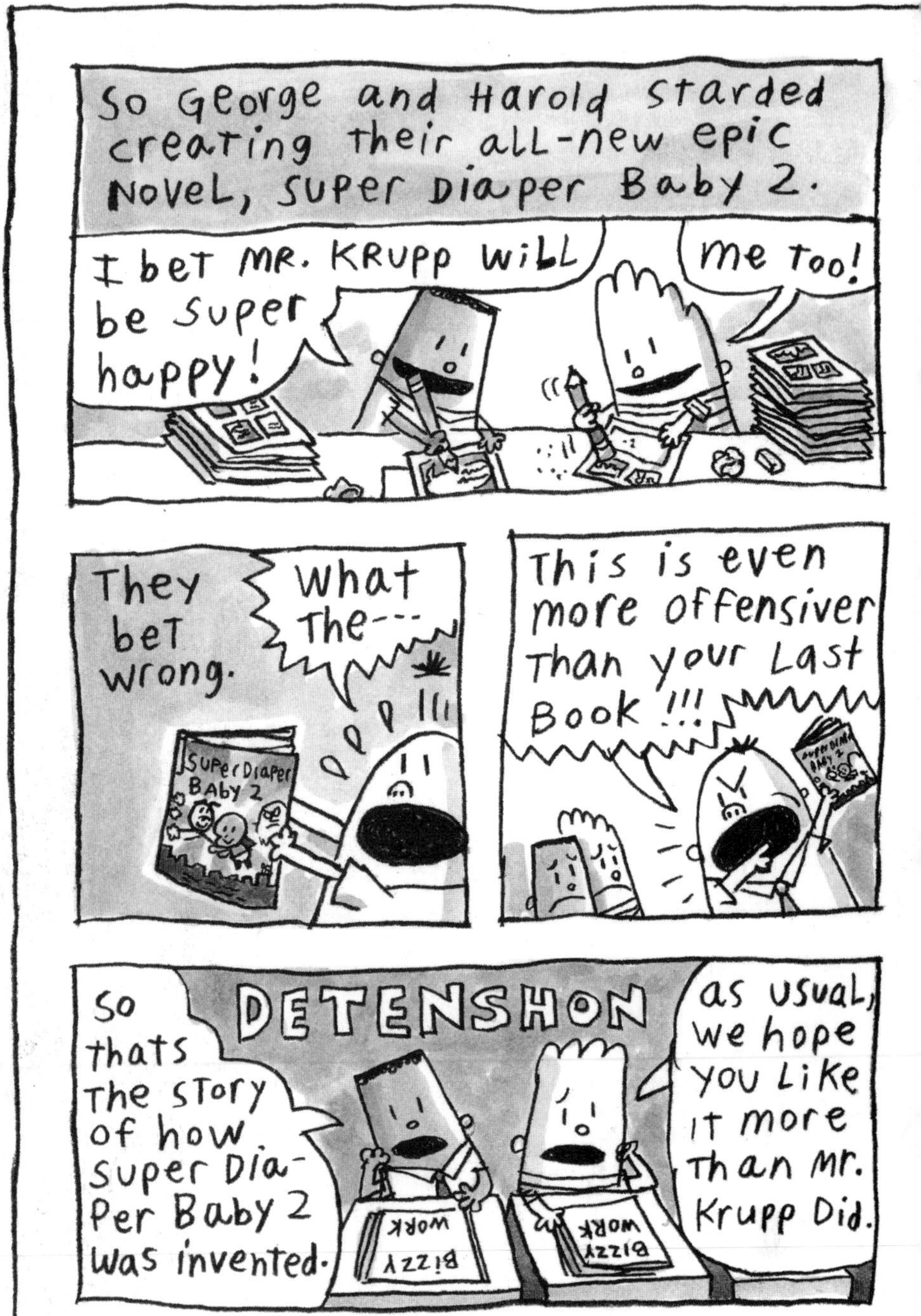
So George and Harold starded creating their all-new epic Novel, Super Diaper Baby 2.
I bet Mr. Krupp will be super happy!
me too!
They bet wrong.
What the---
Super Diaper Baby 2
This is even more offensiver Than your Last Book!!!
So thats the story of how Super Dia-Per Baby 2 was invented.
DETENSHON
as usual, we hope you Like it more Than Mr. Krupp Did.
Bizzy work
Bizzy work

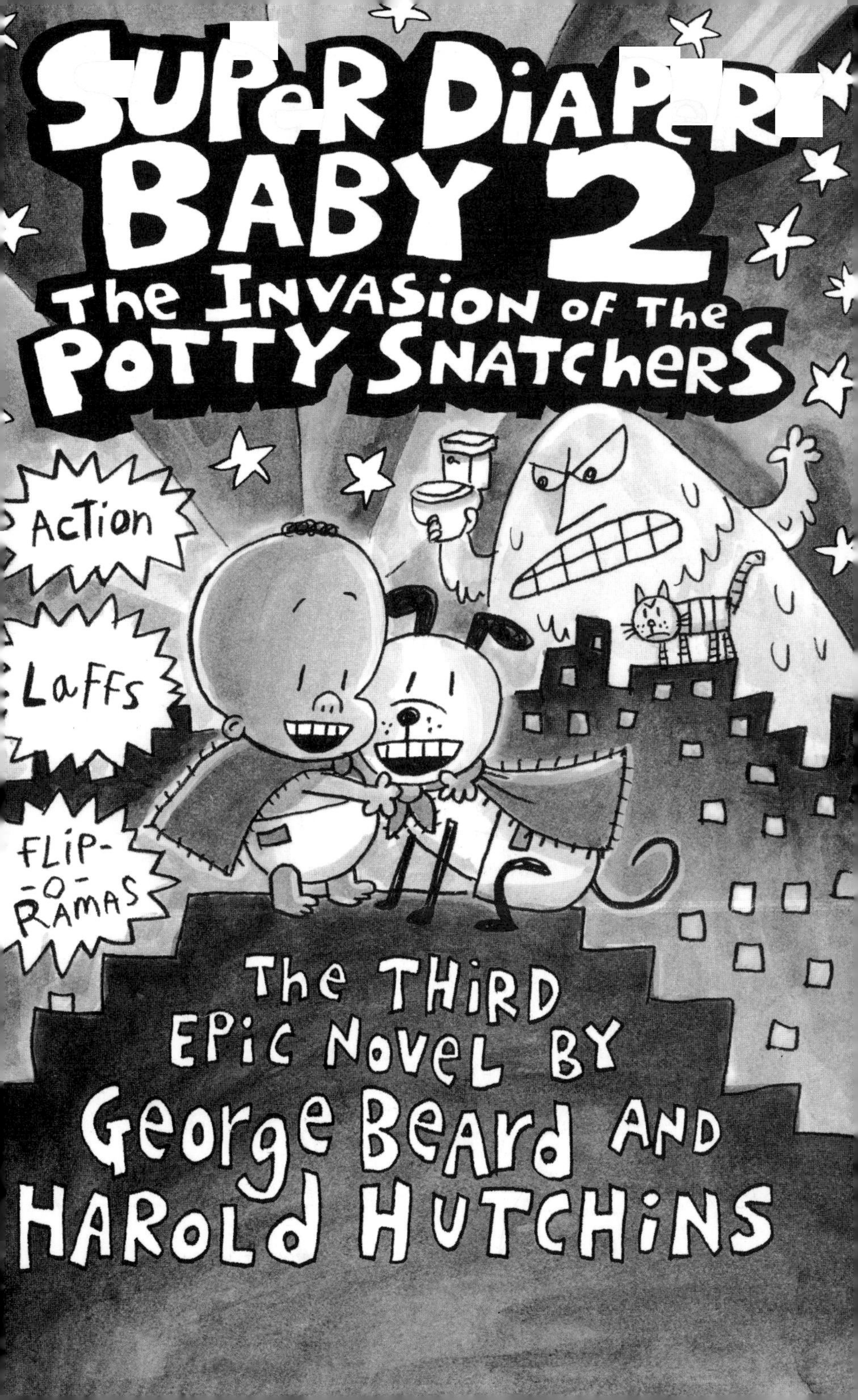
SUPER DIAPER BABY 2
The INVASION of The POTTY SNATCHERS
Action
LaFFs
FLIP-O-RAMAS
The THIRD EPIC NOVEL BY
George Beard AND HAROLD HUTCHINS

Chapters

12

Chapter 1

"A Day at the Park"

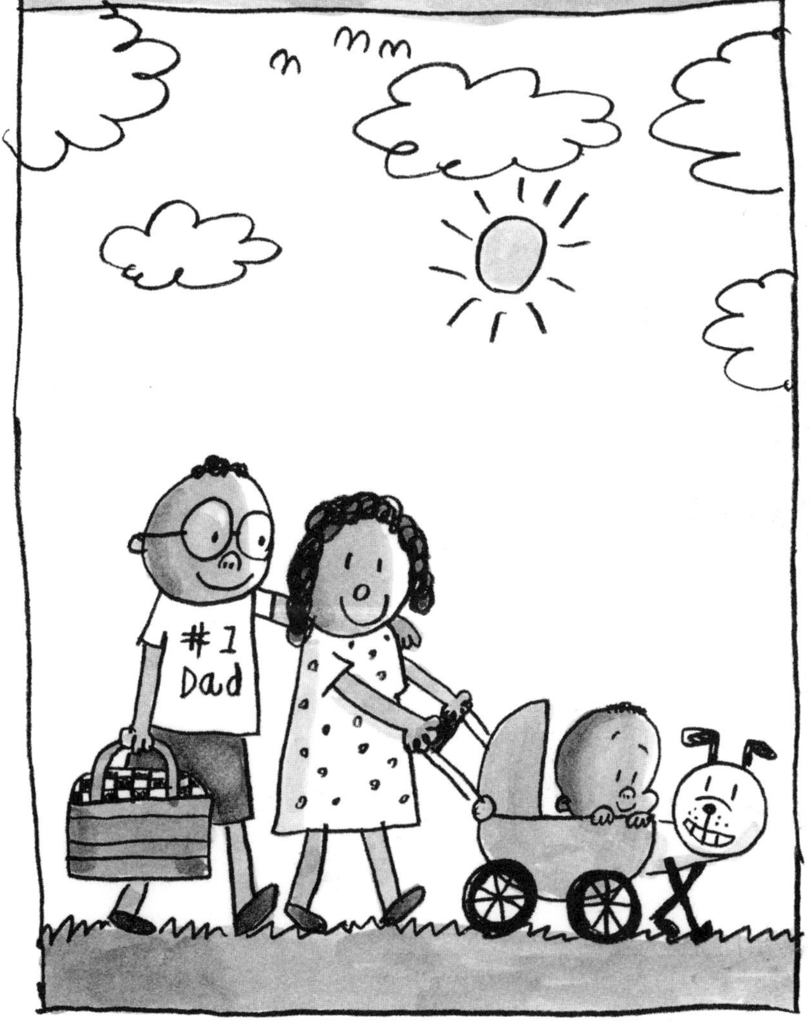

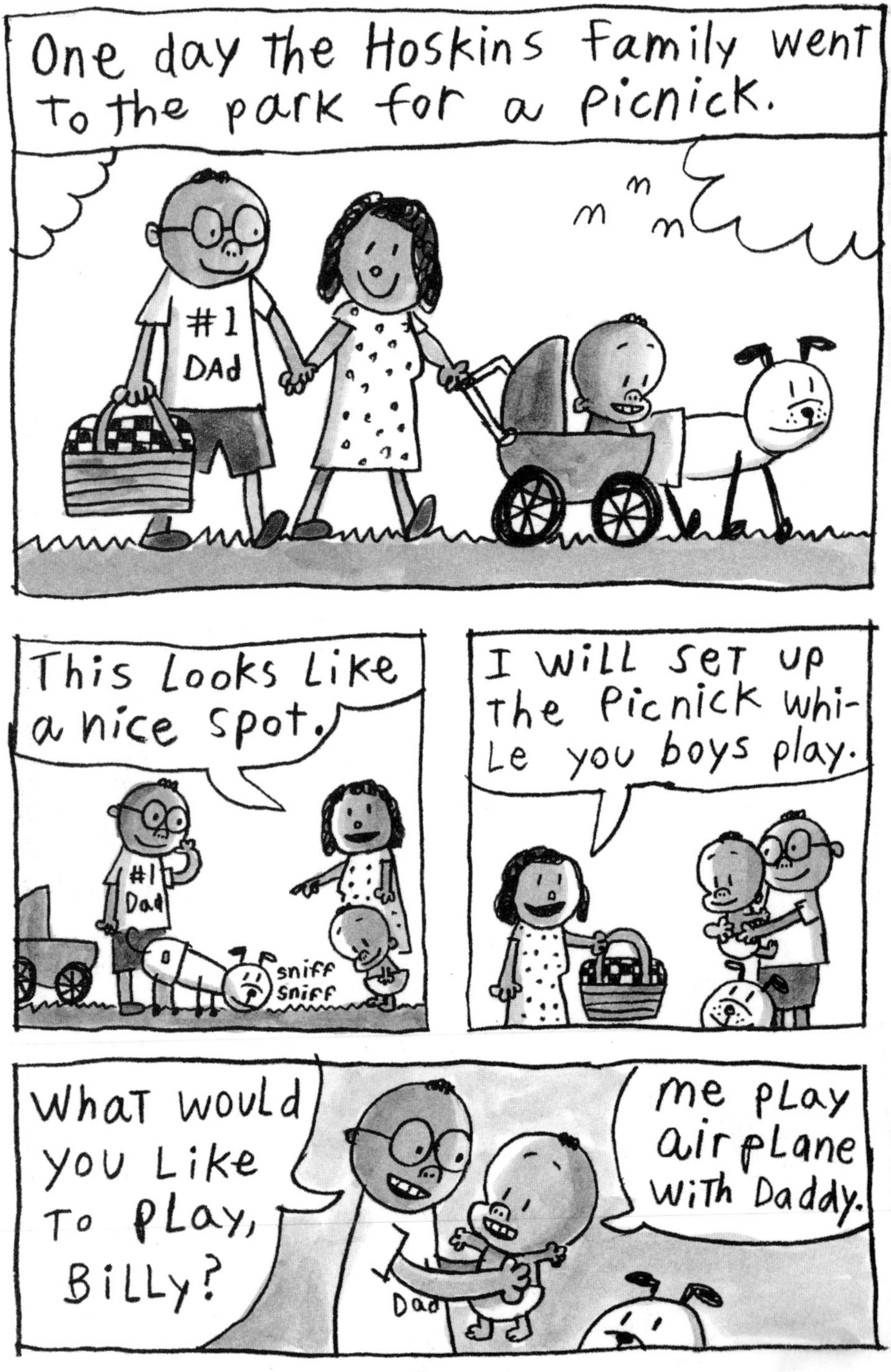
One day the Hoskins family went to the park for a picnick.
#1 DAD
This looks like a nice spot.
#1 Dad
sniff sniff
I will set up the picnick whi-le you boys play.
What would you like to play, Billy?
me play airplane with Daddy.
Dad

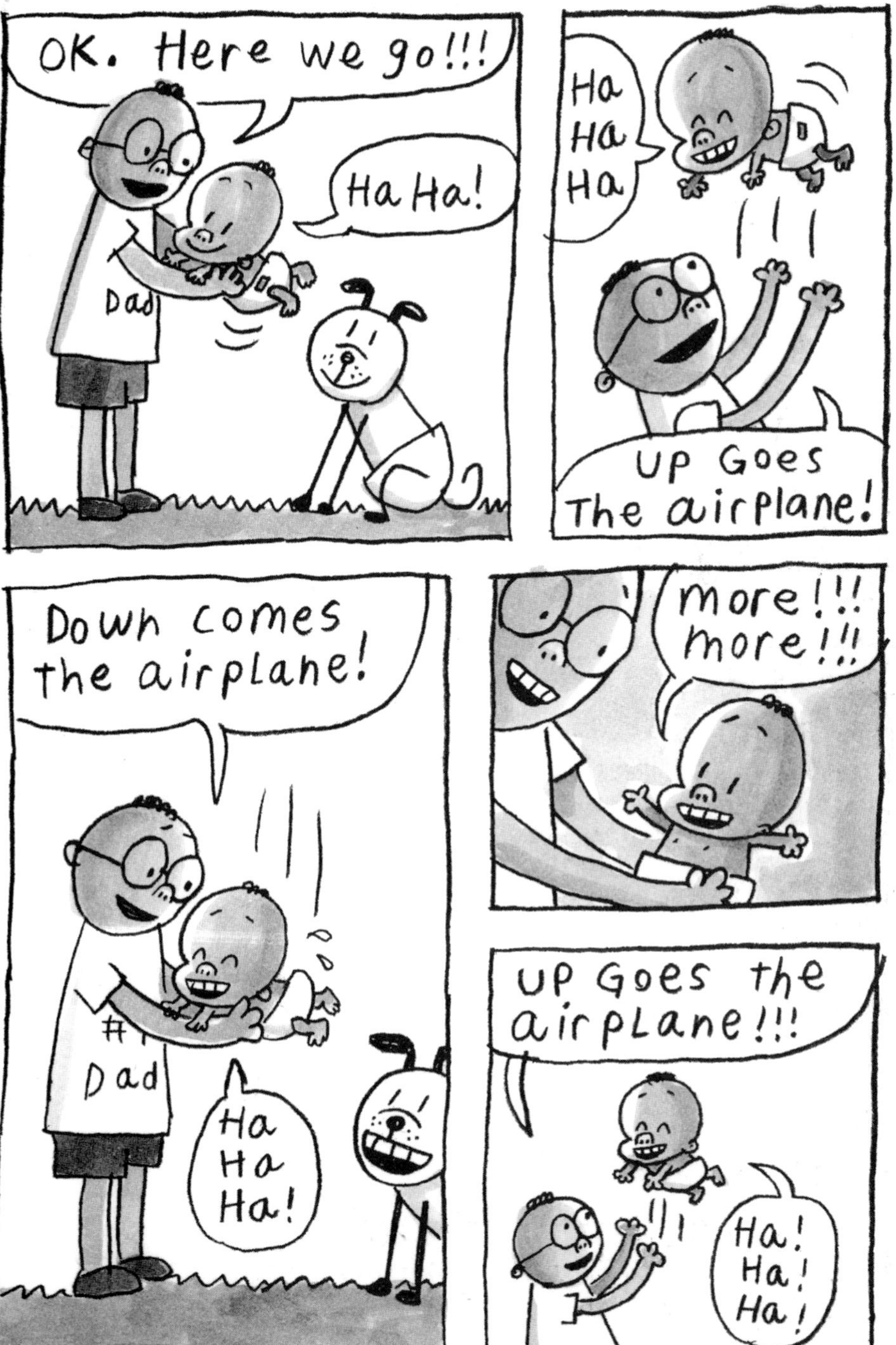
OK. Here we go!!!
Dad
Ha Ha!
Ha Ha Ha
Up Goes The airplane!
Down comes the airplane!
#1 Dad
Ha Ha Ha!
more!!! more!!!
Up Goes the airplane!!!
Ha! Ha! Ha!

Down comes the airplane!
Ha Ha Ha!
Dad
More! More! MORE!

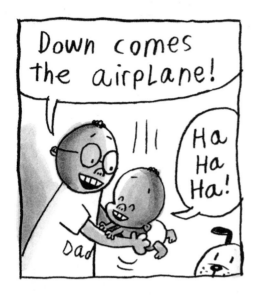

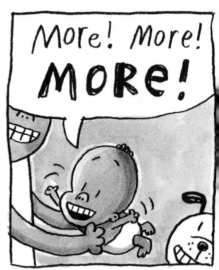

WARNING

The following Flip pages start out "cuteish", but get violentish (and even violentish-er) as this novel goes along.

FLIPPER'S DISGRESHON ADVISED

FLIP·O·RAMA

HEres How it WoRks!!!!

STEP 1
PLace your Left hand inside the dotted Lines marked "Left Hand Here". Hold The Book open FLat.

STEP 2
GRasp the Right-hand Page with Your Right thumb and index finger (inside The dotted Lines marked Right ThumB Here").

STEP 3
NOW Quickly FLip The Right-hand Page back and fourTh UnTiL the Pitcher appears To Be Animated!

(for extra Fun, try adding your own sound Afecks).

FLIP-O-RAMA #1

(pages 19 and 21)

Remember, Flip only page 19. While you are Flipping, be shure you can see the pitcher on page 19 And the one on page 21.

IF you Flip Quickly, The two pitchers will start to Look Like one Animated pitcher.

Dont forget to add your own Sound Afecks!

Left Hand Here

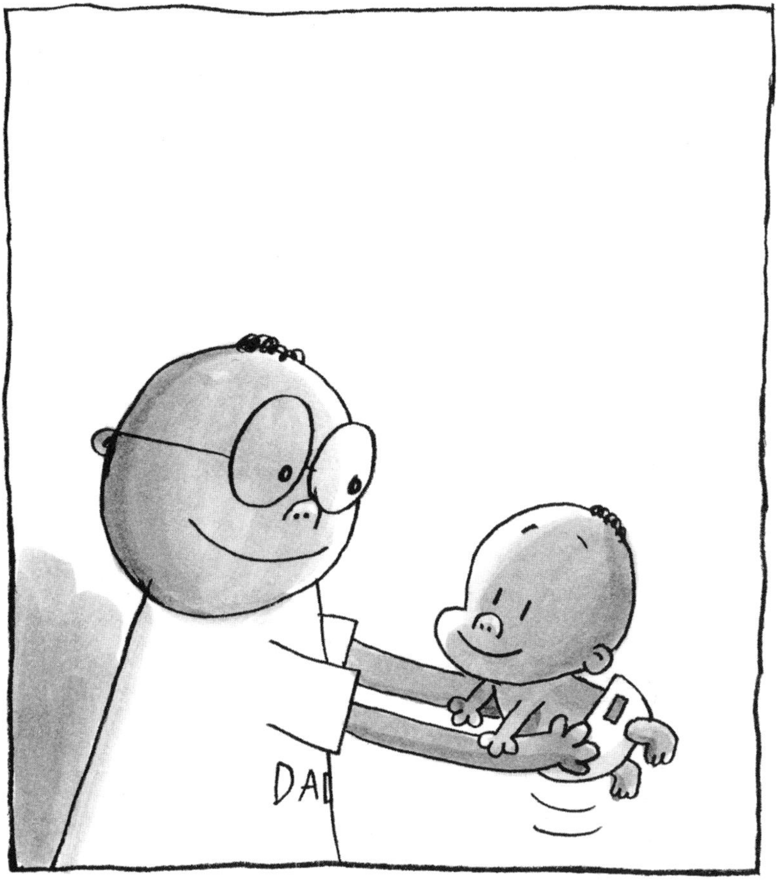
DAD

Down Goes the Airplane...

Right Thumb Here

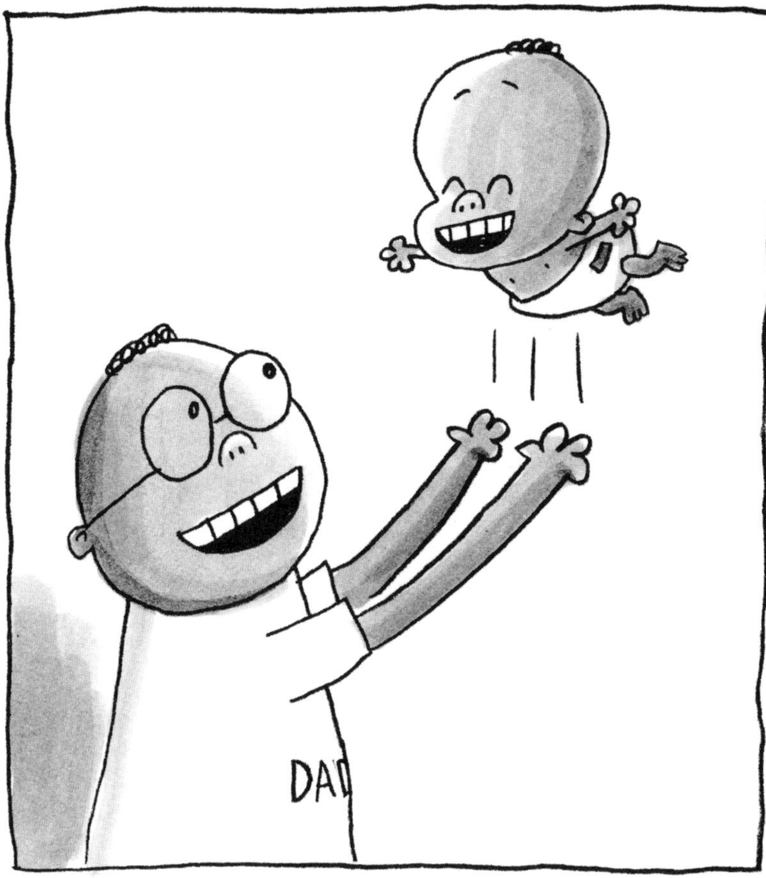
DAD

Up Goes the AirpLane...

Was that fun?
yeah!
Dad
Now Daddys Turn!!!
No—wait!
#1 Dad

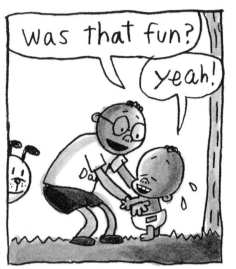

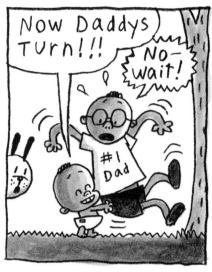

FLiP-O-RAMA 2

Remember---FLip OnLy page 23. while you are FLipping, be shure you can see the pitcher on page 23 and the one on page 25.

If you flip QuickLy, The Two pitchers will start To Look Like one anima-ted pitcher.

DonT Forget Those sound afecks!

Left Hand Here

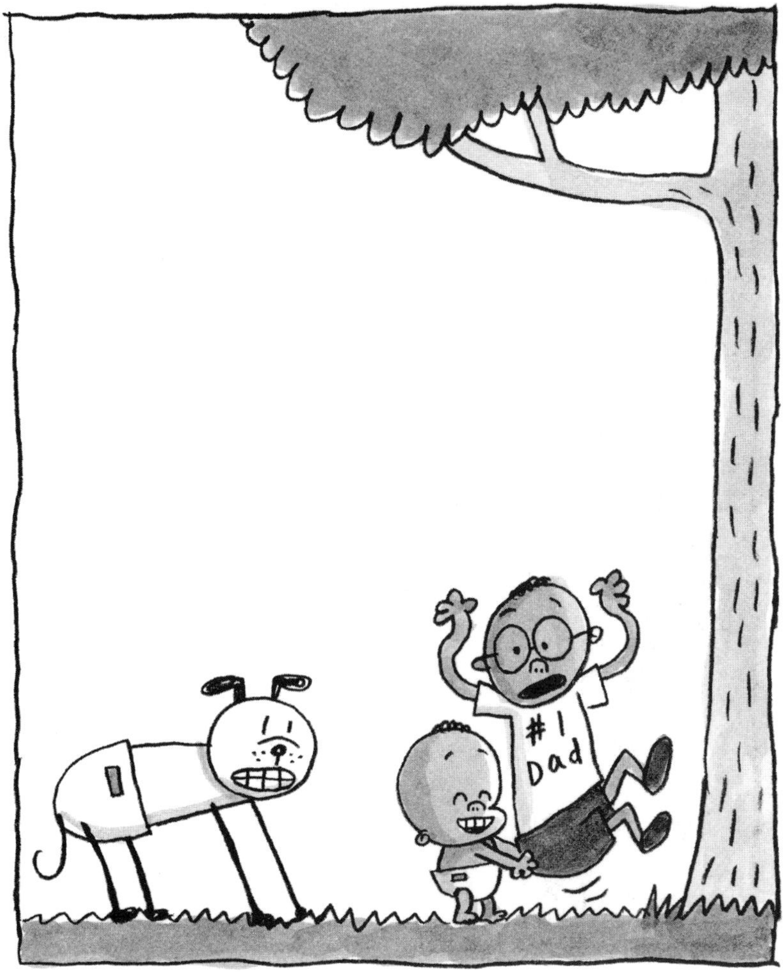
#1 Dad

Down go the airplane

Right Thumb Here

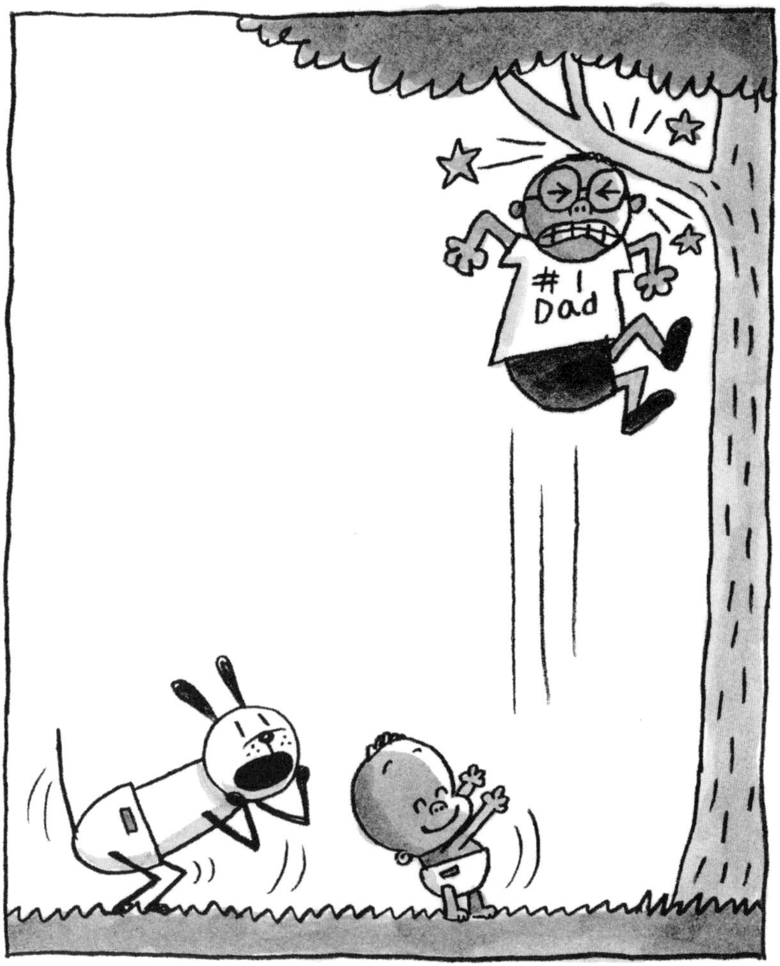
#1
Dad

Up go the airplane

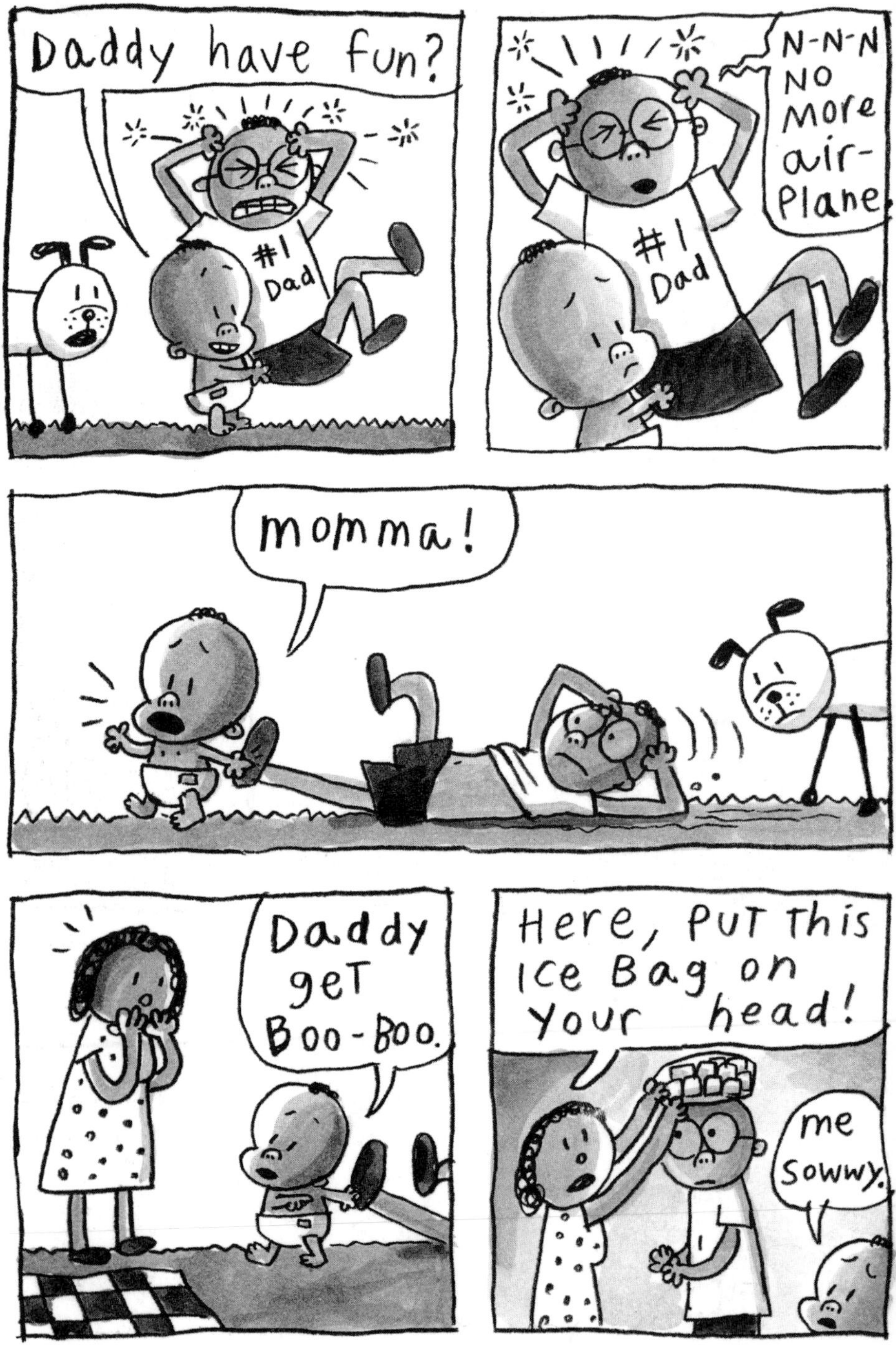
Daddy have fun?
N-N-N NO More air-Plane.
momma!
Daddy geT Boo-Boo.
Here, PUT This Ice Bag on Your head!
me sowwy.

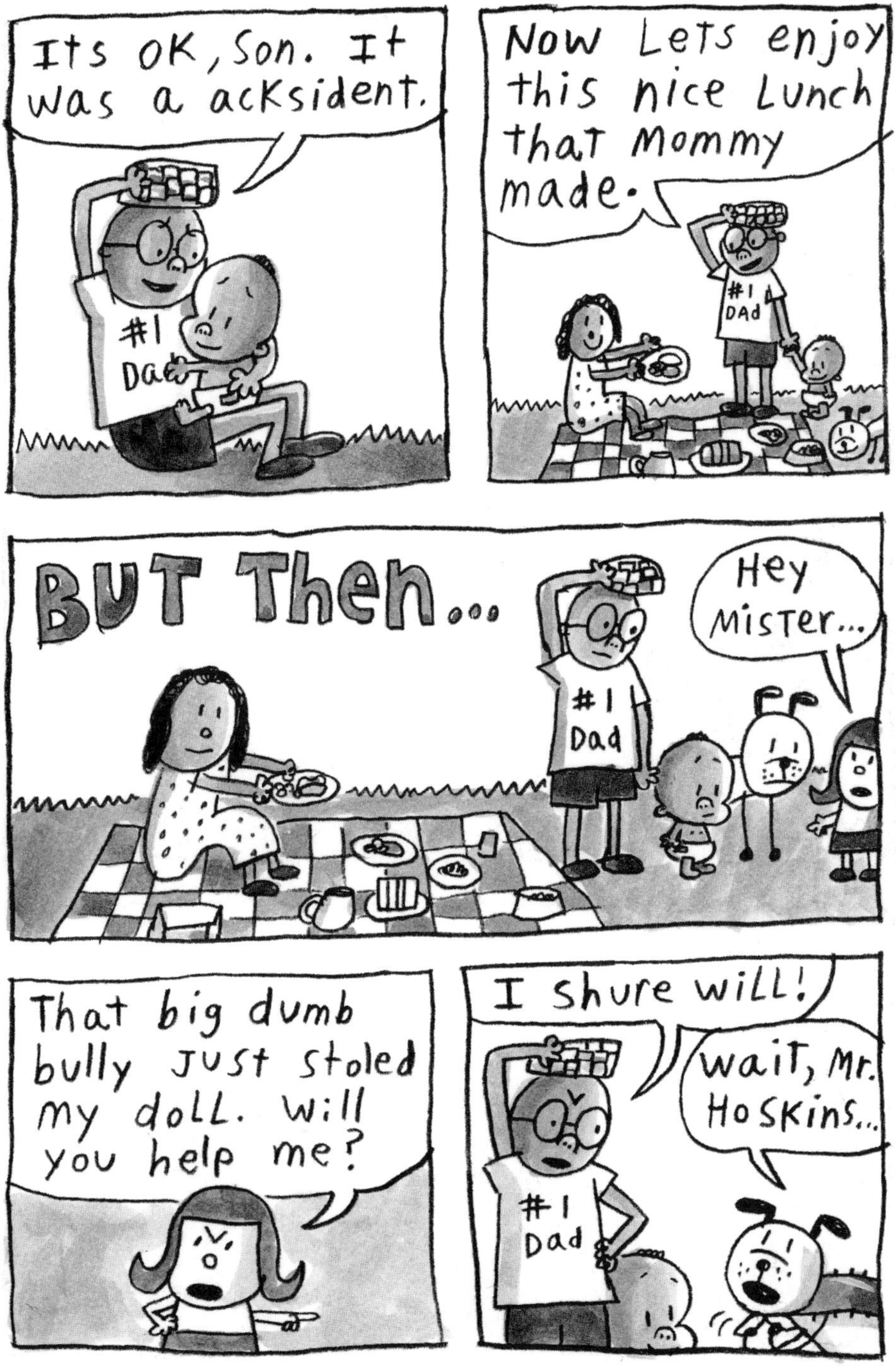
Its OK, Son. It was a acksident.
Now Lets enjoy this nice Lunch that Mommy made.
BUT Then...
Hey Mister...
That big dumb bully JUST stoled my doLL. Will you help me?
I shure wiLL!
wait, Mr. HoSKins...

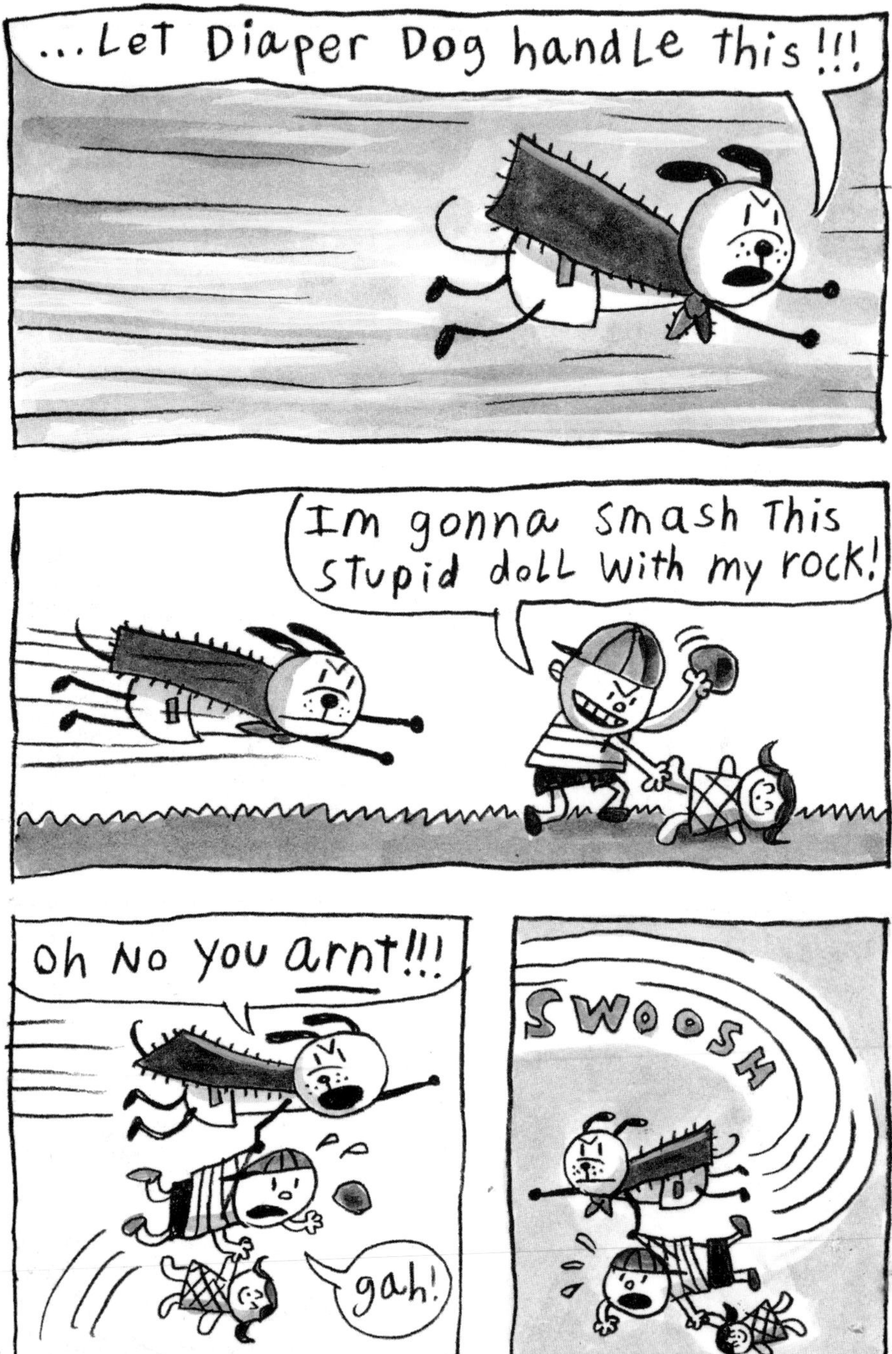
...Let Diaper Dog handle this!!!
Im gonna smash This stupid doll with my rock!
Oh No you arnt!!!
gah!
SWOOSH

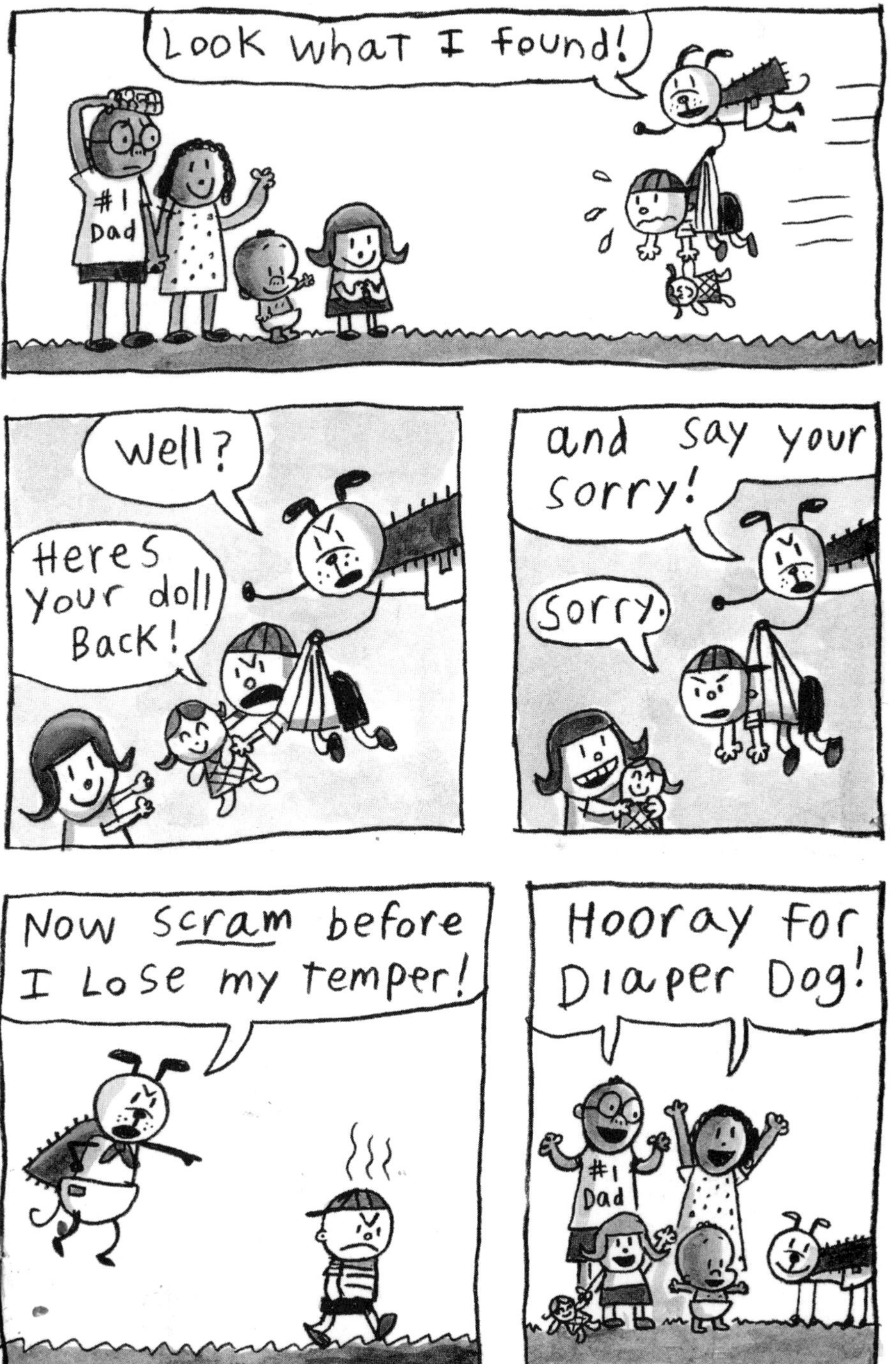
Look what I found!
Well?
Heres your doll Back!
and say your sorry!
Sorry.
Now scram before I Lose my temper!
Hooray for Diaper Dog!

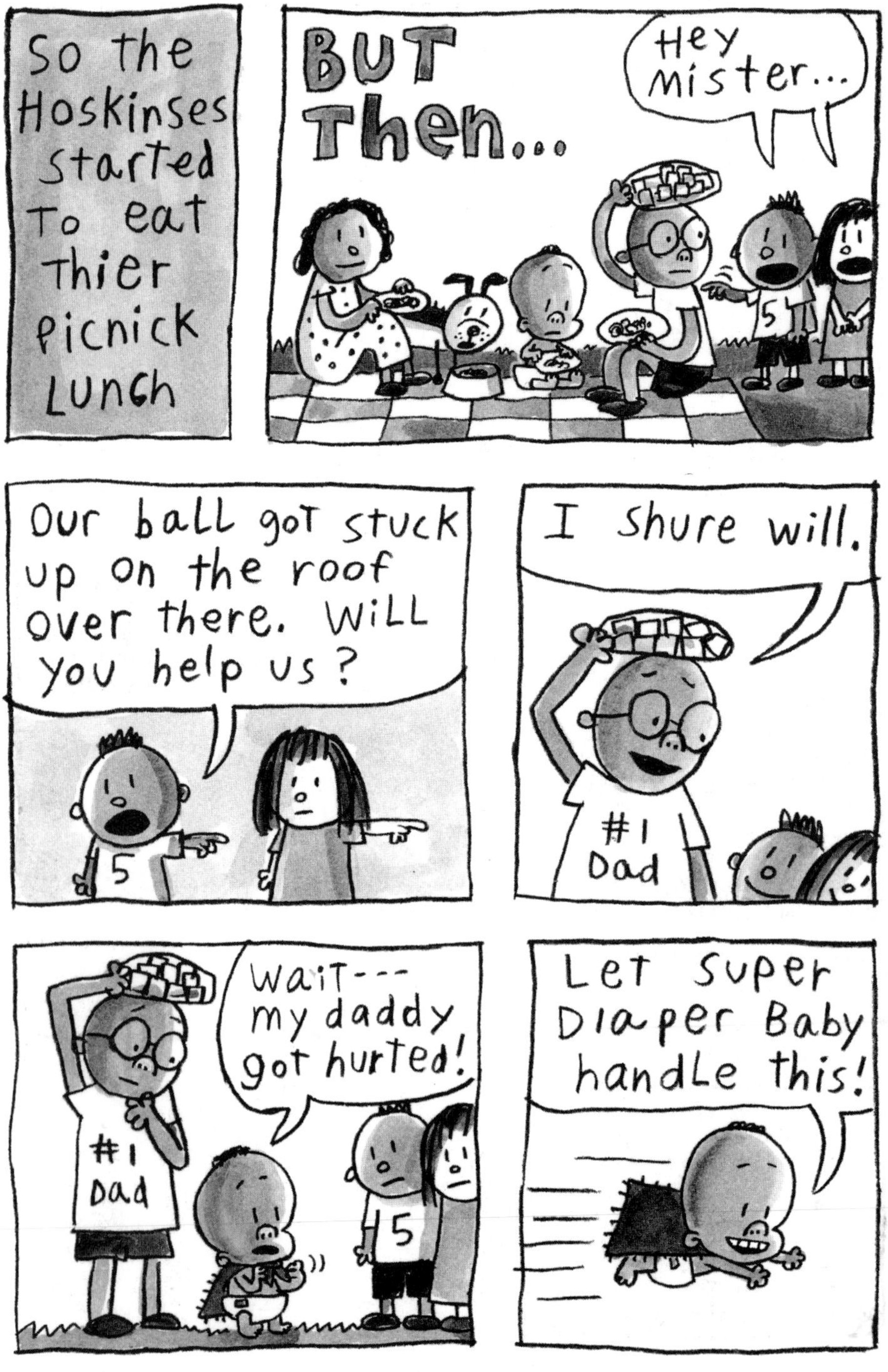
So the Hoskinses started To eat Thier picnick Lunch
BUT Then...
Hey mister...
Our ball got stuck up on the roof over there. Will you help us?
I shure will.
WaiT--- my daddy got hurted!
Let Super Diaper Baby handle this!

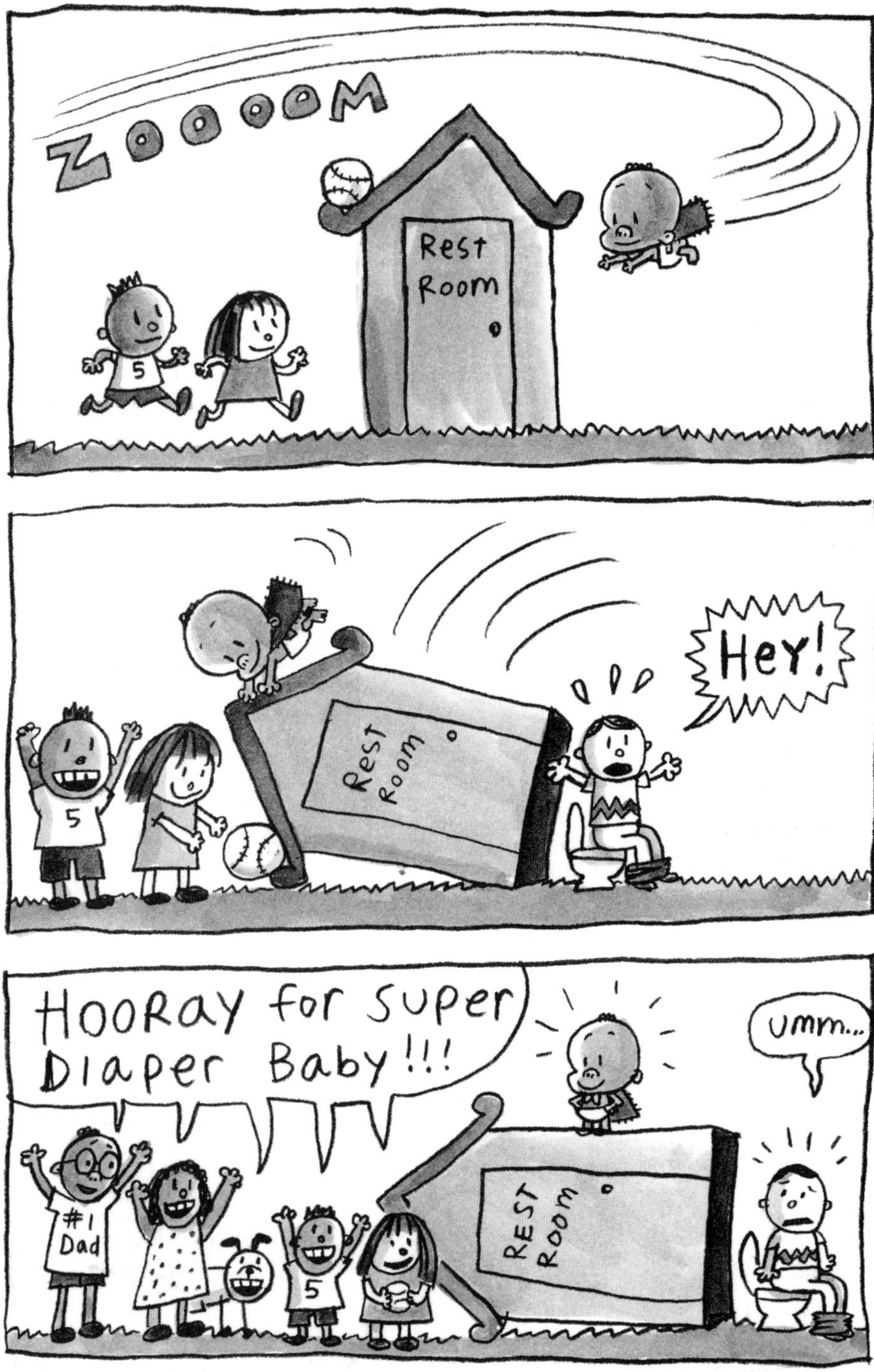
ZOOOOM
Rest Room
Hey!
Rest Room
Hooray for Super Diaper Baby!!!
Umm...
#1 Dad
REST Room

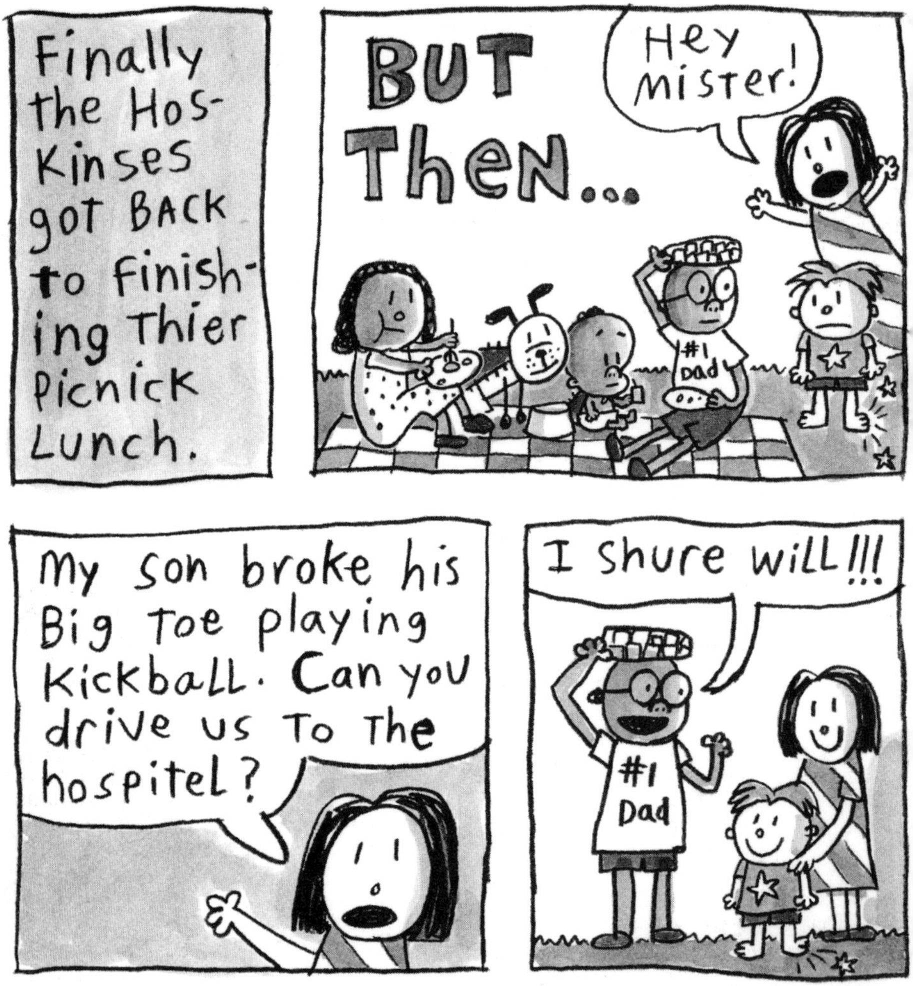
Finally the HosKinses got BACK to Finishing Thier Picnick Lunch.
BUT Then...
Hey Mister!
My son broke his Big Toe playing Kickball. Can you drive us To The hospitel?
I shure will!!!
#1 Dad
Wait, Mr. Hoskins. That will Take Forever!!!

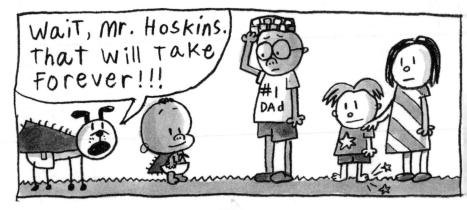

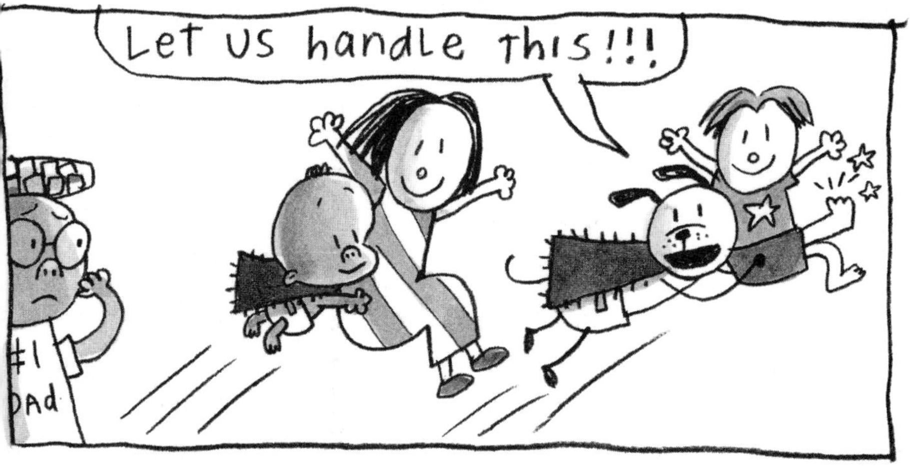
Let us handle this!!!
#1 DAD

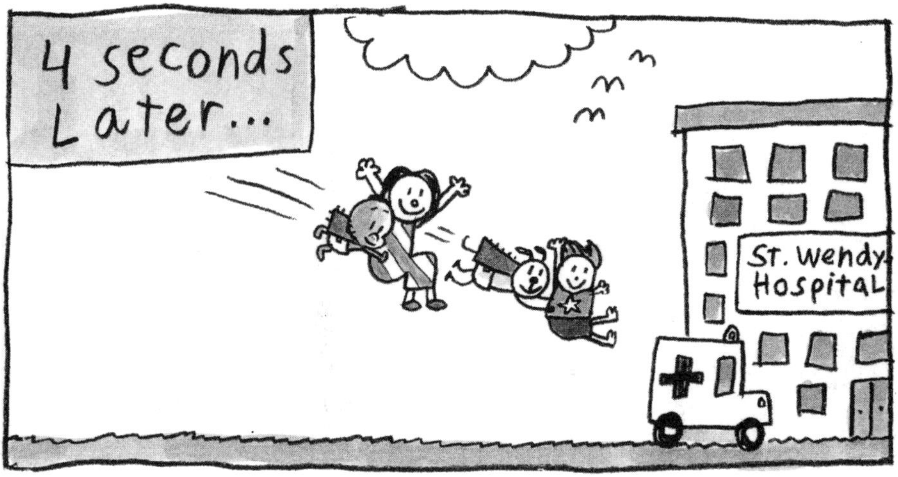
4 seconds Later...
St. Wendy's Hospital

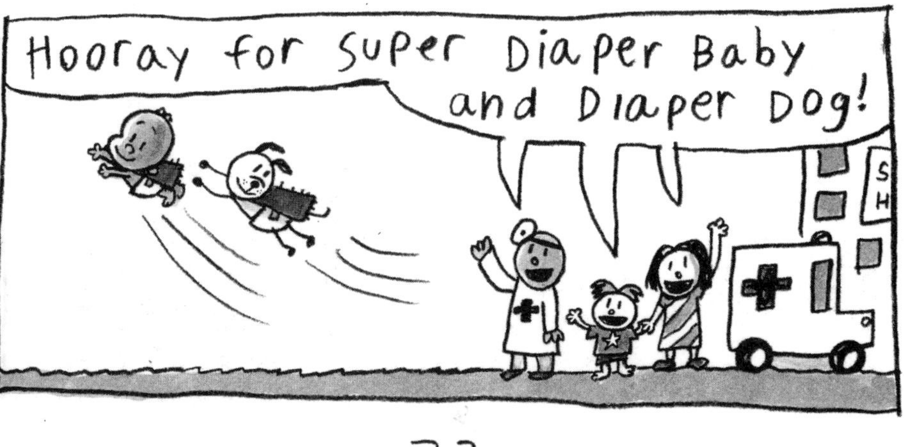
Hooray for Super Diaper Baby and Diaper Dog!

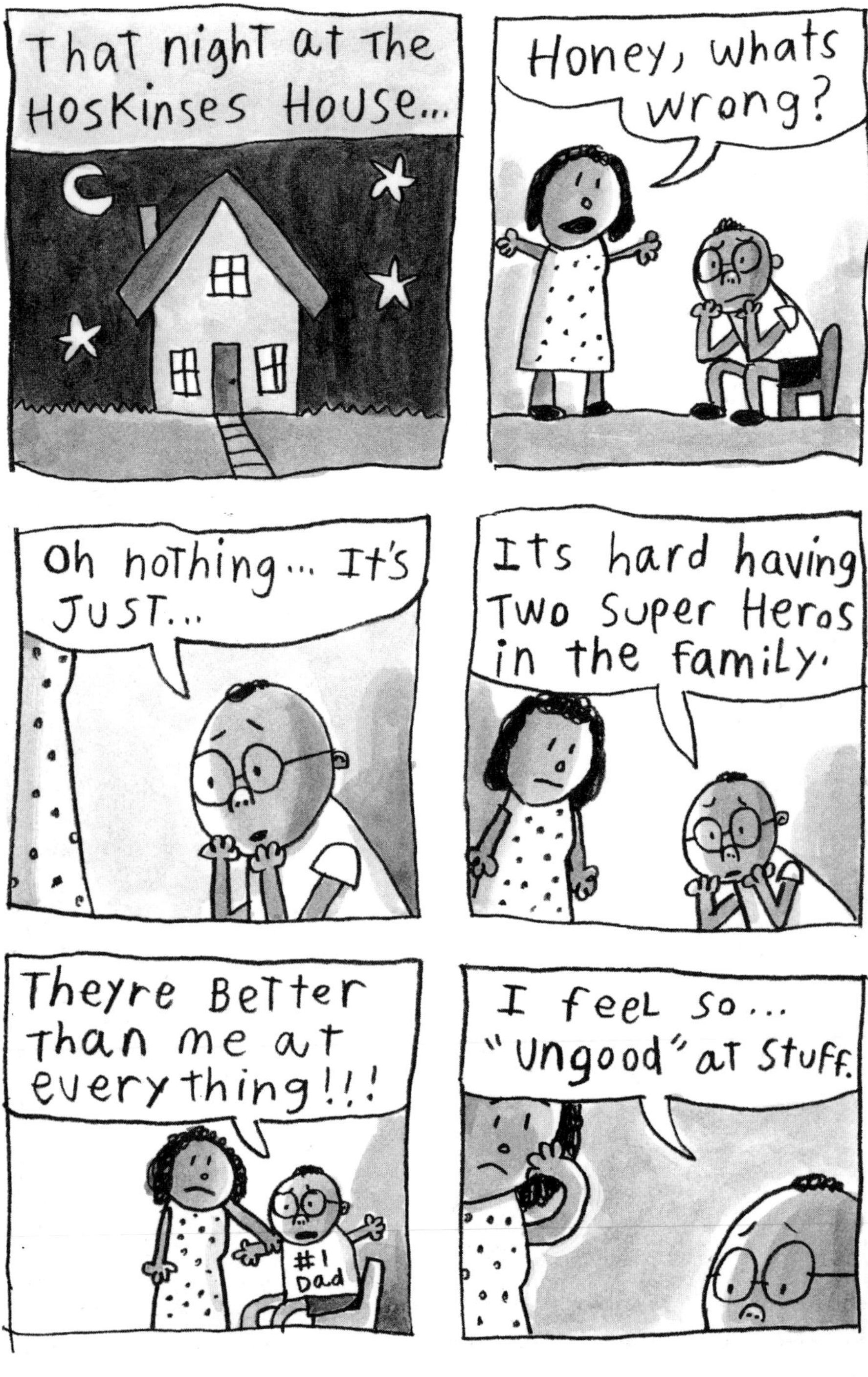
That night at the HosKinses House...
Honey, whats wrong?
Oh nothing... It's JUST...
Its hard having Two Super Heros in the FamiLy.
Theyre Better than me at everything!!!
#1 Dad
I feel so... "Ungood" at Stuff.

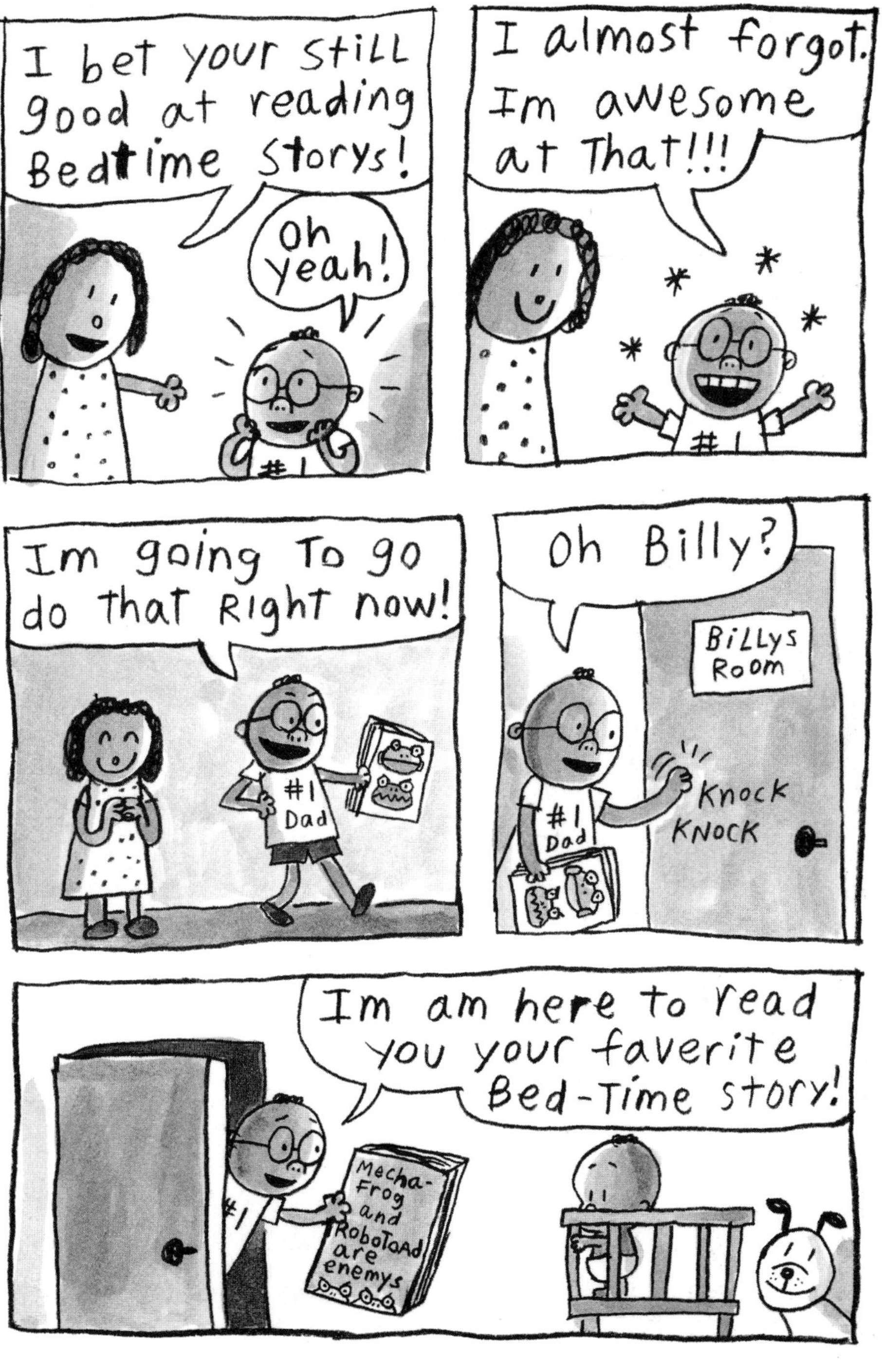
I bet your still good at reading Bedtime Storys!
Oh yeah!
I almost forgot. Im awesome at That!!!
#1
Im going To go do that Right now!
#1 Dad
Oh Billy?
BiLLys Room
#1 Dad
Knock KNOCK
Im am here to read you your faverite Bed-Time story!
Mecha-Frog and RoboToad are enemys
#1

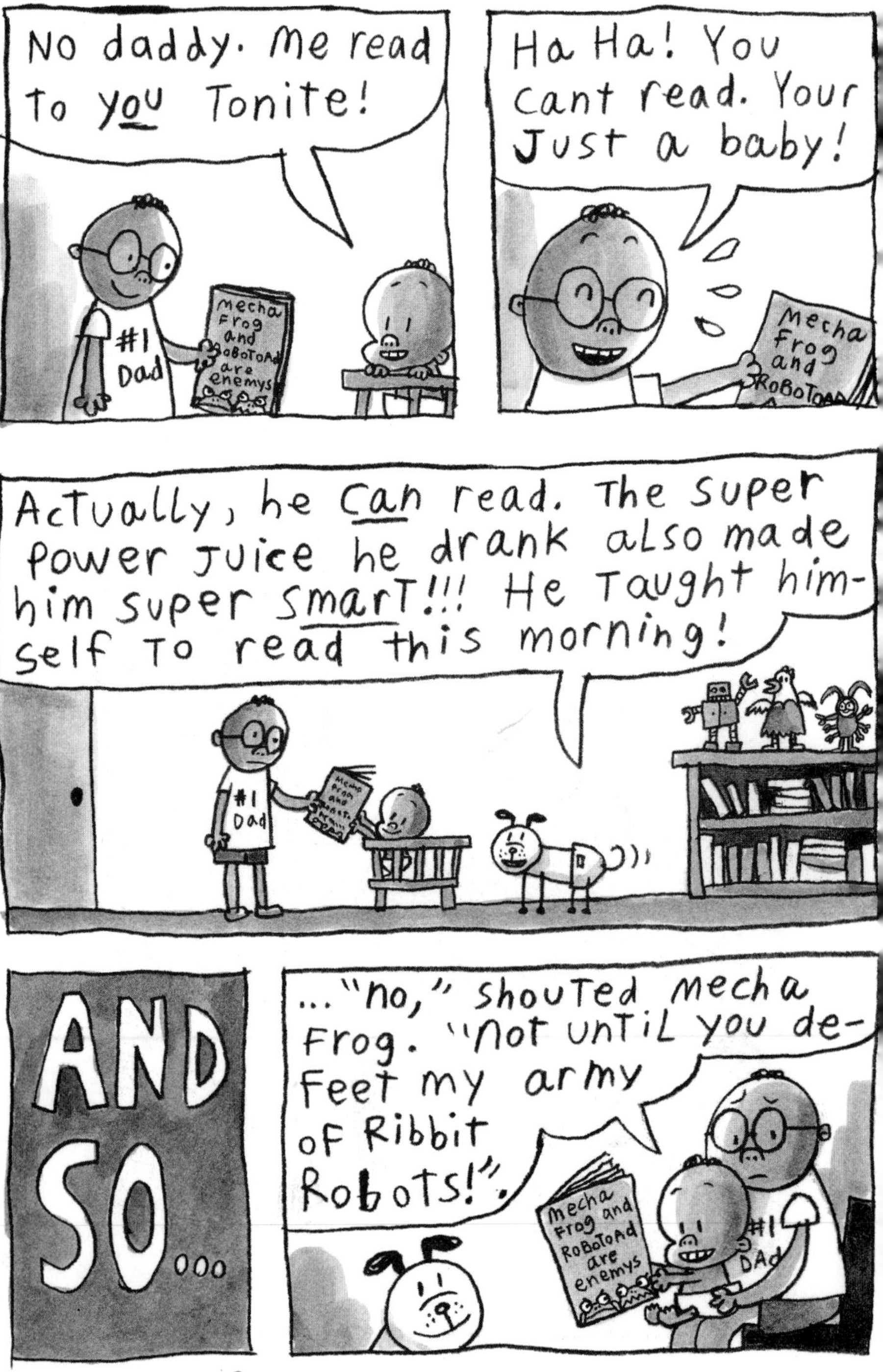
No daddy. Me read to you Tonite!
Mecha Frog and RoboToAd are enemys
Ha Ha! You cant read. Your Just a baby!
Mecha Frog and RoboToAD
Actually, he can read. The super power Juice he drank also made him super smarT!!! He Taught him-self To read this morning!
#1 Dad
AND SO...
..."no," shouted Mecha Frog. "Not until you de-Feet my army of Ribbit Robots!"
Mecha Frog and RoboToAd are enemys
#1 DAd

Chapter 2

Meanwhile…

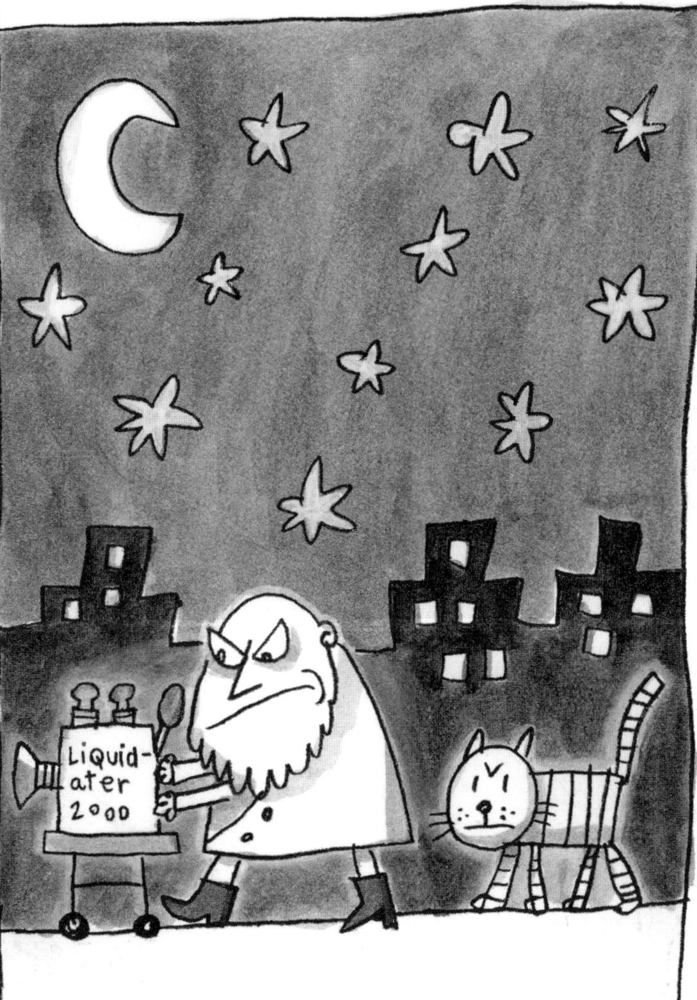
Liquid-
ater
2000

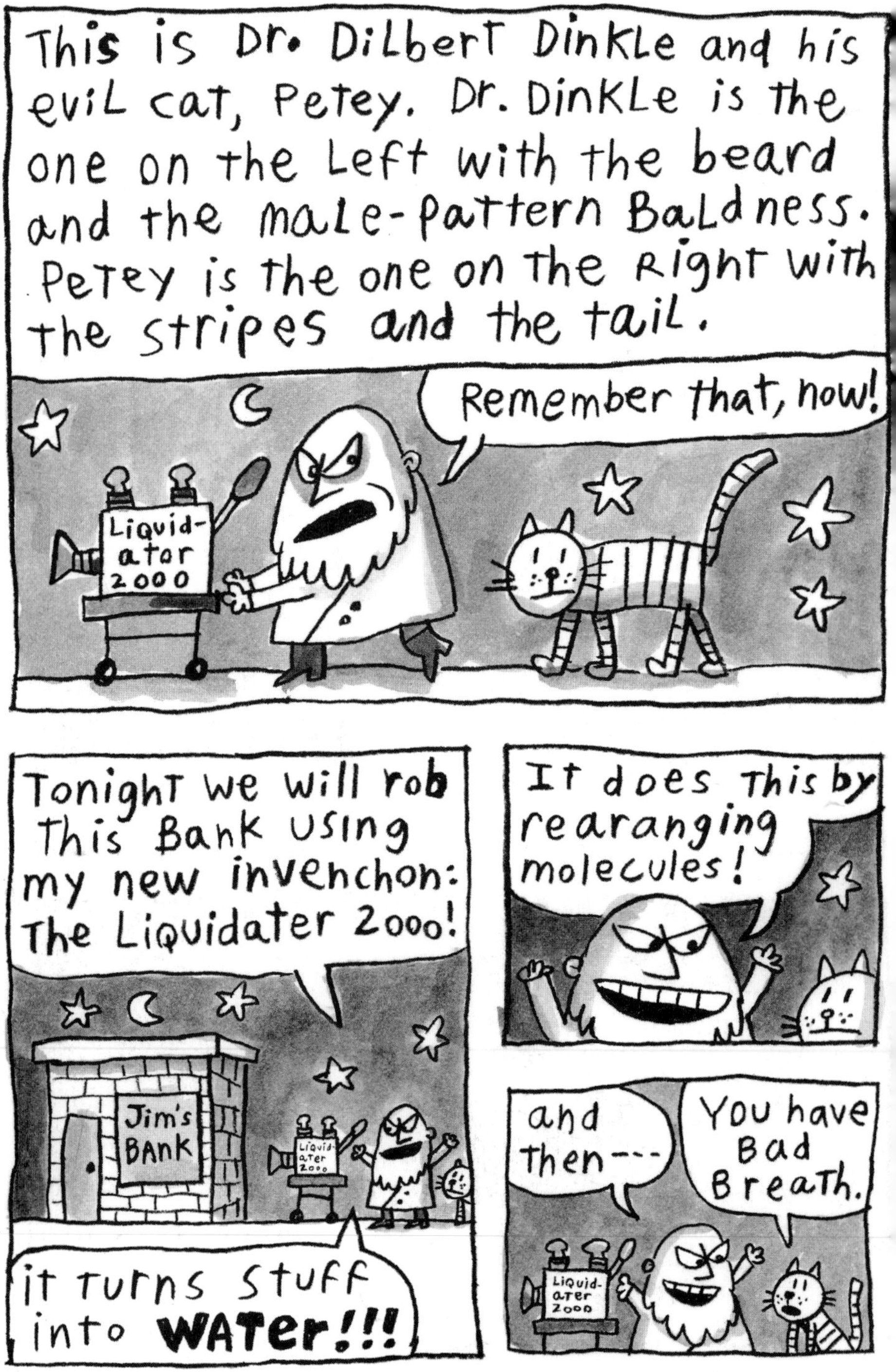
This is Dr. Dilbert Dinkle and his evil cat, Petey. Dr. Dinkle is the one on the left with the beard and the male-pattern baldness. Petey is the one on the right with the stripes and the tail.
Remember that, now!
Liquid-ator 2000
Tonight we will rob this Bank using my new invenchon: The Liquidater 2000!
Jim's BANK
Liquid-ater 2000
it turns stuff into WATer!!!
It does this by rearanging molecules!
and then---
You have Bad Breath.
Liquid-ater 2000

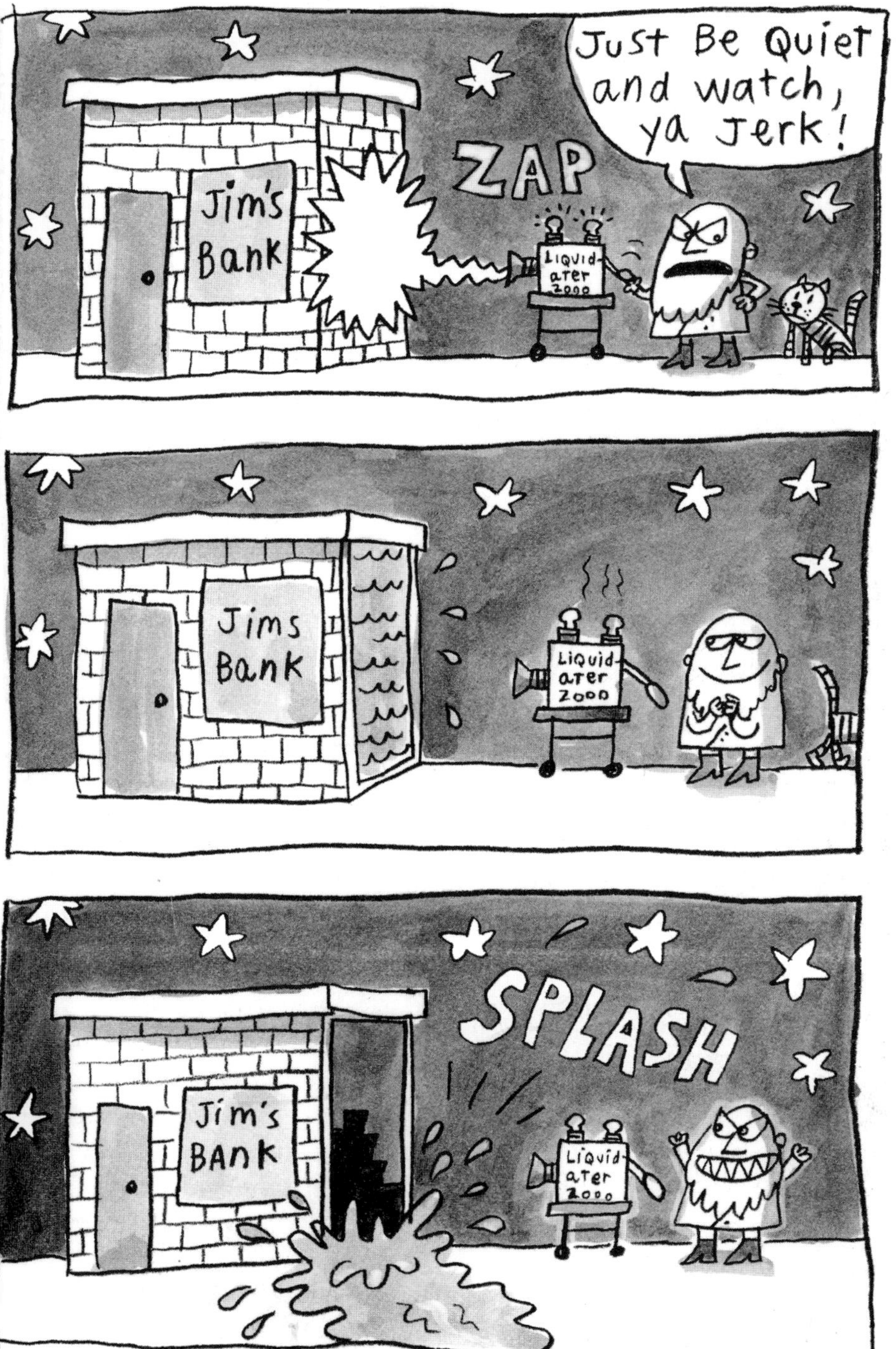
Just Be Quiet and watch, ya Jerk!
ZAP
Jim's Bank
Liquid-ater 2000
Jims Bank
Liquid-ater 2000
SPLASH
Jim's BANK
Liquid-ater 2000

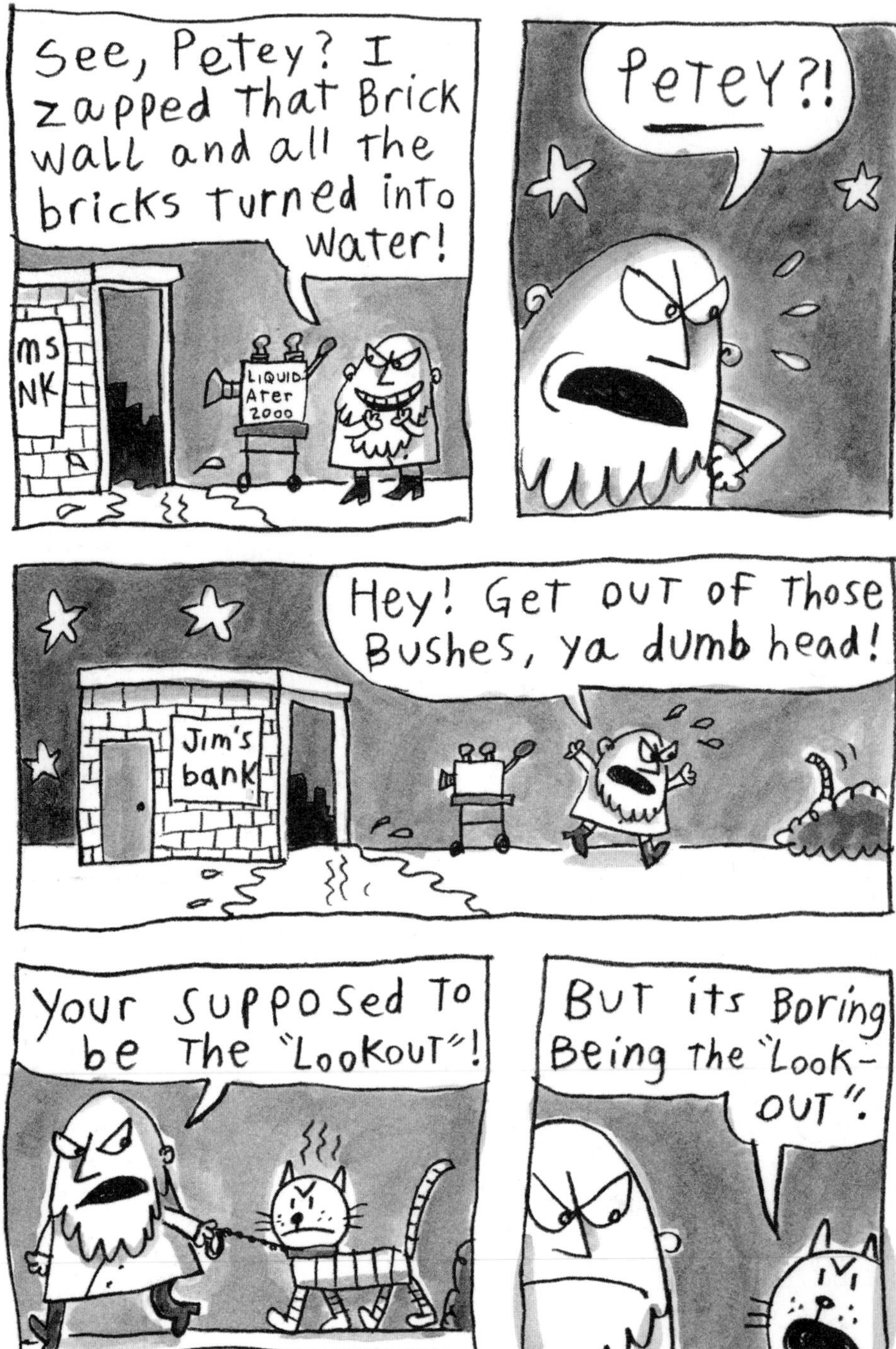
See, Petey? I zapped that Brick wall and all the bricks turned into water!
ms
NK
LIQUID
Ater
2000
PeTeY?!
Hey! Get OUT of Those Bushes, ya dumb head!
Jim's bank
Your SupposeD To be The "LooKouT"!
BuT its Boring Being The "Look-OUT".

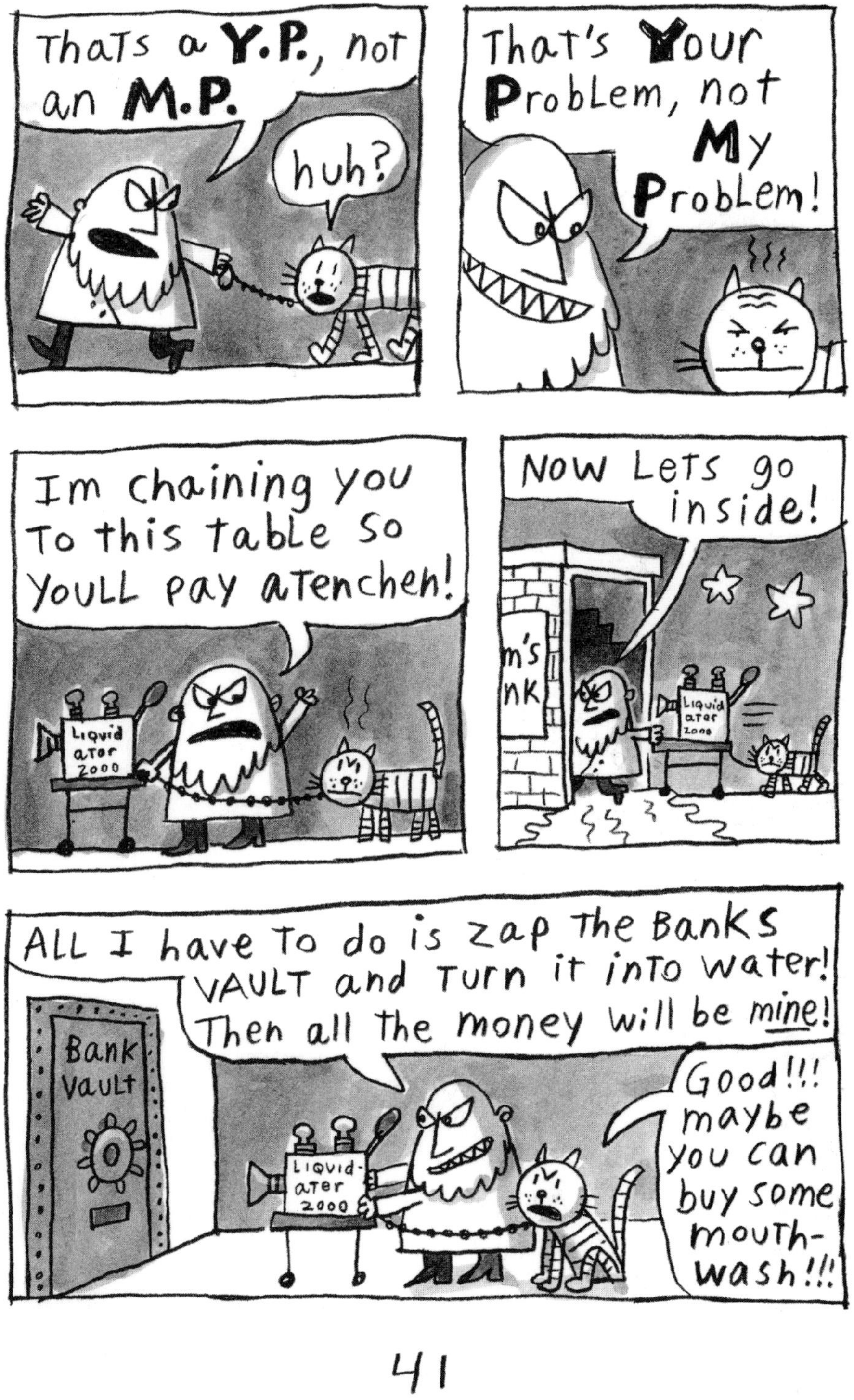
ThaTs a Y.P., not an M.P.
huh?
That's Your Problem, not My Problem!
Im chaining you To this table so youll pay atenchen!
Liquid ater 2000
Now Lets go inside!
Liquid ater 2000
ALL I have To do is zap The Banks VAULT and Turn it into water! Then all the money will be mine!
Bank Vault
LIQUID-ater 2000
Good!!! maybe you can buy some mouth-wash!!!

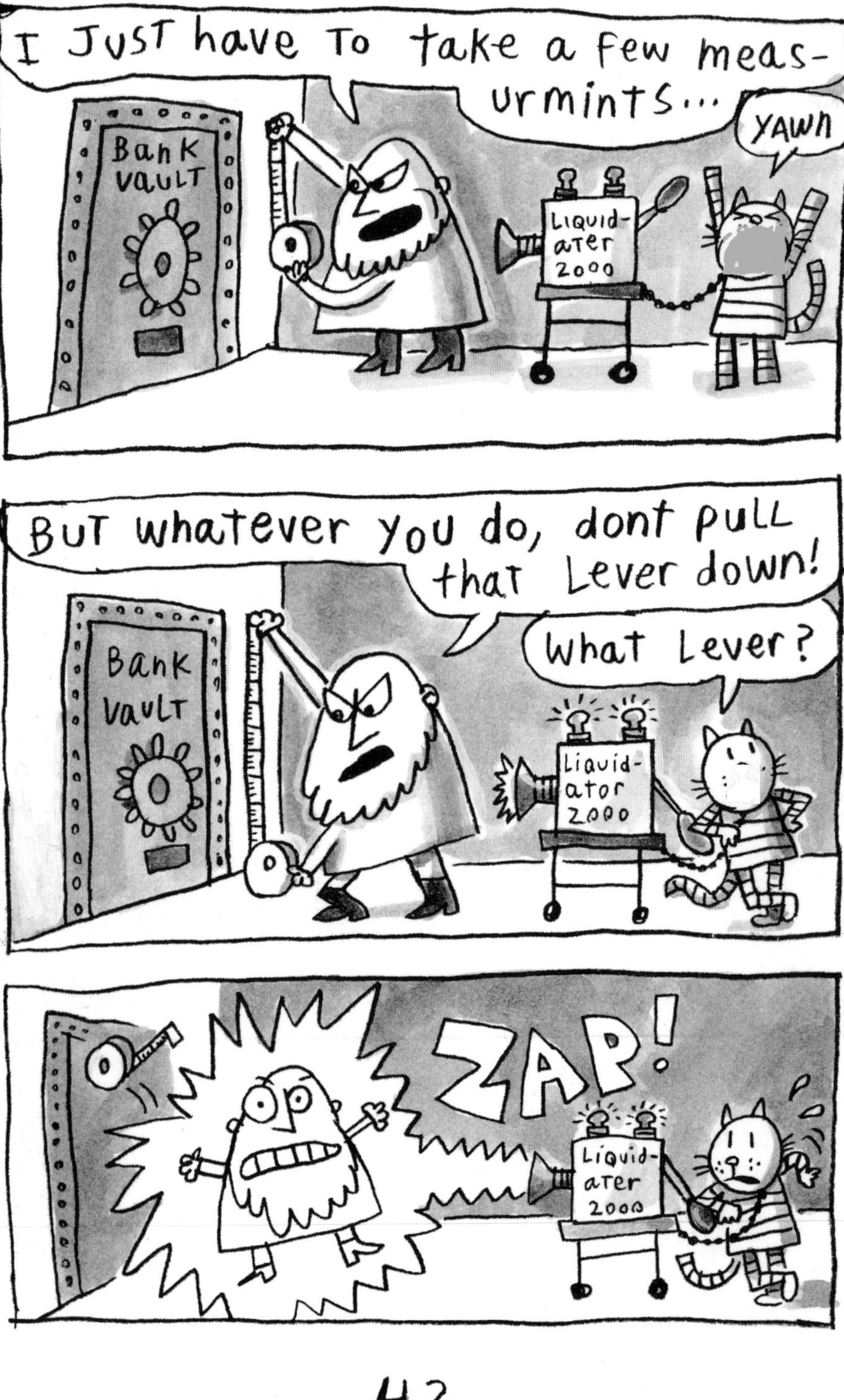
I JUST have To take a few meas-urmints...
YAWN
Bank VAULT
LIQUID-ATER 2000
BUT whatever you do, dont PULL that Lever down!
What Lever?
Bank VAULT
Liquid-ator 2000
ZAP!
Liquid-ater 2000

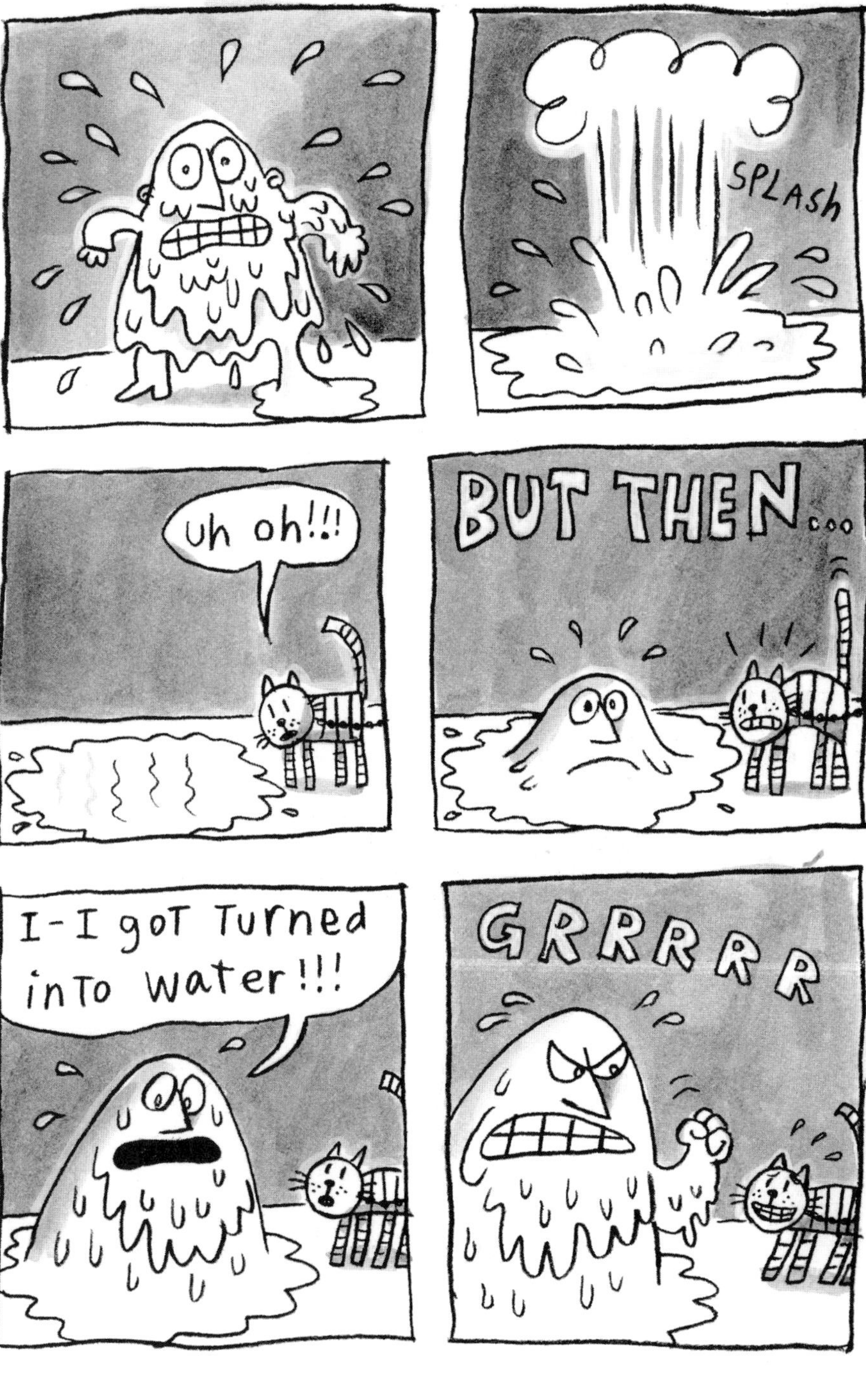
SPLASH
uh oh!!!
BUT THEN...
I-I got Turned into water!!!
GRRRRRR

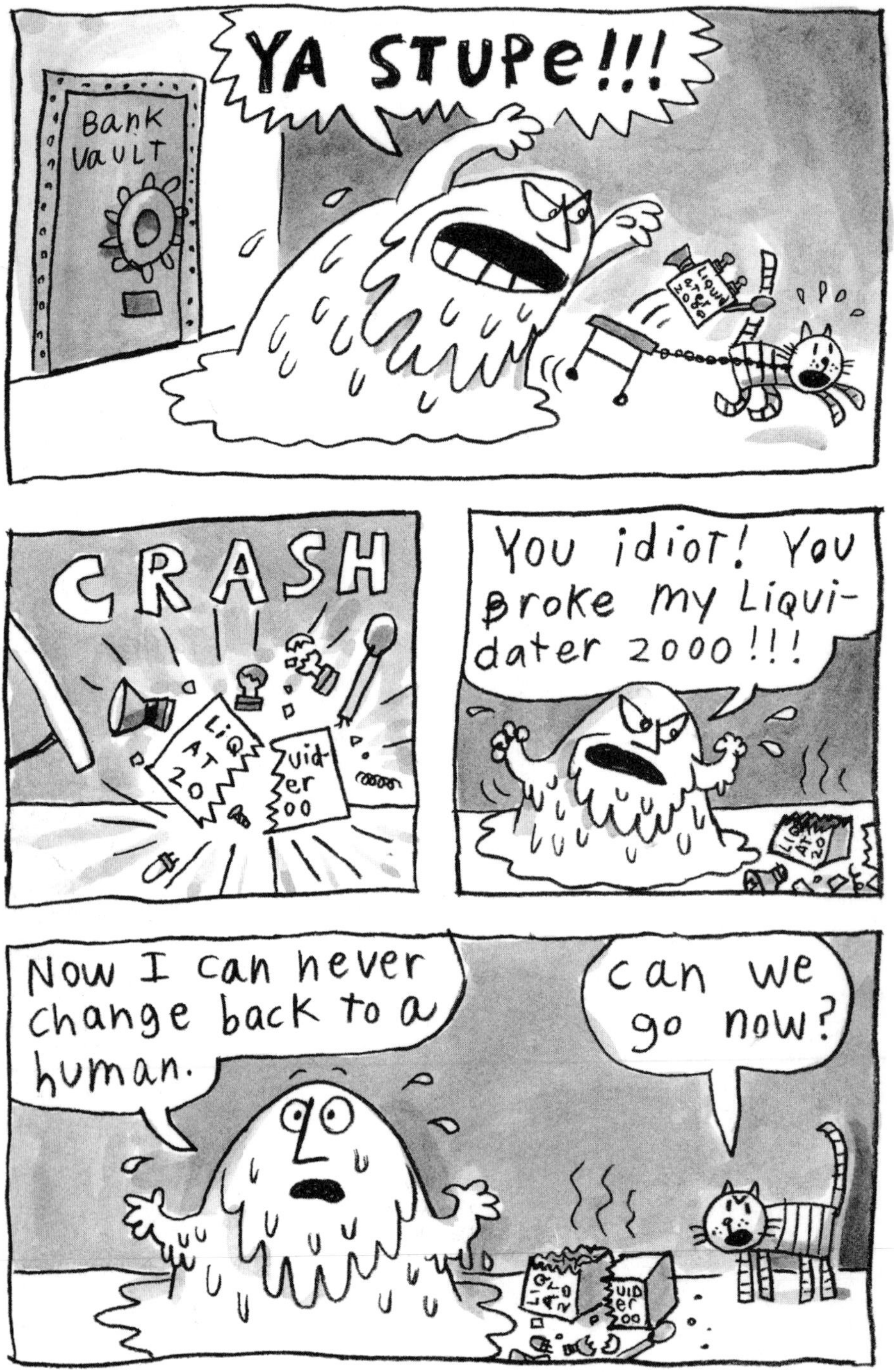
YA STUPE!!!
Bank Vault
CRASH
You idiot! You broke my Liqui-dater 2000!!!
Now I can never change back to a human.
Can we go now?

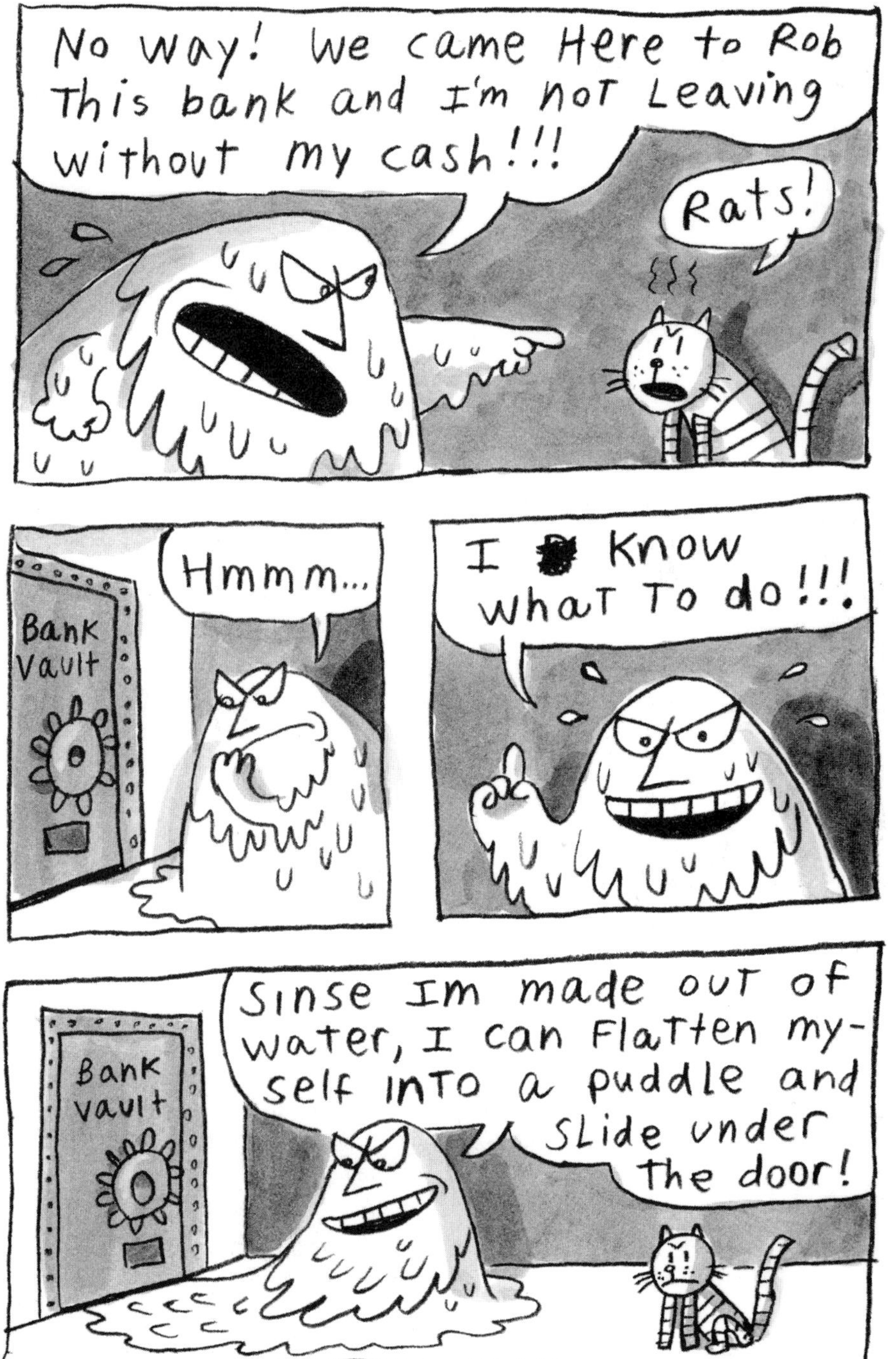
No way! We came Here to Rob This bank and I'm not Leaving without my cash!!!
Rats!
Hmmm...
I Know what To do!!!
Sinse Im made out of water, I can Flatten my-self into a puddle and Slide under the door!
Bank vault

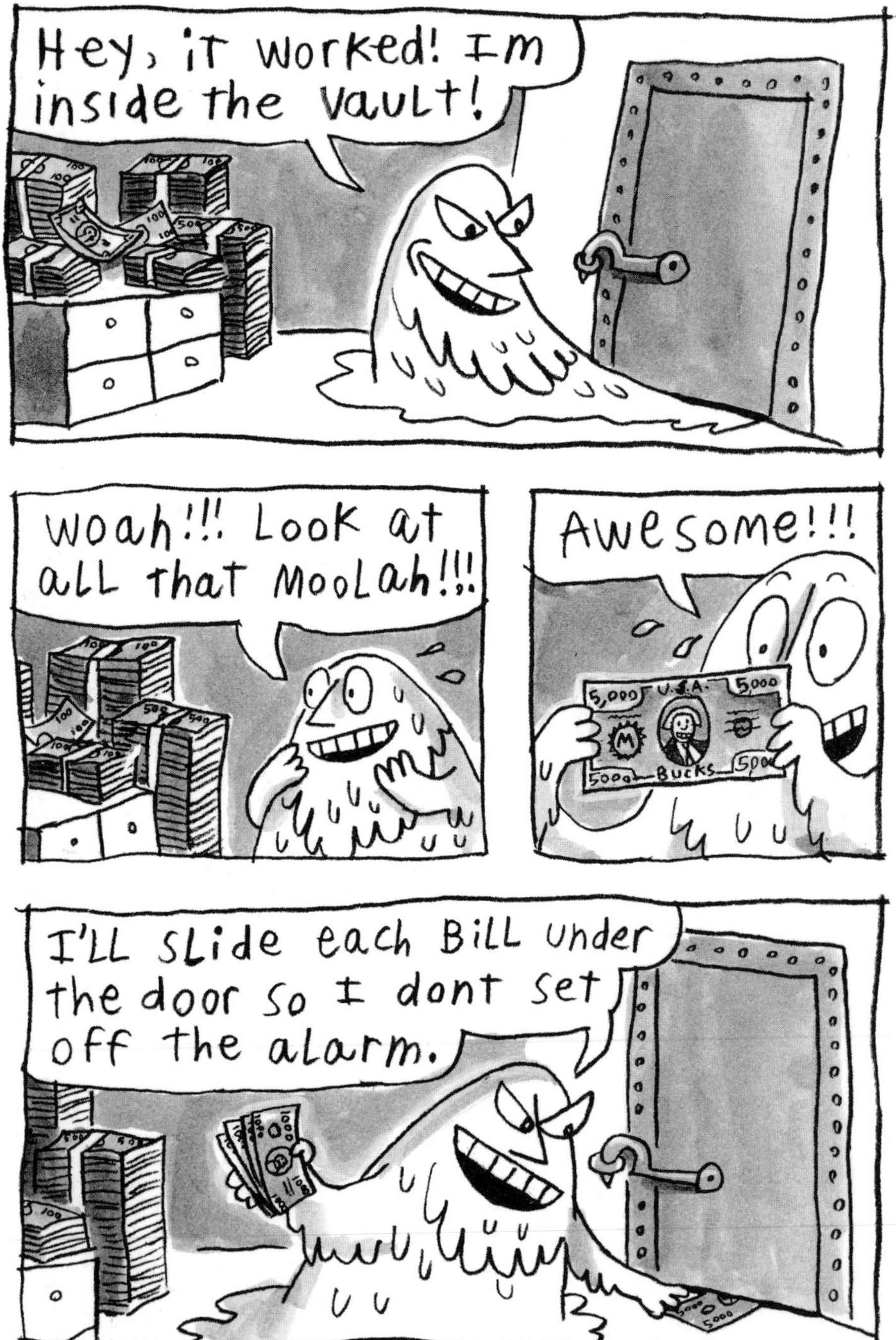
Hey, it worked! I'm inside the vault!
Woah!!! Look at all that Moolah!!!
Awesome!!!
I'll slide each bill under the door so I dont set off the alarm.

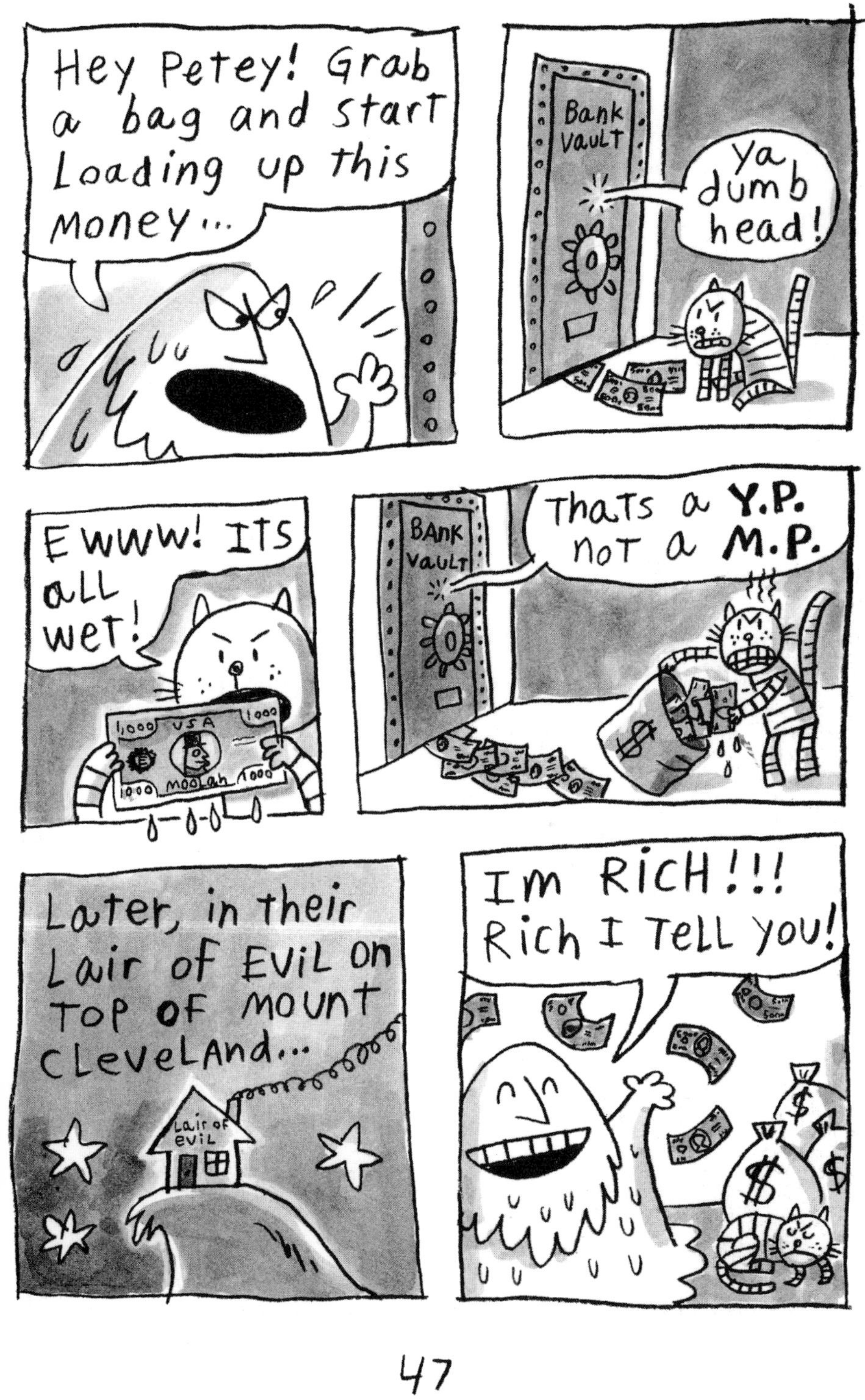
Hey Petey! Grab a bag and start Loading up this Money...
Bank VAULT
Ya dumb head!
Ewww! ITS all wet!
USA
MOOLah
BANK VAULT
Thats a **Y.P.** not a **M.P.**
Later, in their Lair of Evil on Top of Mount Cleveland...
Lair of Evil
Im RICH!!! Rich I TeLL you!

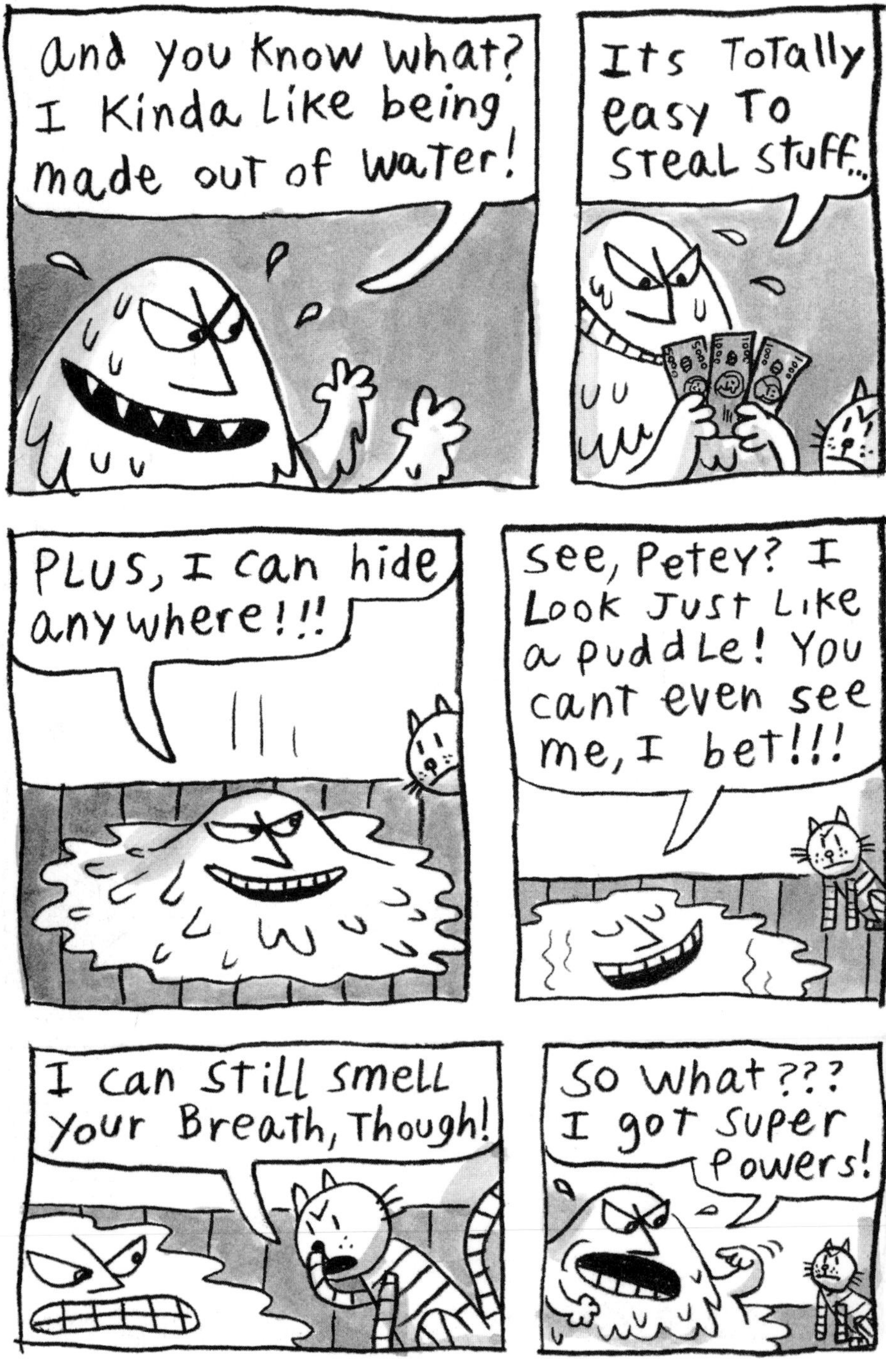
and you know what? I Kinda Like being made out of water!
Its Totally easy To steal stuff...
PLUS, I can hide anywhere!!!
see, Petey? I Look Just Like a puddle! You cant even see me, I bet!!!
I can still smell your Breath, Though!
So what??? I got super Powers!

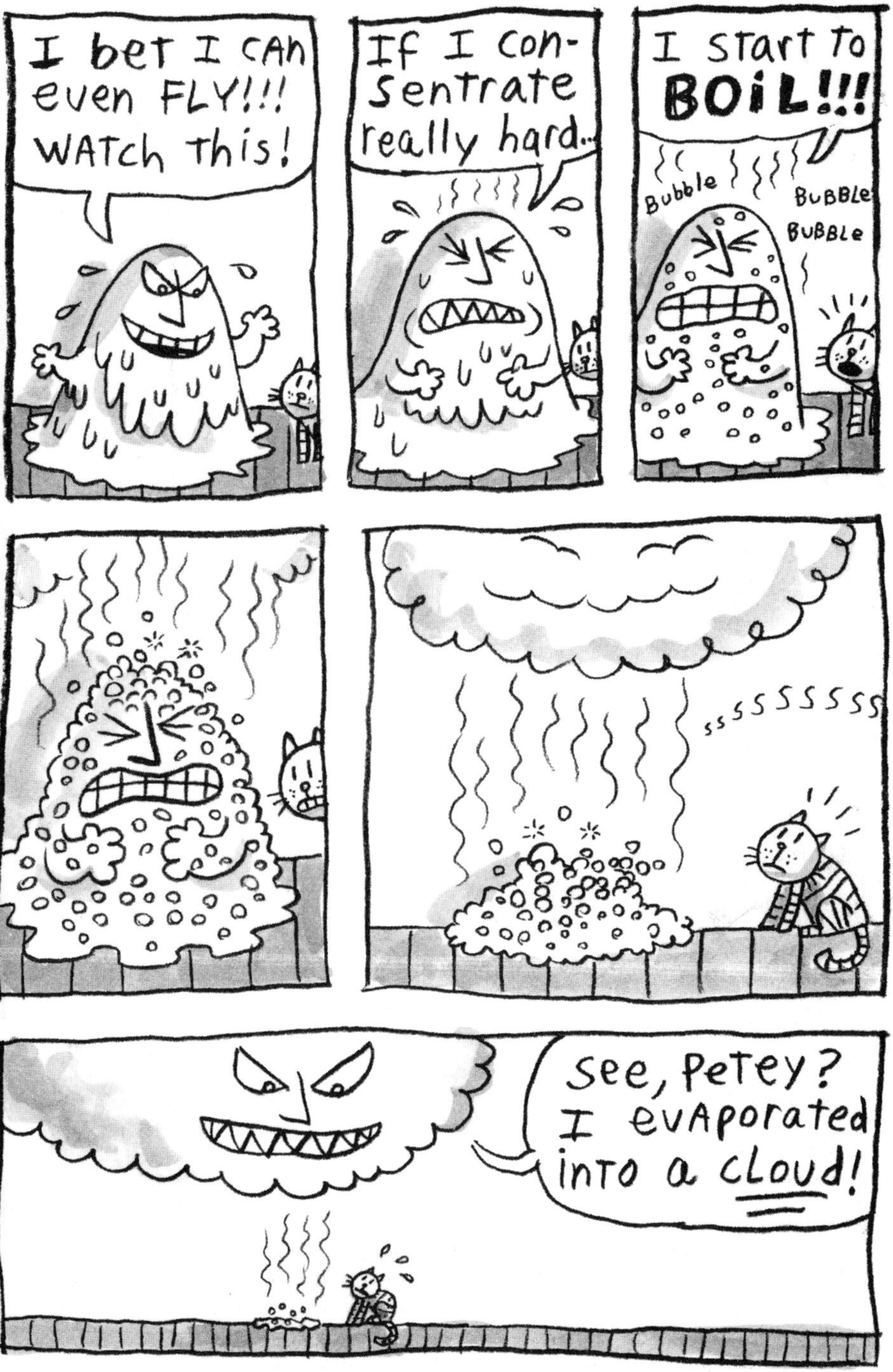
I bet I can even FLY!!! WATCH this!
If I con-sentrate really hard...
I start to BOIL!!!
Bubble
BUBBLE
BUBBLE
sssSSSSSSS
See, Petey? I evaporated into a cloud!

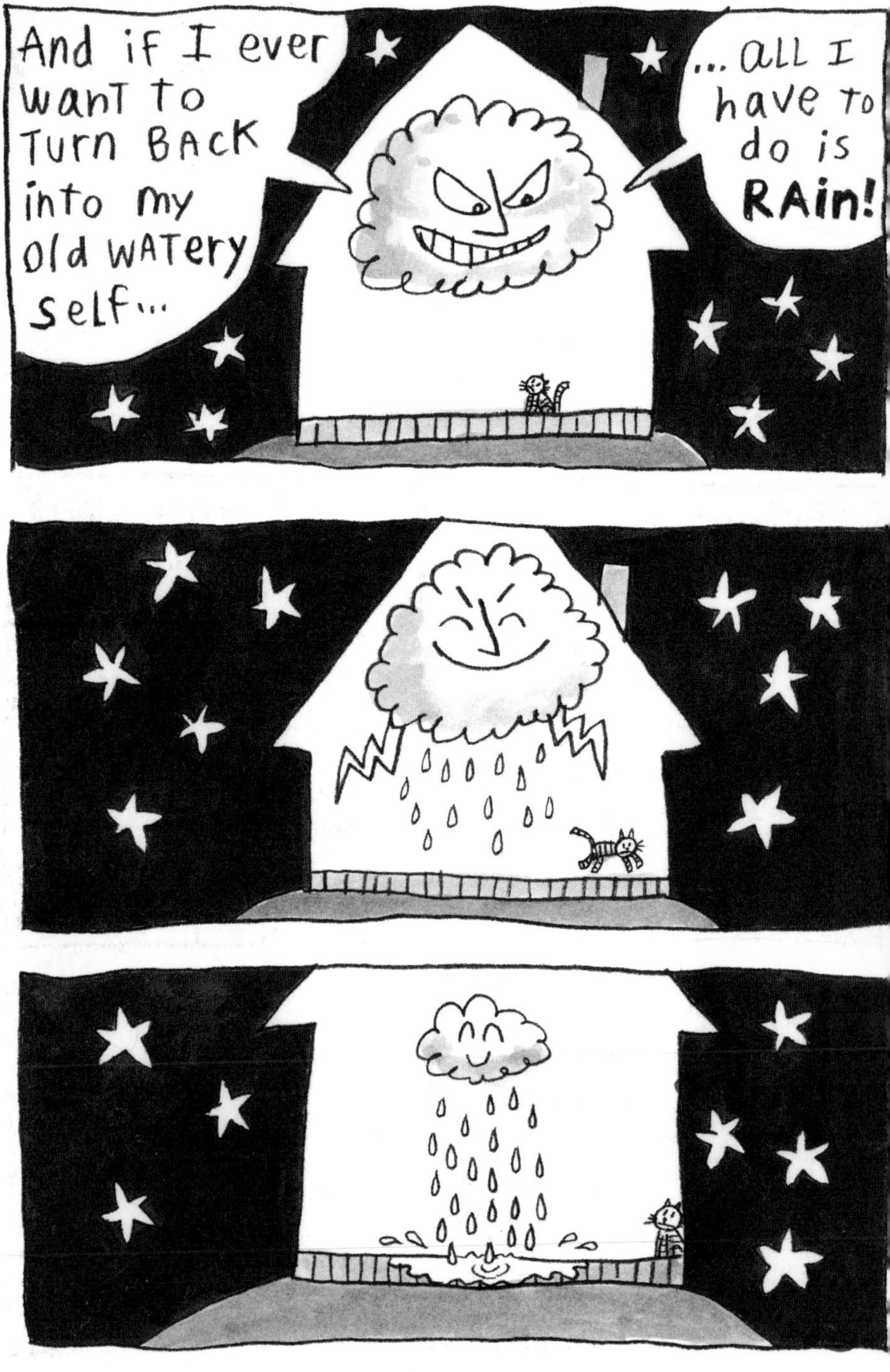
And if I ever want to Turn BACK into my old WATery self...
...all I have to do is RAin!

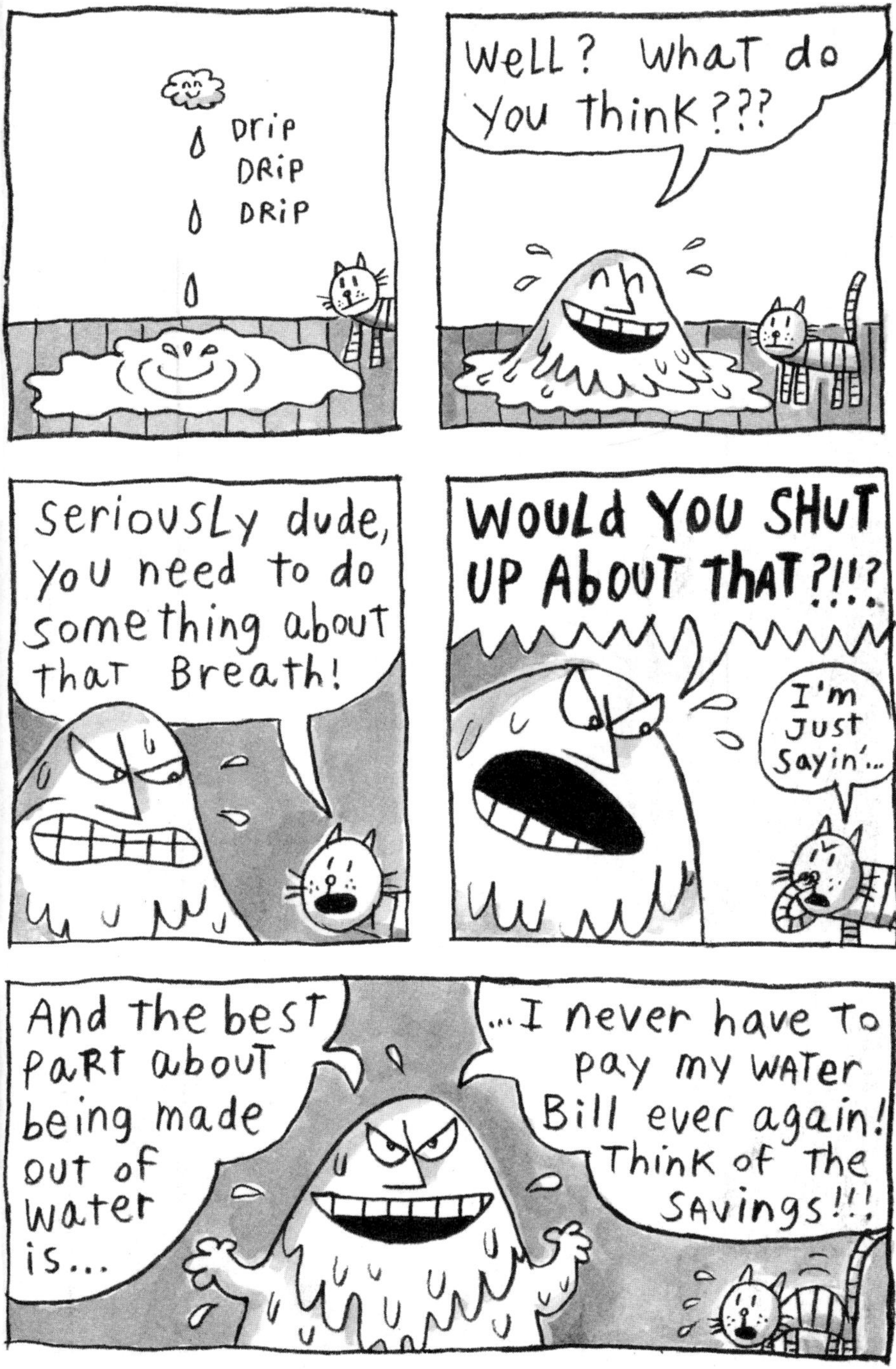
Drip
DRiP
DRiP
Well? What do you think???
Seriously dude, you need to do something about that Breath!
WOULD YOU SHUT UP ABOUT THAT?!!?
I'm Just Sayin'...
And the best part about being made out of water is...
...I never have to pay my water Bill ever again! Think of the Savings!!!

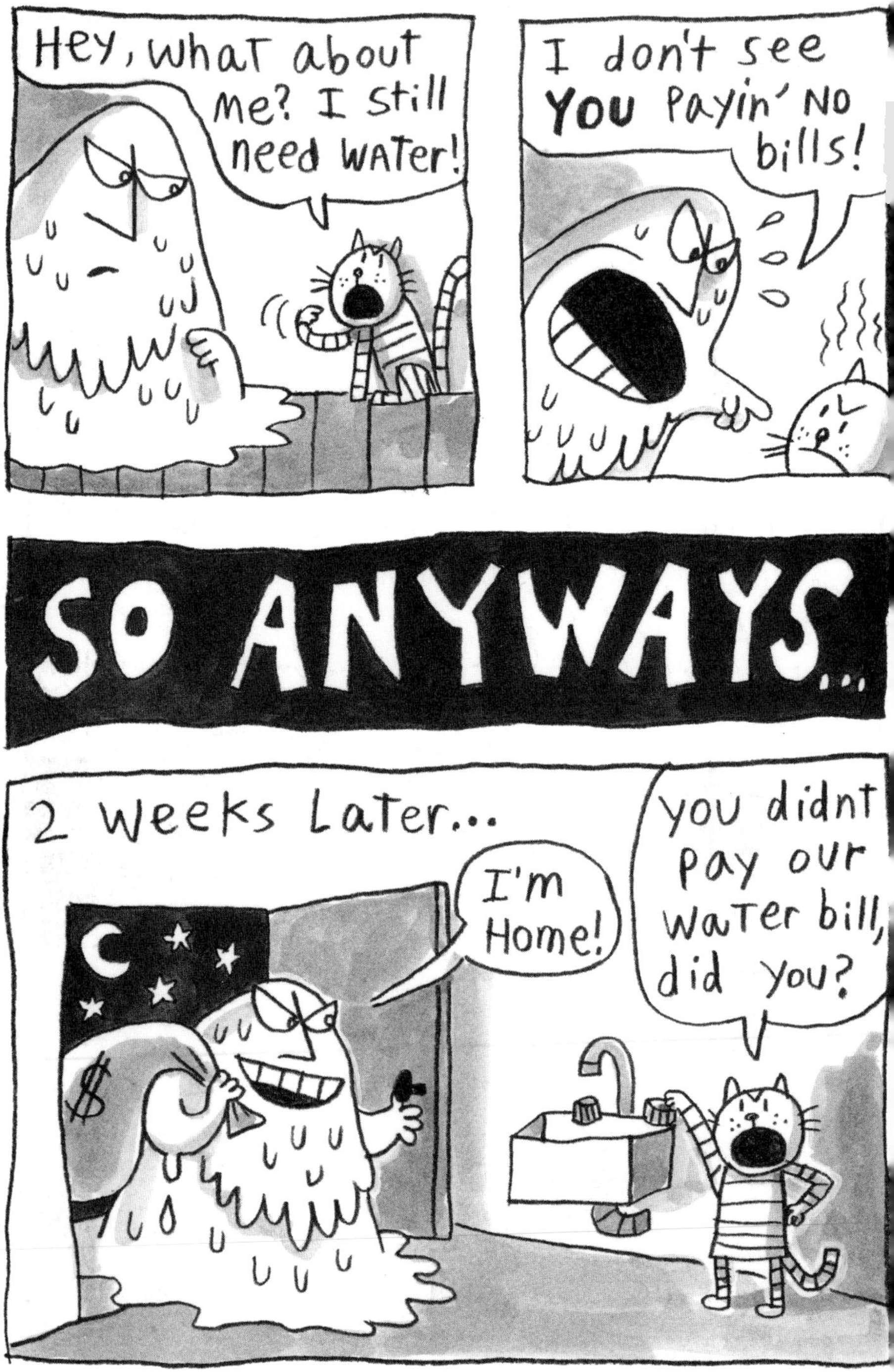
Hey, what about me? I still need water!
I don't see YOU payin' no bills!
SO ANYWAYS...
2 weeks Later...
I'm Home!
you didnt pay our water bill, did you?

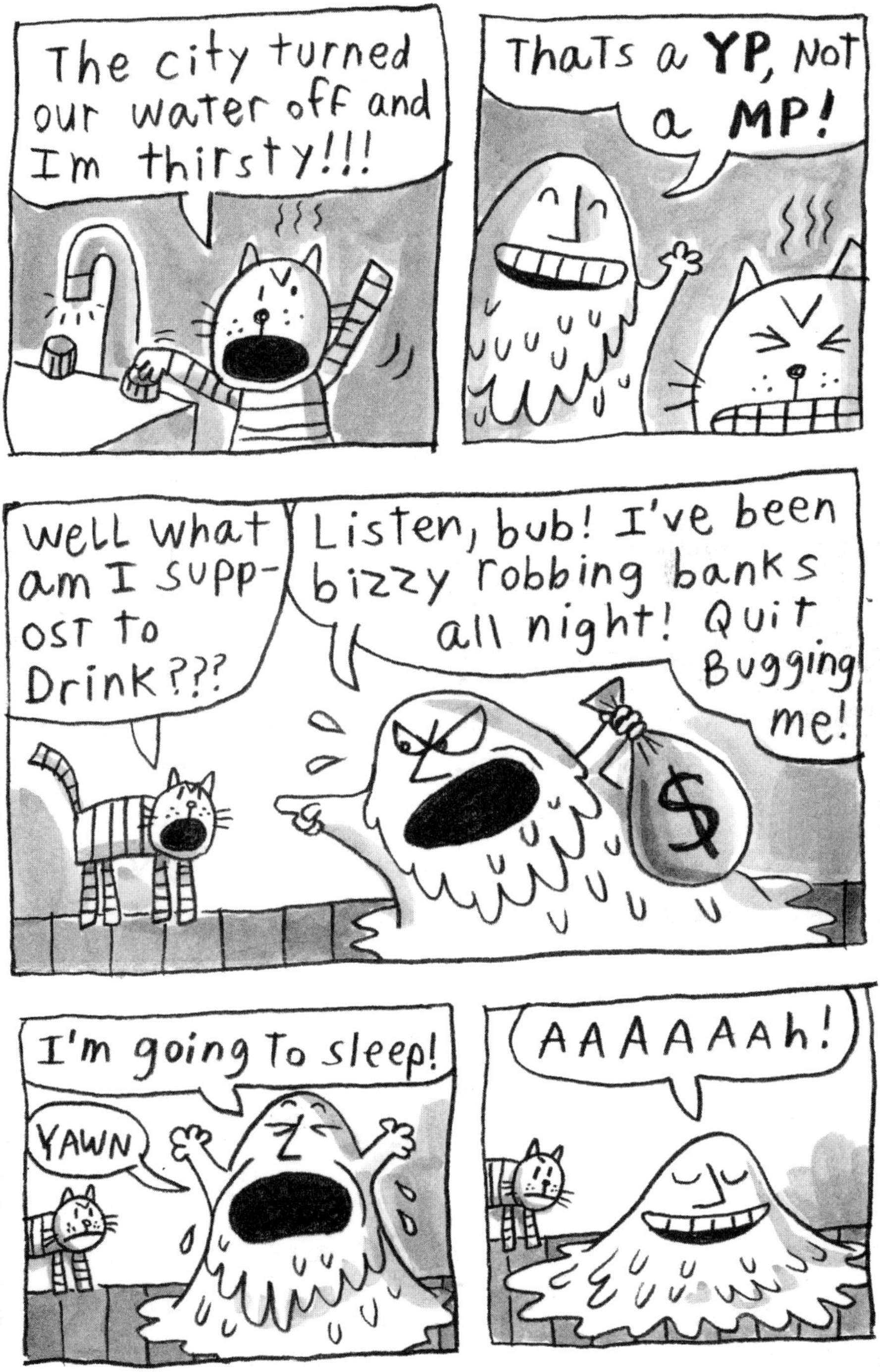
The city turned our water off and I'm thirsty!!!
ThaTs a YP, NoT a MP!
Well what am I supp-ost To Drink???
Listen, bub! I've been bizzy robbing banks all night! Quit Bugging me!
I'm going To sleep!
YAWN
AAAAAAh!

FLiP·O·RAMA 3

If you forgot how to do this already, please see your doctor. Afterwards, Turn to page 17 for further instruckshons.

Left Hand Here.

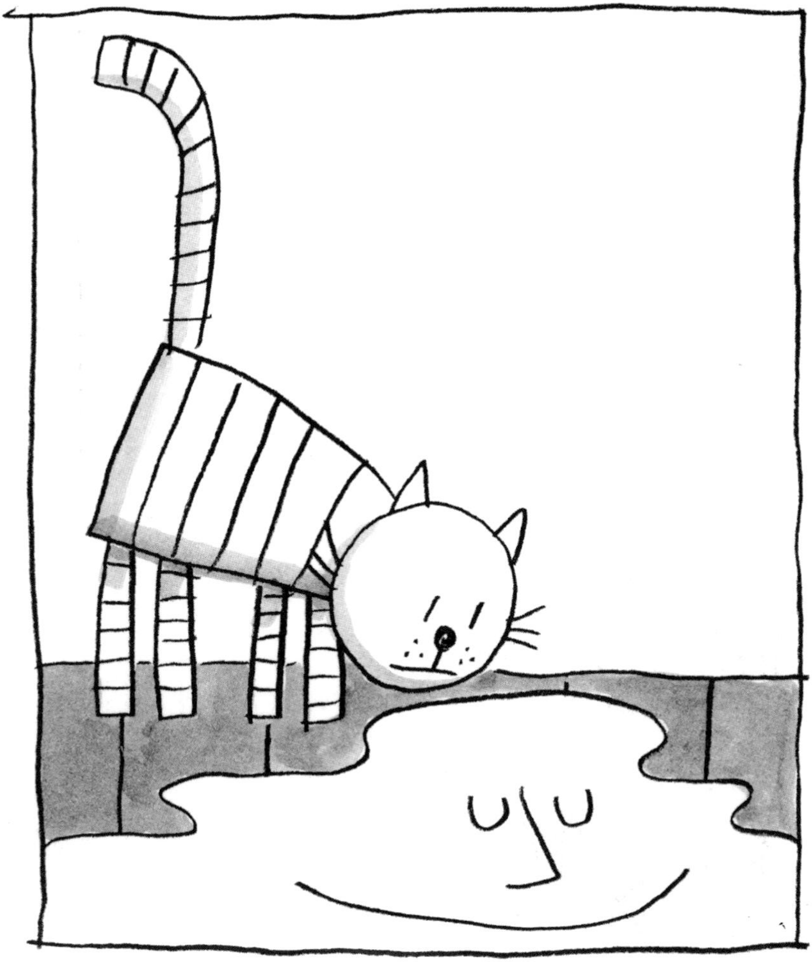

Drinking Dr. Dinkle

Right Thumb Here.

Drinking Dr. Dinkle

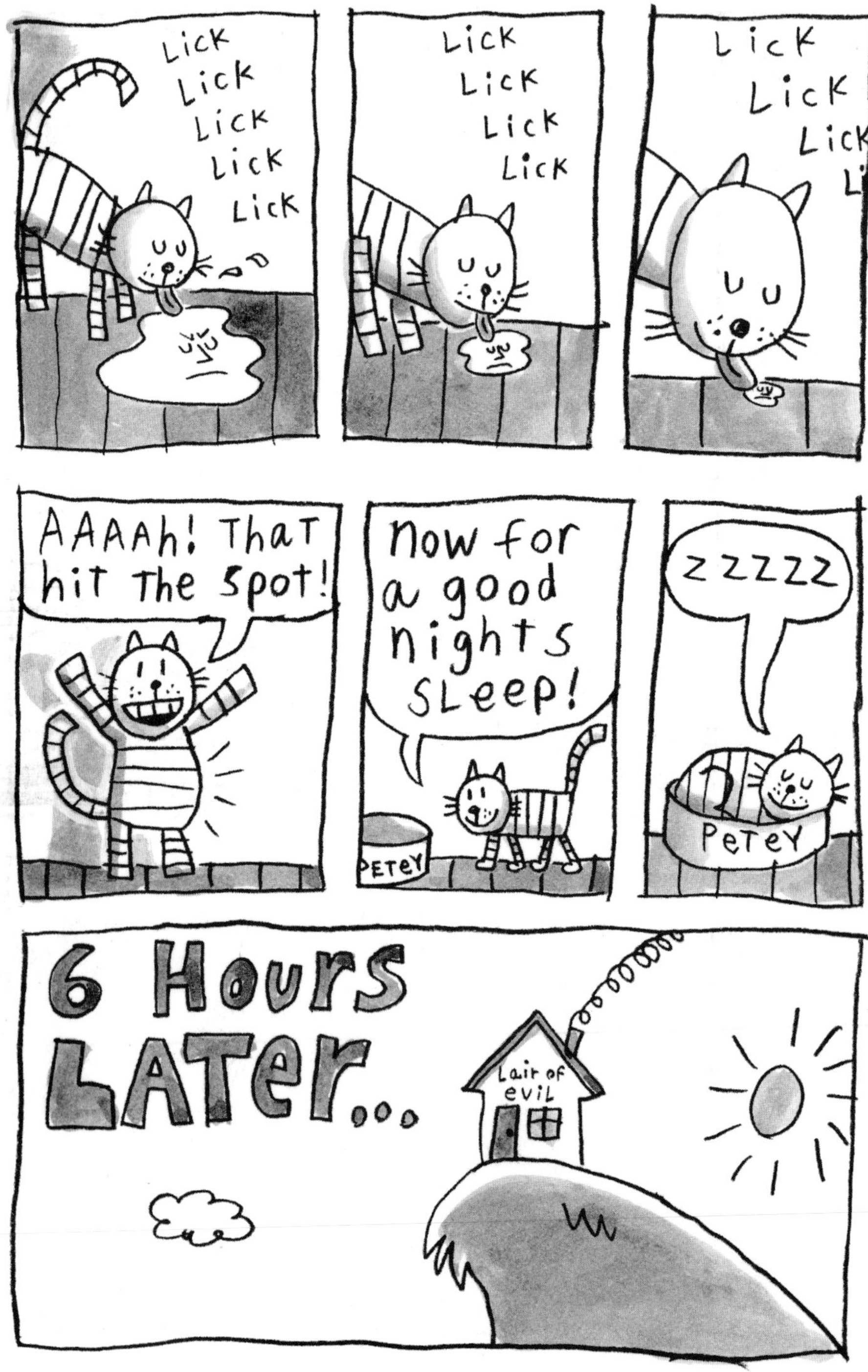
Lick Lick Lick Lick Lick
Lick Lick Lick Lick
Lick Lick Lick
AAAAh! That hit the spot!
Now for a good nights sleep!
PETEY
ZZZZZ
PETEY
6 Hours Later...
Lair of evil

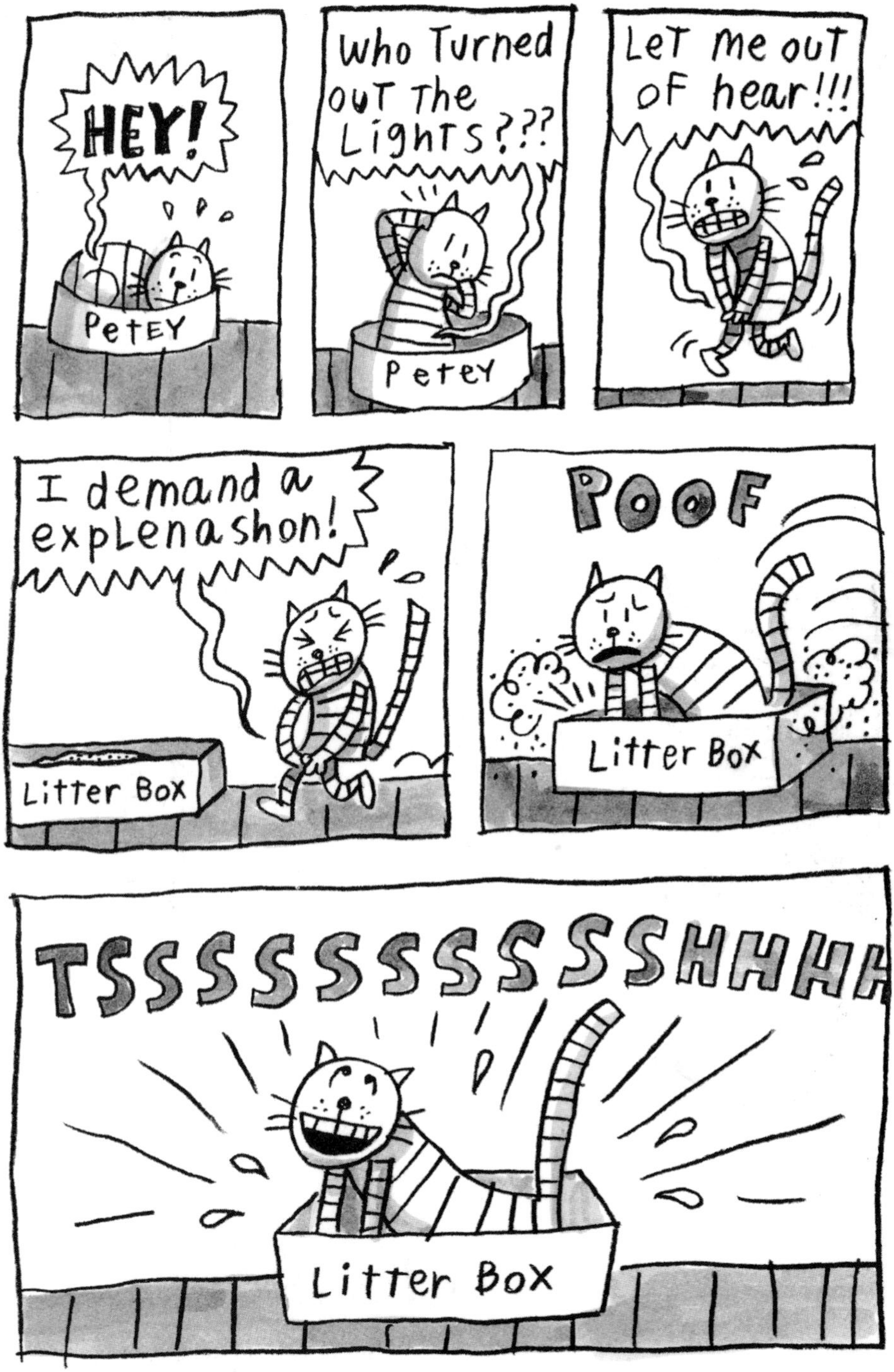
HEY!
PETEY
Who Turned out The Lights???
Petey
LeT me ouT of hear!!!
I demand a explenashon!
Litter Box
POOF
Litter Box
TSSSSSSSSSSHHHH
Litter Box

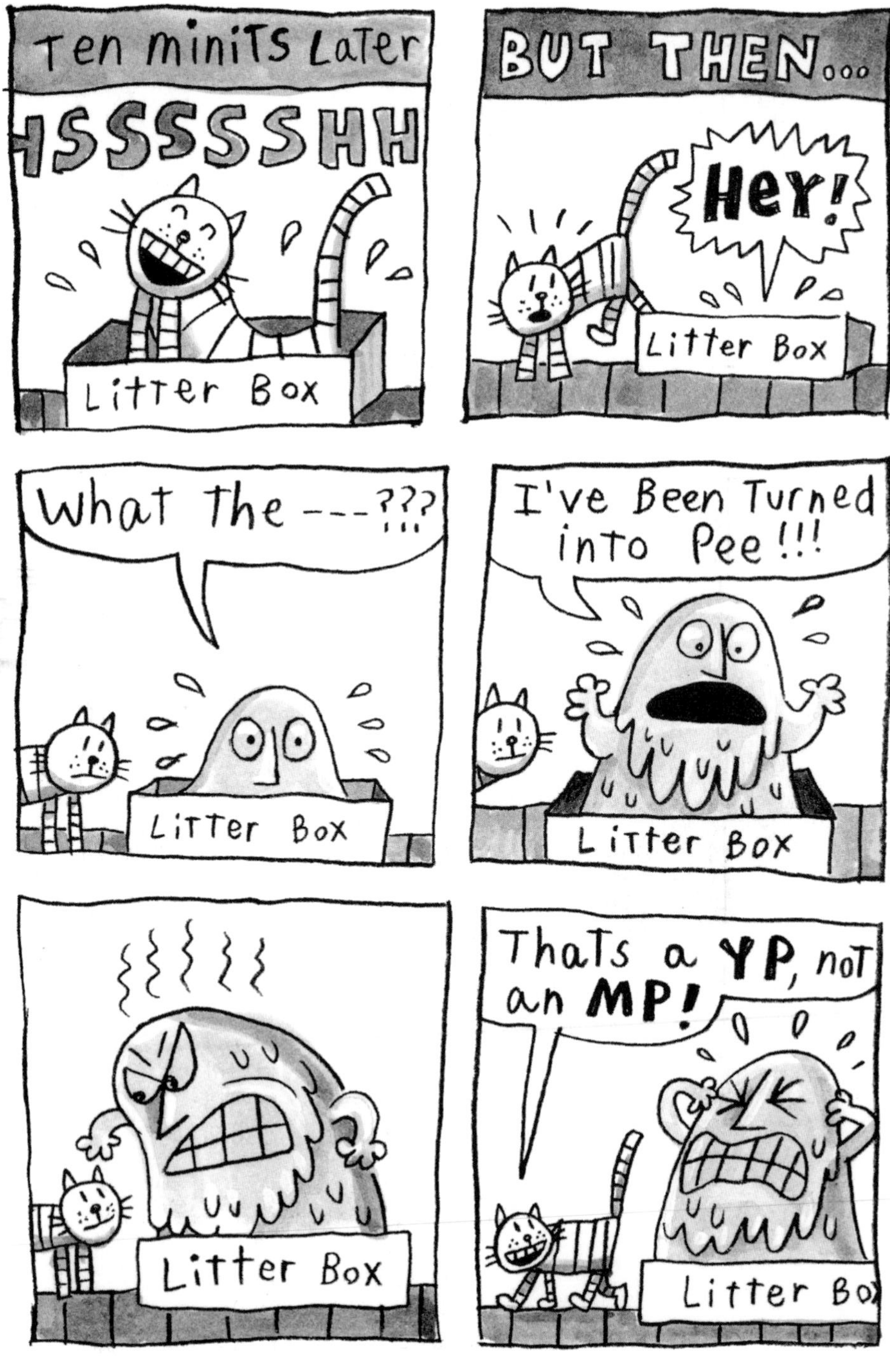
Ten minits Later
HSSSSSHH
Litter Box
BUT THEN...
HEY!
Litter Box
What the ---???
Litter Box
I've Been Turned into Pee!!!
Litter Box
Litter Box
Thats a YP, not an MP!
Litter Bo

ChAPTer 3

Daddy DiLema

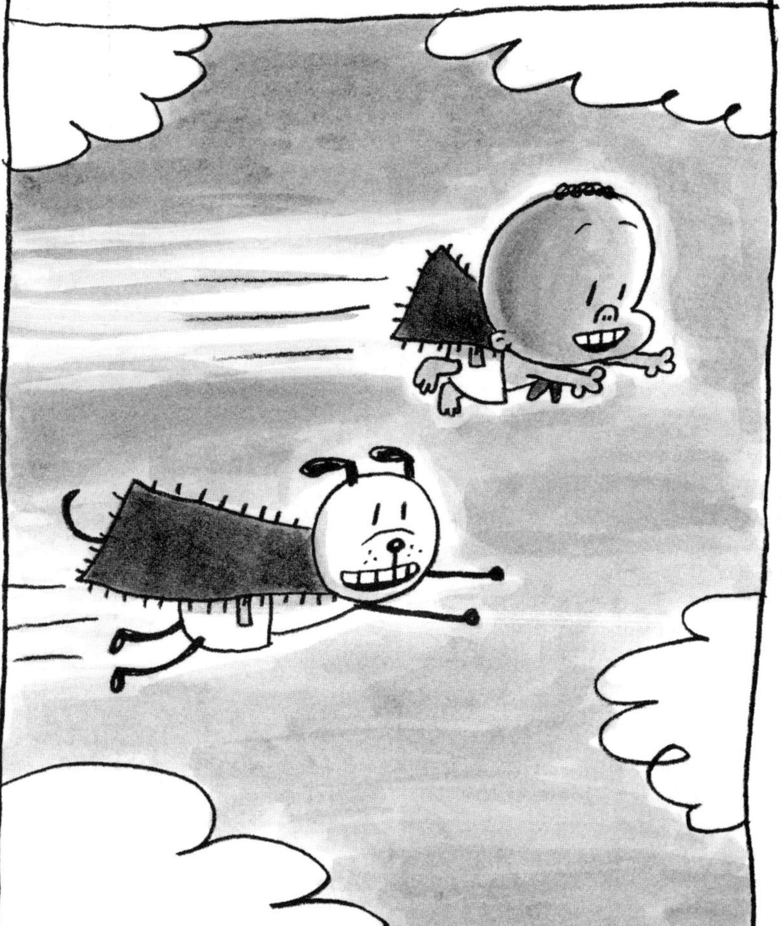

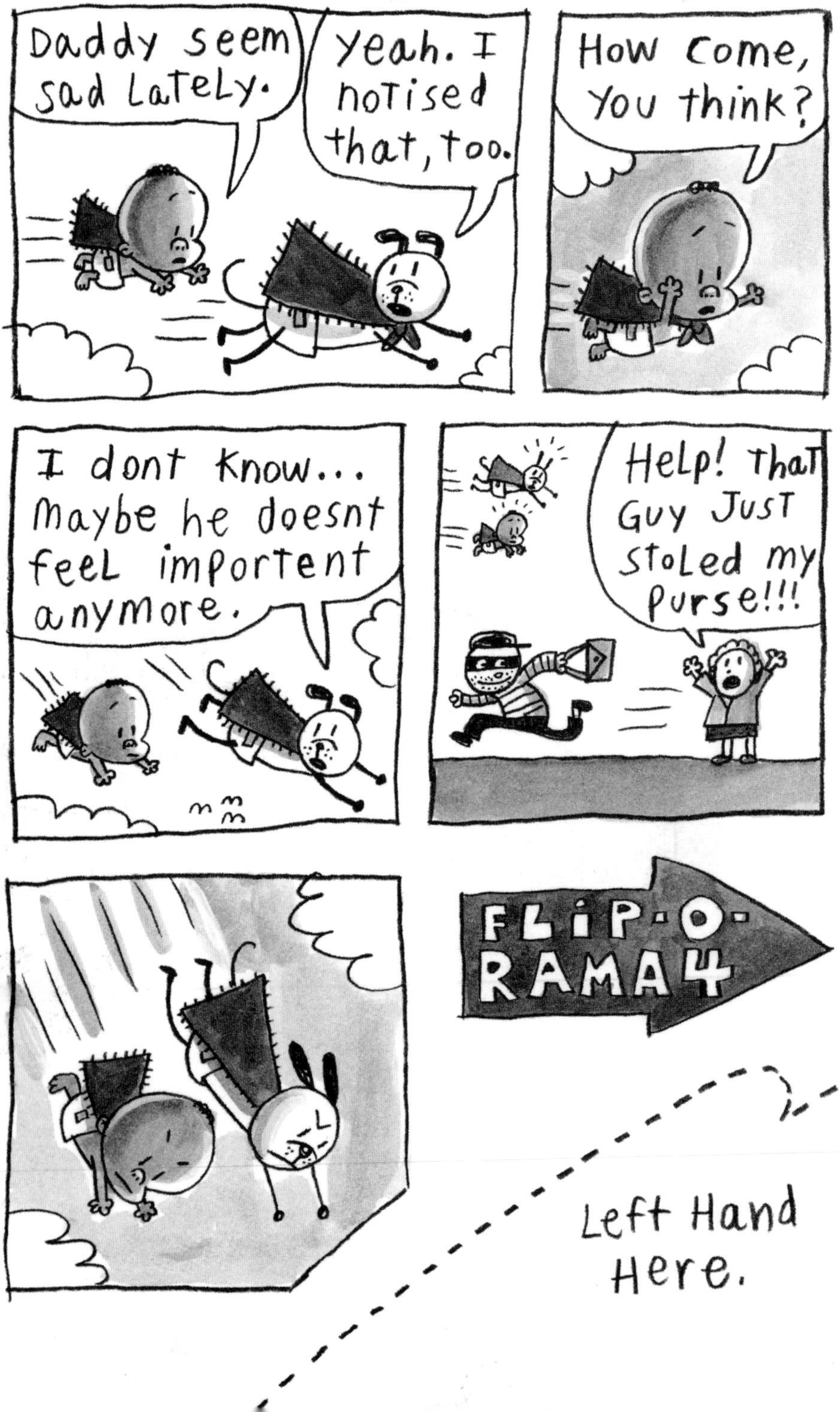

Daddy seem sad Lately.
Yeah. I notised that, too.
How come, You think?
I dont know... maybe he doesnt feeL importent anymore.
Help! That Guy JusT stoLed my purse!!!
FLIP-O-RAMA 4
Left Hand Here.

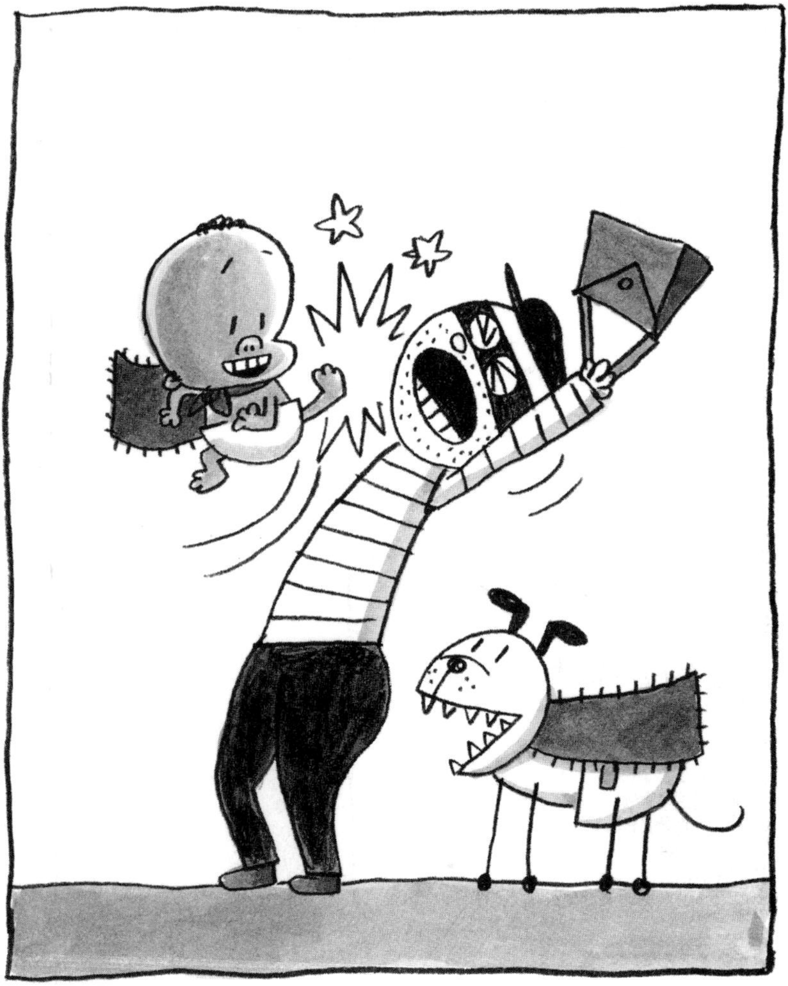

Snatcher Catchers

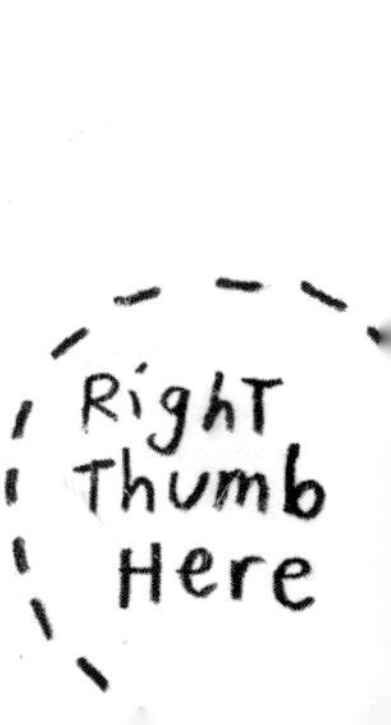
Right
Thumb
Here

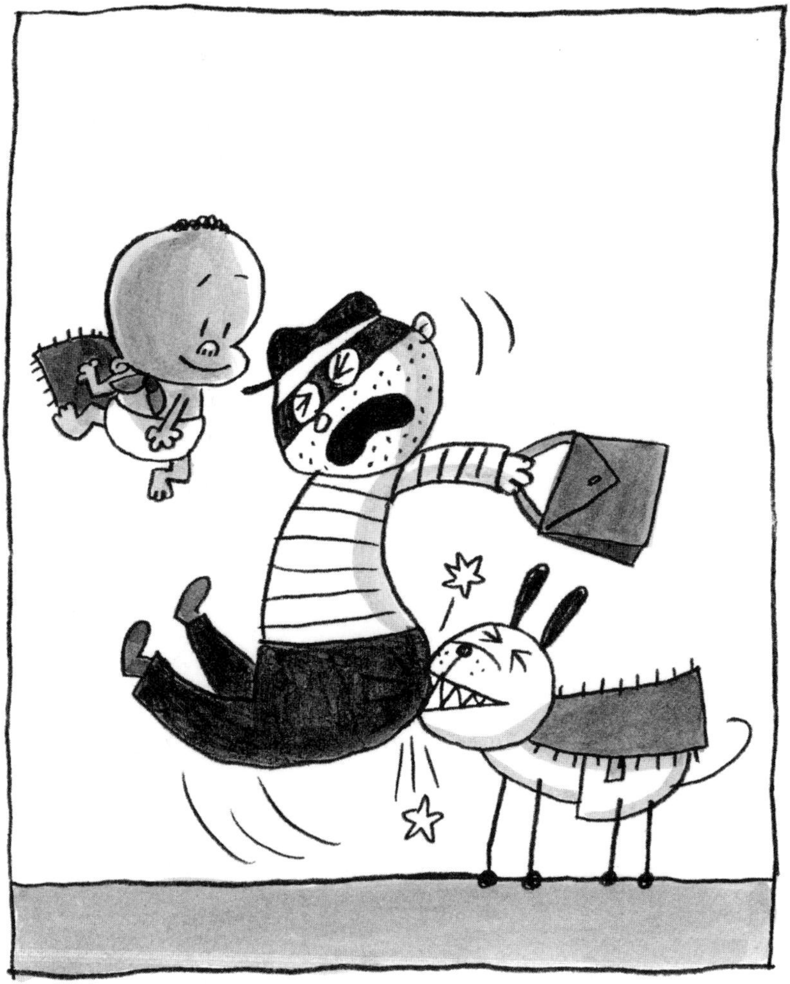

Snatcher Catchers

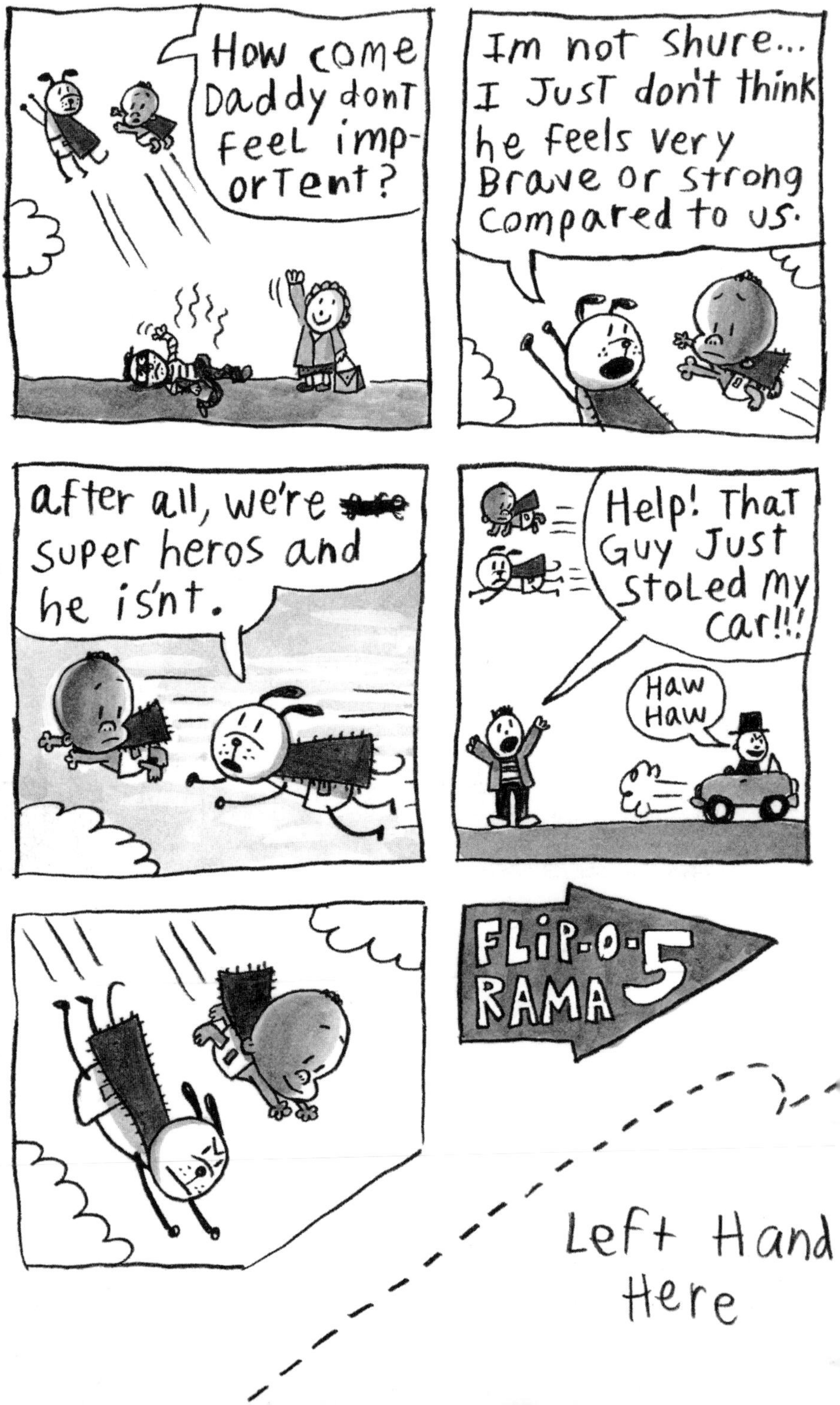
How come Daddy dont feel imp-orTent?
Im not shure... I JusT don't think he feels very Brave or strong compared to us.
after all, we're super heros and he isn't.
Help! That Guy Just stoLed my car!!!
Haw Haw
FLiP-O-RAMA 5
Left Hand Here

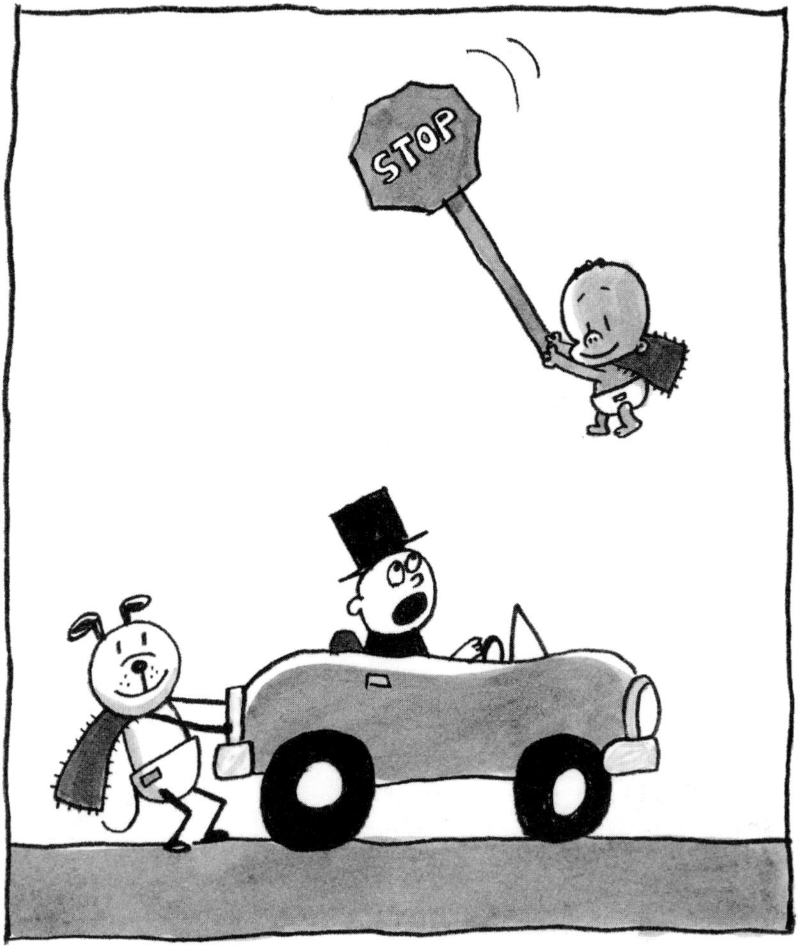
STOP

Jacker Smackers

Right
Thumb
Here

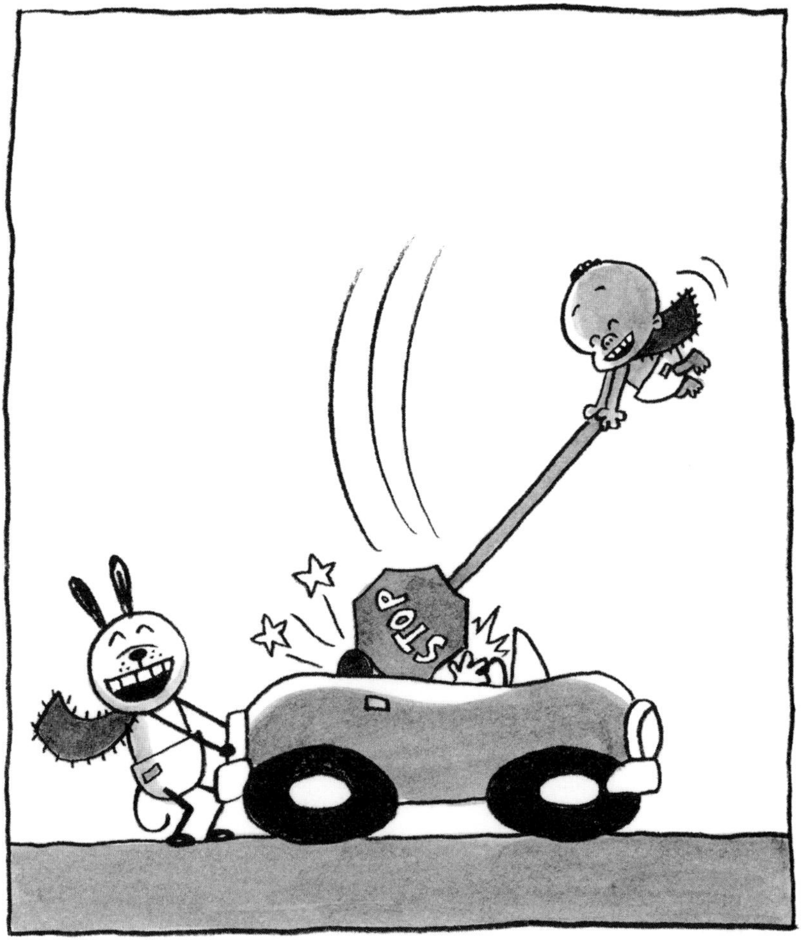
STOP

Jacker Smackers

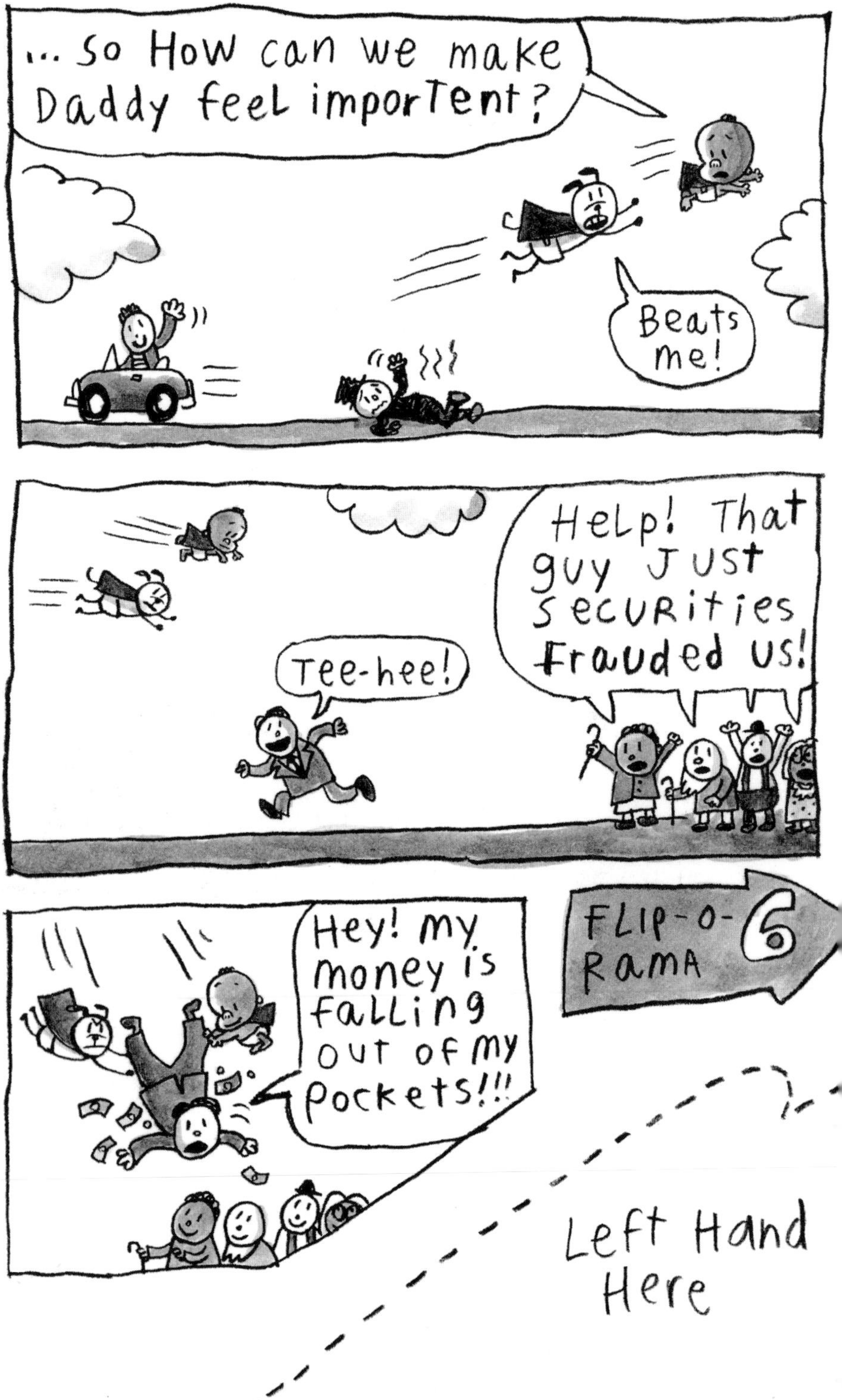
... So How can we make Daddy feel imporTent?
Beats me!
Help! That guy JUST securities Frauded us!
Tee-hee!
Hey! my money is falling out of my pockets!!!
FLIP-O-RAMA 6
Left Hand Here

Cheater Beaters!

Right
thumb
Here

Cheater Beaters!

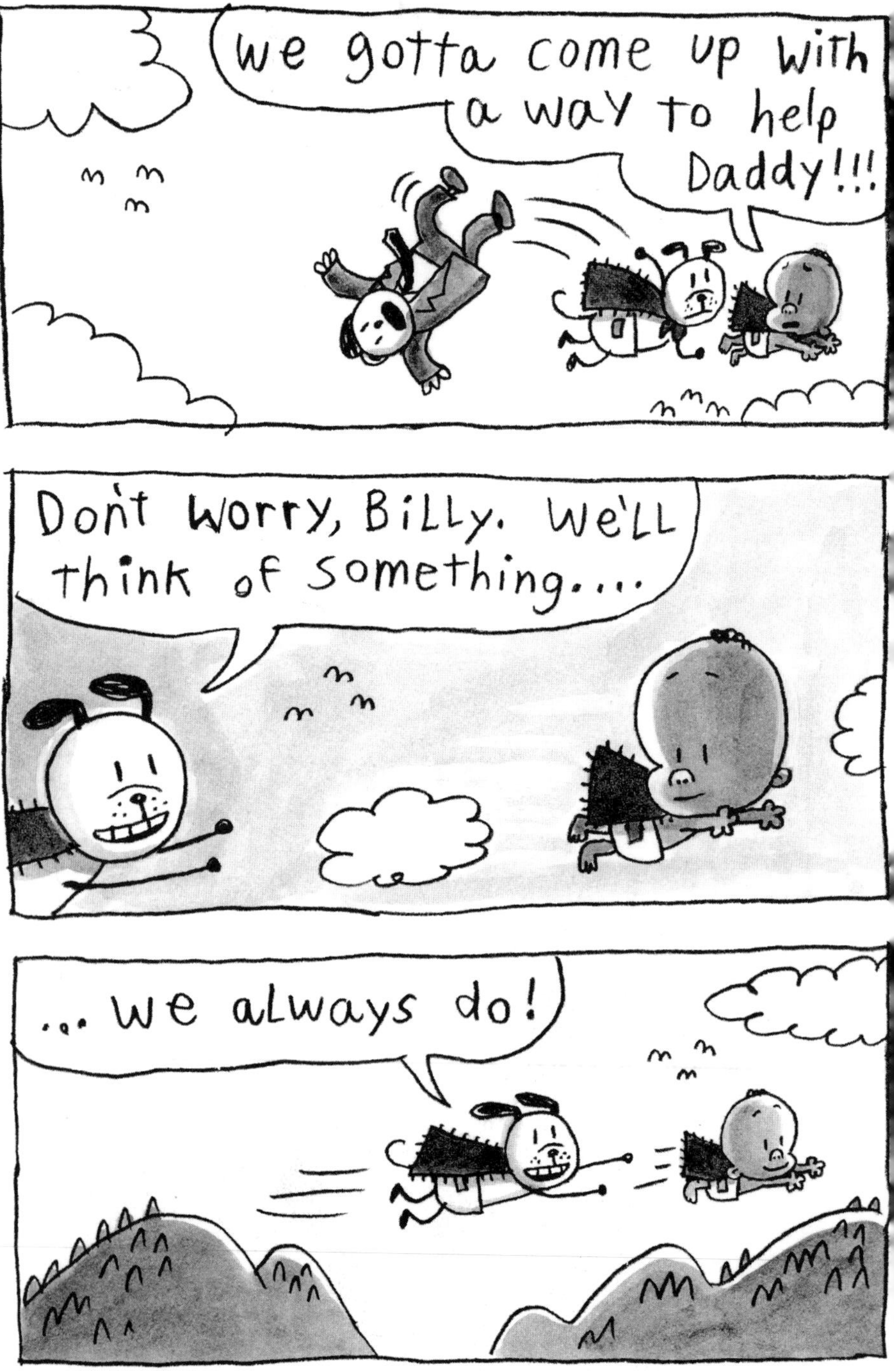
we gotta come up with a way to help Daddy!!!
Don't worry, Billy. We'll think of something....
...we always do!

Chapter 4 (Part 1)

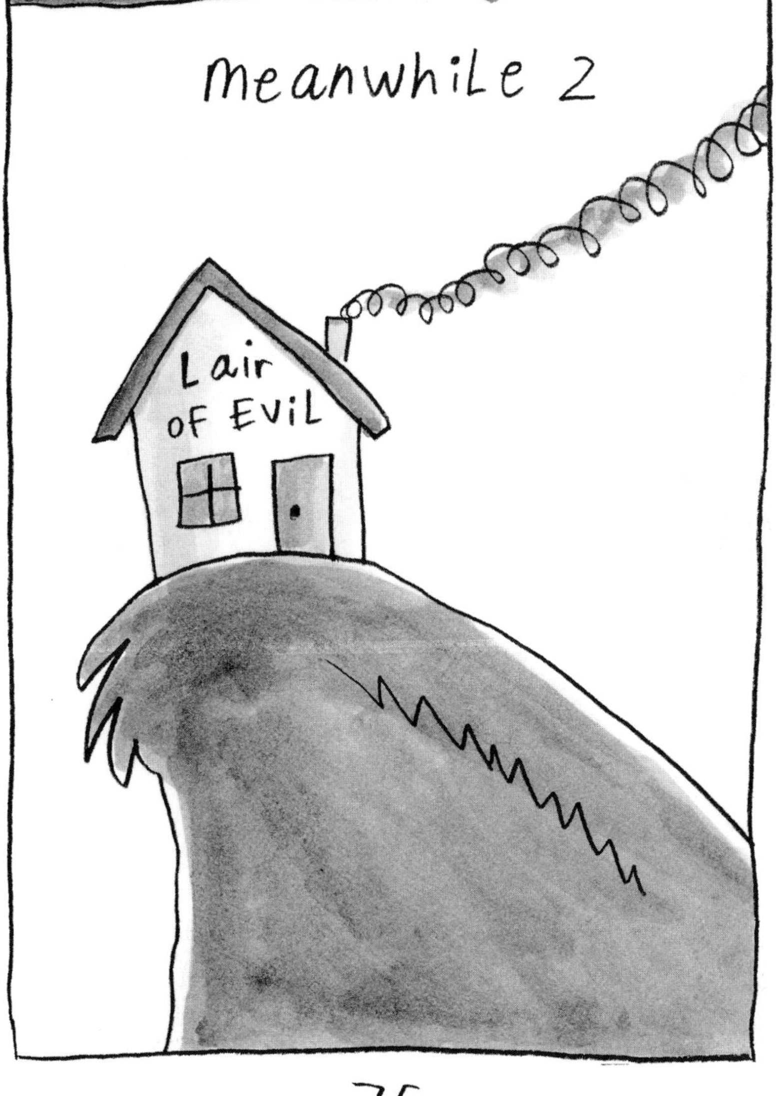

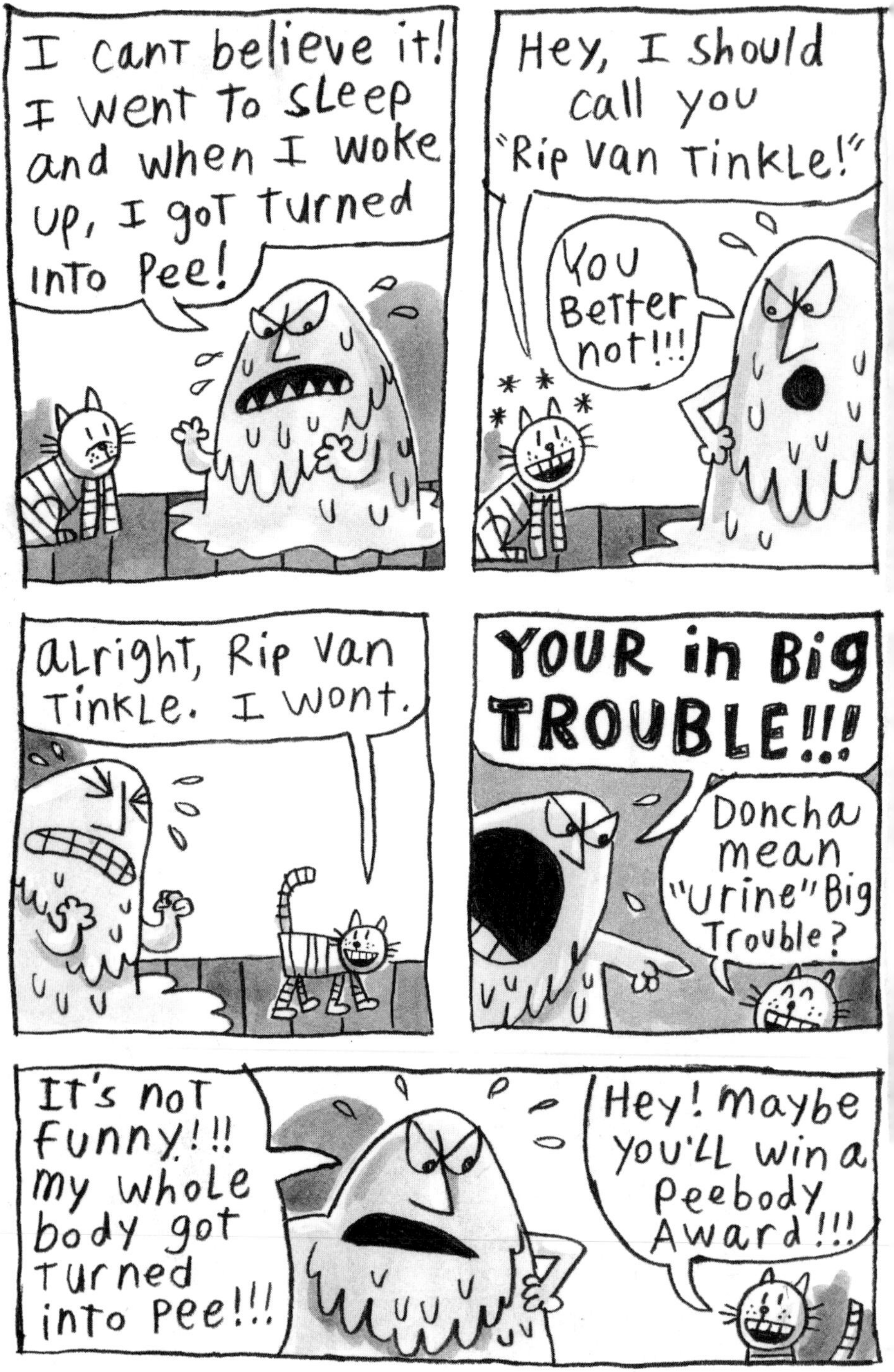
I cant believe it! I went to sleep and when I woke up, I got turned into Pee!
Hey, I should call you "Rip Van Tinkle!"
You Better not!!!
alright, Rip Van Tinkle. I wont.
YOUR in Big TROUBLE!!!
Doncha mean "Urine" Big Trouble?
It's not funny!!! my whole body got turned into Pee!!!
Hey! maybe you'll win a Peebody Award!!!

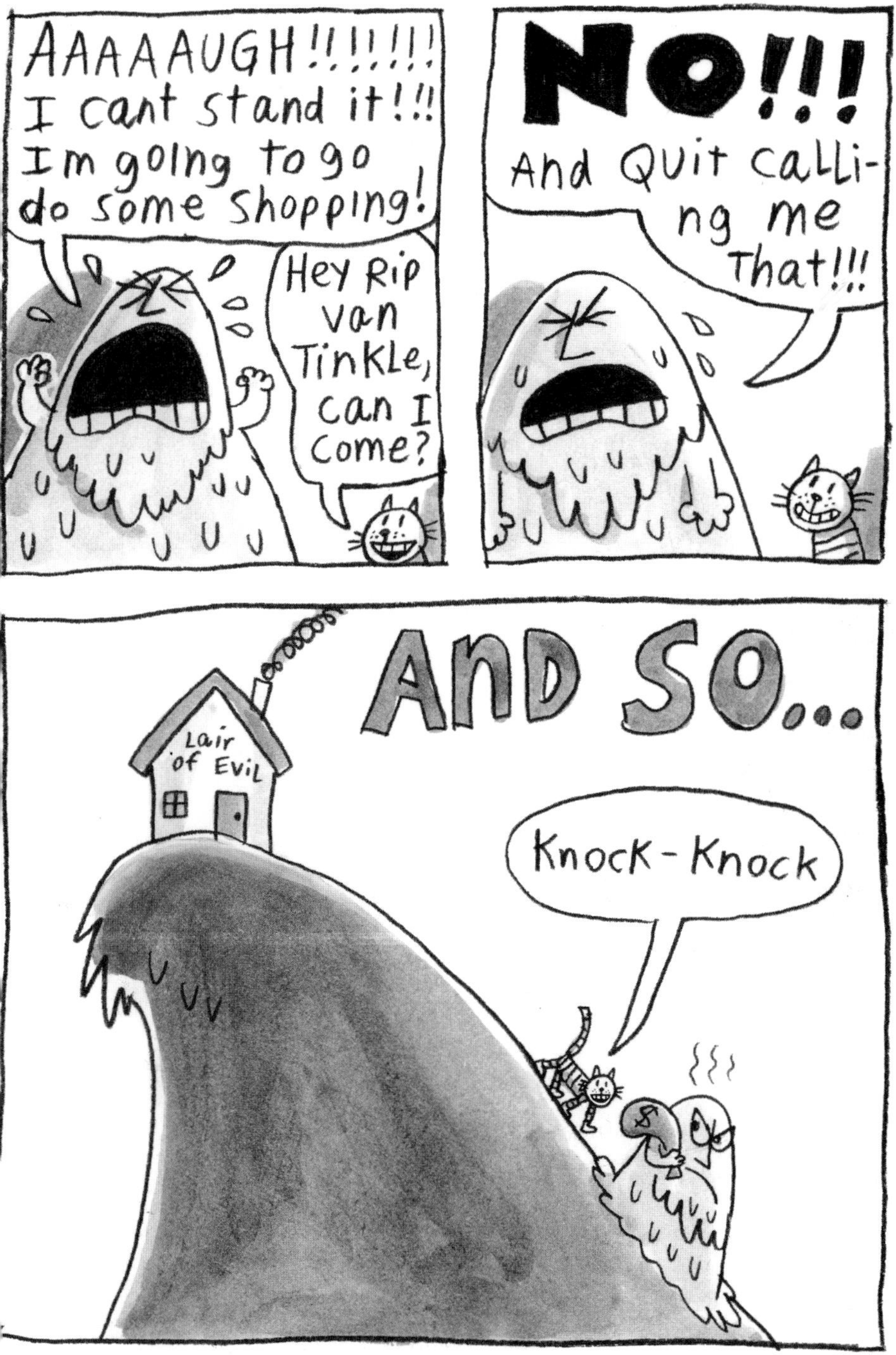
AAAAAUGH!!!!!!!
I cant stand it!!!
Im going to go do some shopping!
Hey Rip van Tinkle, can I come?
NO!!!
And QUIT calli-ng me That!!!
AND SO...
Lair of EVIL
Knock-Knock

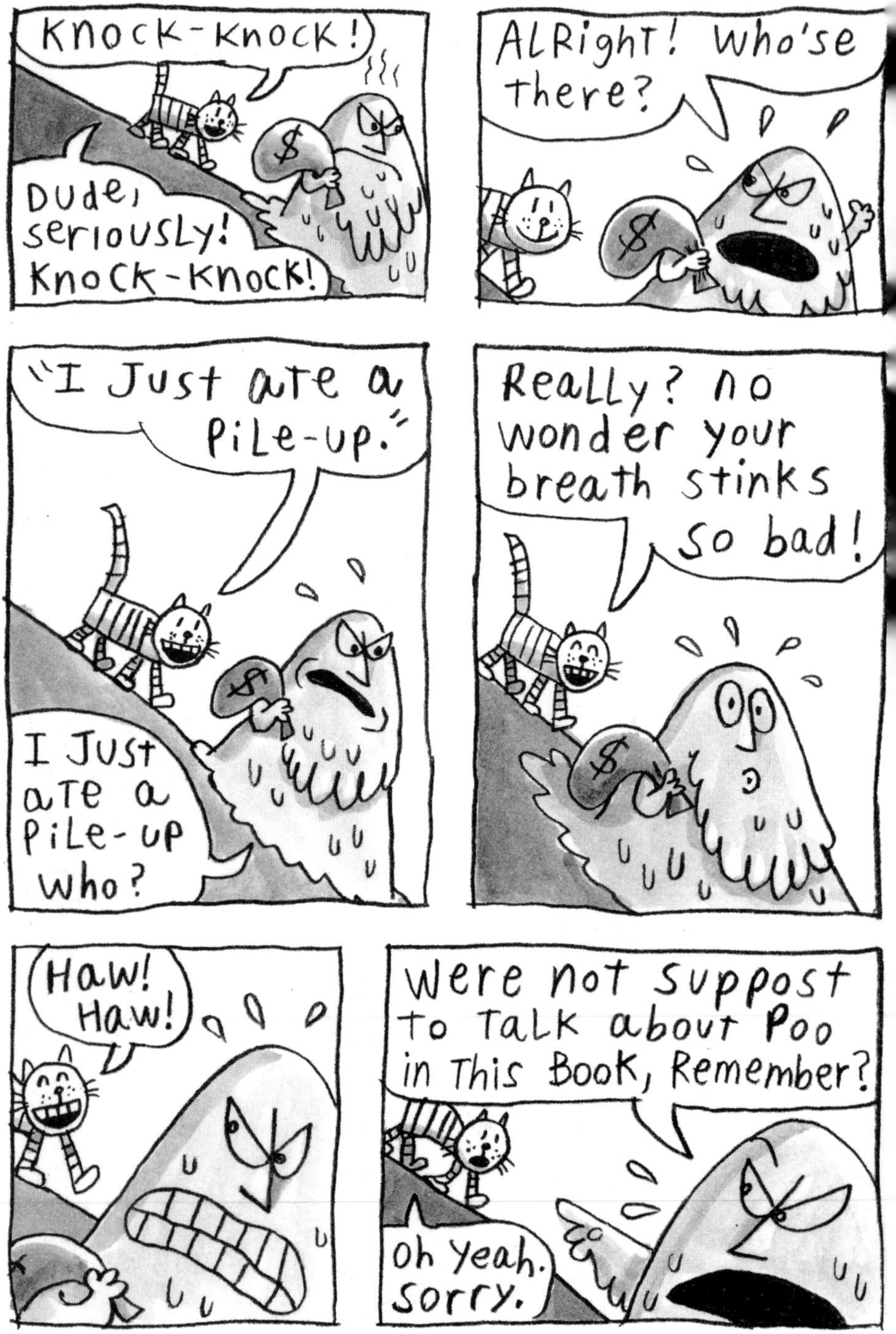
Knock-Knock!
Dude, seriously! Knock-Knock!
ALRight! Who'se there?
"I Just ate a Pile-up."
I Just ate a Pile-up who?
Really? no wonder your breath stinks so bad!
Haw! Haw!
Were not suppost to Talk about Poo in This Book, Remember?
Oh Yeah. Sorry.

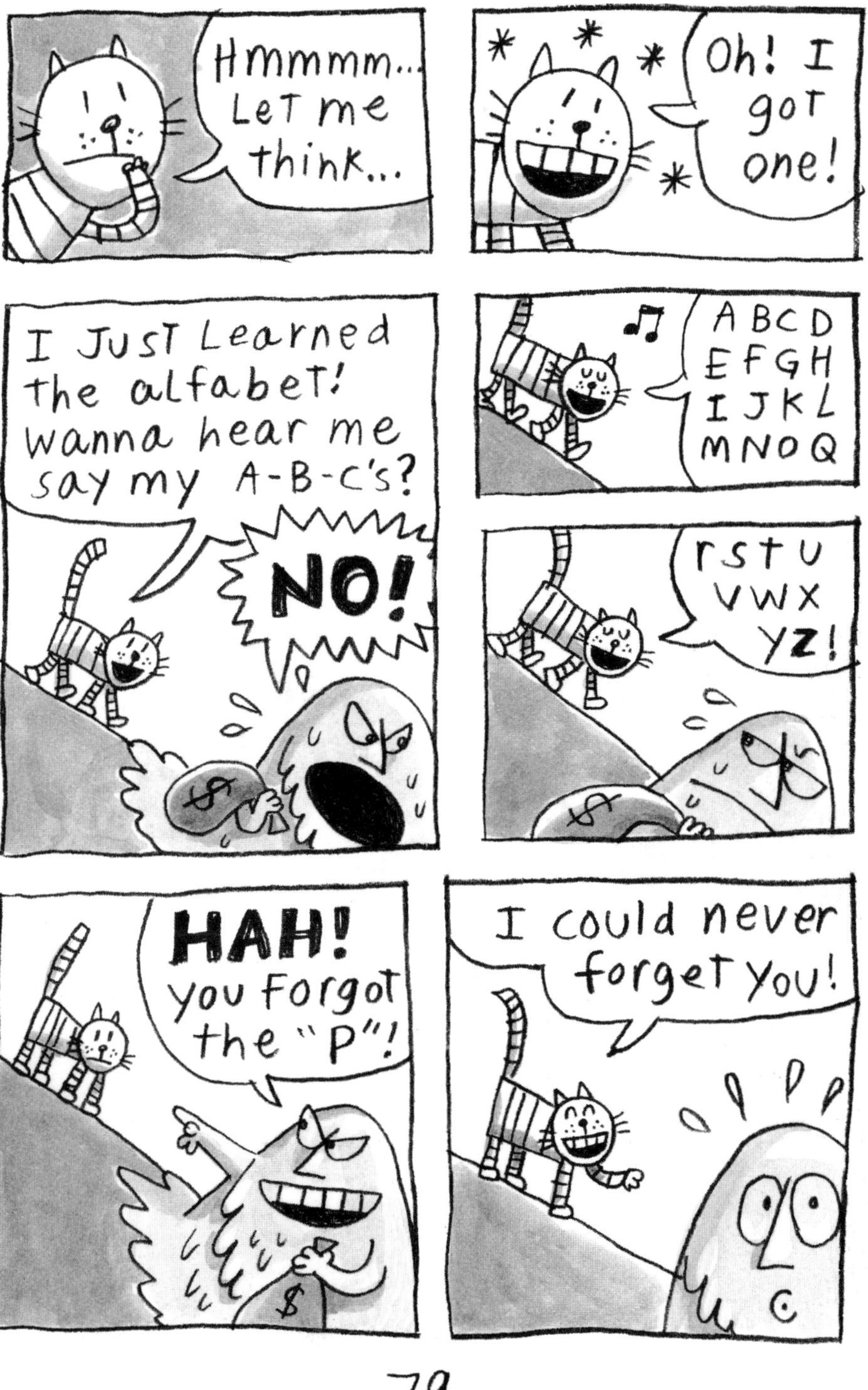
Hmmmm... Let me think...
Oh! I got one!
I JUST Learned the alfabet! wanna hear me say my A-B-C's?
NO!
A B C D E F G H I J K L M N O Q
r s t u v w x y z!
HAH! you Forgot the "P"!
I could never forget you!

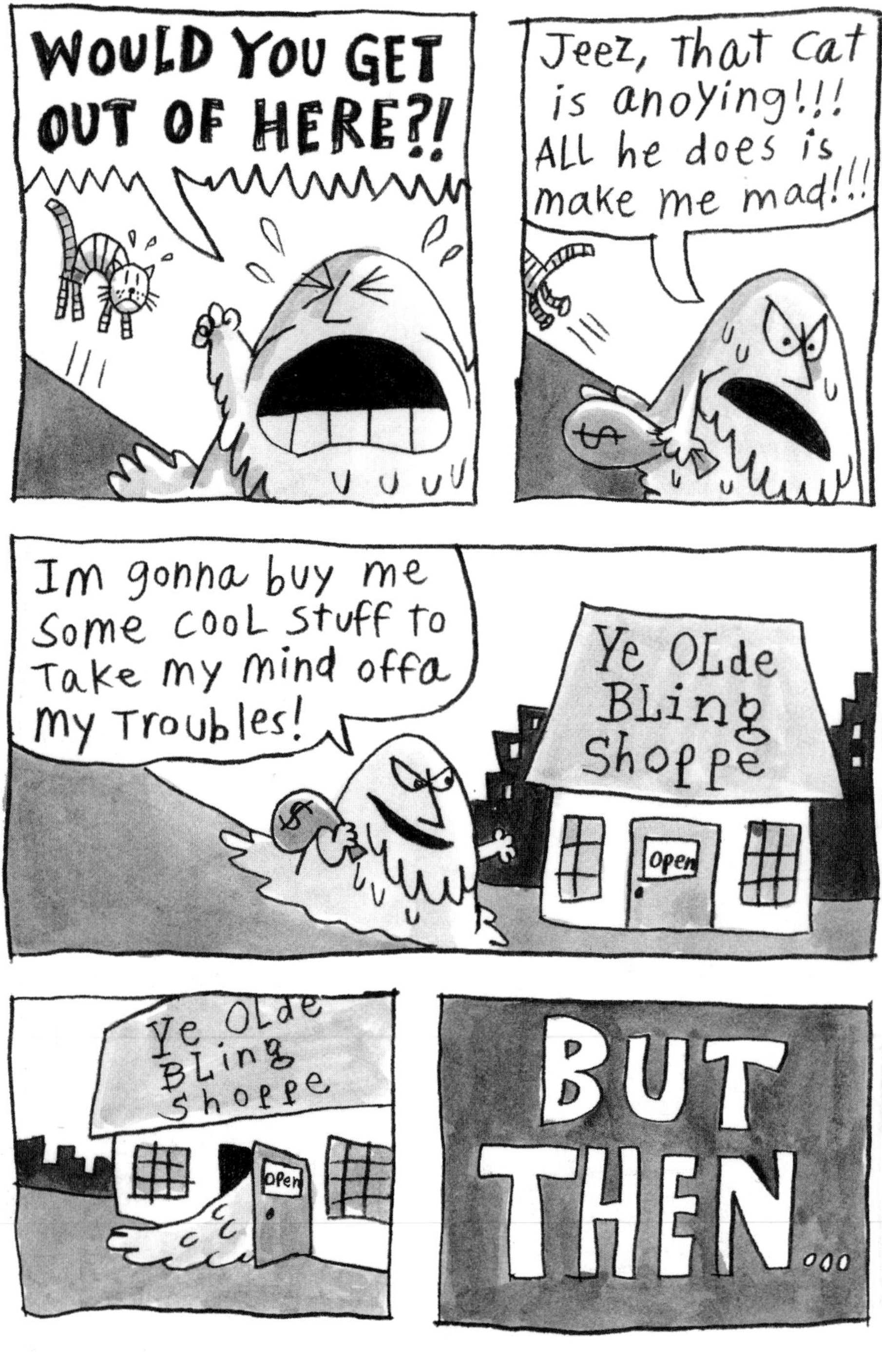
WOULD YOU GET OUT OF HERE?!
Jeez, That cat is anoying!!! ALL he does is make me mad!!!
Im gonna buy me some cool stuff to Take my mind offa my Troubles!
Ye OLde BLing Shoppe
Open
Ye OLde BLing Shoppe
Open
BUT THEN...

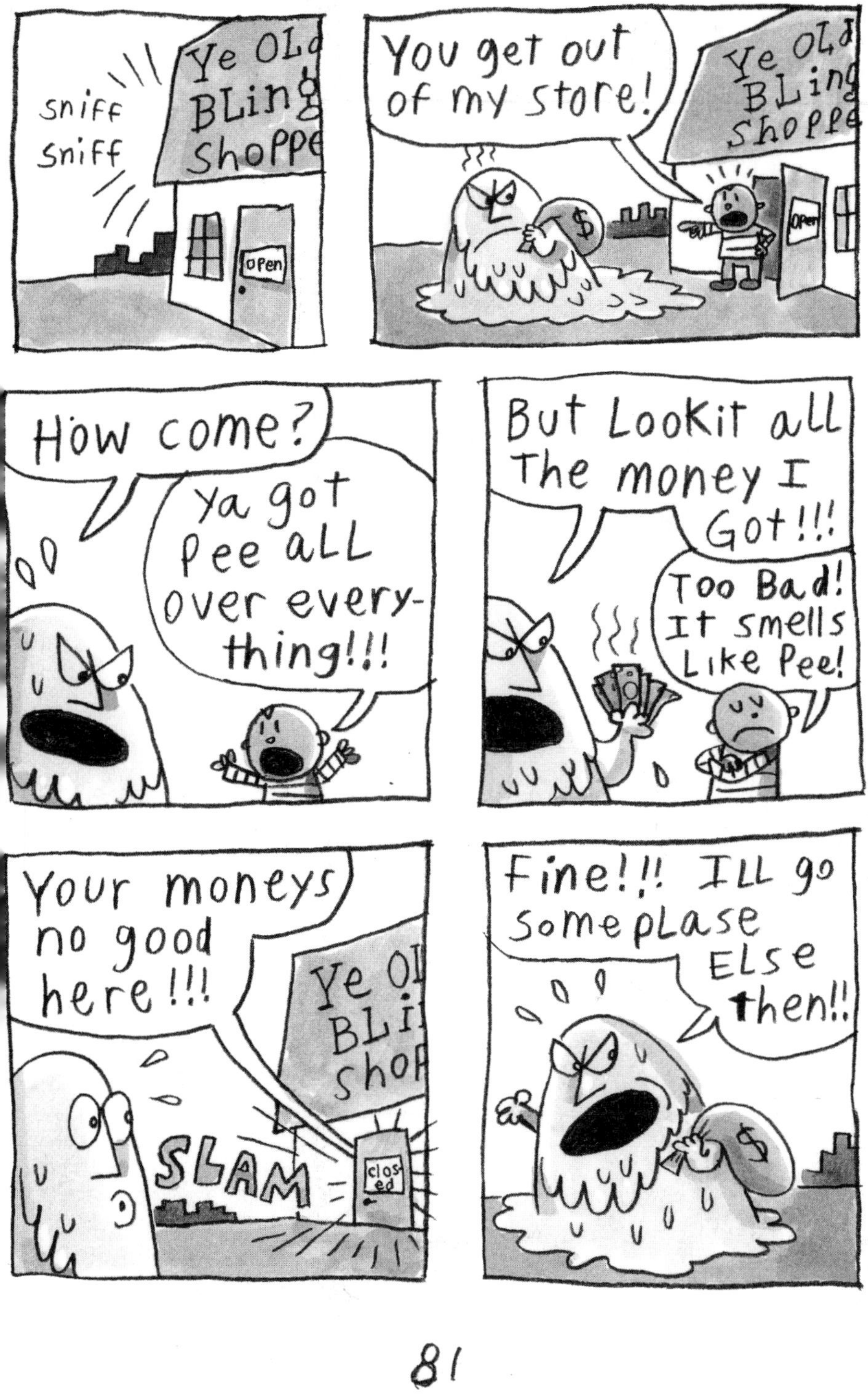
Ye OLd BLing Shoppe
sniff sniff
open
You get out of my store!
Ye OLd BLing Shoppe
Open
How come?
Ya got pee aLL over every-thing!!!
But Lookit all The money I Got!!!
Too Bad! It smells Like Pee!
Your moneys no good here!!!
Ye OL BLi Shop
SLAM
clos ed
Fine!!! ILL go someplase Else then!!

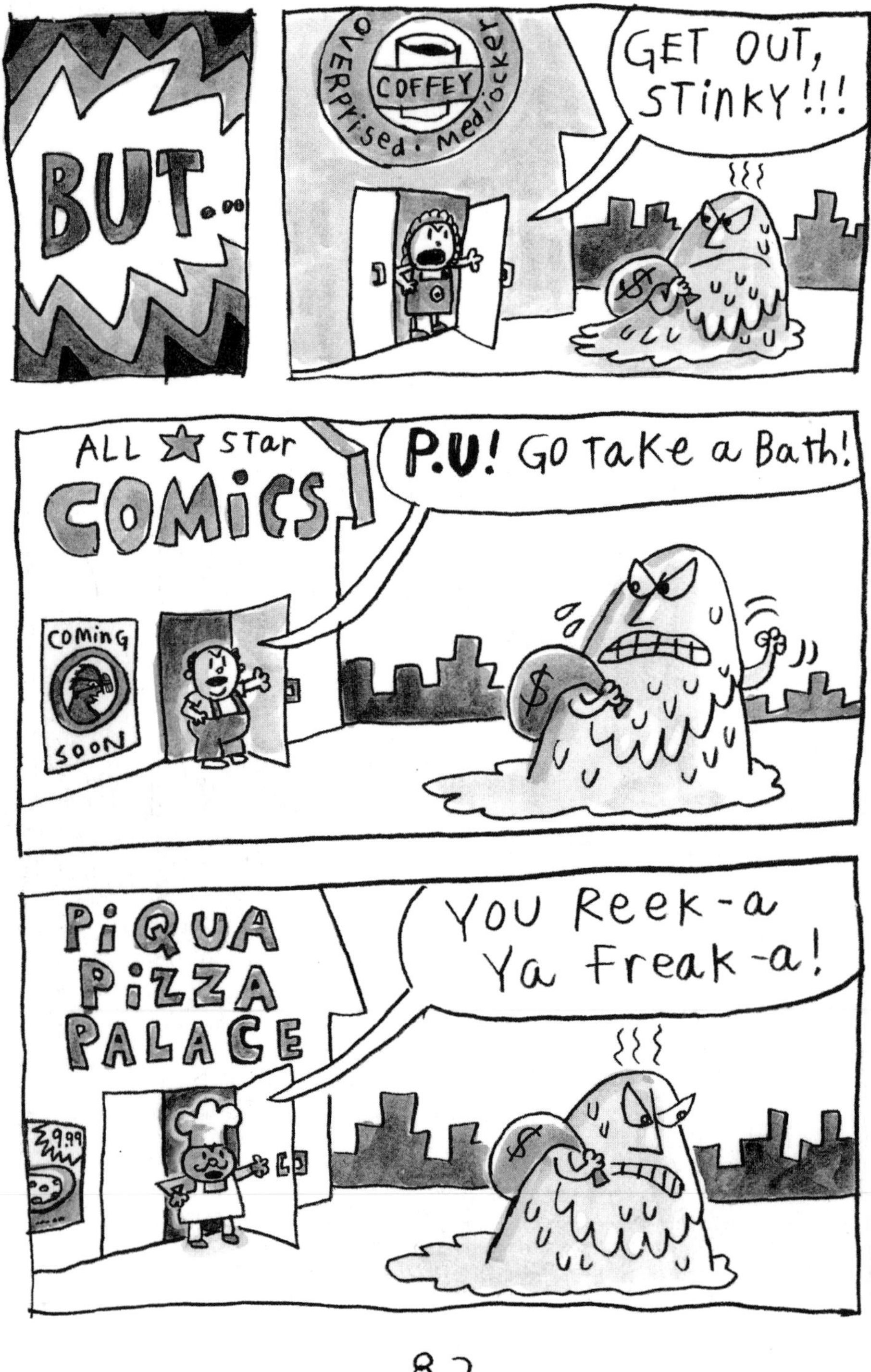
BUT...
OVERPRYSED • MEDIOCKER
COFFEY
GET OUT, STINKY!!!
ALL ★ STAR COMICS
COMING SOON
P.U! GO TAKE A BATH!
PIQUA PIZZA PALACE
$9.99
YOU REEK-A YA FREAK-A!

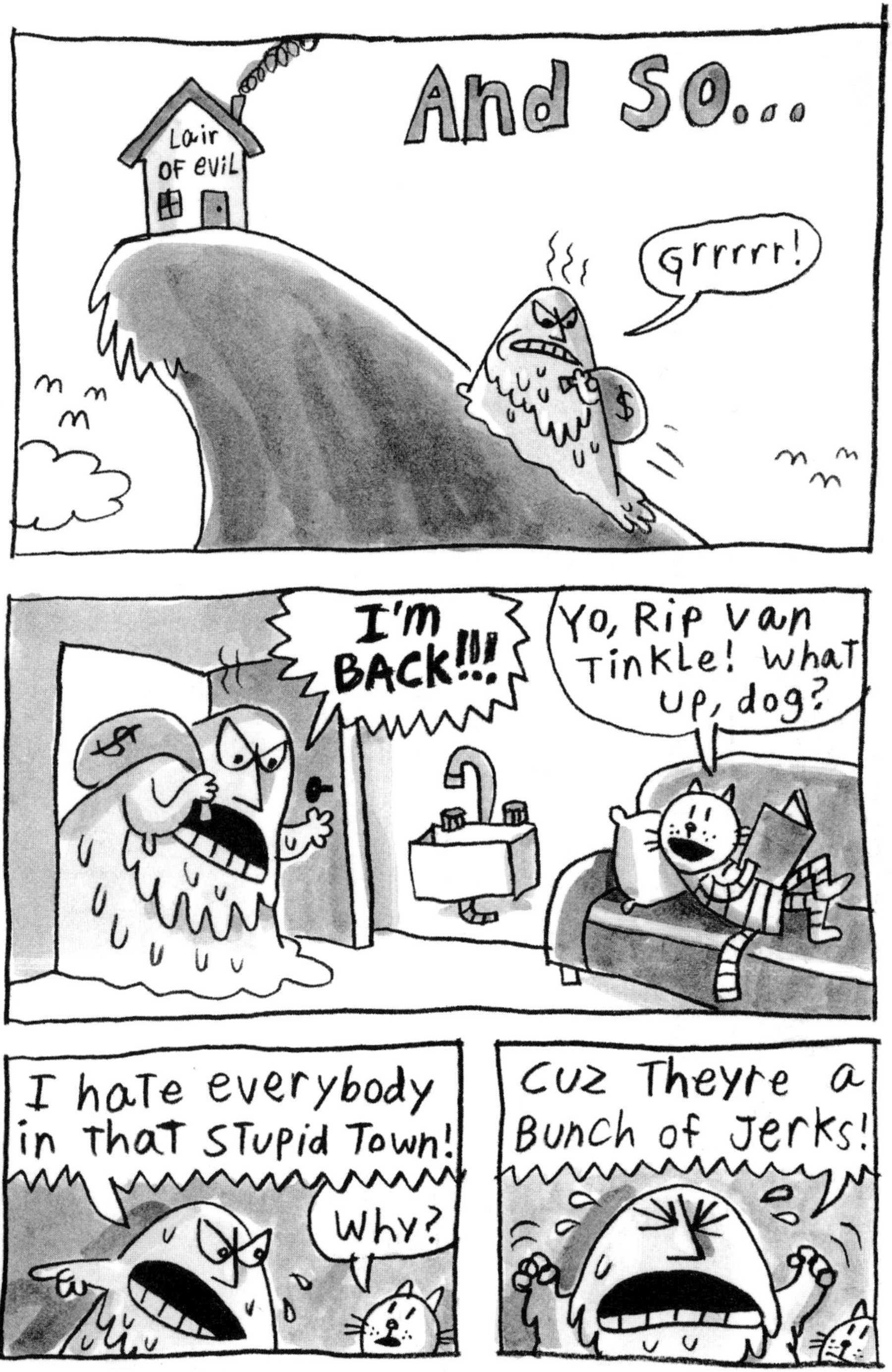
And so...
Lair OF evil
Grrrrr!
I'm BACK!!!
Yo, Rip van Tinkle! What up, dog?
I hate everybody in that Stupid Town!
Why?
Cuz Theyre a Bunch of Jerks!

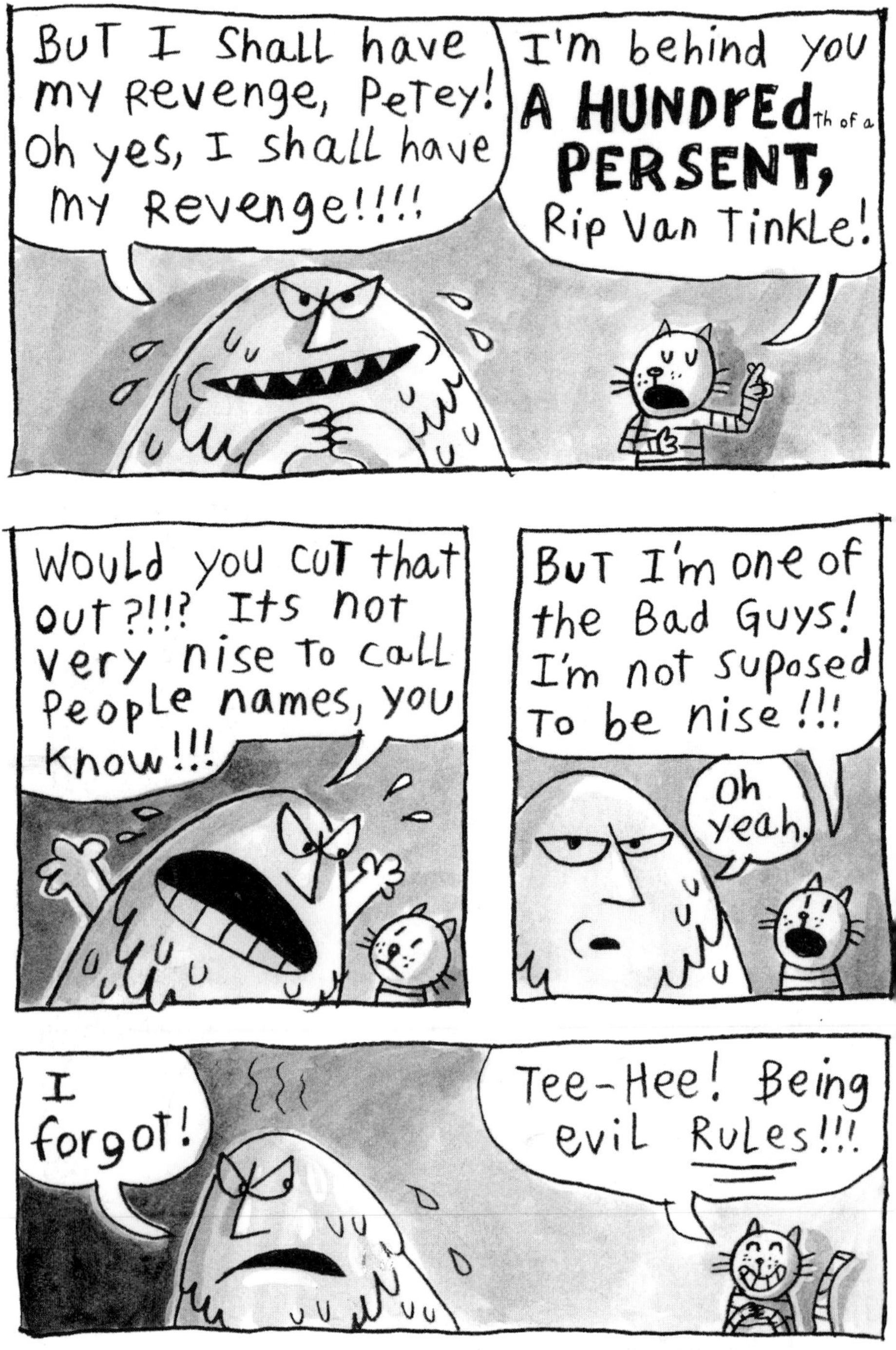
BuT I Shall have my Revenge, PeTey! Oh yes, I shall have my Revenge!!!!
I'm behind you A HUNDrED Th of a PERSENT, Rip Van Tinkle!
WouLd you cuT that out?!!? Its not very nise To call PeopLe names, you Know!!!
BuT I'm one of the Bad Guys! I'm not suposed To be nise!!!
Oh yeah.
I forgot!
Tee-Hee! Being evil RuLes!!!

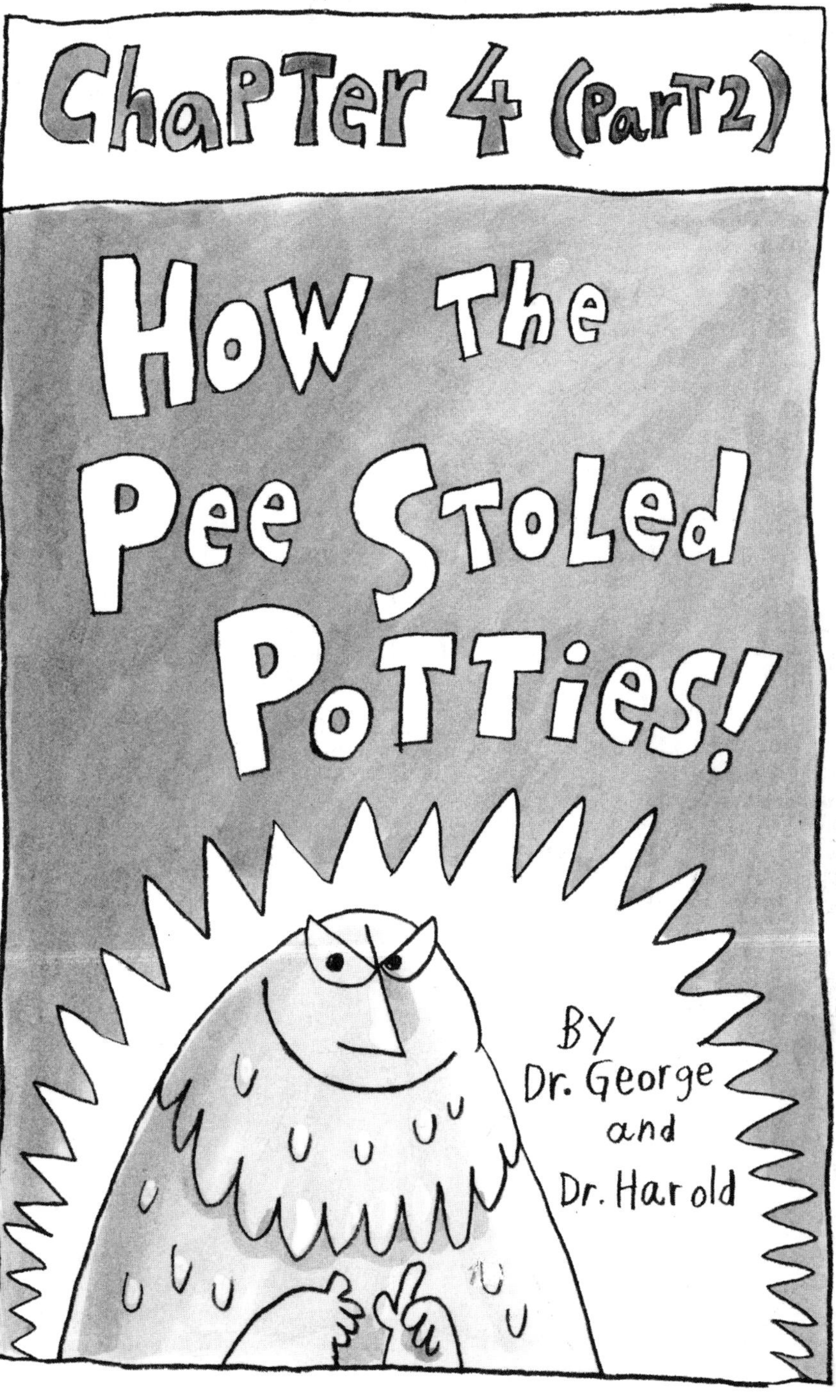
Chapter 4 (Part 2)
How the Pee Stoled Potties!
By Dr. George and Dr. Harold

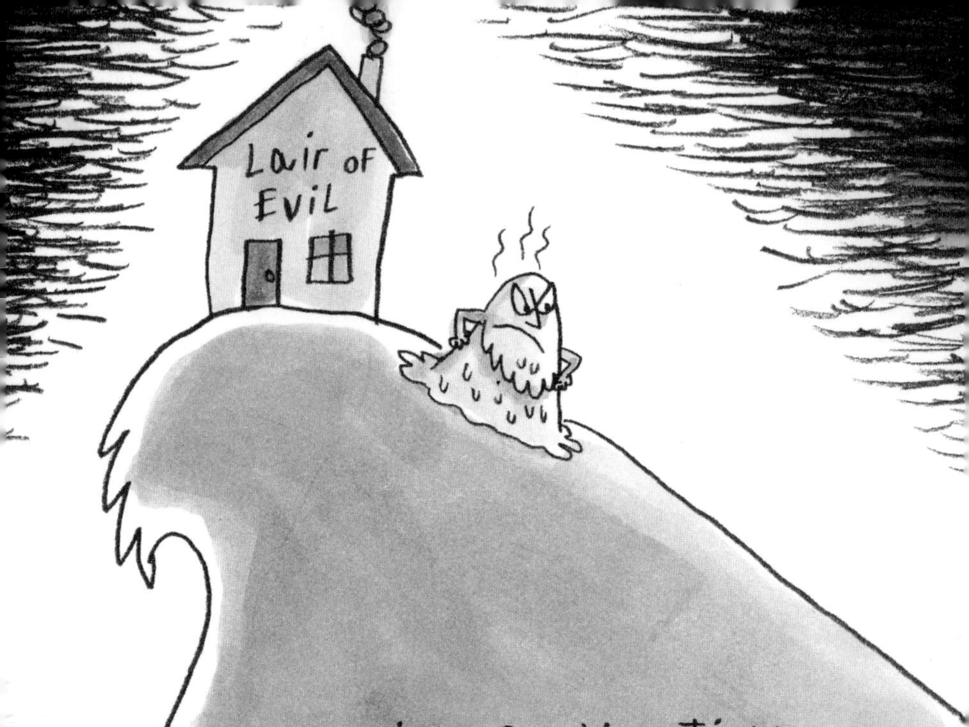
Lair of Evil

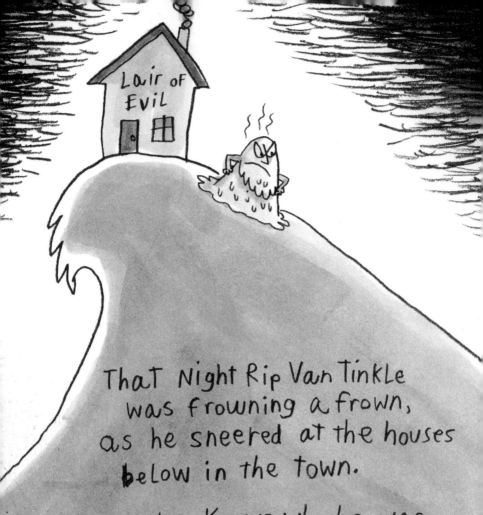

That Night Rip Van Tinkle
was frowning a frown,
as he sneered at the houses
below in the town.

No one Knows why he was
feeling so ruthless...
It could be because all his
money was useless.

Or maybe because he was
JUST feeling cranky.
Or possibly cuz his bad breath
was so stanky.
But we think the very best
reason might be
that he smelled like a bucket
of twelve-day-old pee.

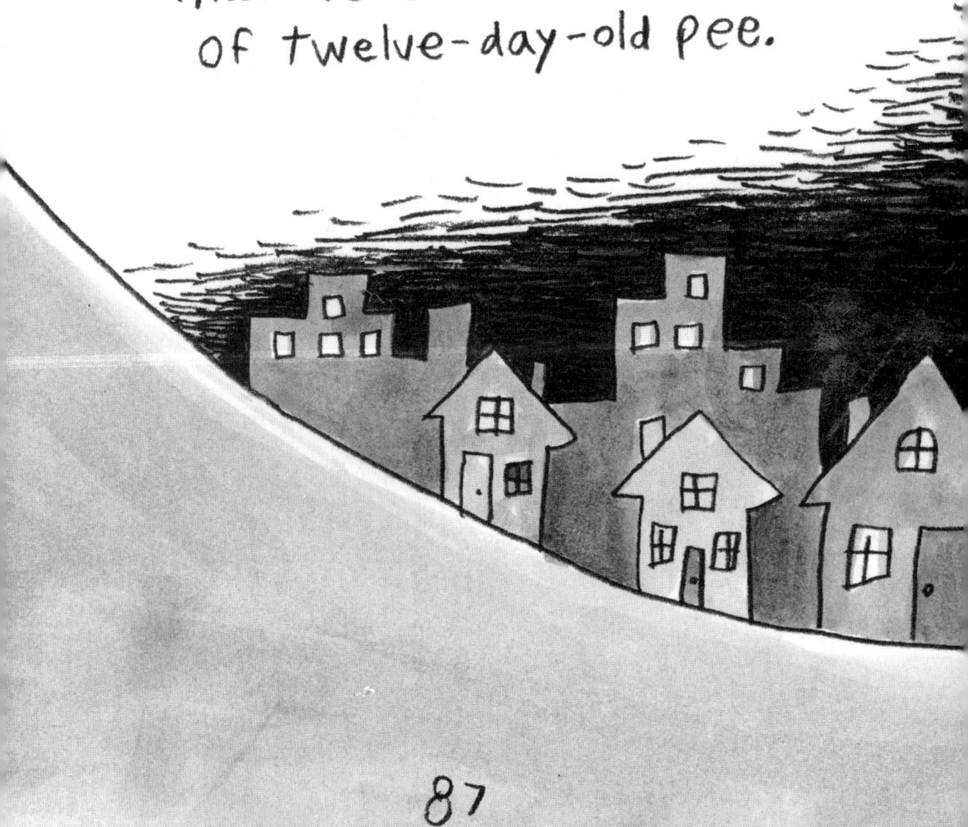

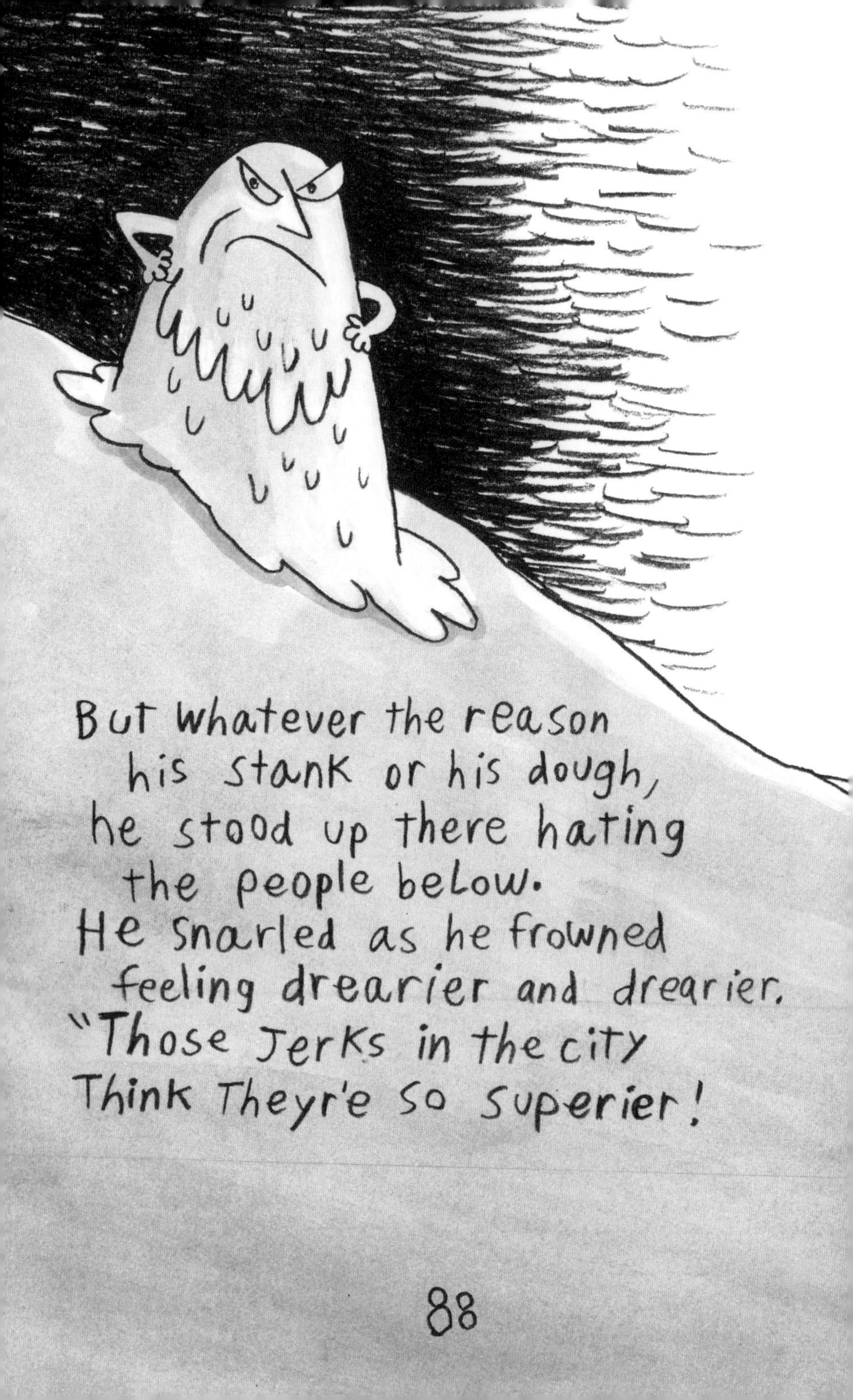

But whatever the reason
his stank or his dough,
he stood up there hating
the people below.
He snarled as he frowned
feeling drearier and drearier.
"Those Jerks in the city
Think Theyr'e so superier!

"They all be hatin'!
   But heres what I think:
 I think things would change
   if they started to stink!

If all of those idiots
   smelled just like pee,
they wouldent be goin' Round
 disrespectin' me!!!"

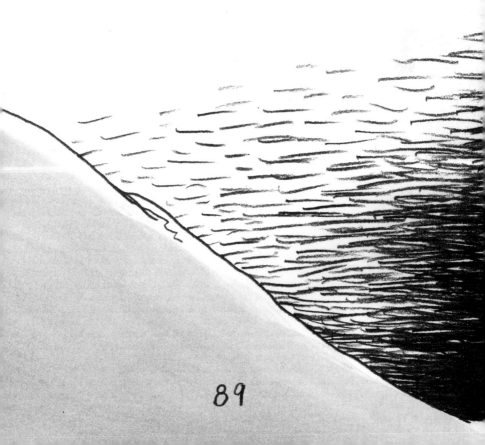

89

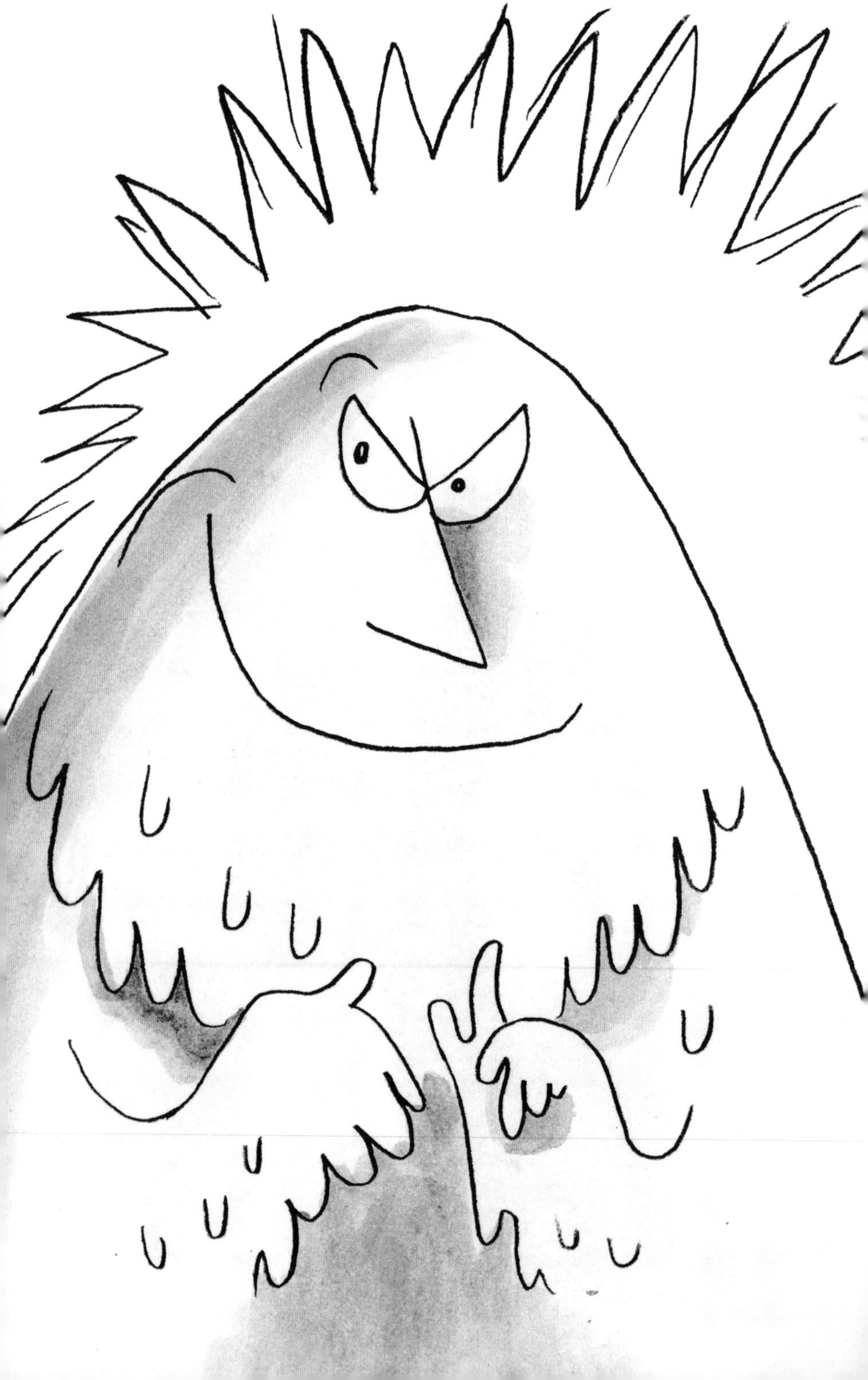

And Then Rip Van Tinkle
    Thought up a idea.
BuT we couldent Think up
    a rhyme for "idea".

"I Know just what to do"
    he started professin'.
"I'LL teach all of those good-
    smelling people a Lessen!"

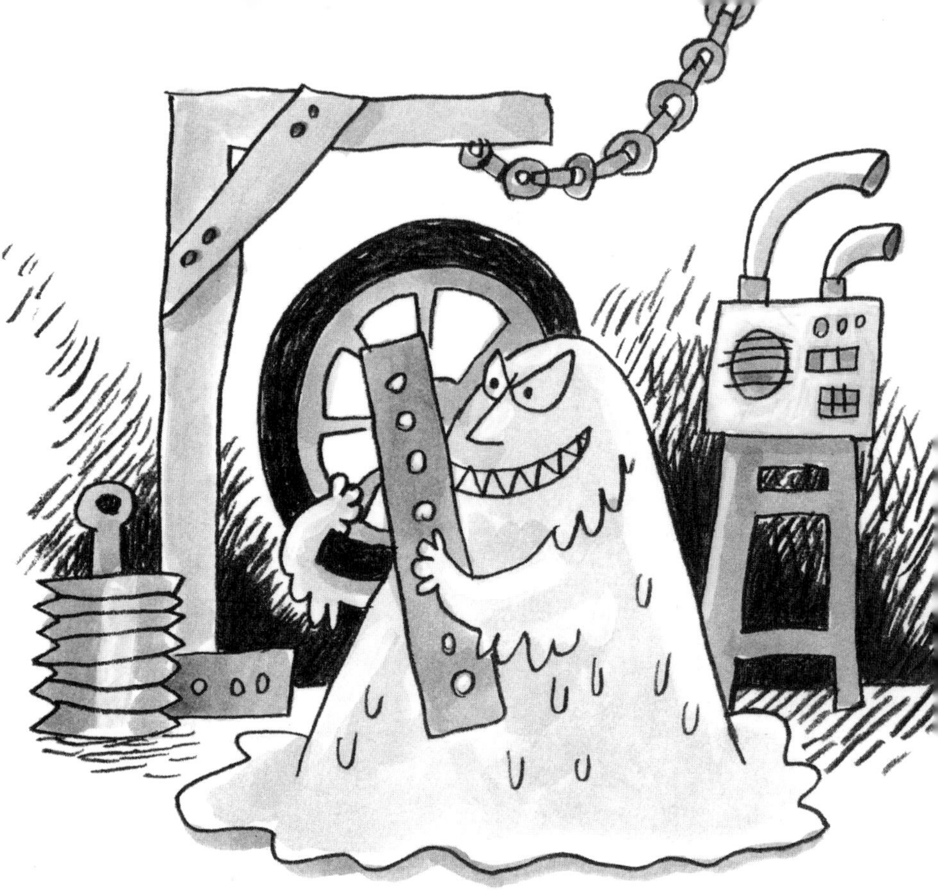

So he Took Some scrap metal
and used an old wheel
To build a contrapshon
with Teeth made of steel.

He hammered its tail
and sharpened its claws,
and welded its wiskers
and titened its Jaws.

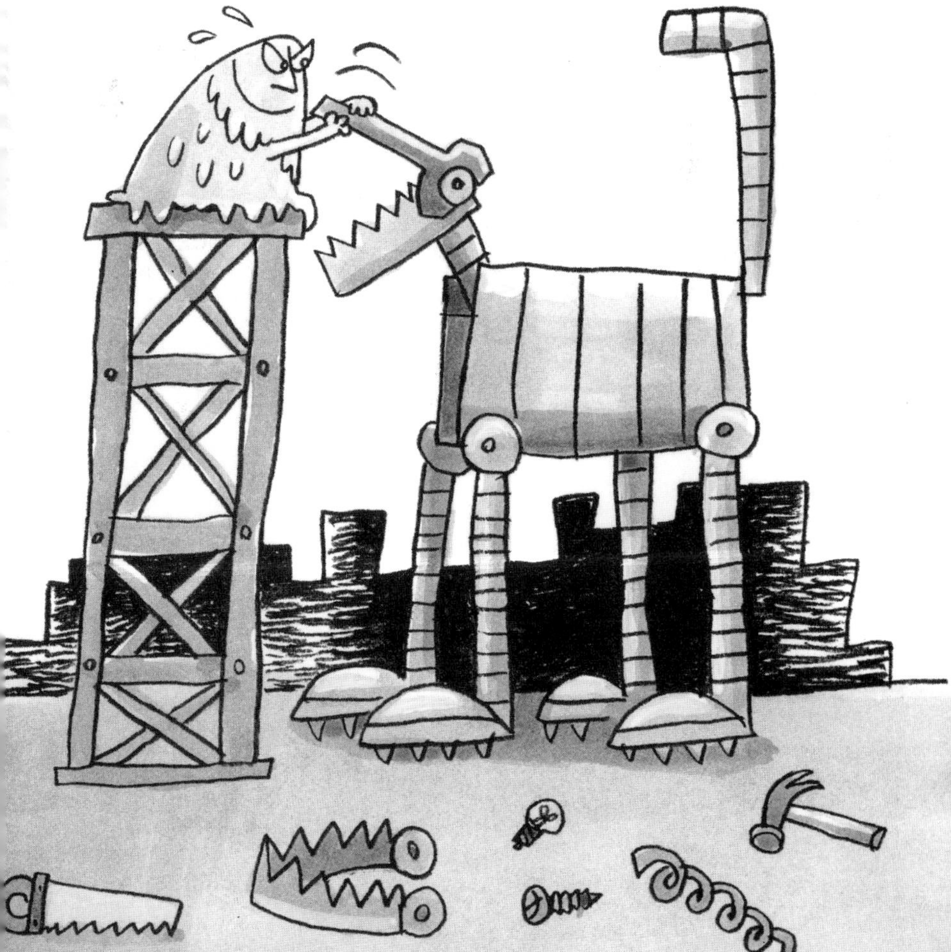

It took 24 hours
  From when he'd begun,
'Till the Robo-Kitty
  Three Thousand was done.
"ALL I need is a driver.
  I need someone mean.
I need someone evil ❤
  to run my machine".

So he took his cat "Petey"
  and strapped him in tight...

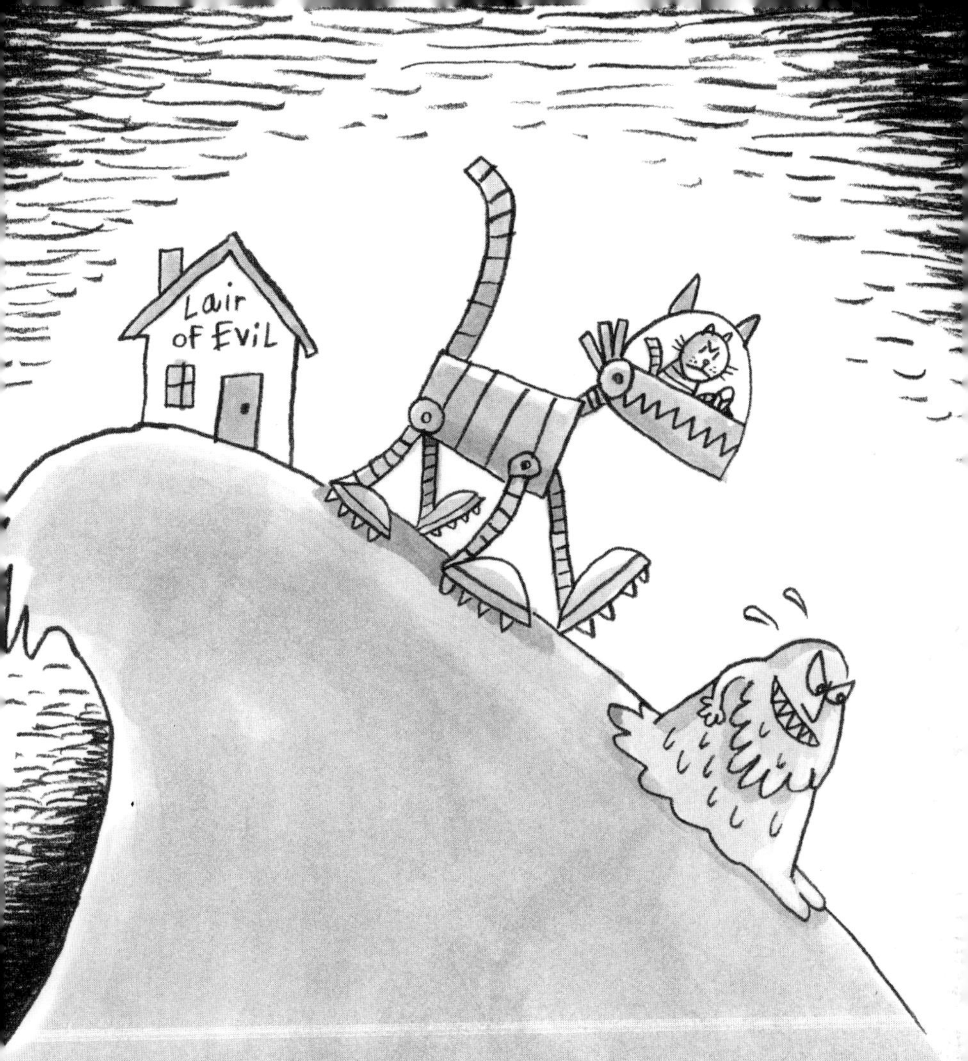
Lair of EviL

...Then both of those villens sneaked out in the night.

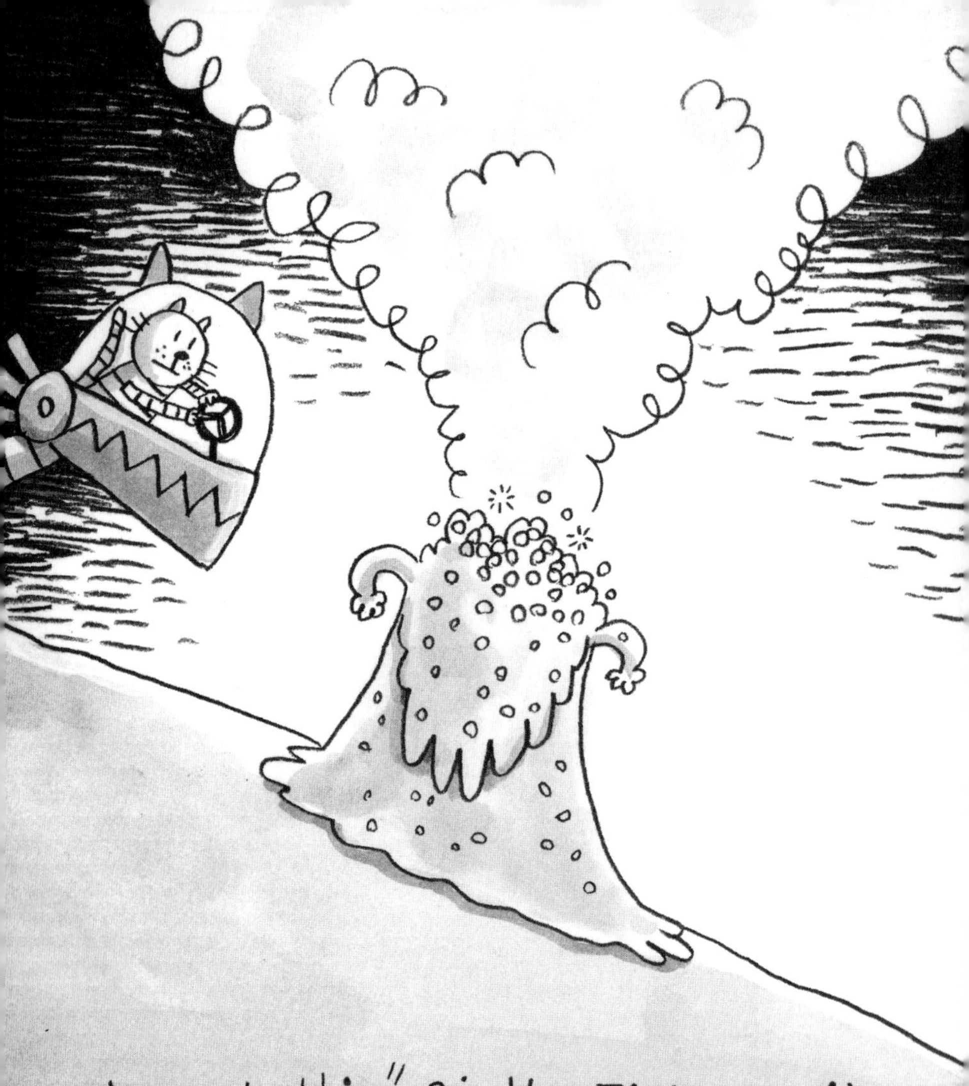

"Watch this," Rip Van Tinkle said
Laffing out Loud...
and soon he began to
turn into a cloud.

And when the pee cloud
was over the town,
The thunderclaps crashed
and the pee drops rained down.

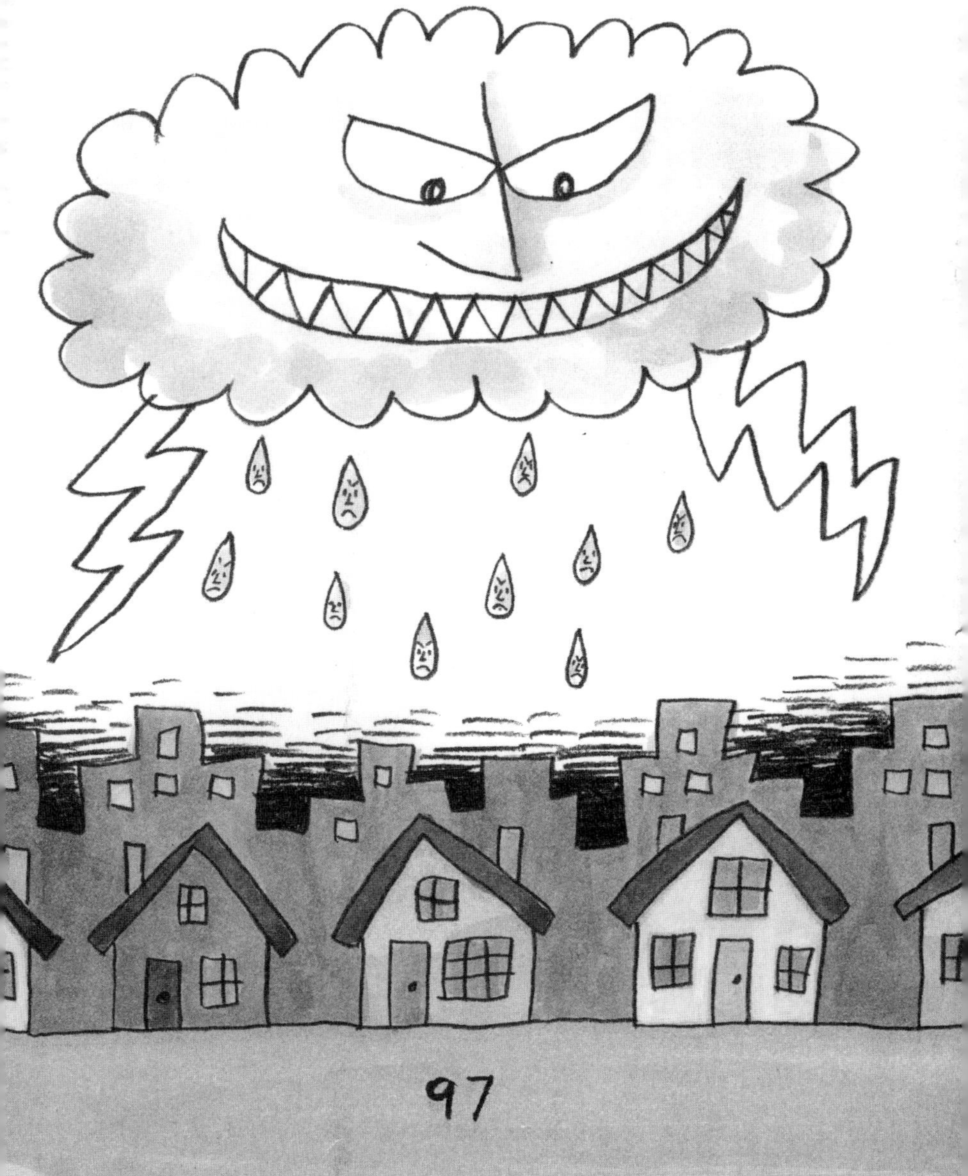

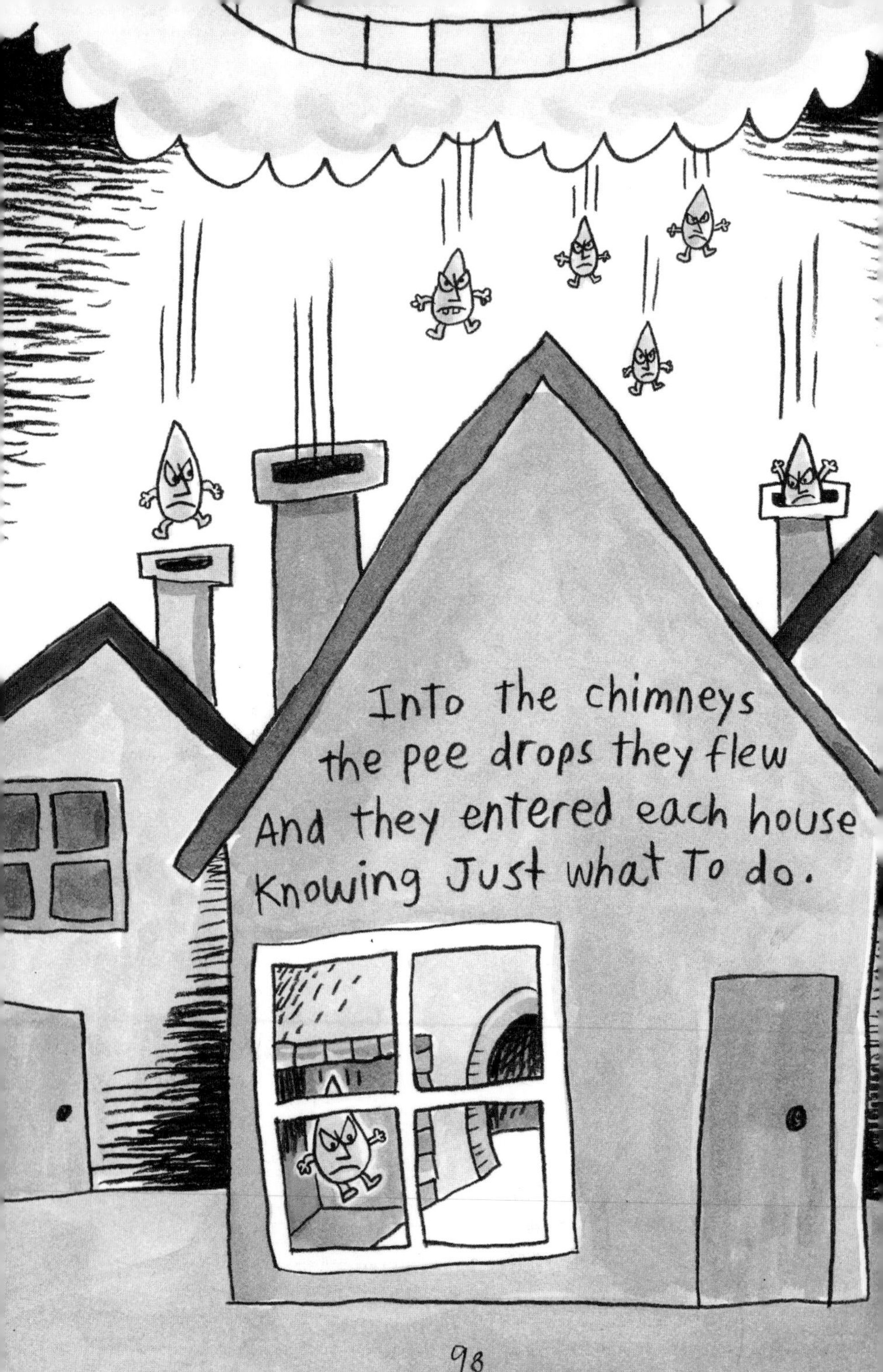
Into the chimneys
the pee drops they flew
And they entered each house
Knowing Just what To do.

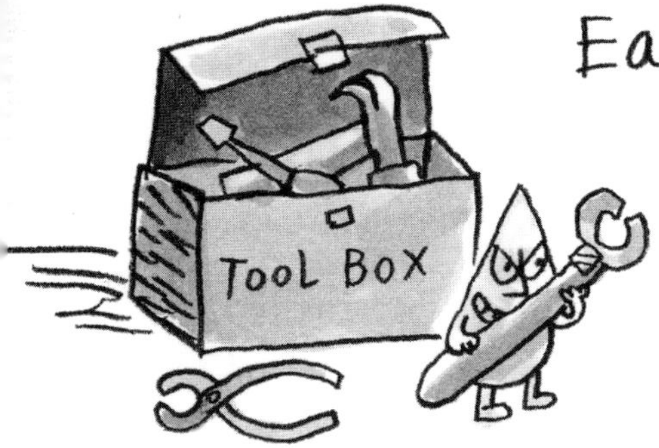
TOOL BOX

Each drop found a wrench...

... and each wrench found a bolt...

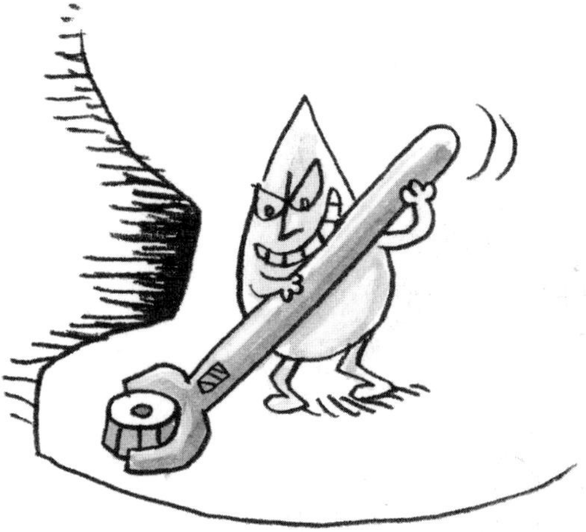

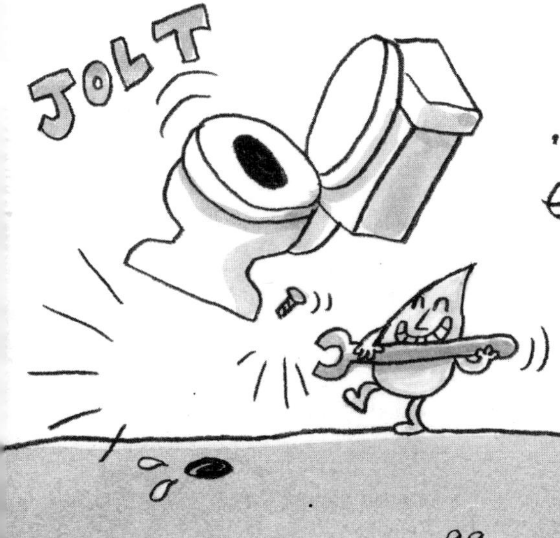
JOLT

...and soon every Toilet popped up with a JoLt!

They carried each toilet
  Right out of each house, and
Into the jaws of the
  Kitty Three thousend.

Crunch! Crunch! went the robot
without too much trouble
and soon every potty
was crushed into rubbel!

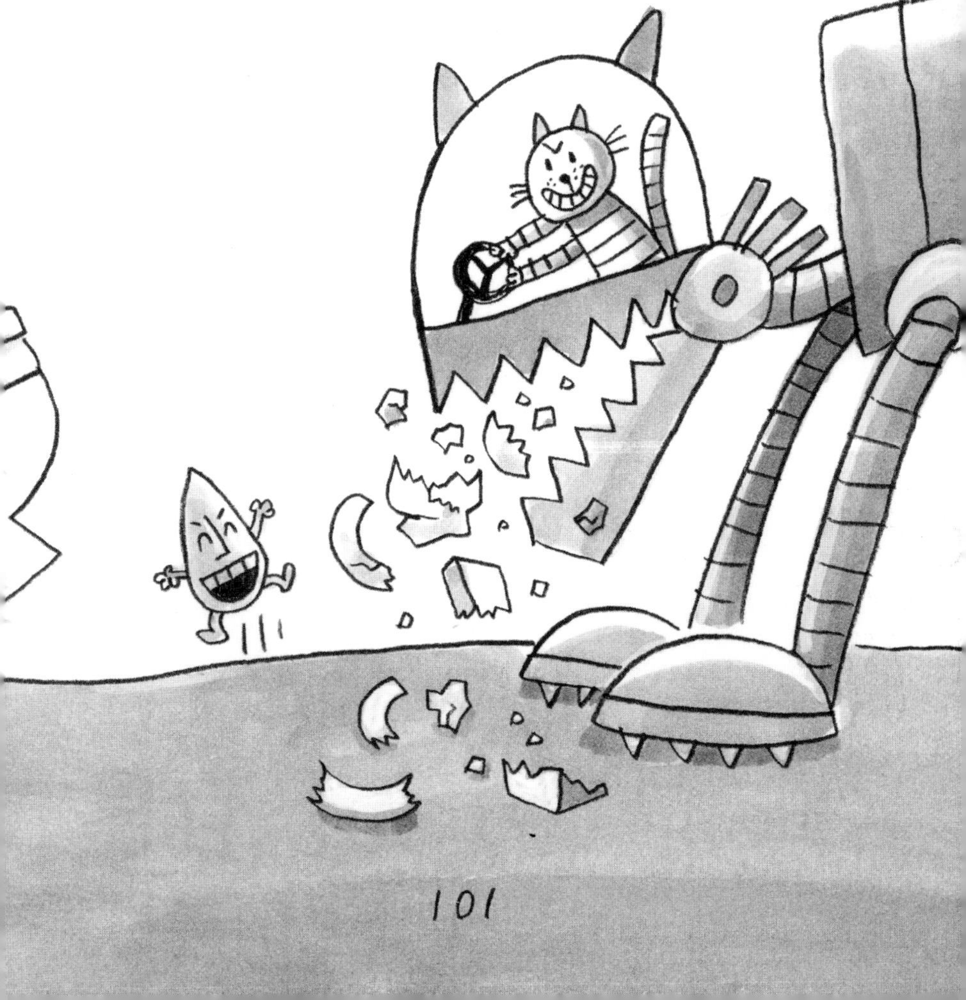

But in one little house,
on one little street,
One drip heard the sounds
of two little feet.

The pee drop looked up
and what did it see?
but a cute little tot
with a fluffy blankie.

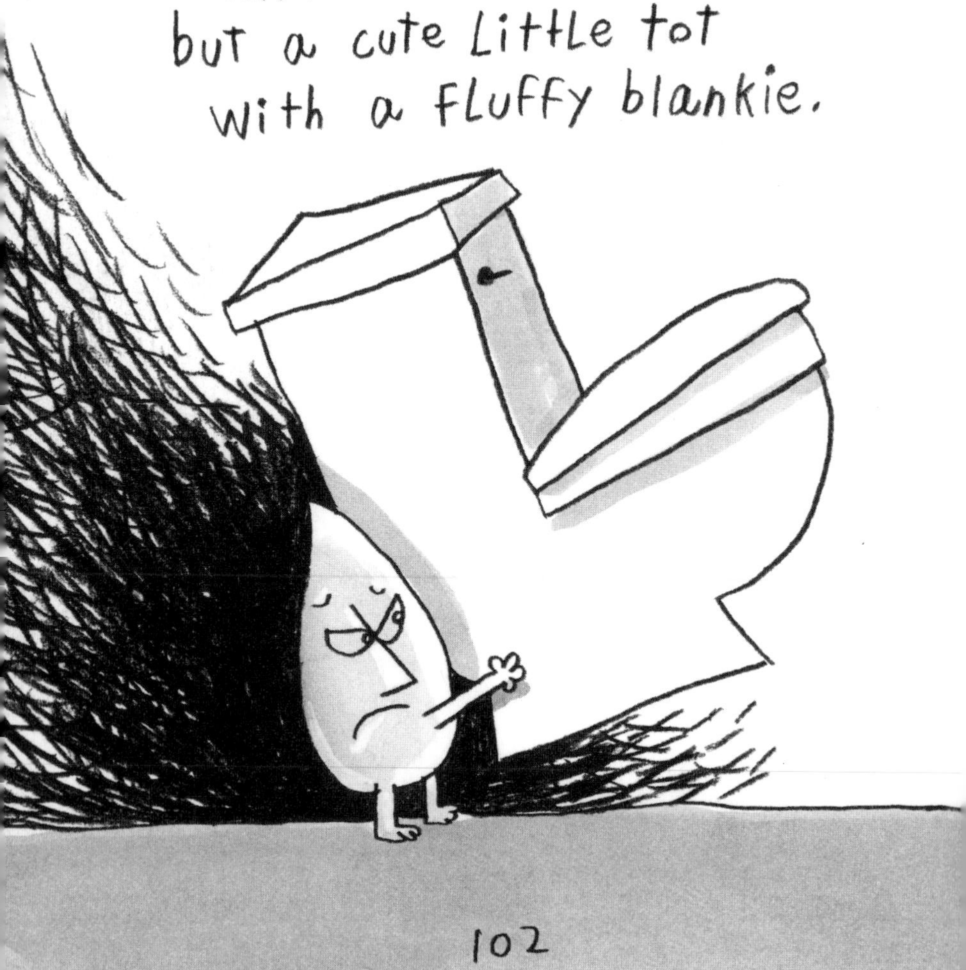

The baby looked down and said, "MR. Pee, Hey! Why are you taking our toiLet away?"

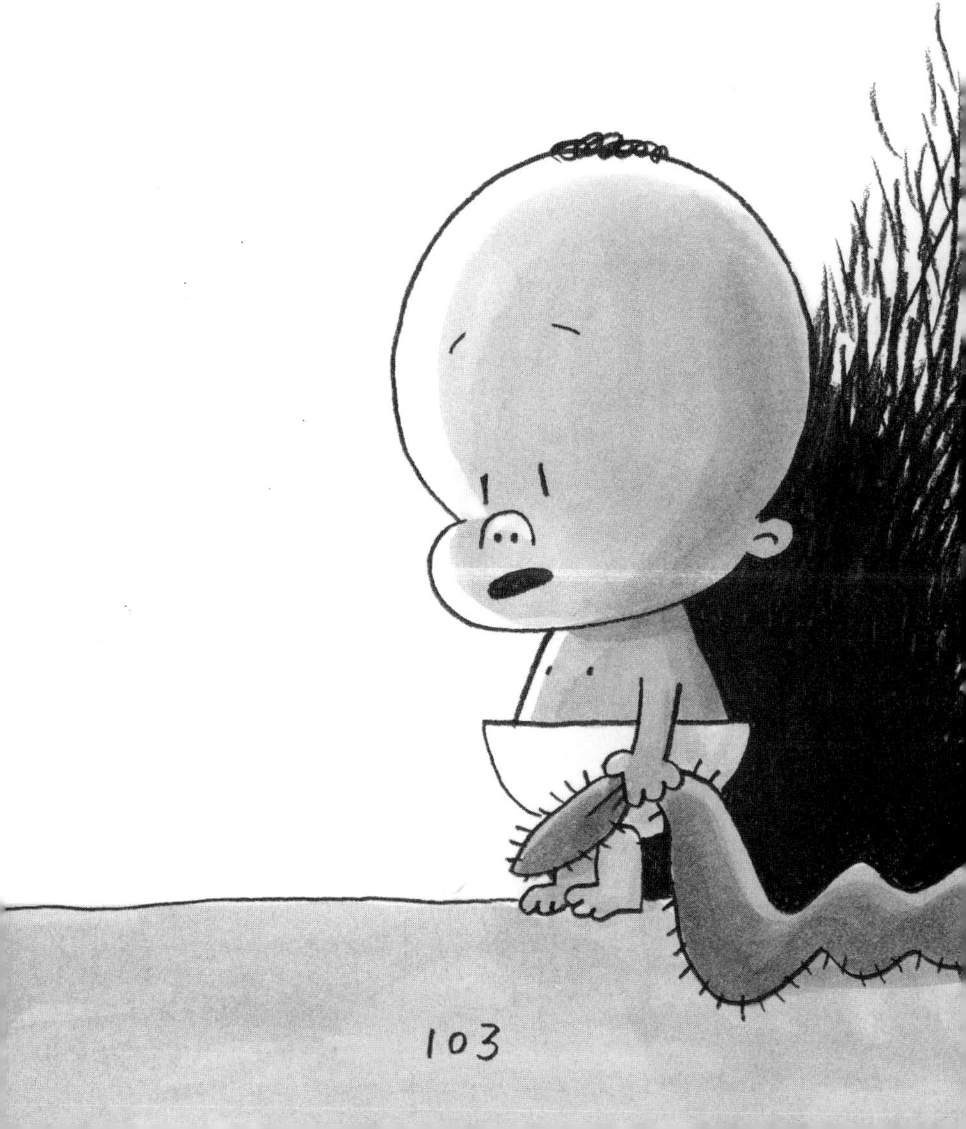

And that mean Little drip,
do you Know what it did?
Why, it made up a Lie
and it said to the Kid:

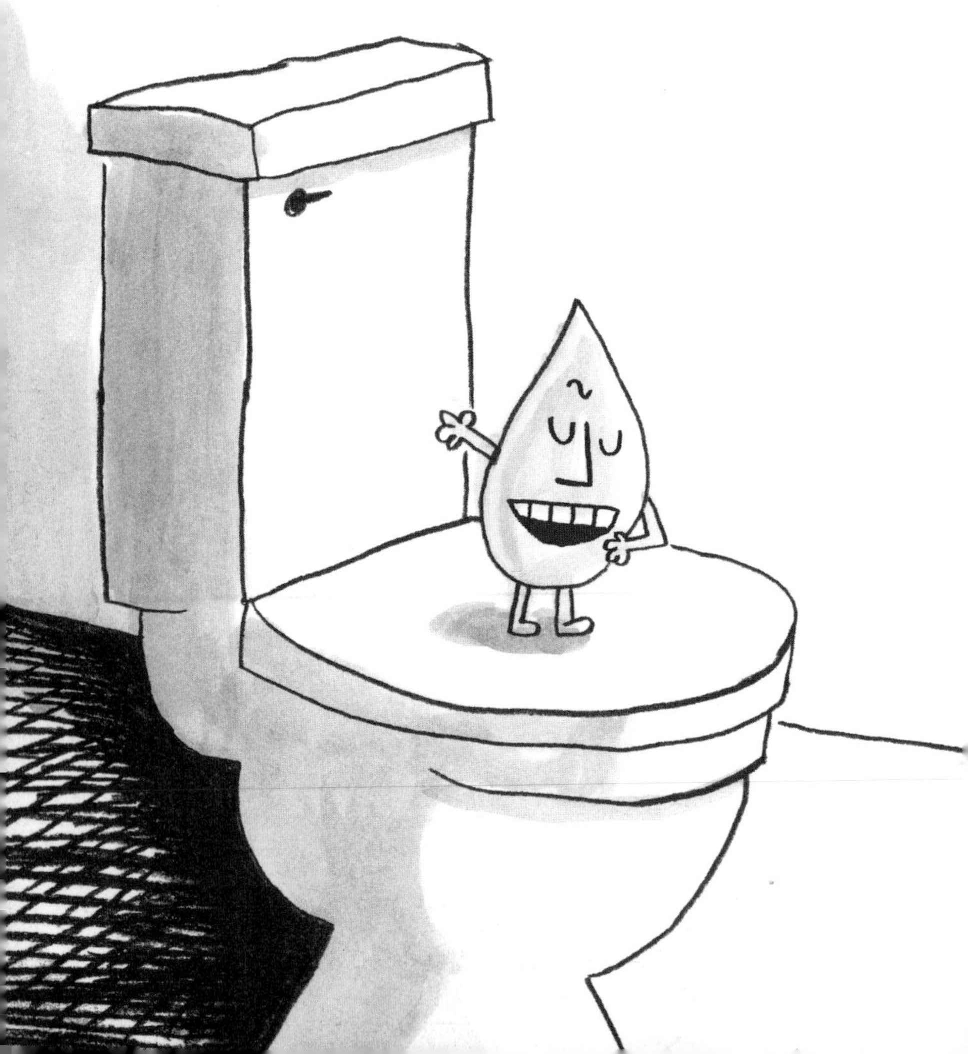

"Your toilet is broken---
 it squeaks when you flush it.
I'LL take it away and I'LL
 cLean it and brush it.

I'LL shine it right up
 -I'LL fix it and oiL it,
and soon I'LL return with a
 Good-as-new toilet."

And the baby believed what the pee drop had said. So it got him a juice box and took him to bed.

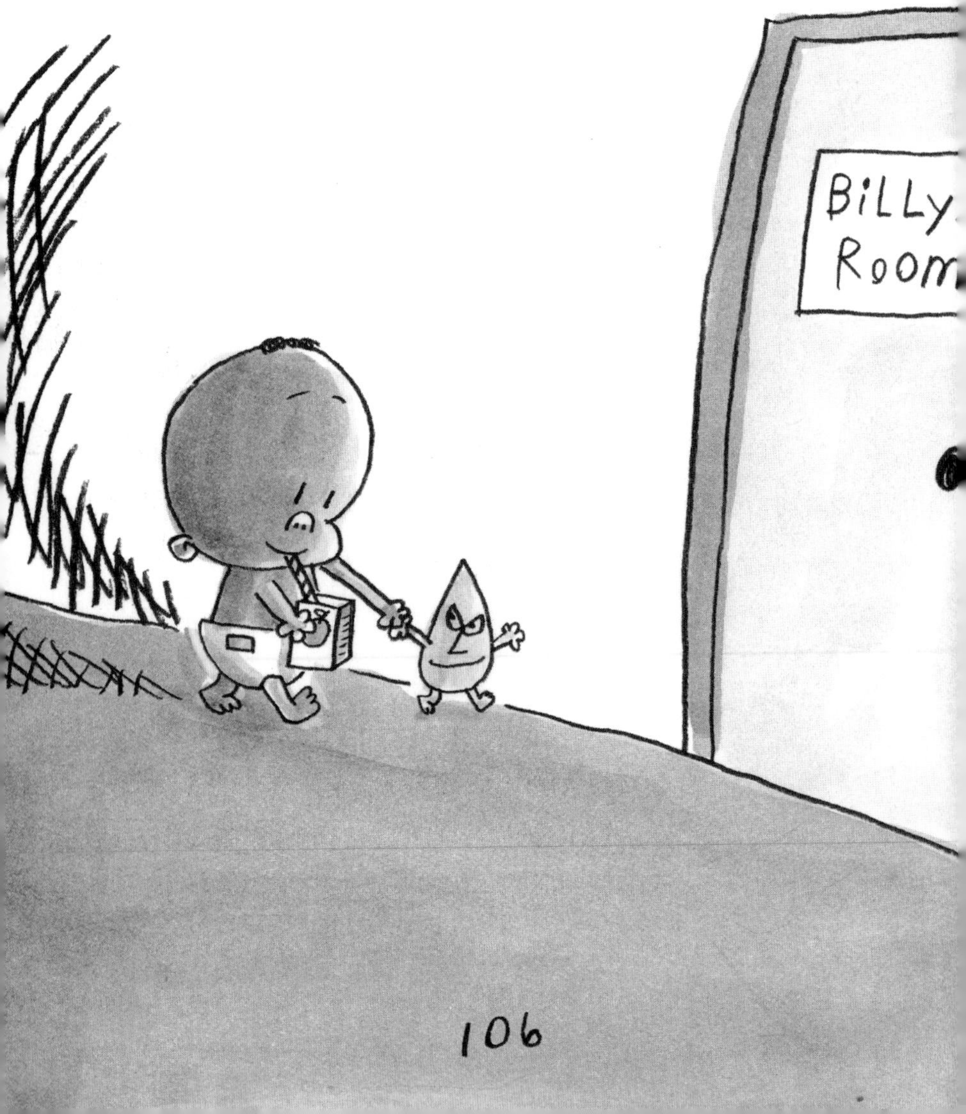
BiLLy
Room

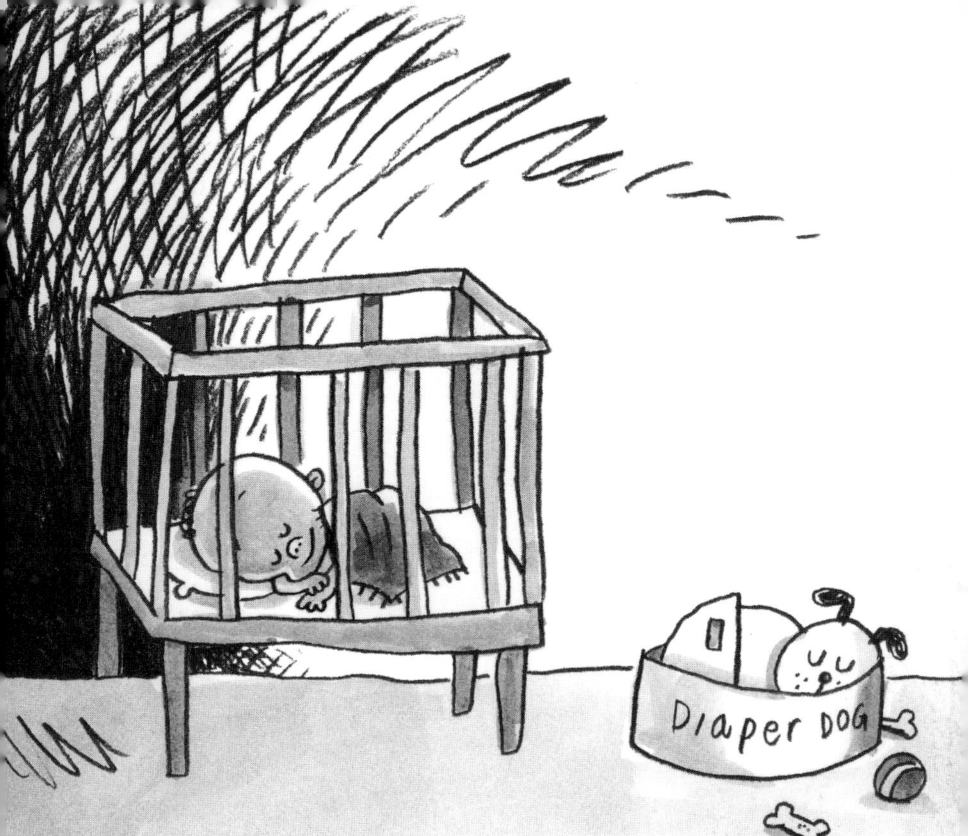
Diaper Dog

And at Last when the baby
was sleeping and dreaming,
That nasty old pee drop
went on with its skeeming!

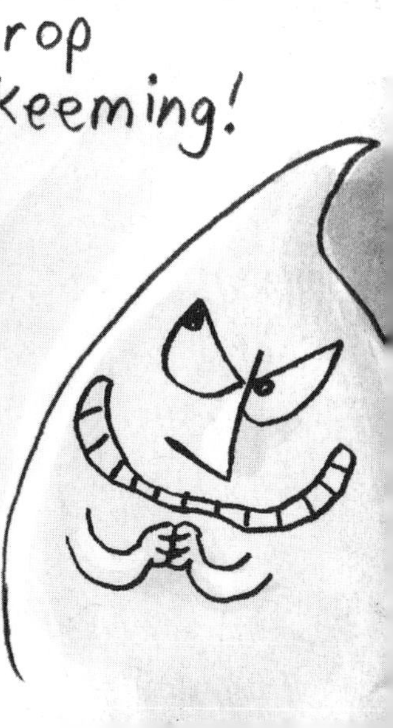

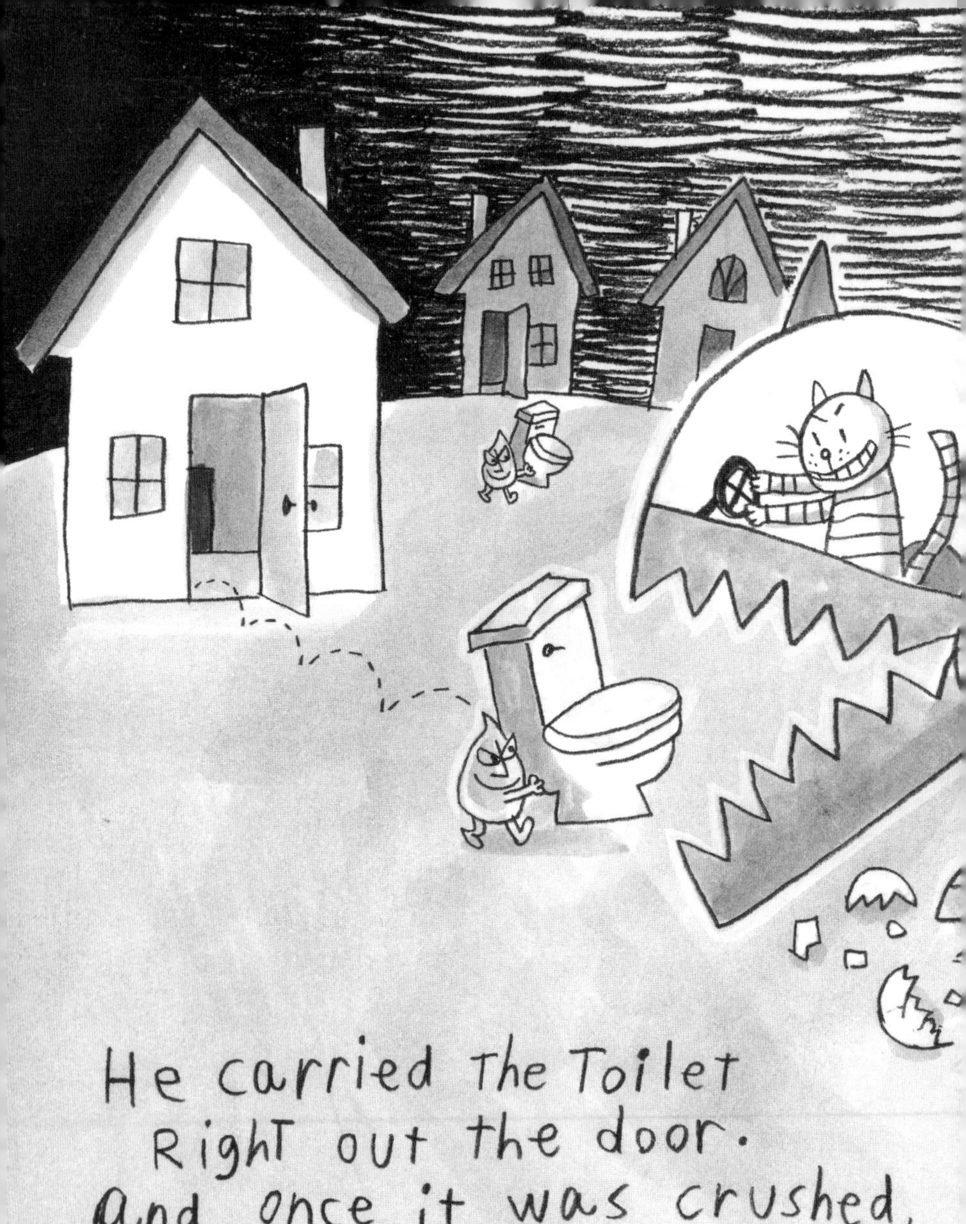

He carried the Toilet
Right out the door.
And once it was crushed,
He went back to get more.

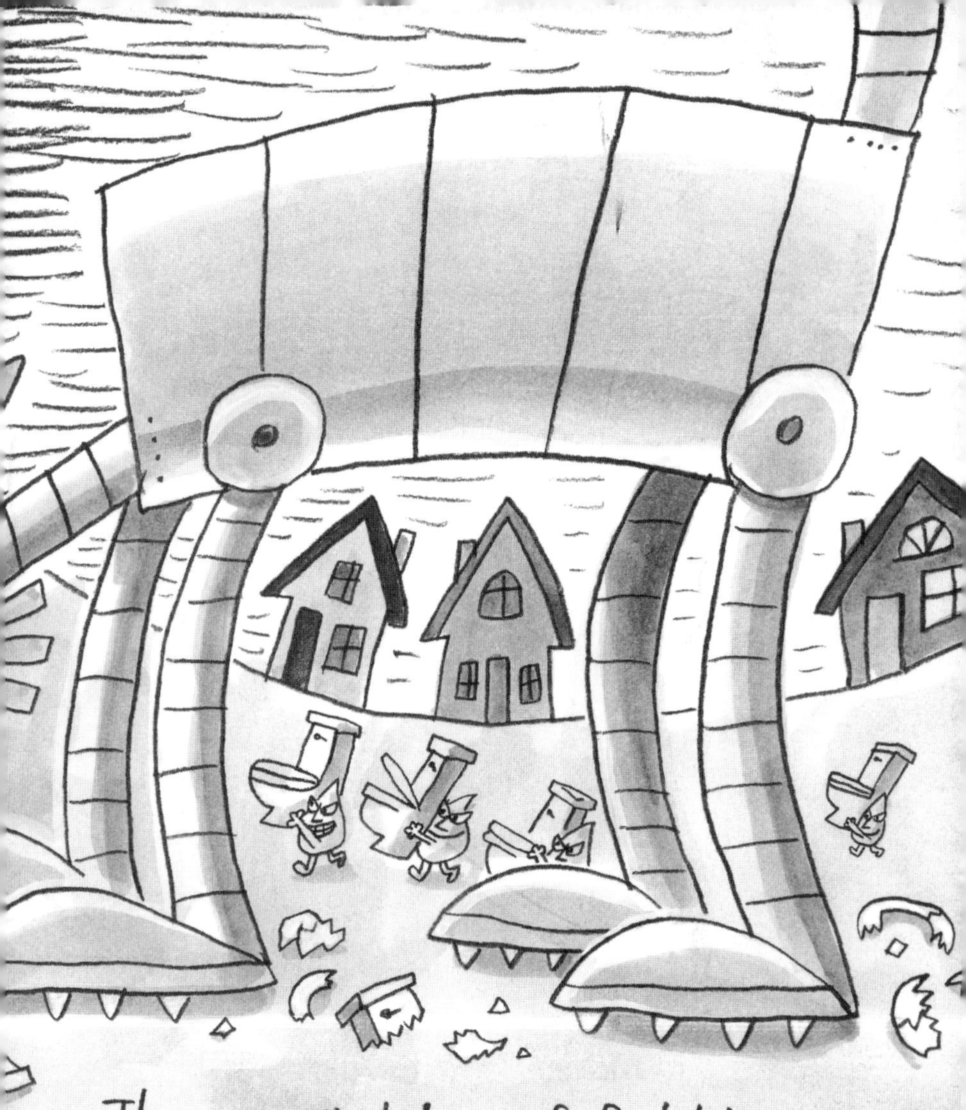

The snatching of Potties
went on through the night,
And into the dawn of the
Mornings first Light.

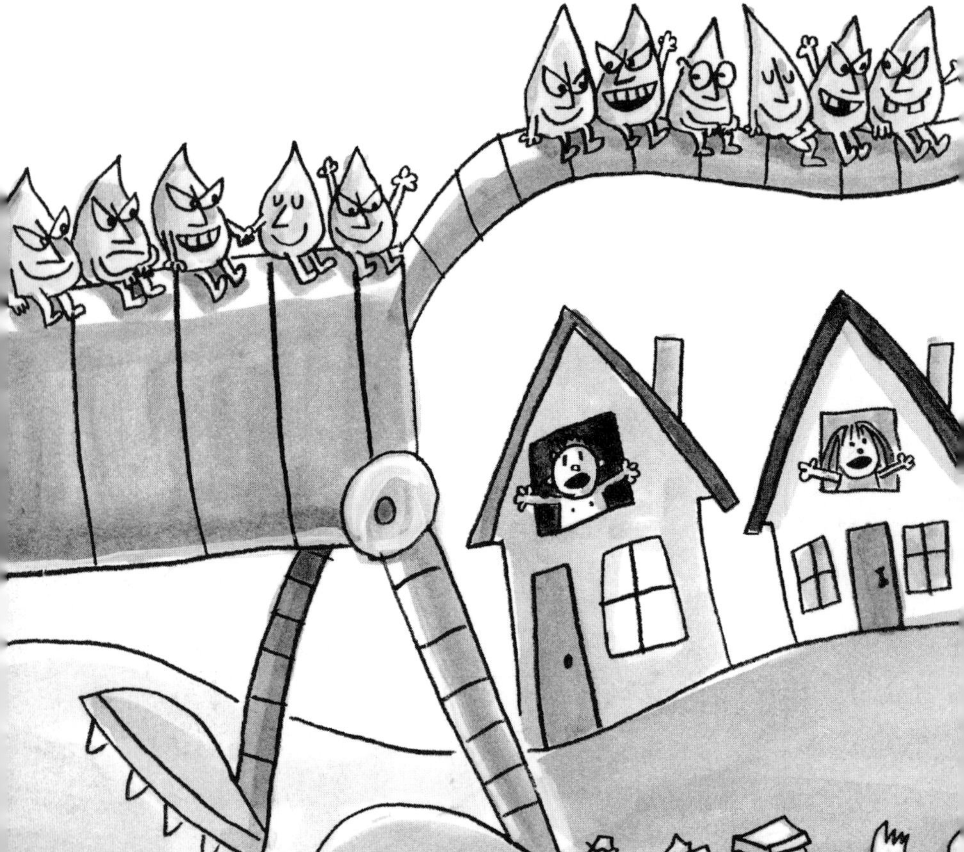

And Once Every Toilet
was crushed by the cat,
The people awoke and cried,
"What up wit' dat?"

"Our Toilets are gone!
Weve got to go Potty!
Oh, we do not Like this!
Oh, no we do notty!"

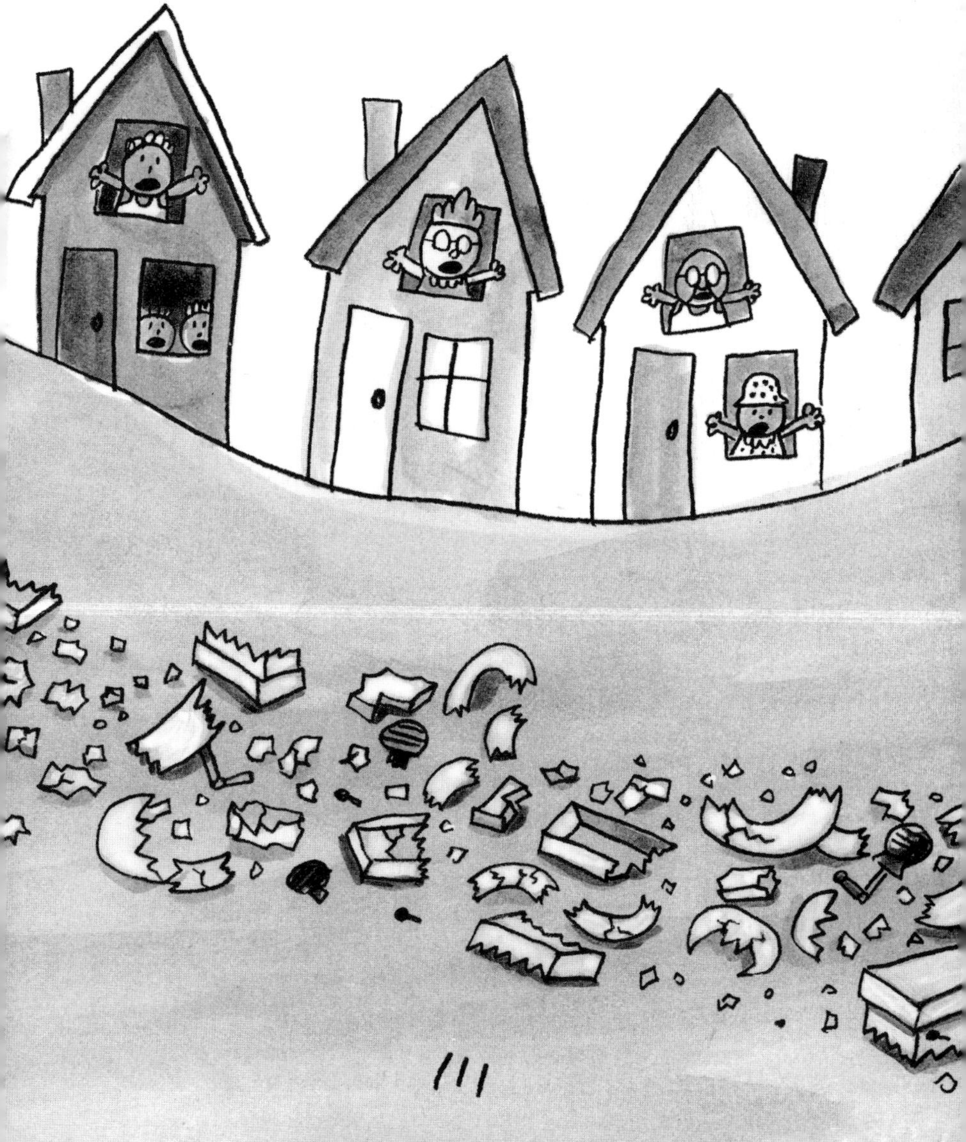

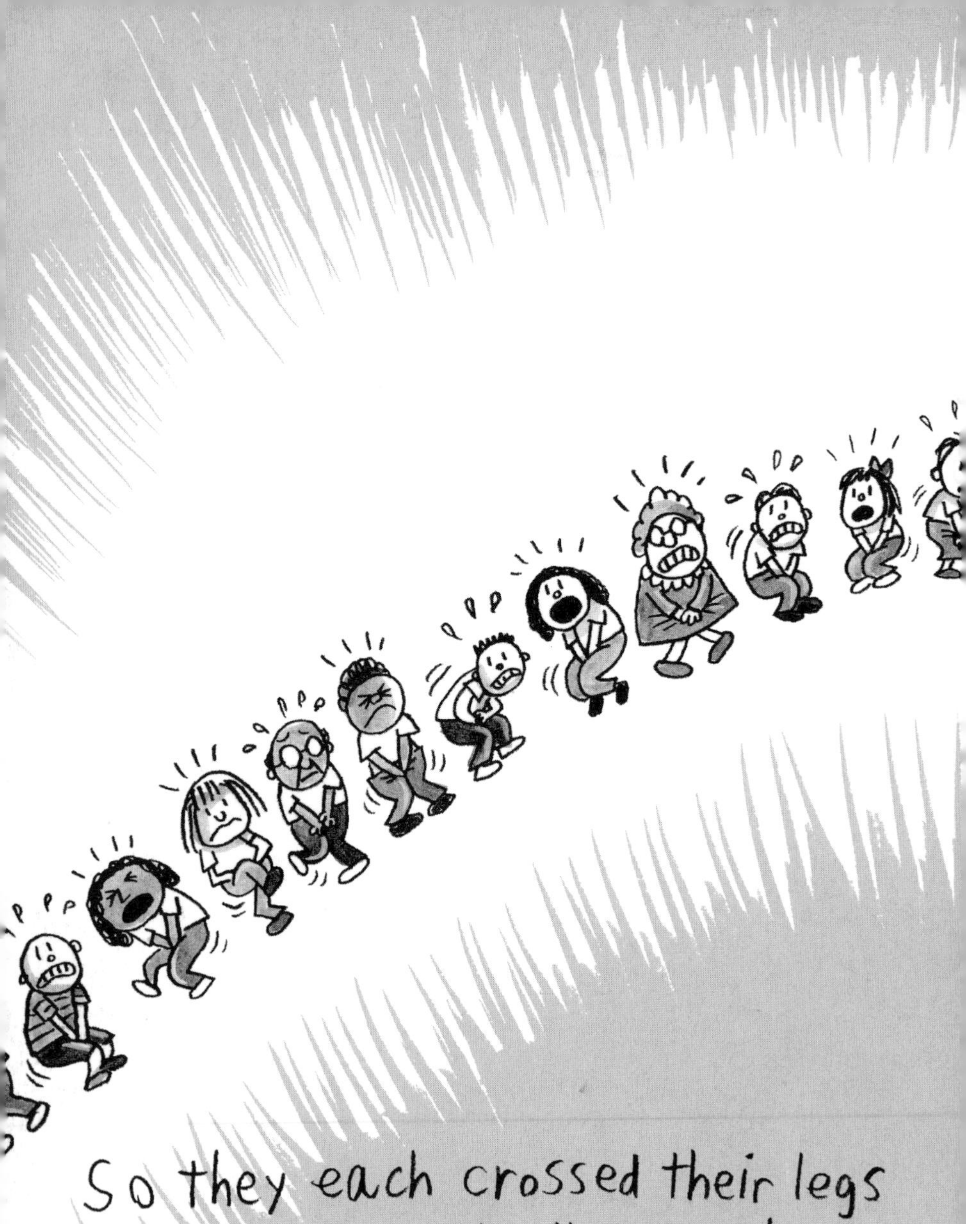

So they each crossed their legs
and squirmed all around,
And they squeezed and they clenched,
and they bobbed up and down.

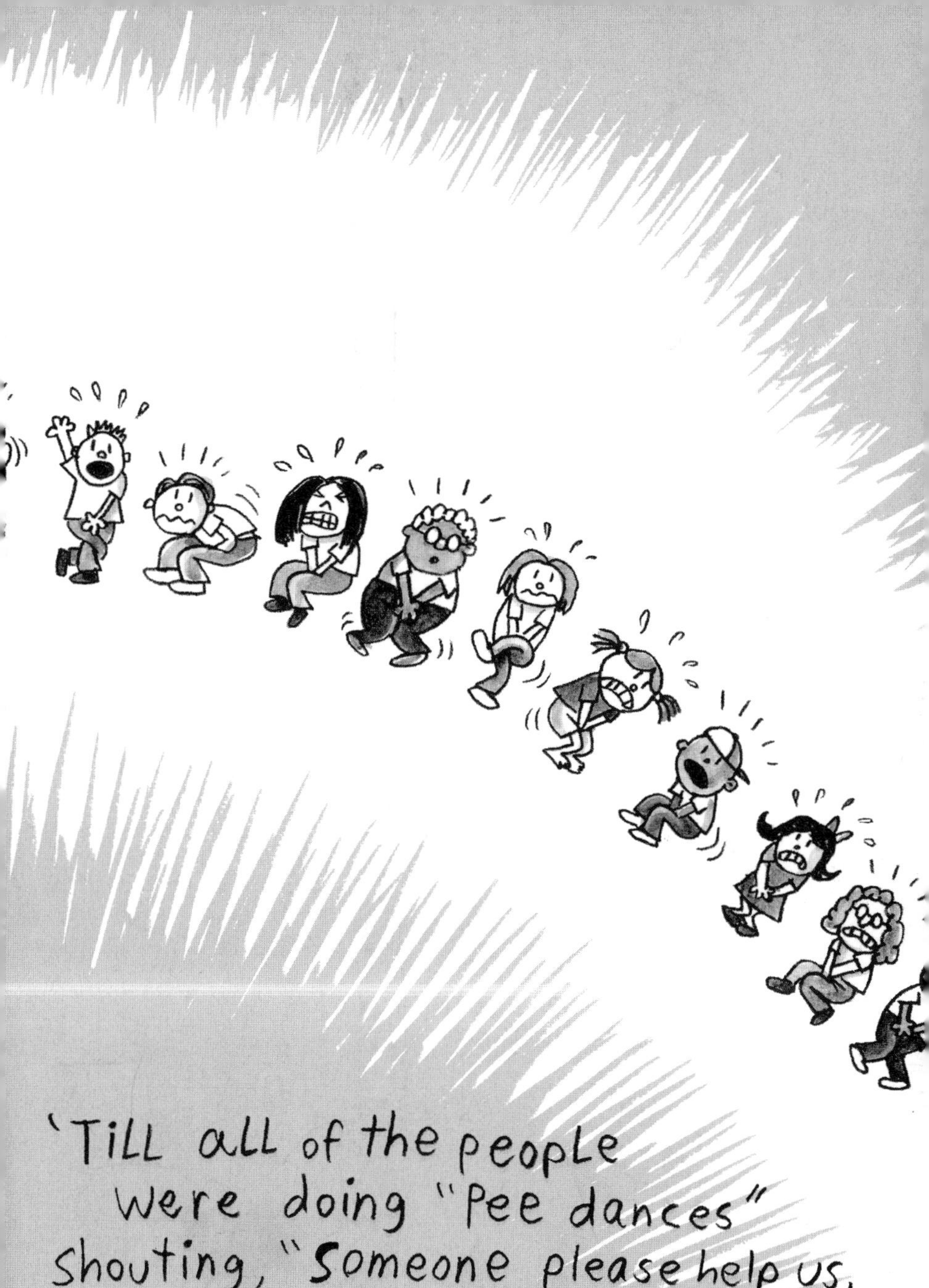

'Till all of the people
were doing "pee dances"
Shouting, "Someone please help us,
or we'll wet our pantses!"

They wiggled all morning
    in torment and Trauma,
Just like they're doing
    in this Flip-o-Rama →

Left Hand
Here

Pee-Dance
RevoLushon

Right
Thumb
Here

Pee-Dance
RevoLushon

soon, warm Liquid streams
   with yellowish Hues
Flowed down their Legs
   and filled up their shoes.

And they sobbed as they stood
   in their puddles of piddle,
But no one could help them.
   Not even a Little.

118

Chapter 5

the Aftermath

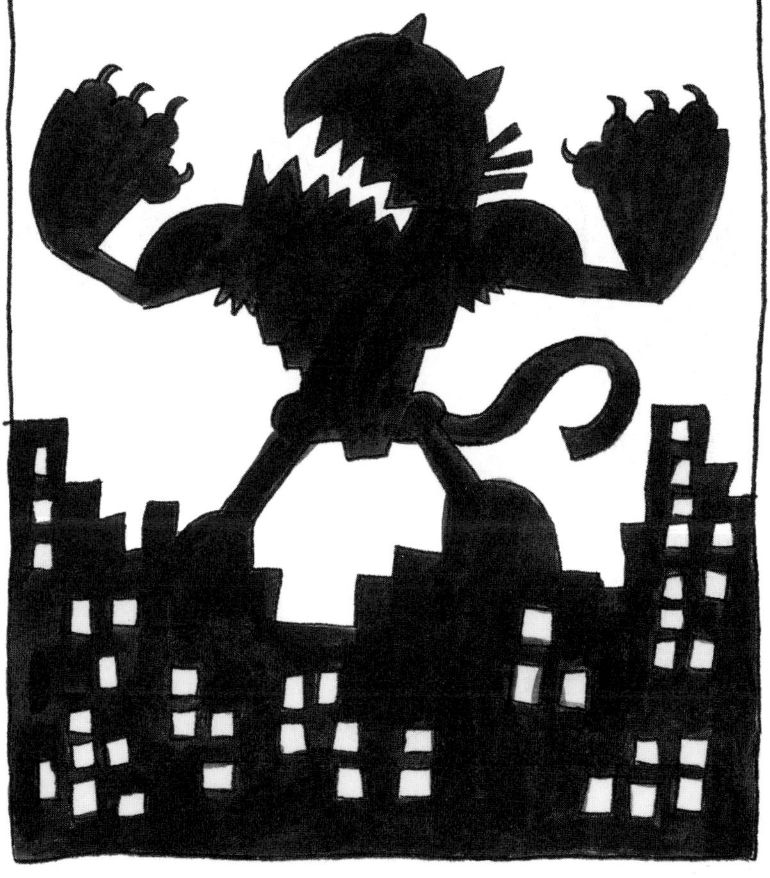

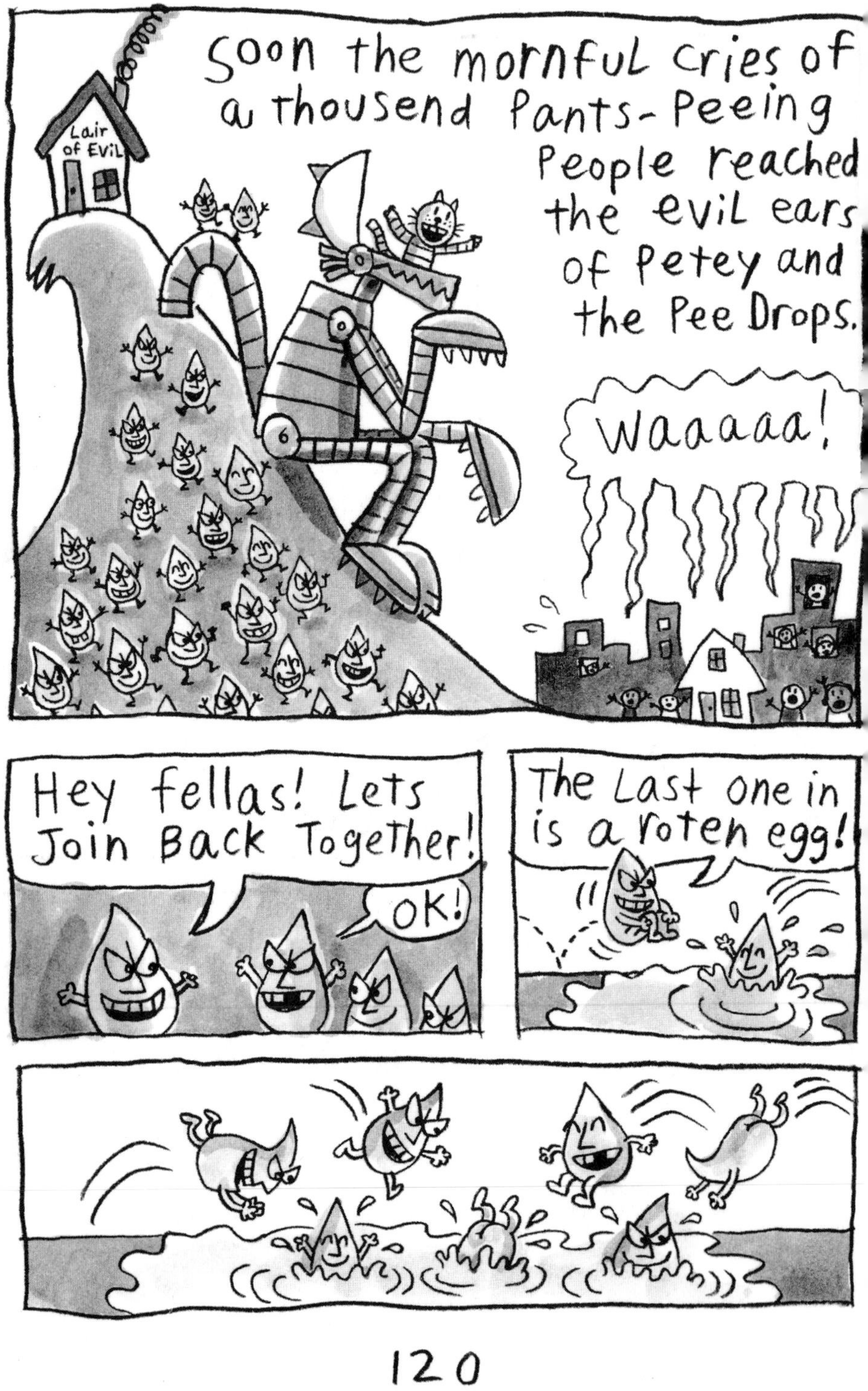
Lair of EVIL
Soon the mornful cries of a thousend Pants-Peeing People reached the evil ears of Petey and the Pee Drops.
Waaaaa!
Hey fellas! Lets Join Back Together!
OK!
The Last one in is a roten egg!

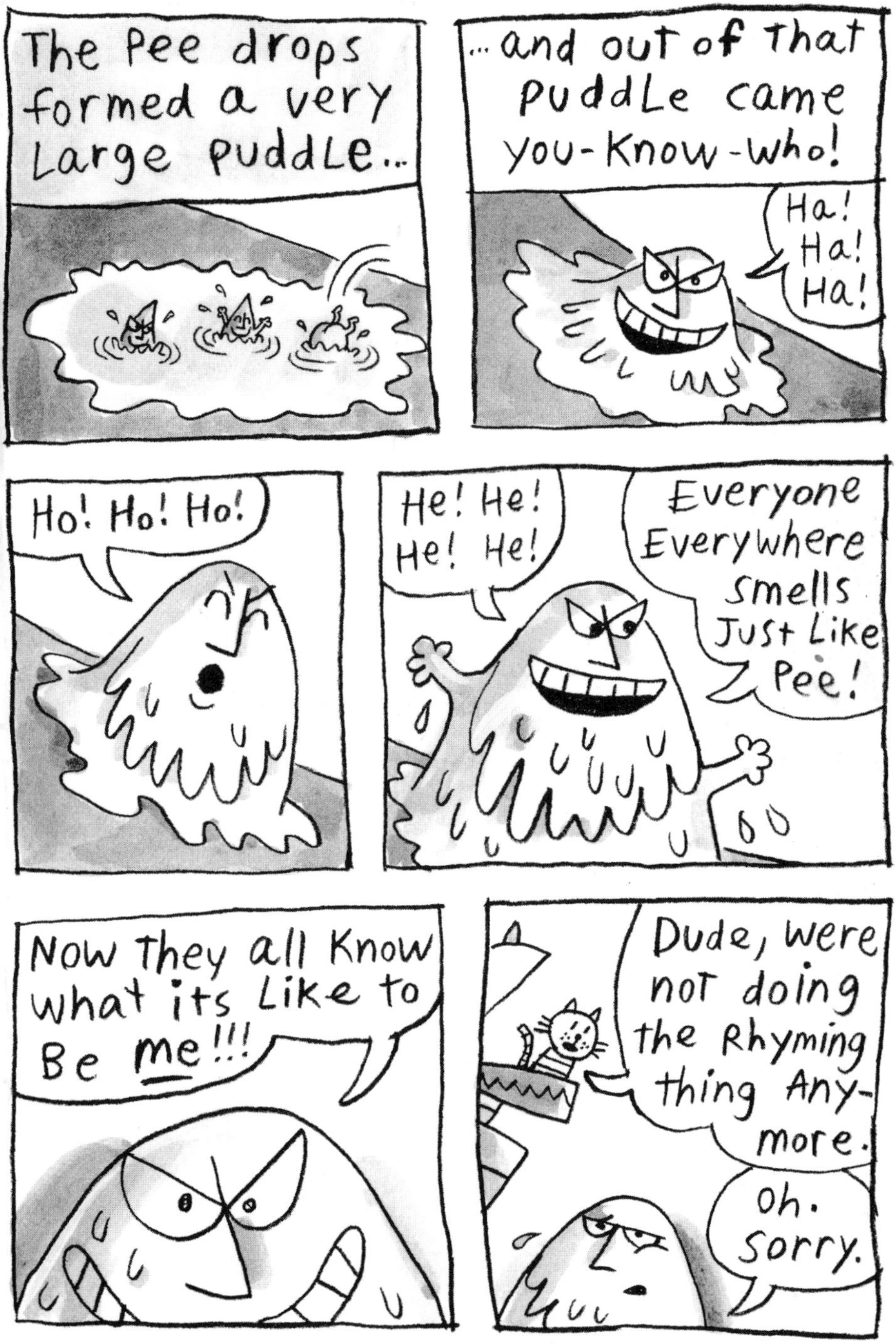
The Pee drops formed a very Large puddLe...
...and out of That puddLe came you-Know-who!
Ha! Ha! Ha!
Ho! Ho! Ho!
He! He! He! He!
Everyone Everywhere smells Just Like Pee!
Now They all Know what its Like to Be me!!!
Dude, were not doing the Rhyming thing Any-more.
Oh. Sorry.

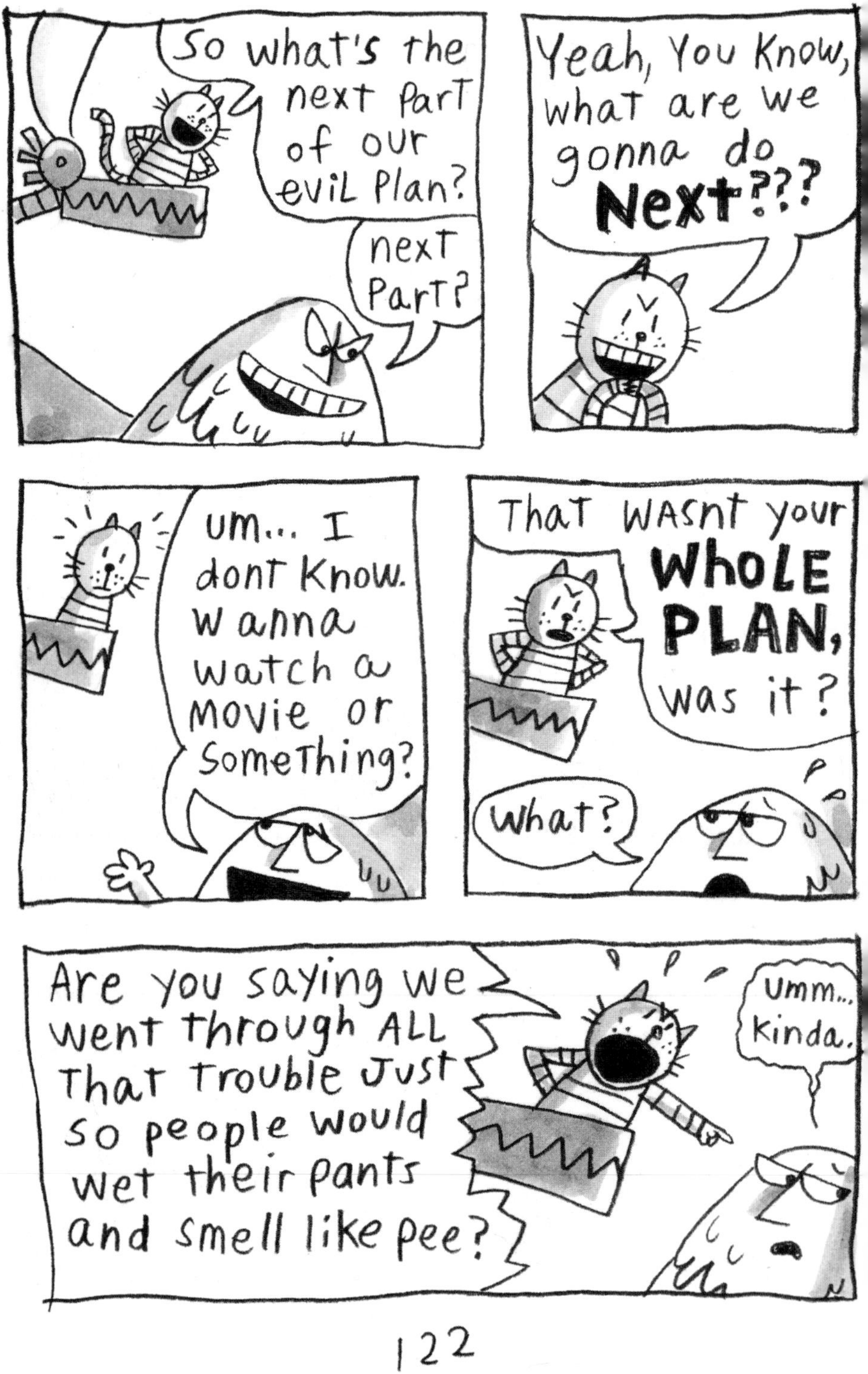
So what's the next Part of our evil Plan?
next Part?
Yeah, You Know, what are we gonna do NEXT???
um... I dont Know. Wanna watch a Movie or Something?
That WASnt your WHOLE PLAN, was it?
What?
Are you saying we went through ALL That Trouble Just so people would wet their pants and smell like pee?
Umm... Kinda.

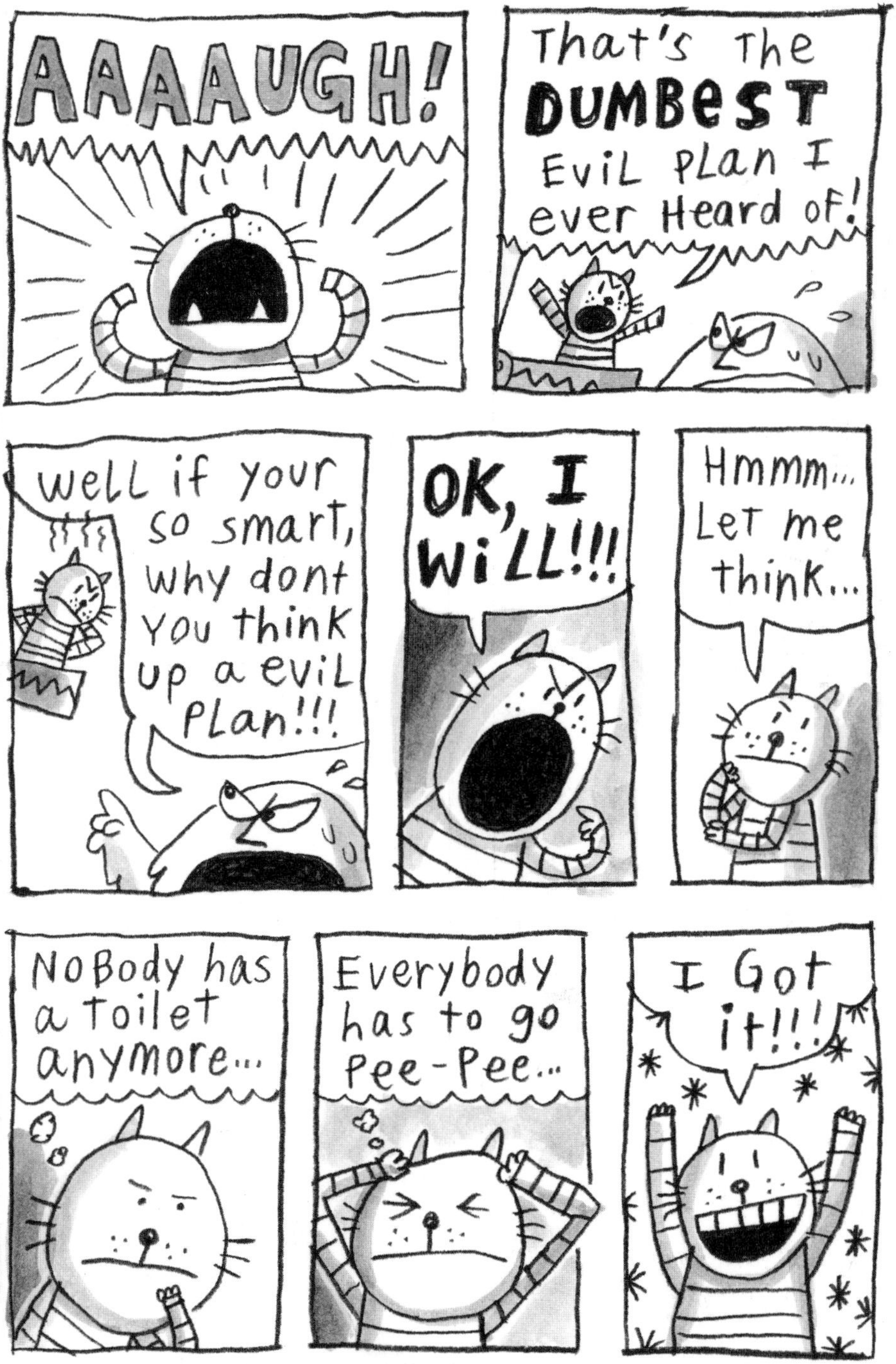
AAAAUGH!
That's The DUMBesT EviL PLan I ever Heard oF!
well if your so smart, why dont You think up a eviL PLan!!!
OK, I WiLL!!!
Hmmm... Let me think...
NoBody has a Toilet anymore...
Everybody has to go Pee-Pee...
I Got it!!!

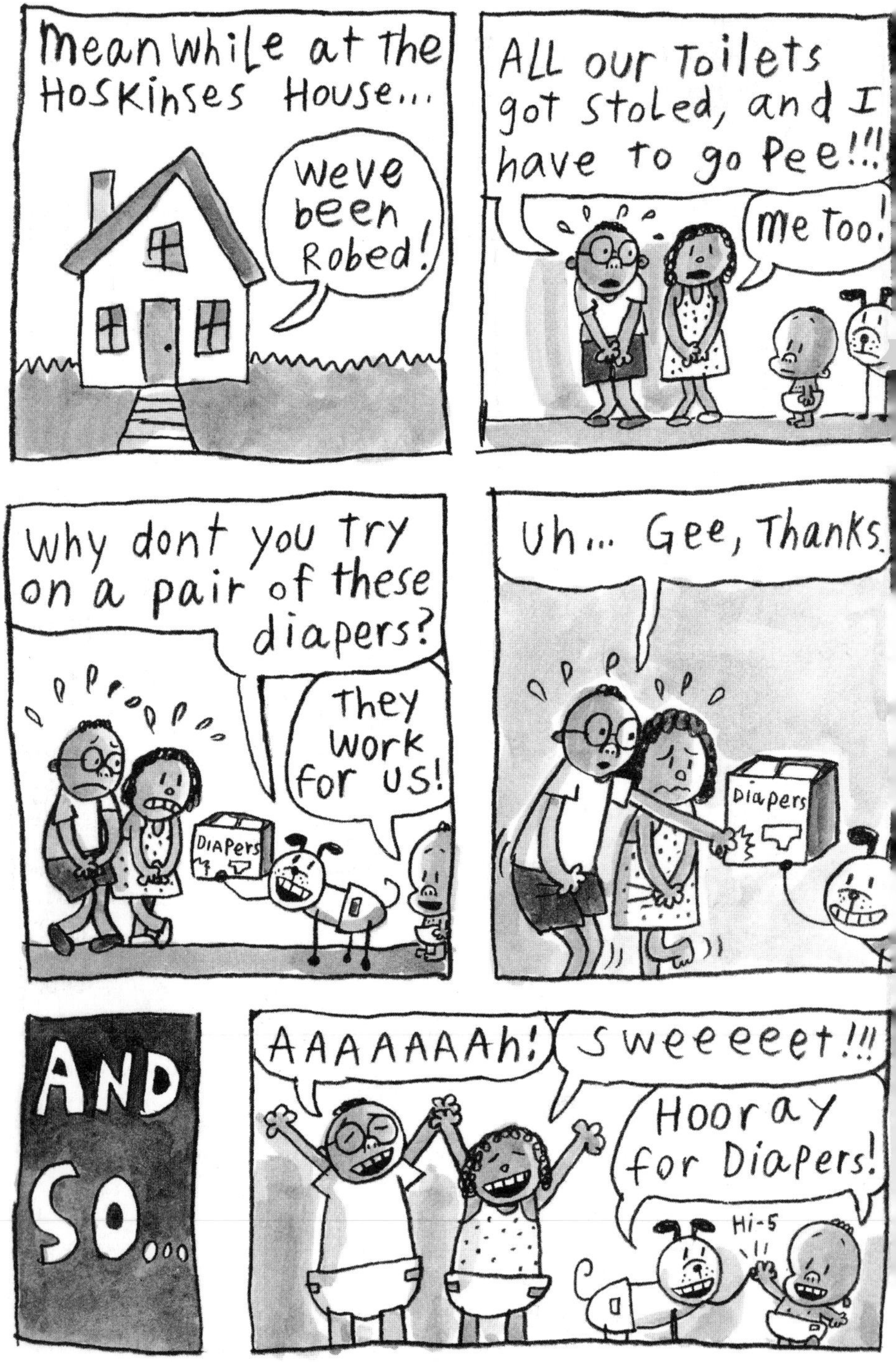
Meanwhile at the Hoskinses House...
Weve been Robed!
ALL our Toilets got Stoled, and I have to go Pee!!!
me Too!
Why dont you try on a pair of these diapers?
They work for US!
DIAPers
Uh... Gee, Thanks.
Diapers
AND SO...
AAAAAAAh!
Sweeeeet!!!
Hooray for Diapers!
Hi-5

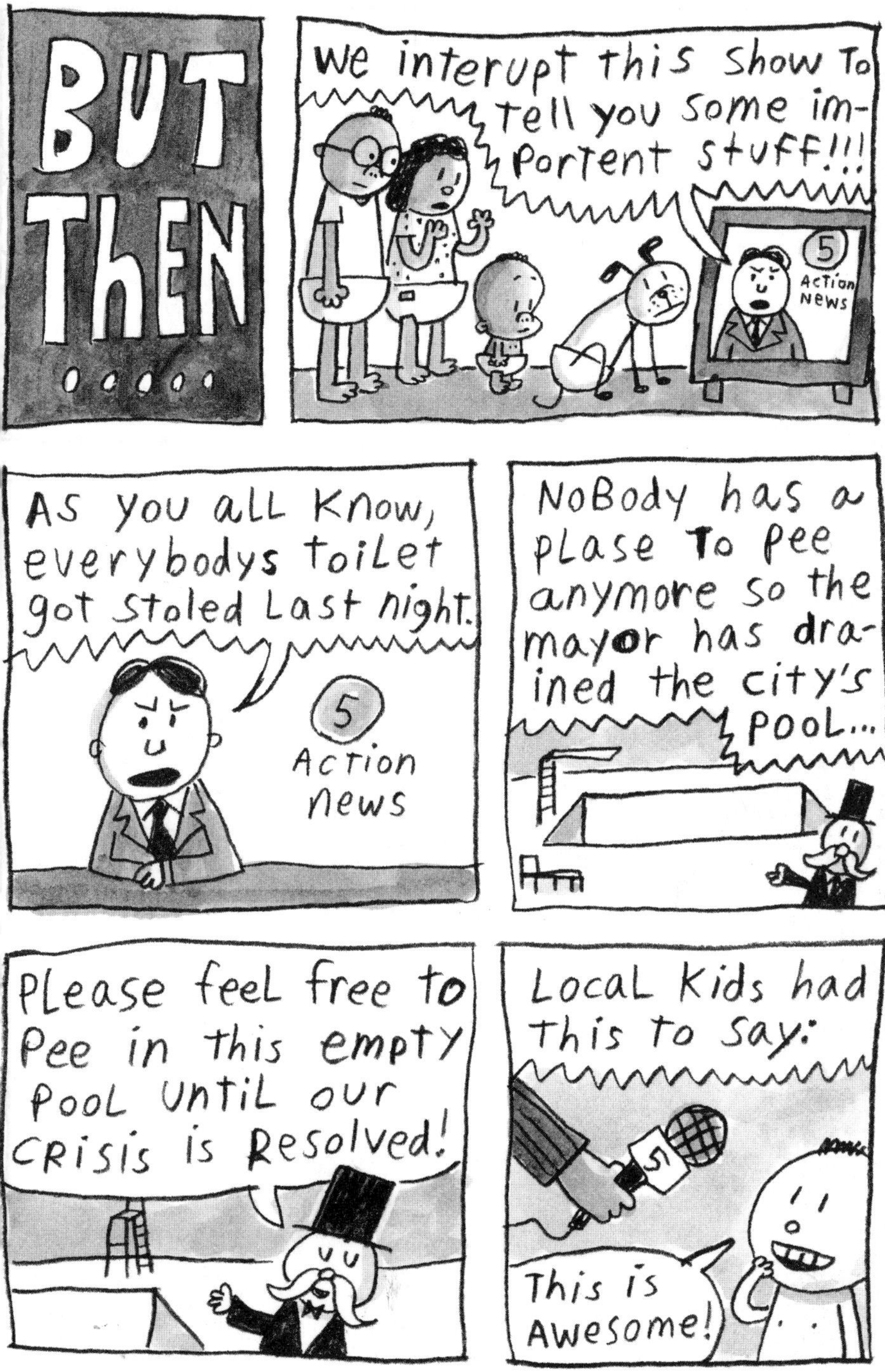
BUT
ThEN
......
We interupt this Show To tell you some im-portent stuff!!!
5 Action news
As you all know, everybodys toilet got stoled last night.
5 Action news
NoBody has a plase To pee anymore so the mayor has dra-ined the city's pool...
Please feel free to Pee in this empty Pool until our crisis is Resolved!
Local Kids had this to say:
5
This is Awesome!

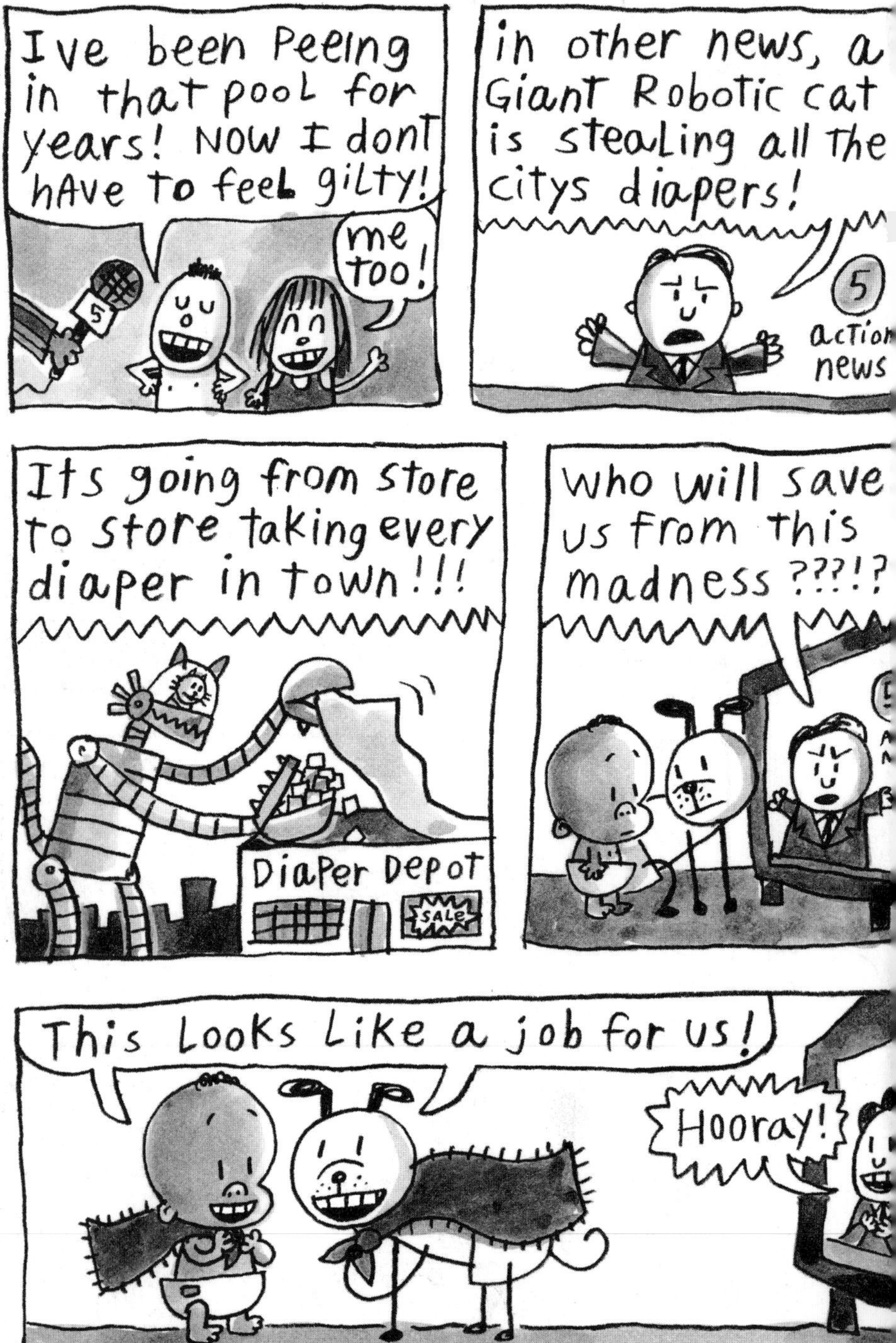
Ive been Peeing in that pool for years! NOW I dont hAve to feel gilty!
me too!
in other news, a Giant Robotic cat is stealing all the citys diapers!
5 action news
Its going from store to store taking every diaper in town!!!
Diaper Depot
SALE
Who will save us from this madness???!?
This Looks Like a job for us!
Hooray!

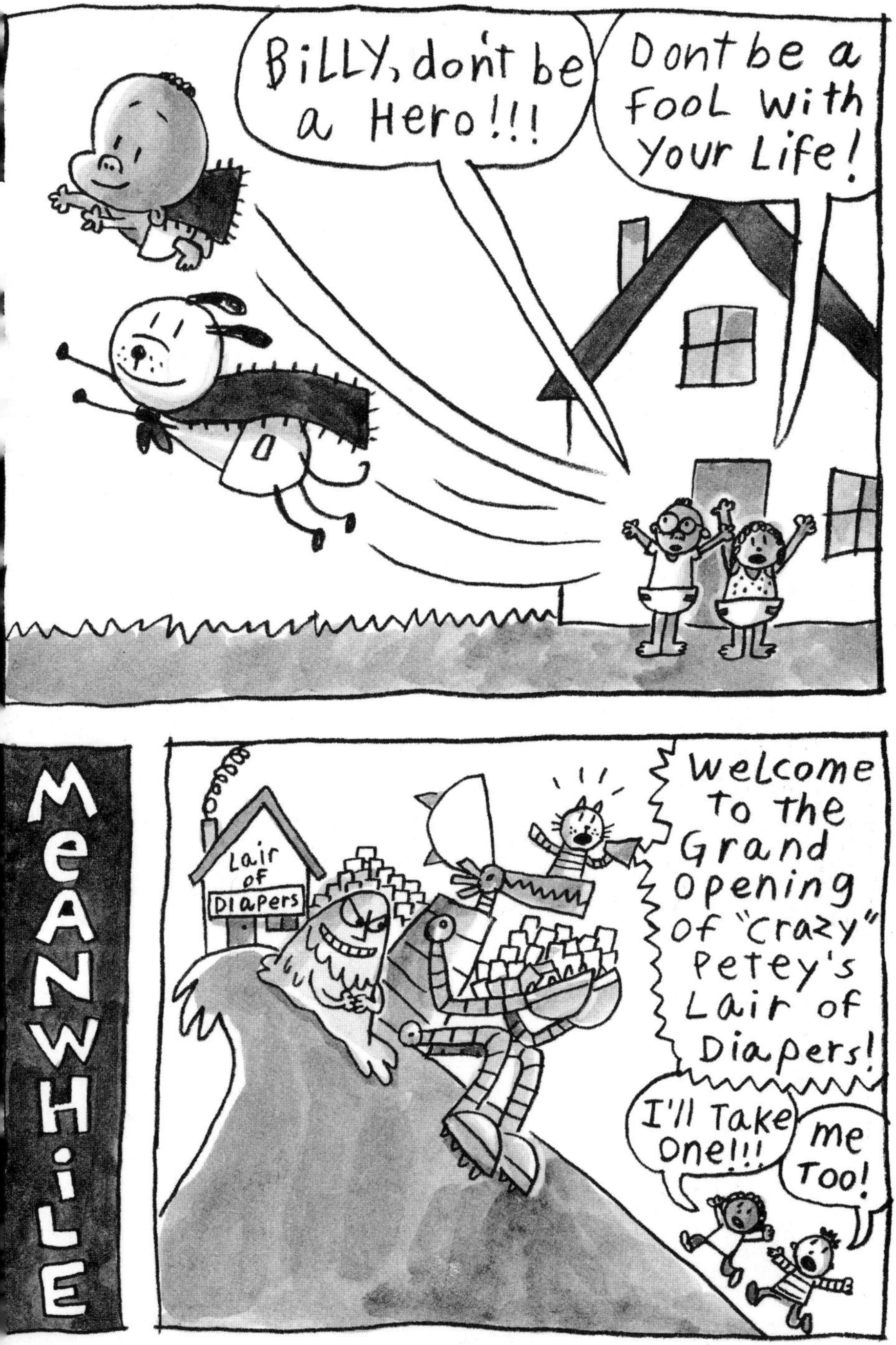
BiLLY, don't be a Hero!!!
Dont be a FooL with Your Life!
MEANWHiLE
Lair of Diapers
Welcome to the Grand Opening of "crazy" Petey's Lair of Diapers!
I'll Take One!!!
me Too!

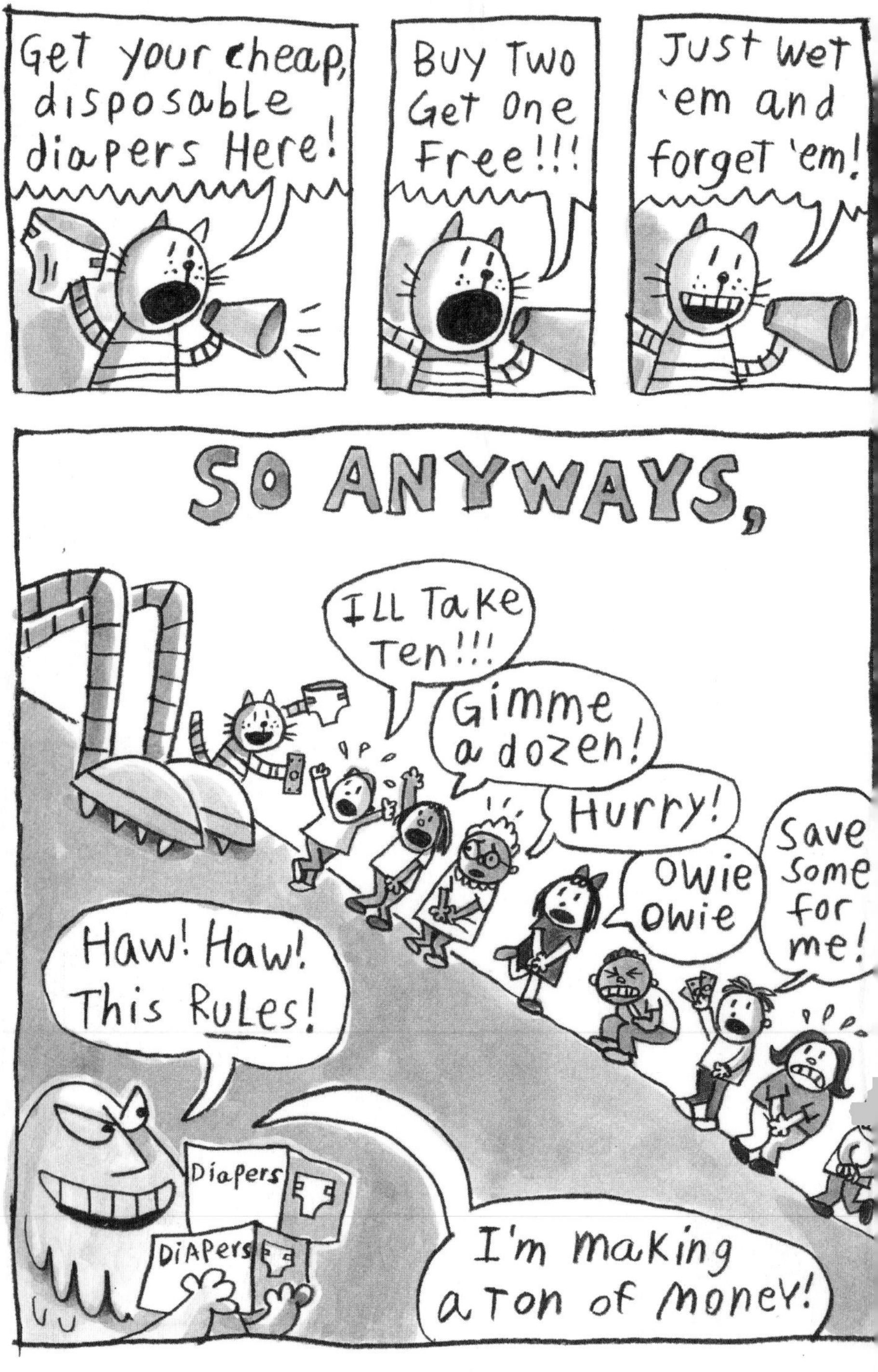
Get your cheap, disposable diapers Here!
Buy Two Get One Free!!!
Just wet 'em and forget 'em!
SO ANYWAYS,
I'LL Take Ten!!!
Gimme a dozen!
Hurry!
Owie Owie
Save some for me!
Haw! Haw! This Rules!
Diapers
DiAPers
I'm making a Ton of money!

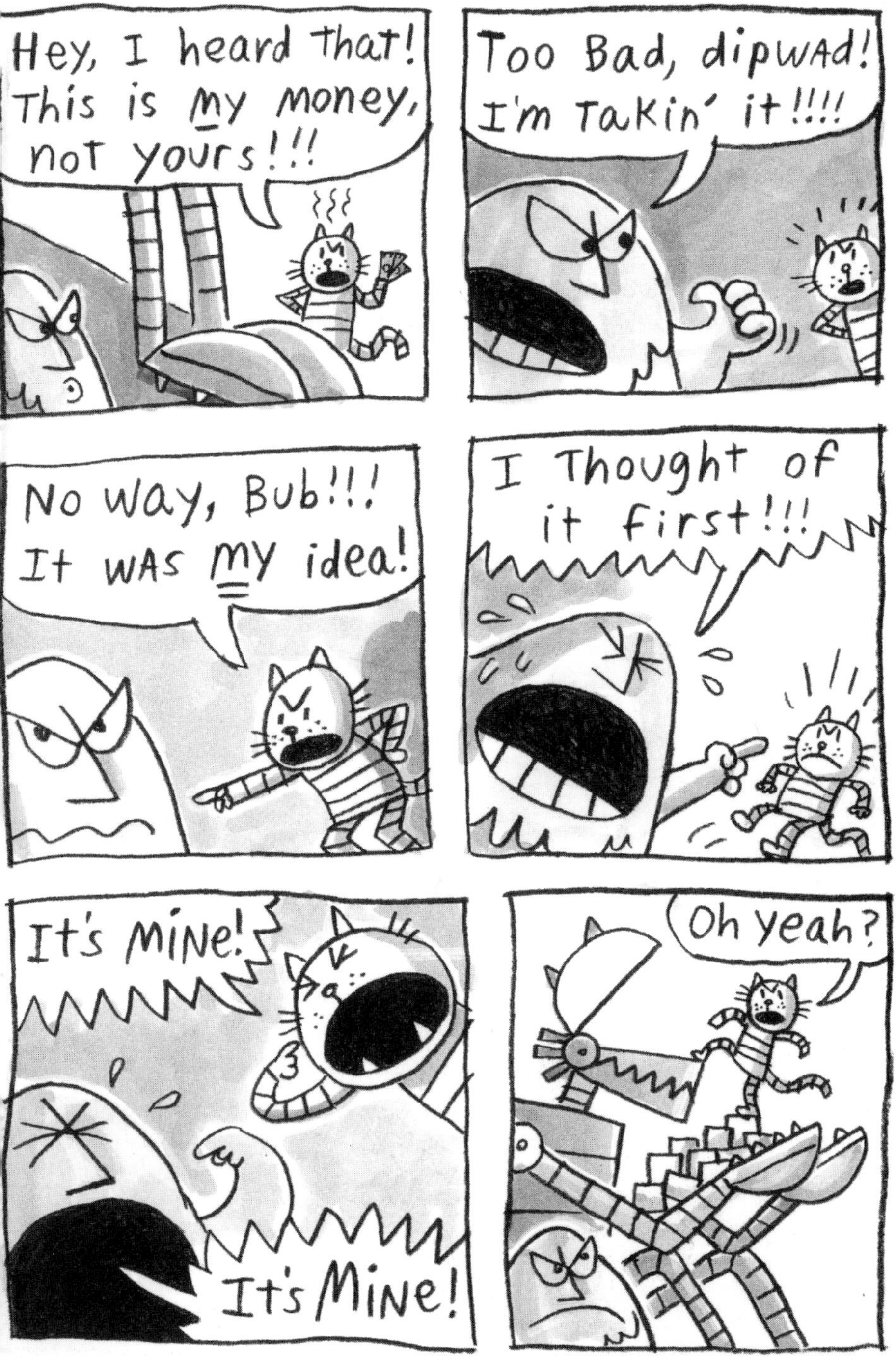
Hey, I heard that! This is my money, not yours!!!
Too Bad, dipwad! I'm Takin' it!!!!
No way, Bub!!! It was my idea!
I Thought of it first!!!
It's mine!
It's Mine!
Oh yeah?

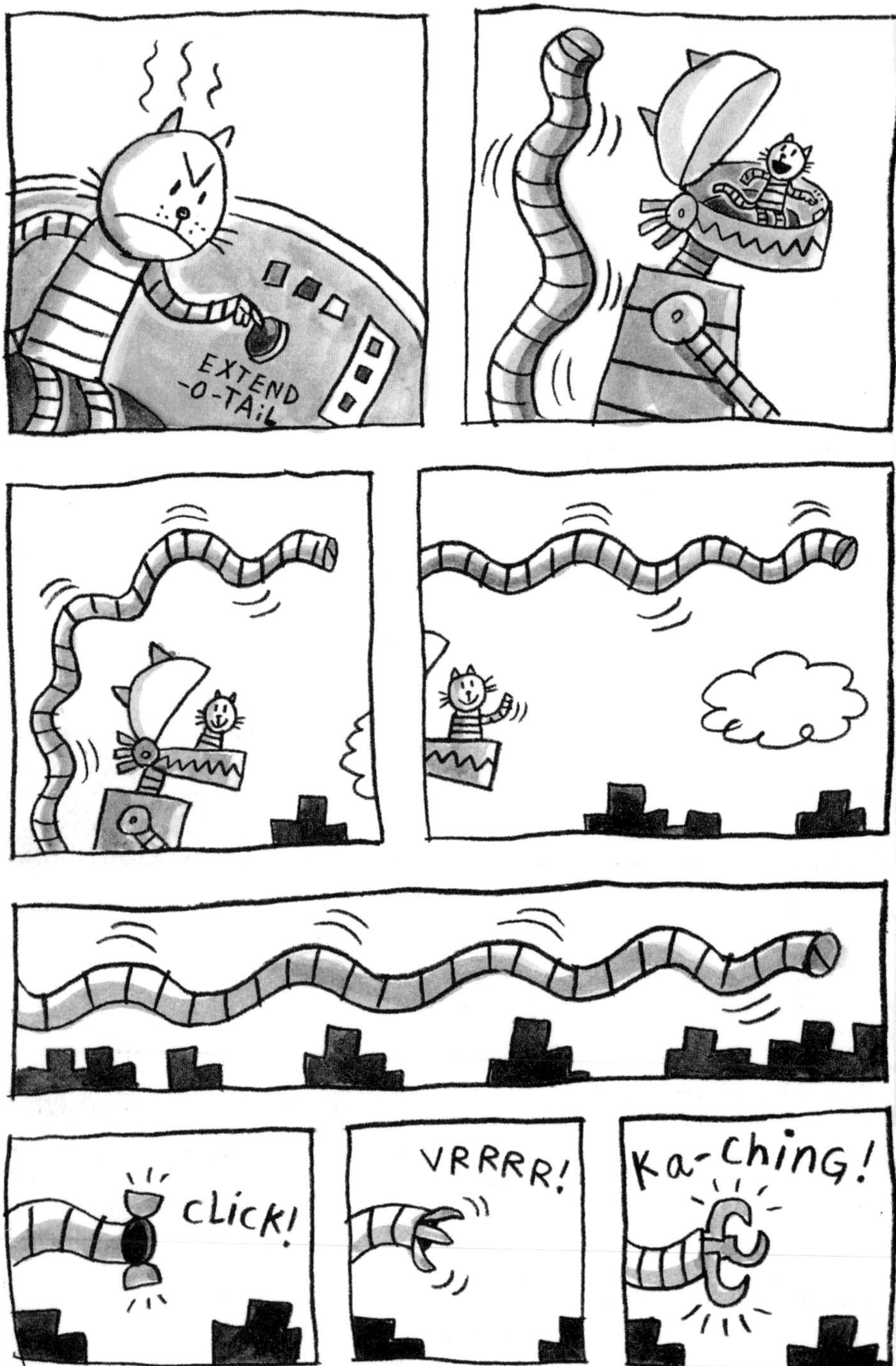
EXTEND
-O-TAIL
CLICK!
VRRRR!
KA-CHING!

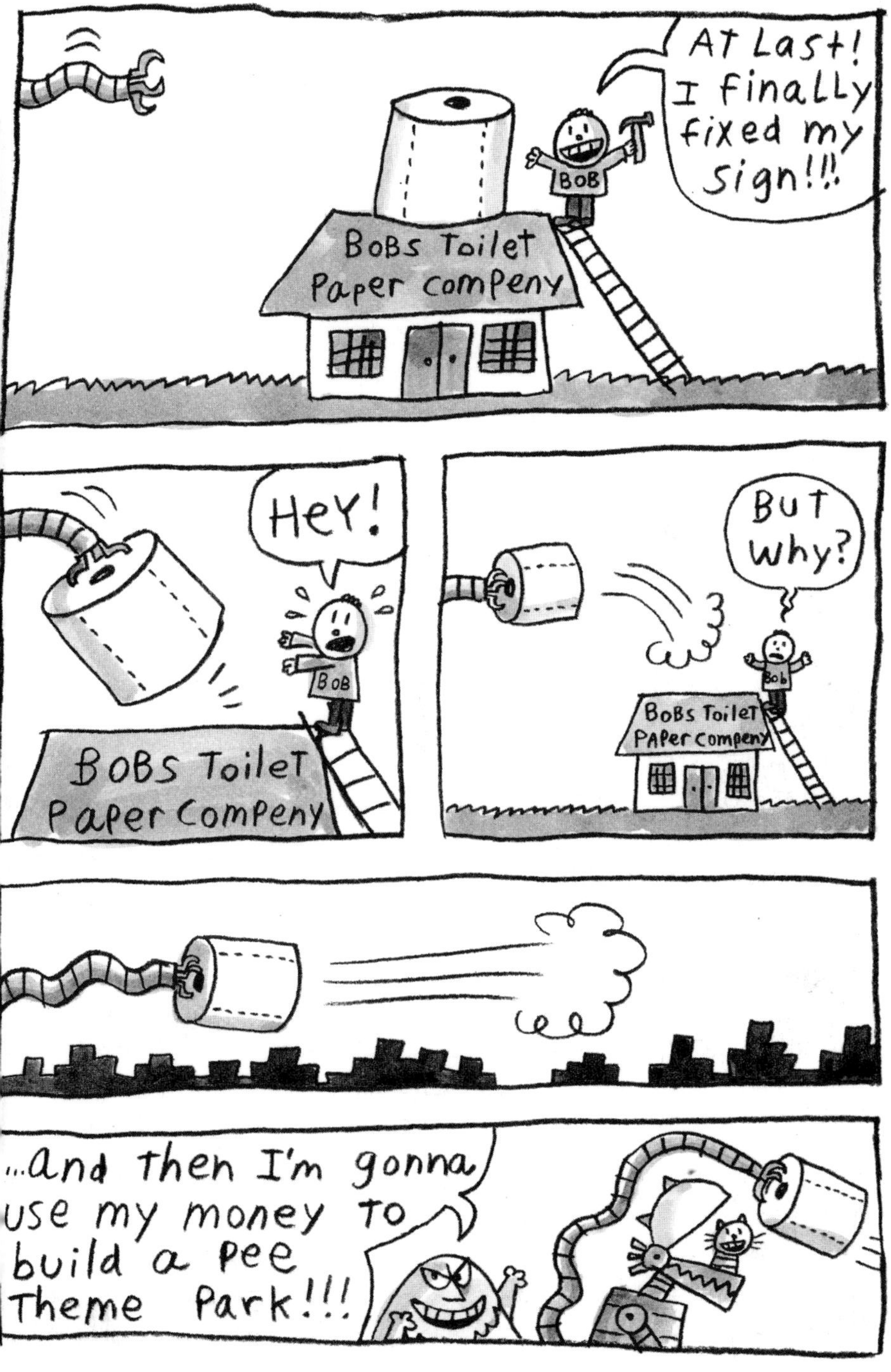
At Last! I finally fixed my sign!!!
BOB
BoBs Toilet Paper compeny
HeY!
BOB
BOBS ToileT Paper Compeny
But why?
Bob
BoBs ToileT PAper compeny
...and then I'm gonna use my money to build a pee Theme Park!!!

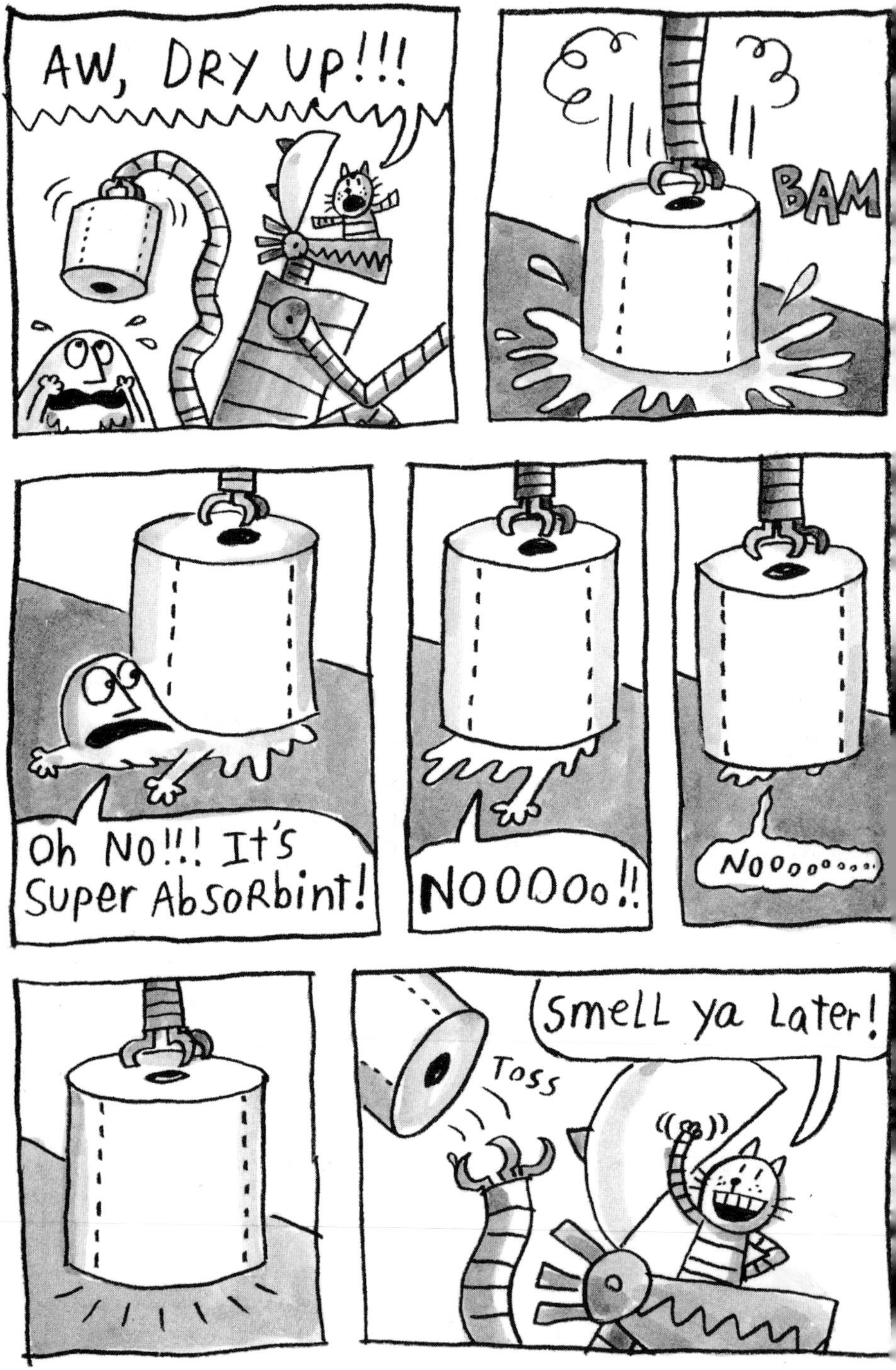
AW, DRY UP!!!
BAM
Oh No!!! It's Super Absorbint!
NOOOOo!!
NOoooooooo
Smell ya Later!
Toss

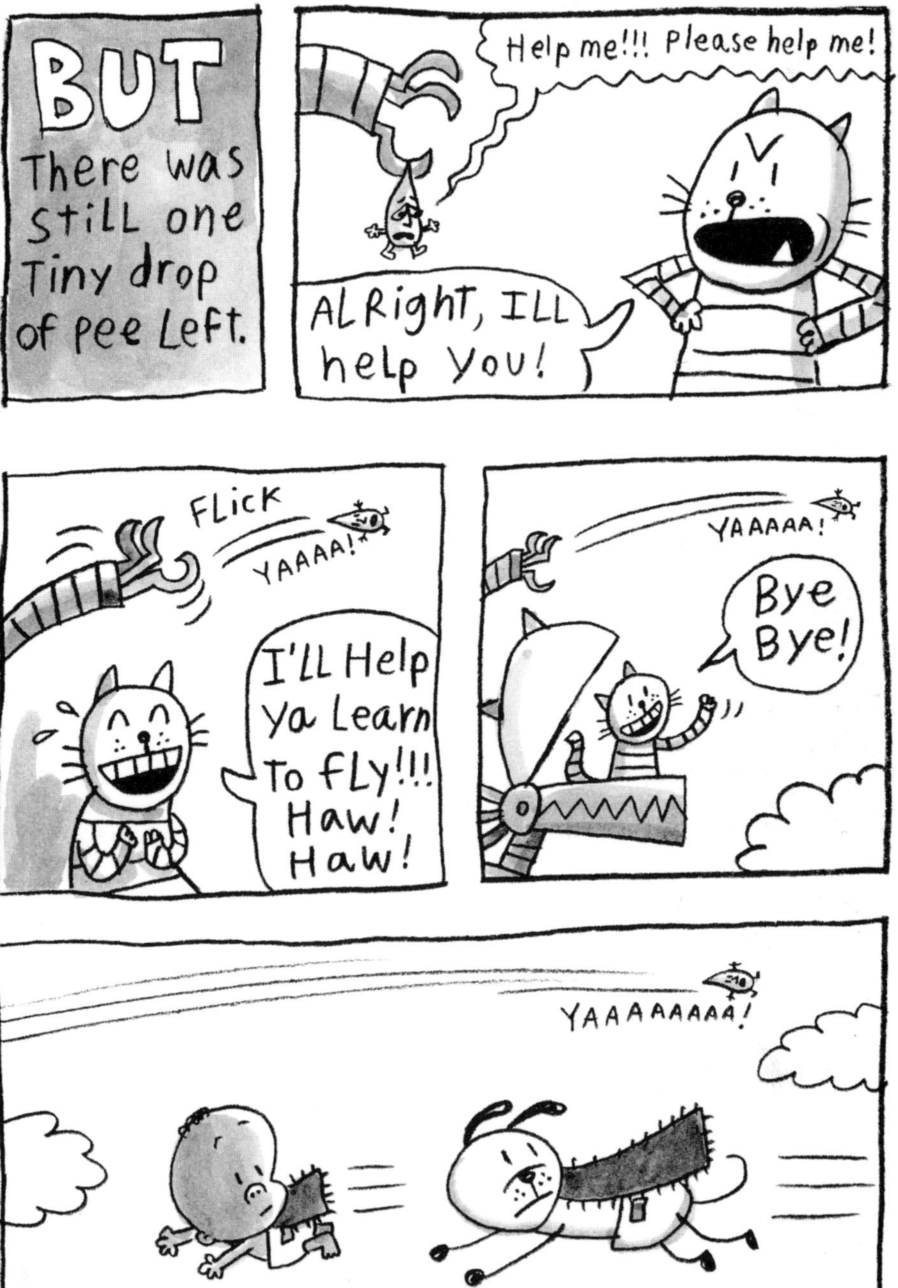
BUT There was still one Tiny drop of pee Left.
Help me!!! Please help me!
ALRight, ILL help You!
FLick
YAAAA!
I'LL Help Ya Learn To FLy!!! Haw! Haw!
YAAAAA!
Bye Bye!
YAAAAAAAA!

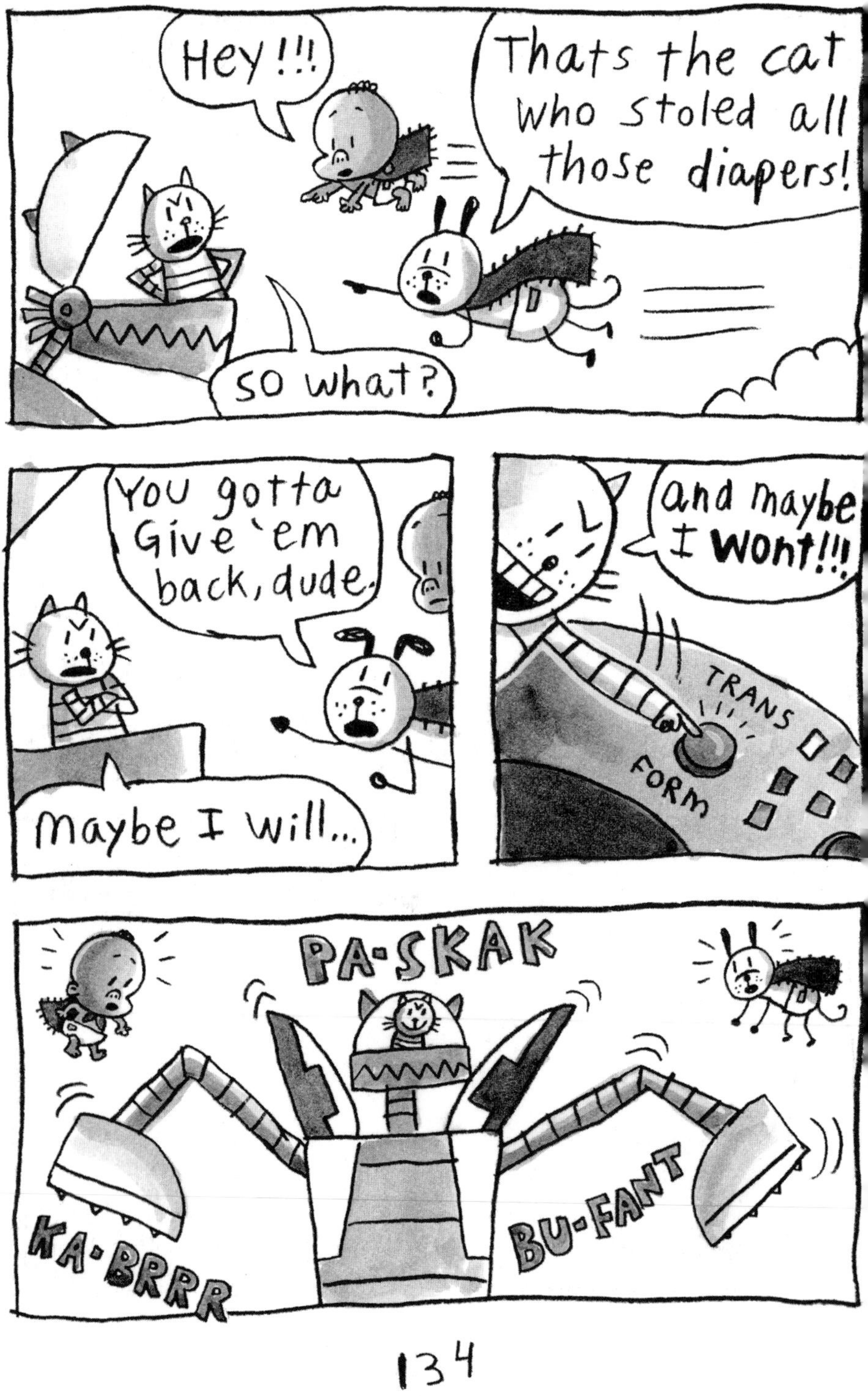
Hey!!!
Thats the cat who stoled all those diapers!
SO what?
You gotta Give 'em back, dude.
maybe I will...
and maybe I wont!!!
TRANS
FORM
PA·SKAK
KA·BRRR
BU·FANT

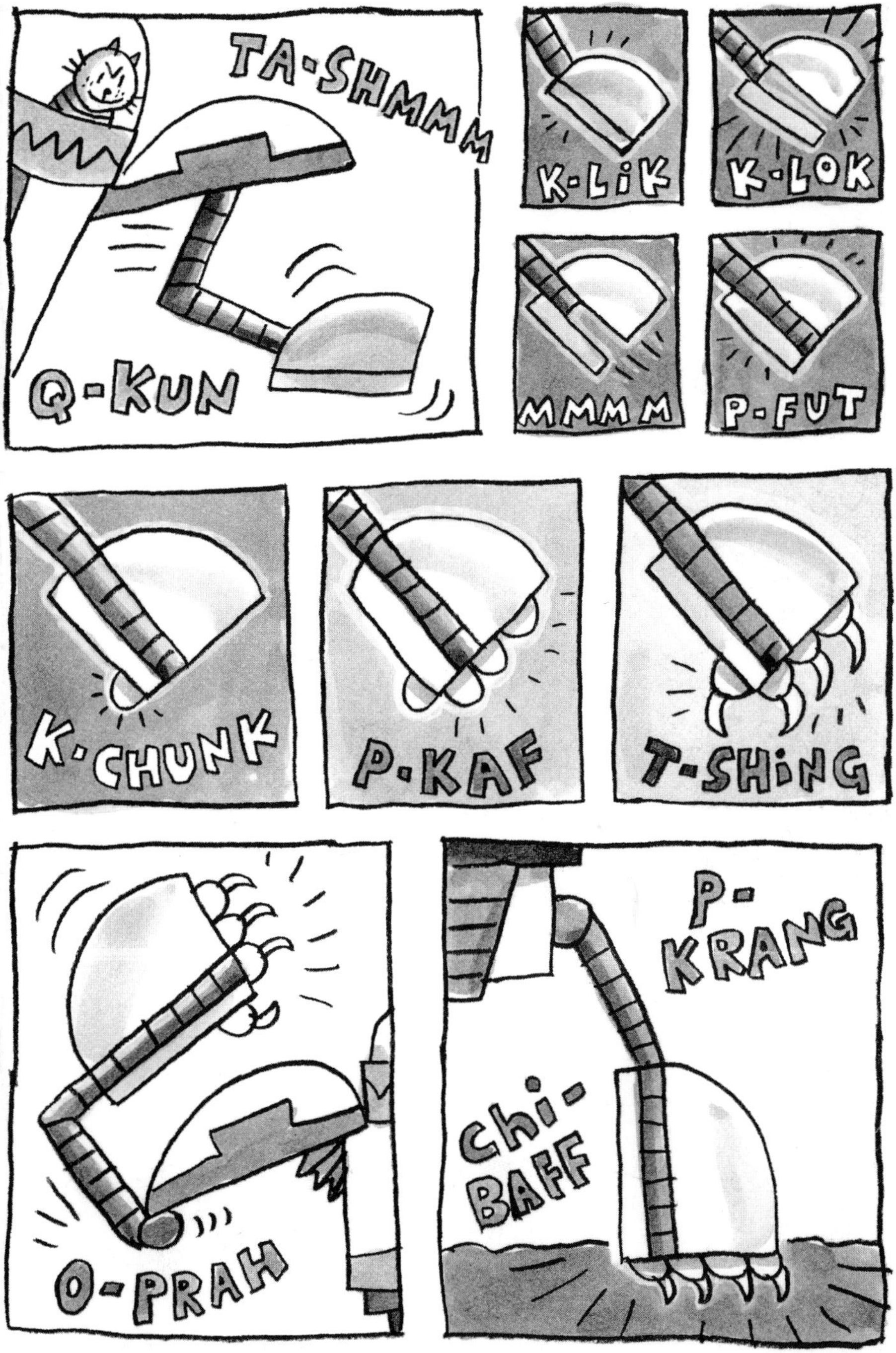
TA-SHMMMM
Q-KUN
K-LIK
K-LOK
MMMM
P-FUT
K-CHUNK
P-KAF
T-SHING
O-PRAH
P-KRANG
CHI-BAFF

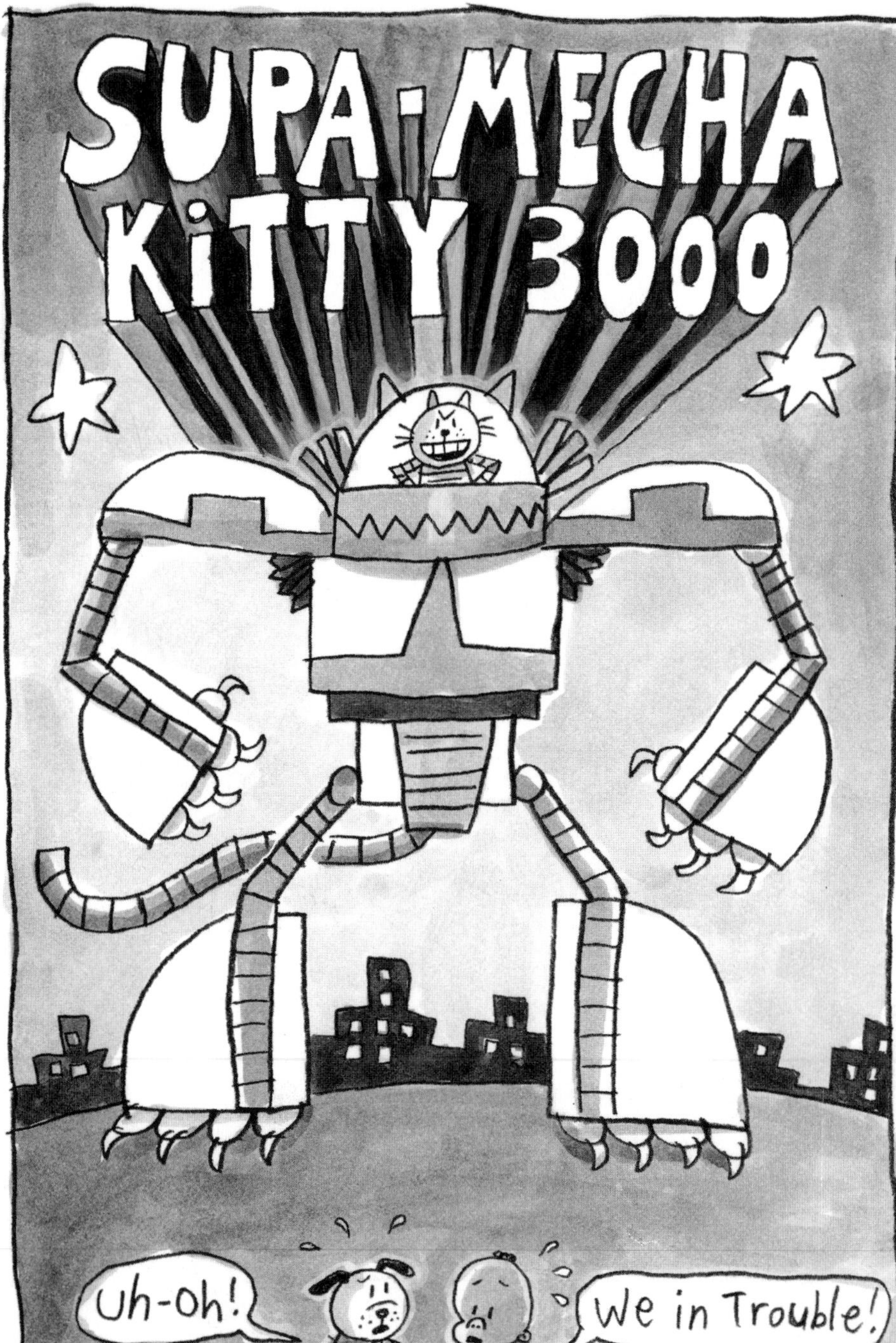
SUPA-MECHA
KITTY 3000
Uh-Oh!
We in Trouble!

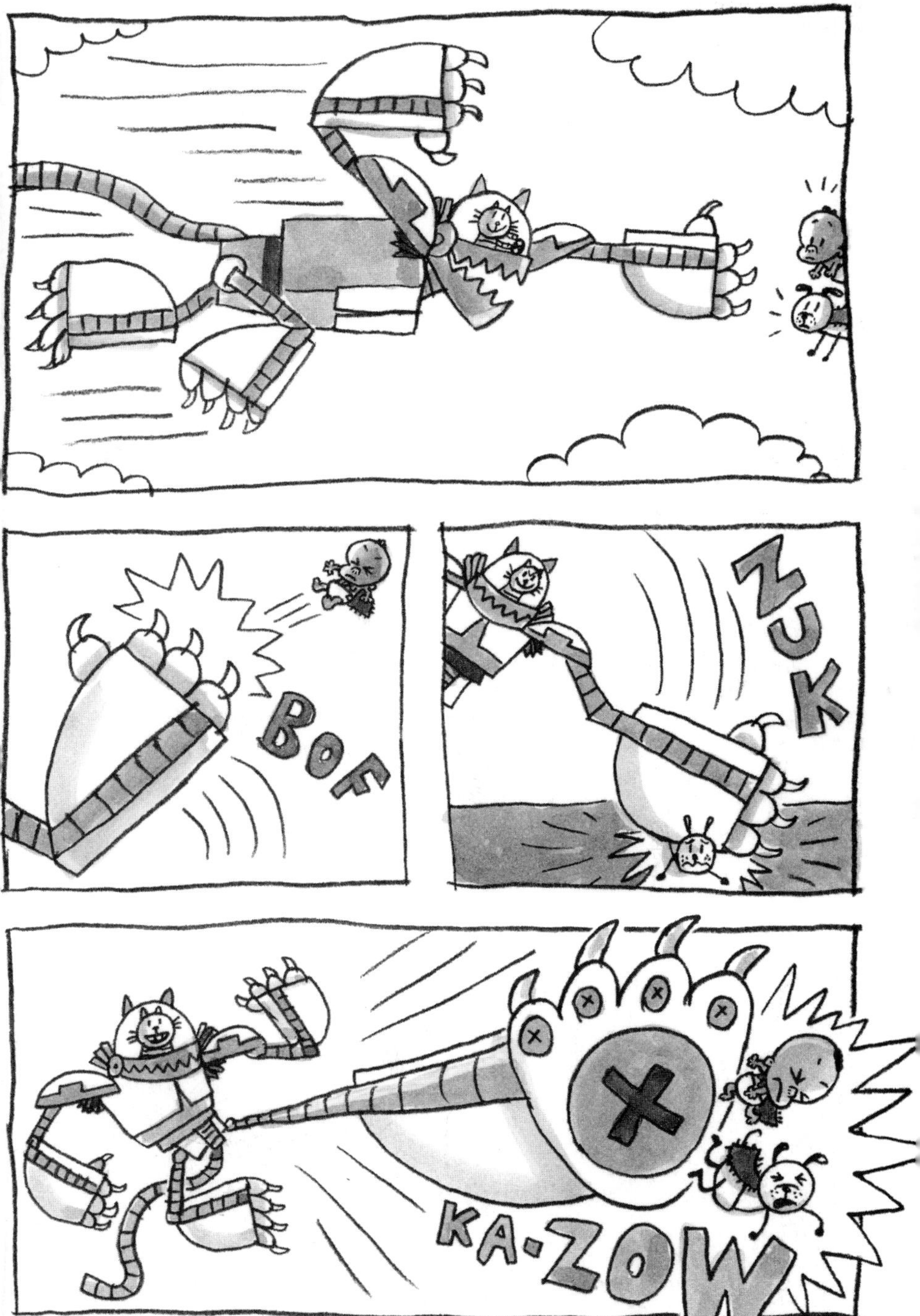
BOF
NUK
KA-ZOW

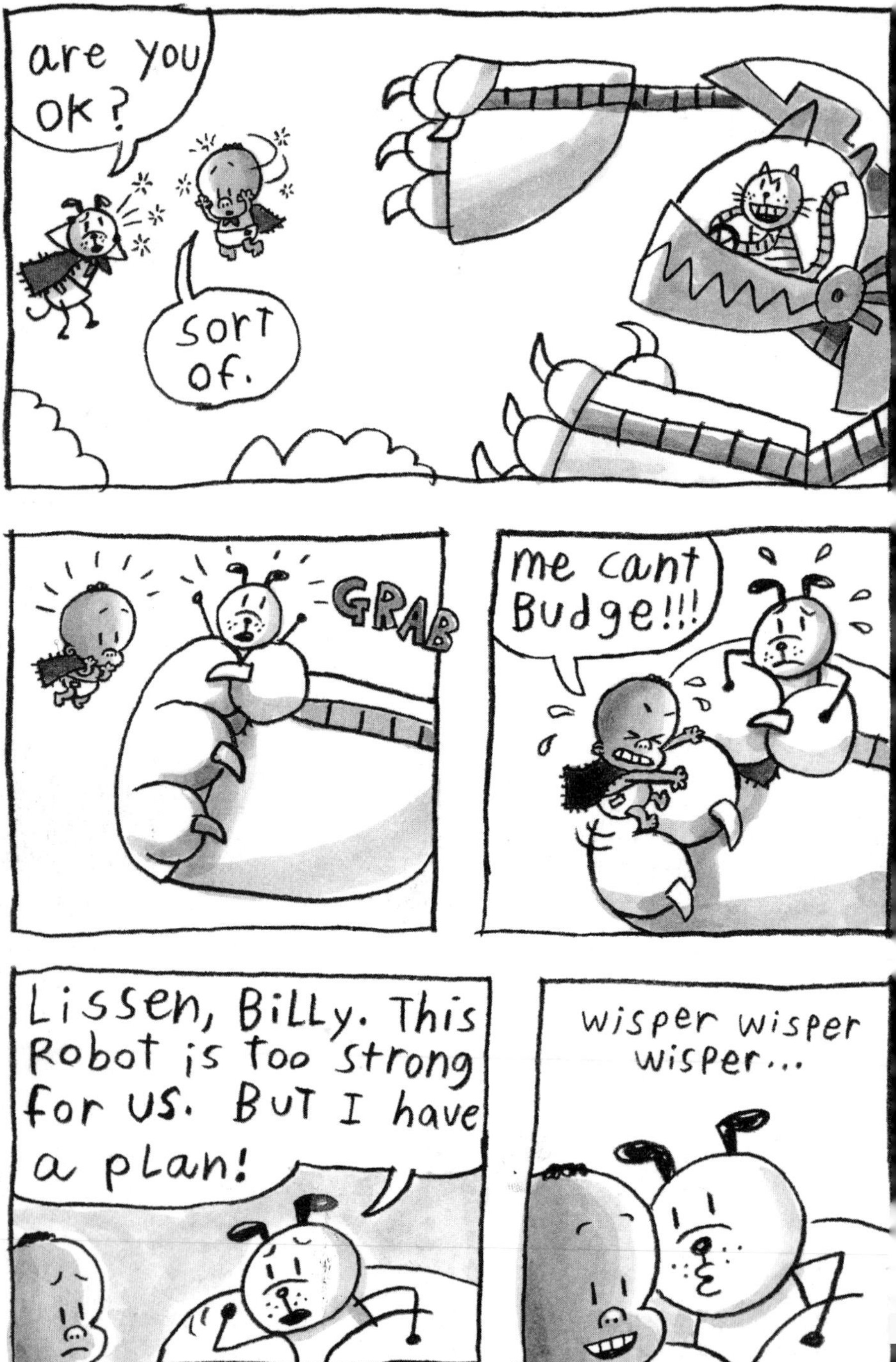
are you OK?
sort of.
GRAB
me cant Budge!!!
Lissen, Billy. This Robot is too strong for us. But I have a plan!
wisper wisper wisper...

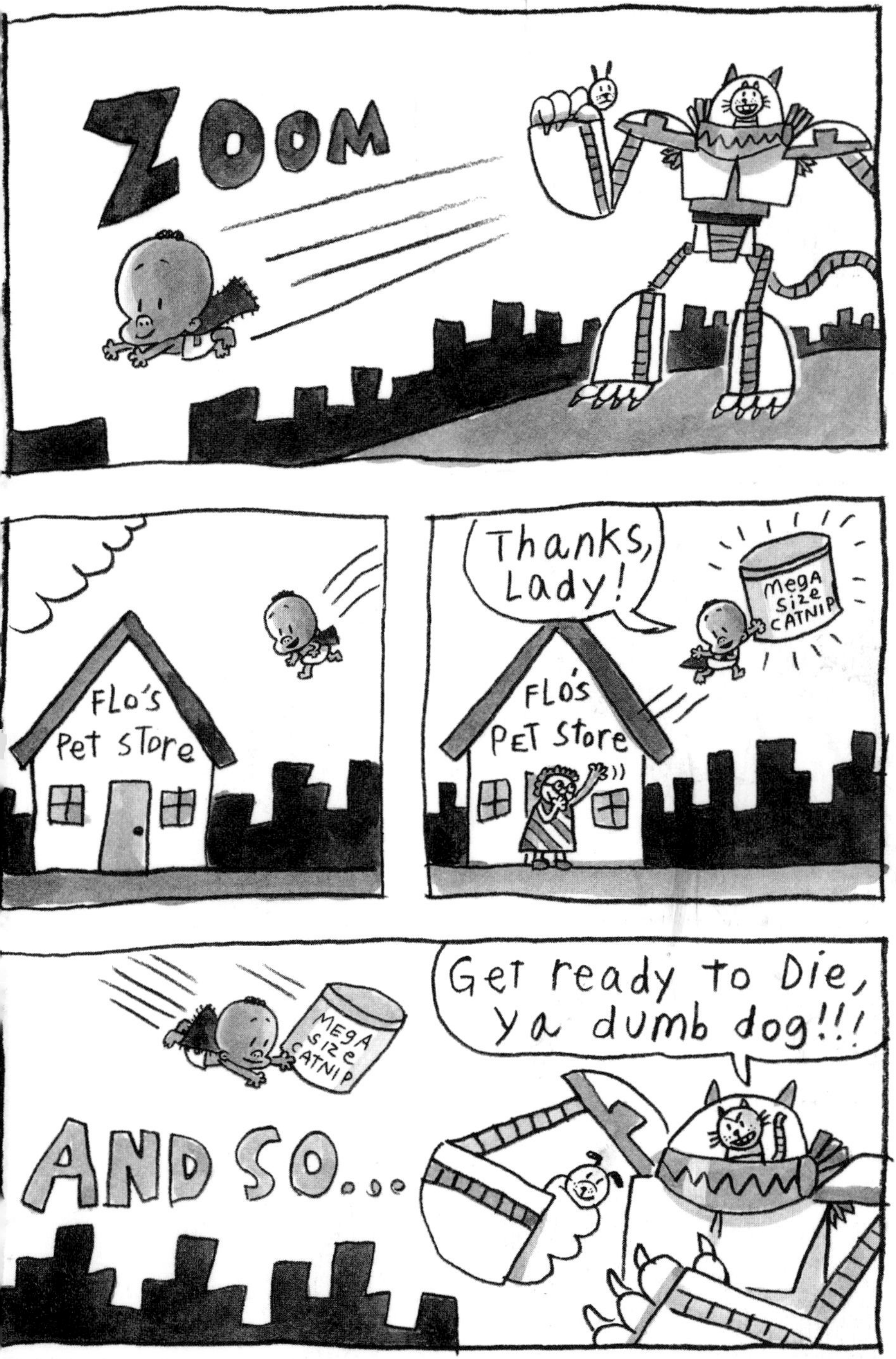
ZOOM
FLO'S
Pet Store
Thanks, Lady!
FLO'S
PET Store
MEGA Size CATNIP
MEGA Size CATNIP
AND SO...
Get ready to Die, ya dumb dog!!!

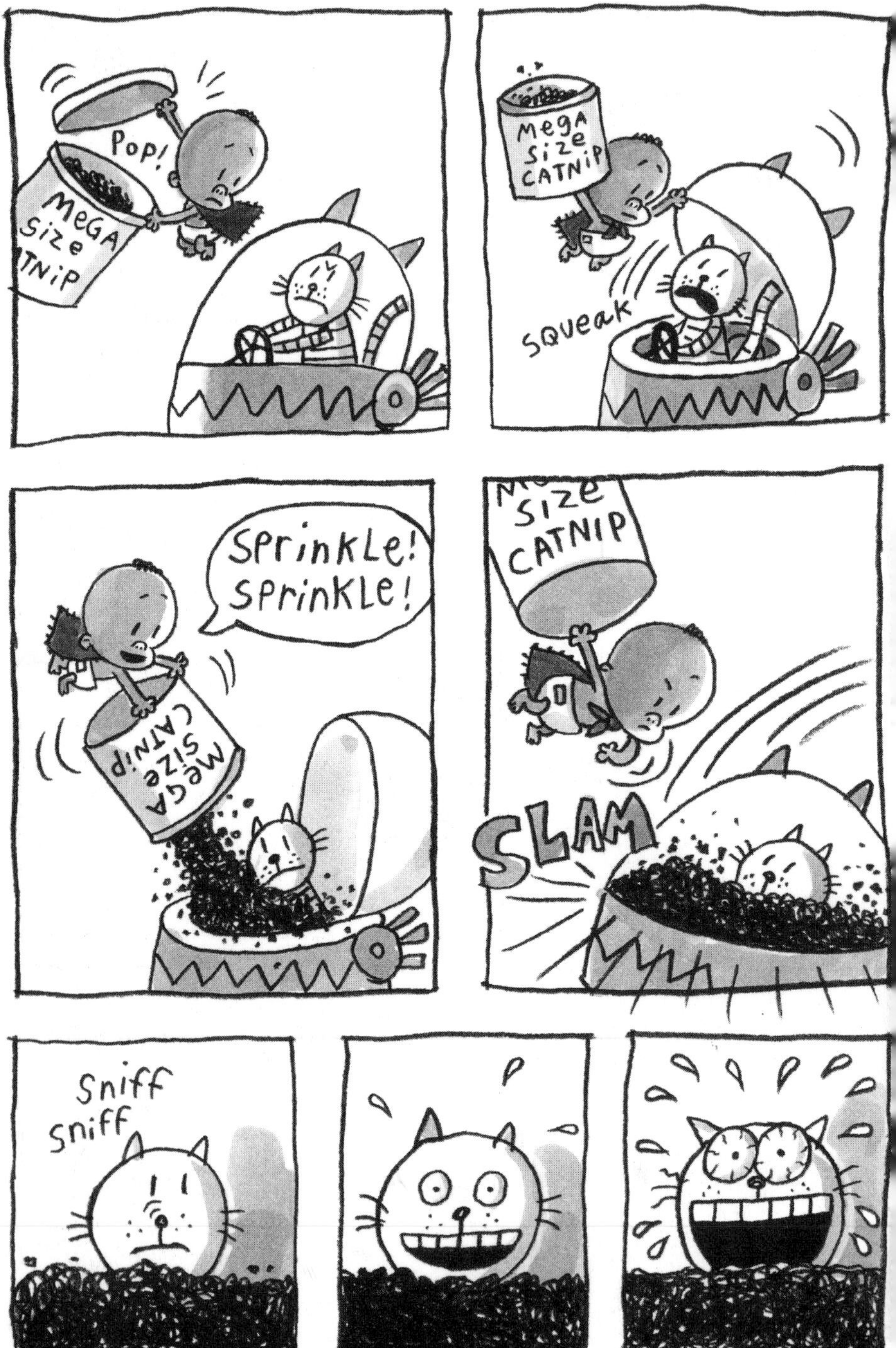
Pop!
MEGA Size [C]ATNIP
MEGA Size CATNIP
SQUEAK
Sprinkle! Sprinkle!
MEGA Size CATNIP
Size CATNIP
SLAM
Sniff sniff

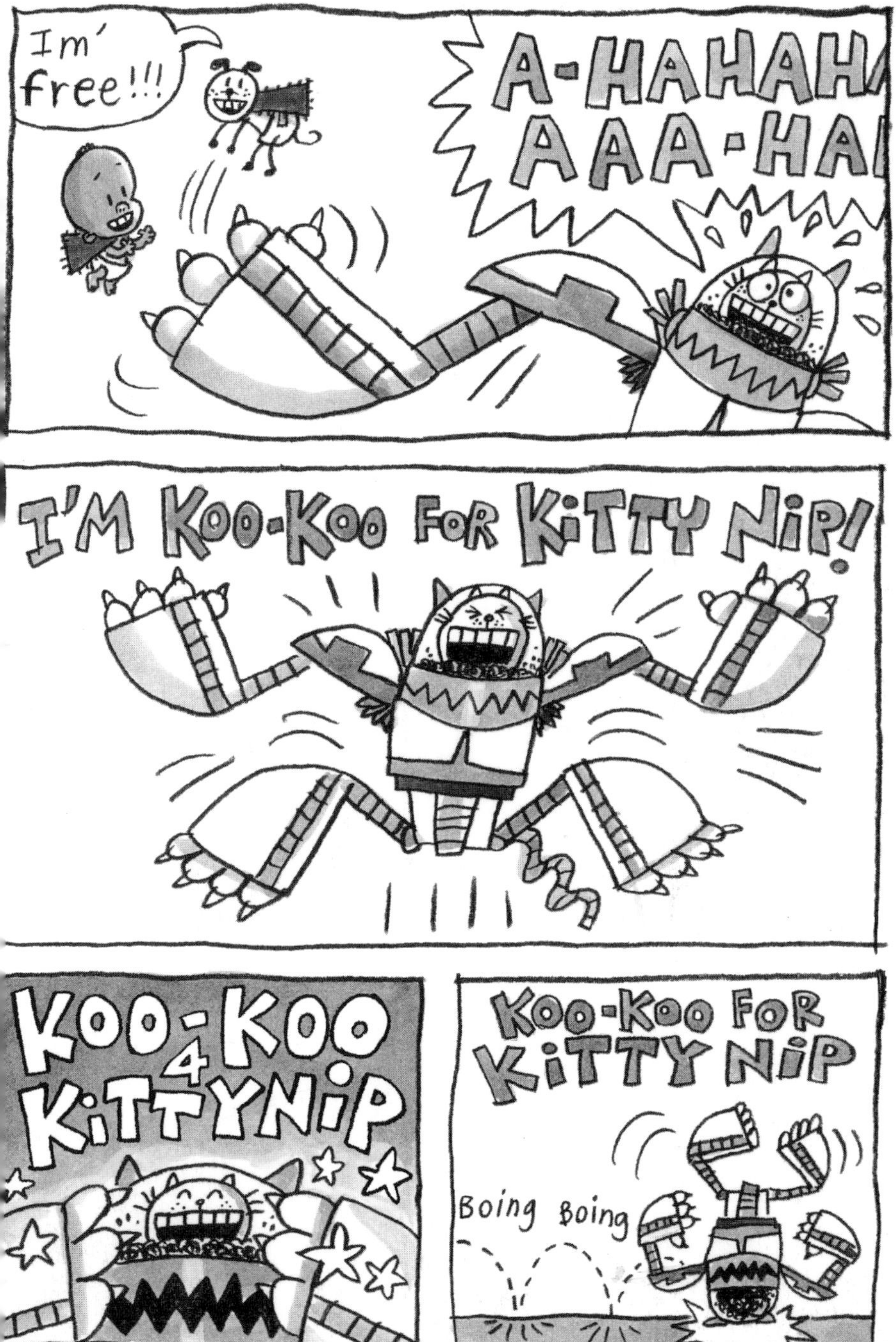
I'm free!!!
A-HAHAH AAA-HA
I'M KOO-KOO FOR KITTY NIP!
KOO-KOO 4 KITTYNIP
KOO-KOO FOR KITTY NIP
Boing Boing

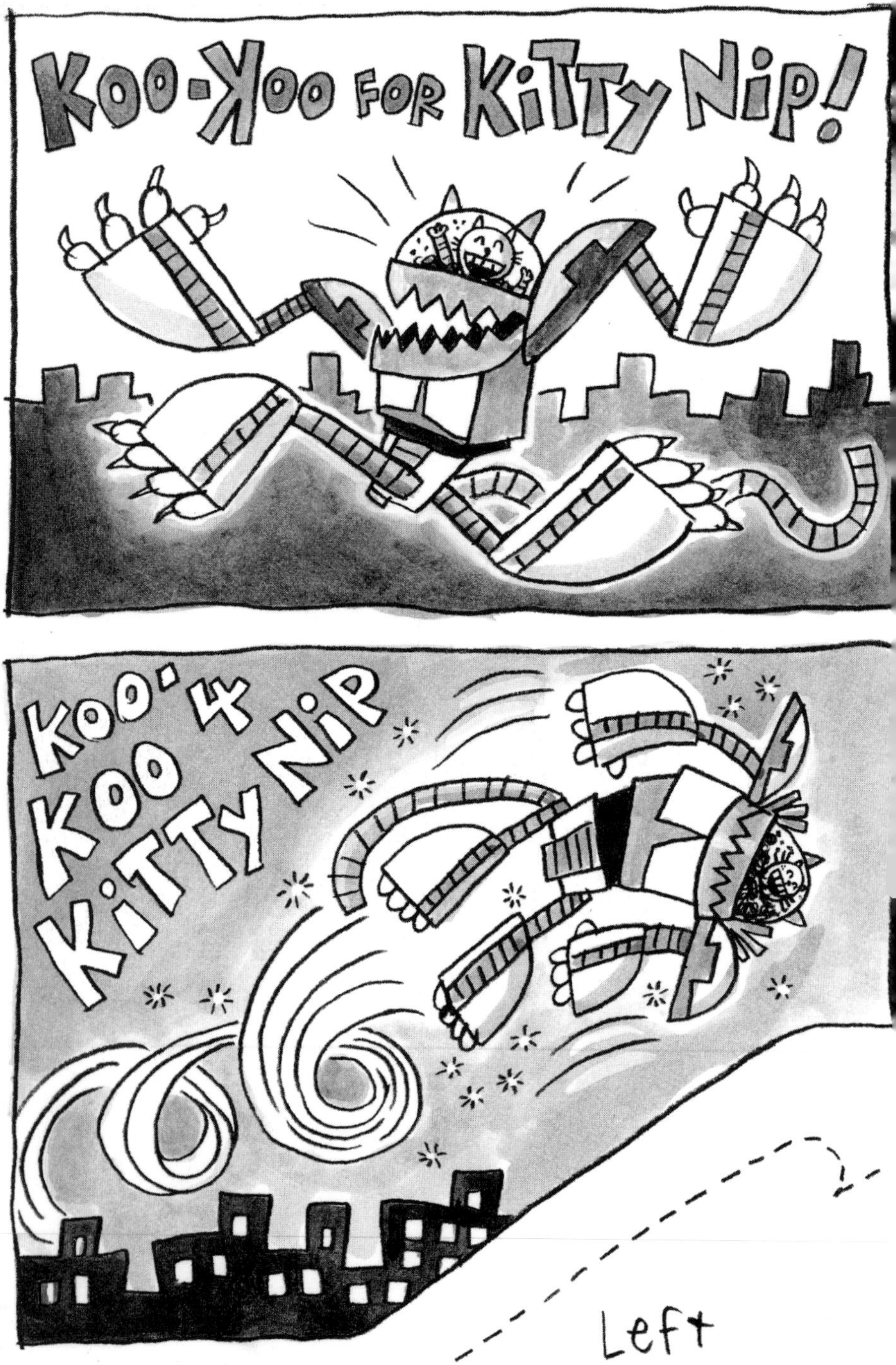
KOO-KOO FOR KITTY NIP!
KOO-KOO 4 KITTY NIP

Left
Hand Here

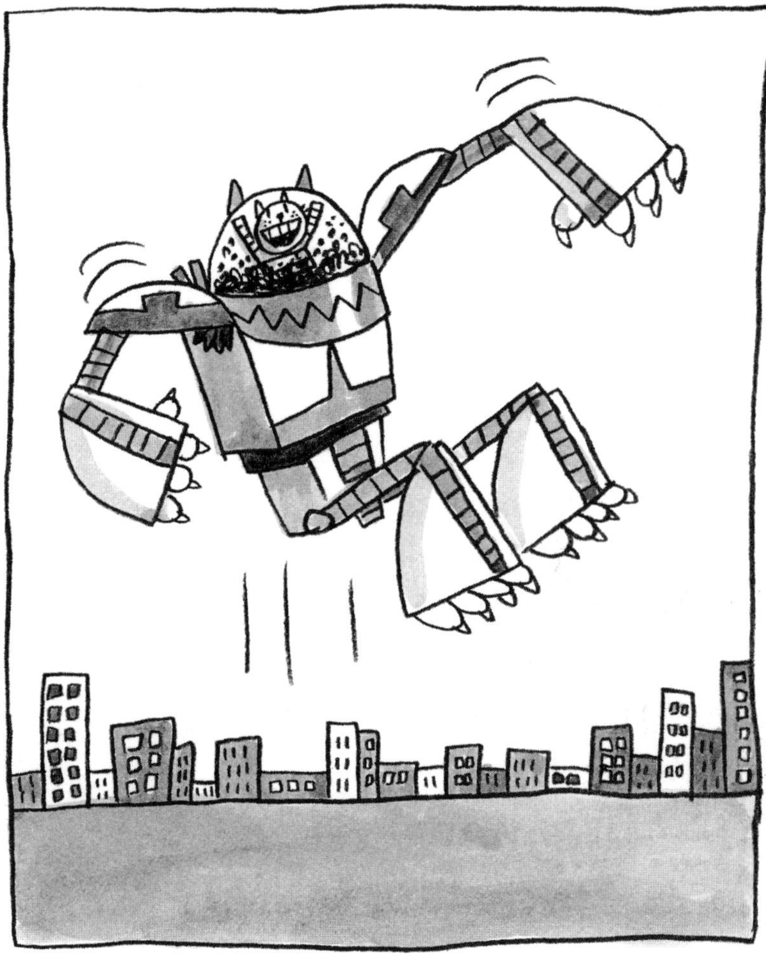

Koo-Koo For Kitty Nip!

Right thumb Here

Koo-Koo For Kitty Nip!

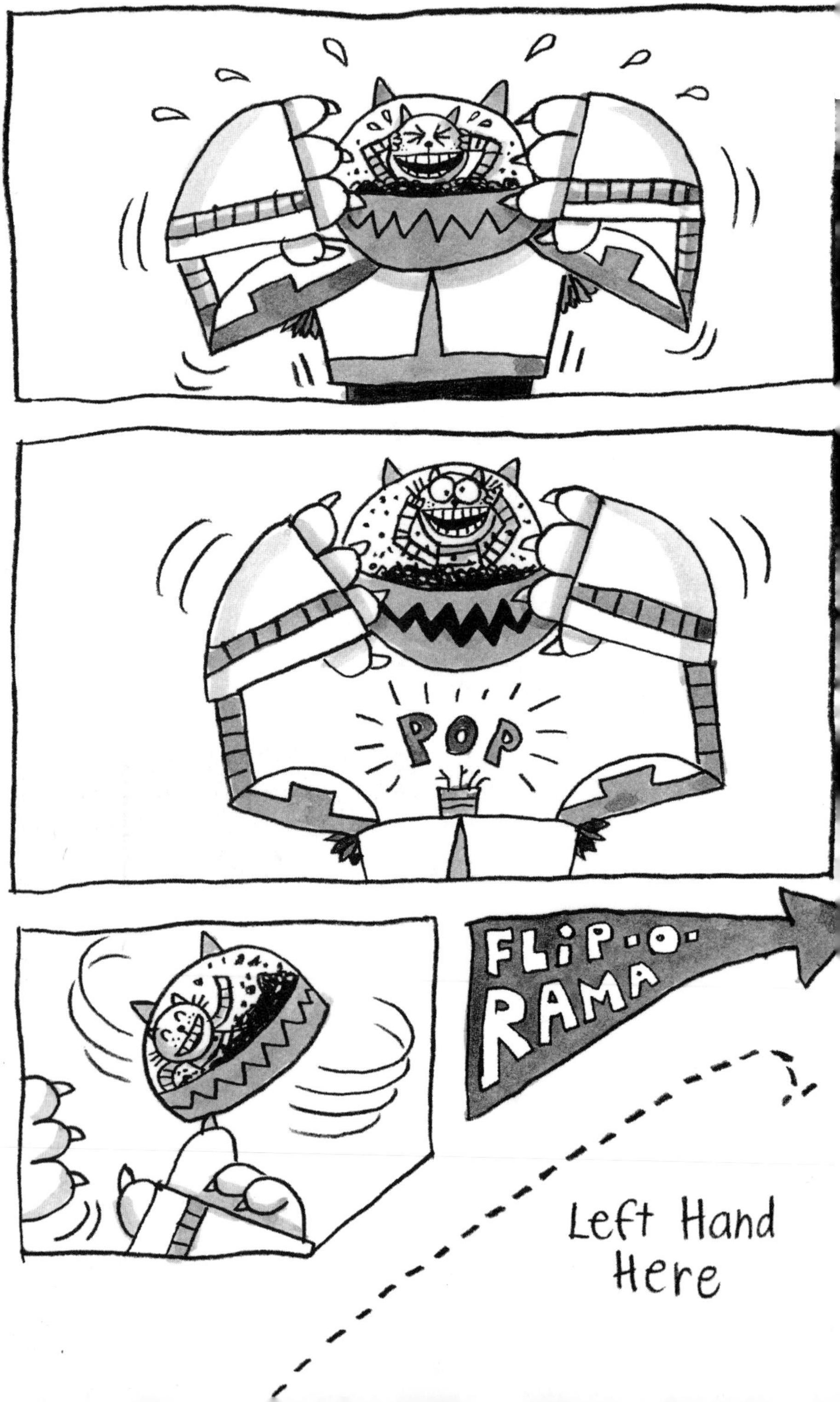
POP
FLIP-O-RAMA
Left Hand
Here

Kitty for Koo-Koo Nip!

147

Right thumb Here.

Kitty For Koo-Koo Nip!

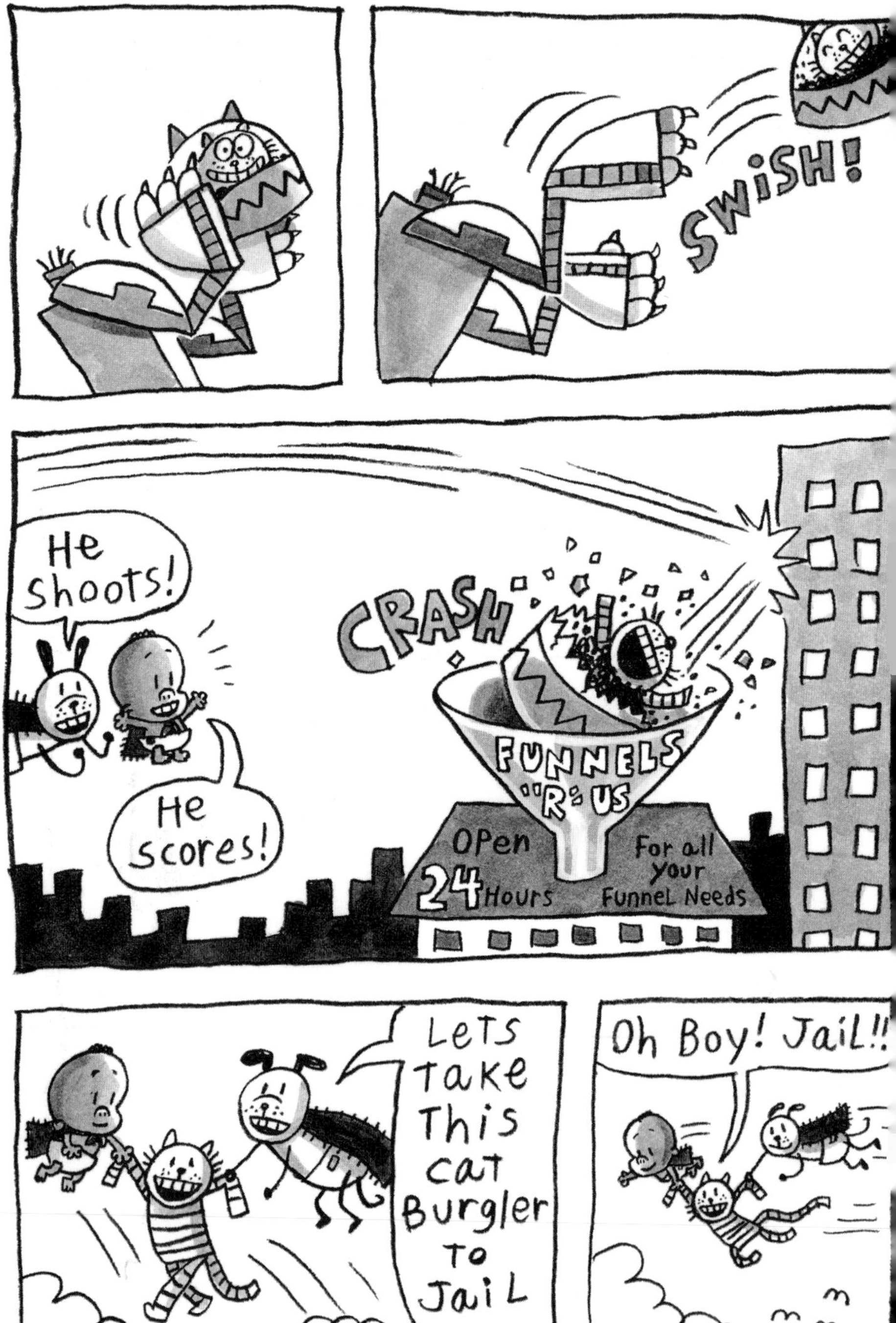
SWISH!
He shoots!
CRASH
He scores!
FUNNELS "R" US
Open 24 Hours
For all your Funnel Needs
Lets Take This cat Burgler To JaiL
Oh Boy! JaiL!!

CHAPTER 6

The Revenge of Rip Van Tinkle

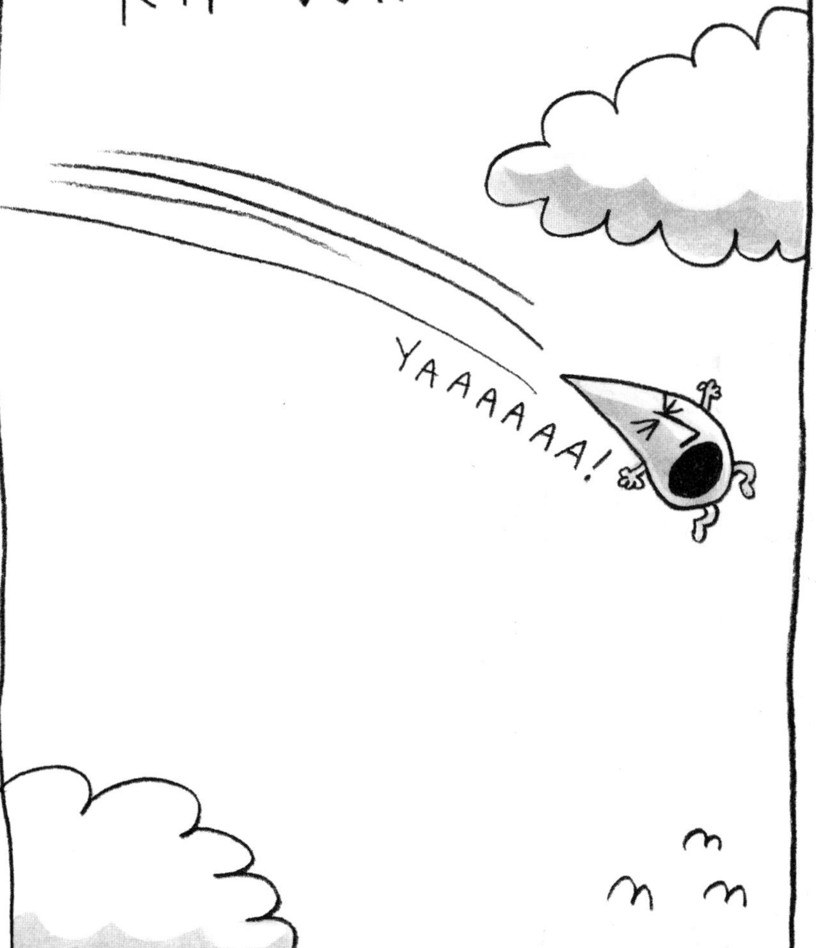
YAAAAAAA!

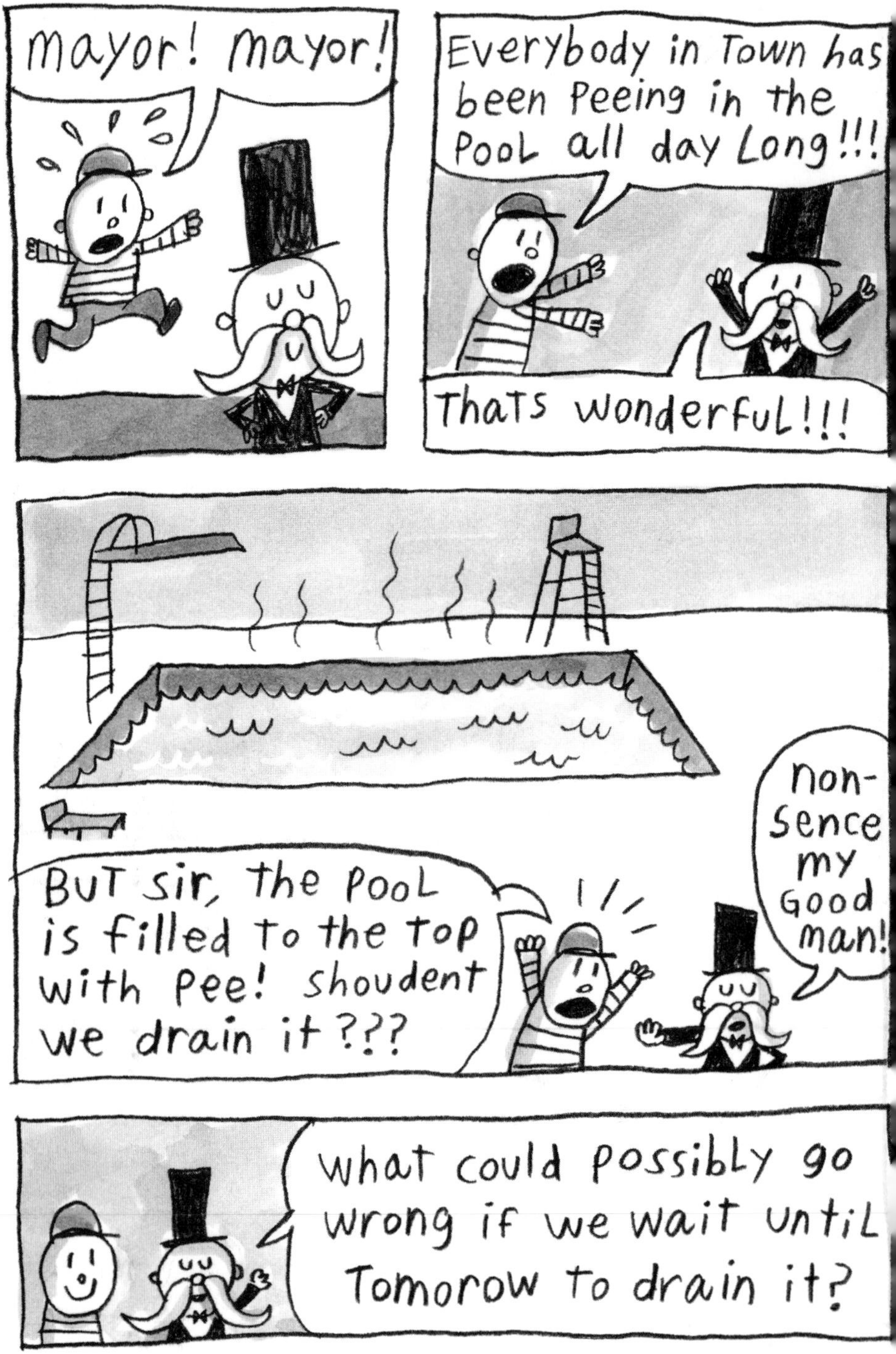
mayor! mayor!
Everybody in Town has been Peeing in the PooL all day Long!!!
ThaTs wonderfuL!!!
BuT sir, the PooL is filled To the Top with Pee! shoudent we drain it???
non-sence my Good man!
what could possibLy go wrong if we wait untiL Tomorow To drain it?

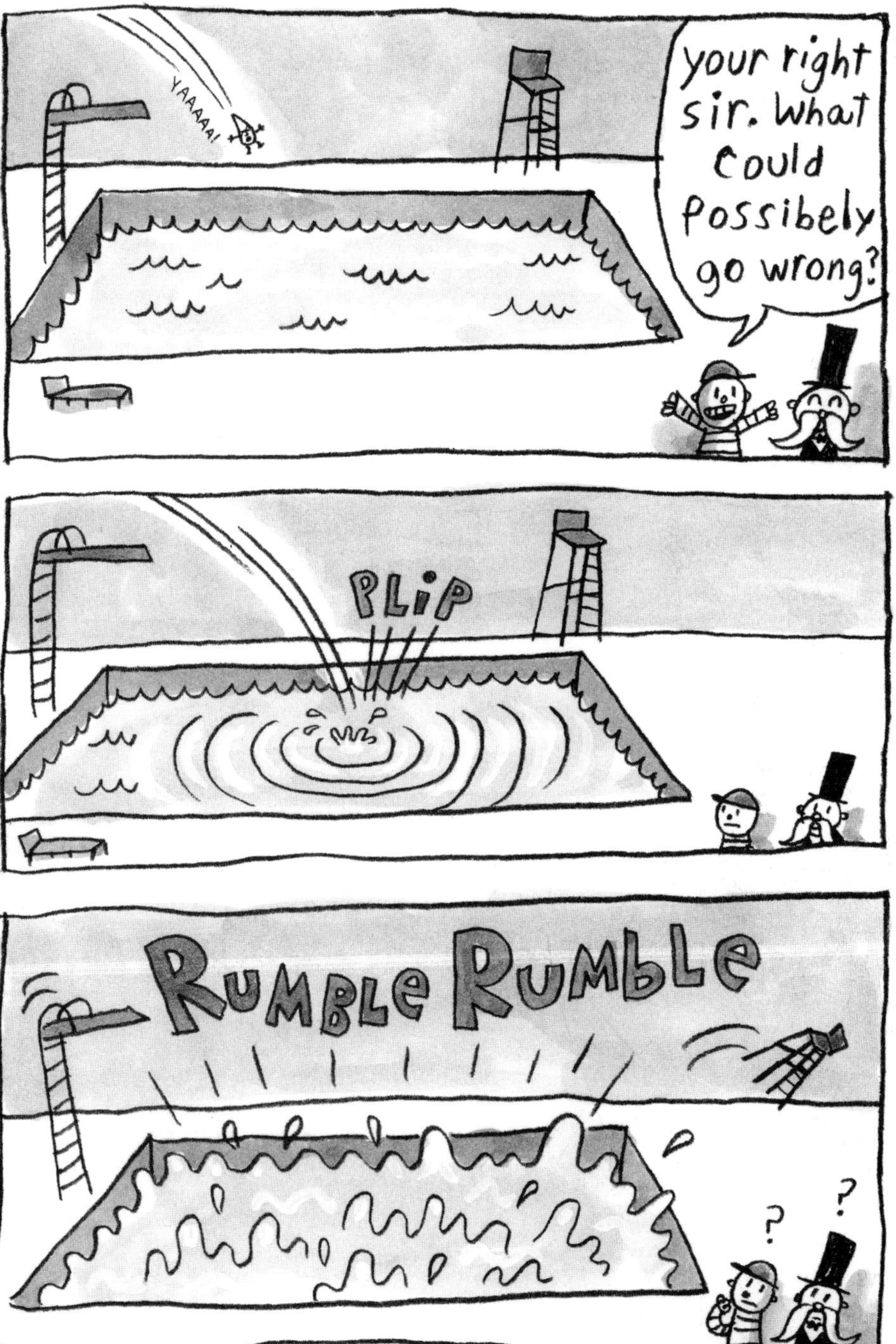
YAAAAA!
your right sir. What Could Possibely go wrong?
PLiP
RUMBLE RUMBLE
?
?

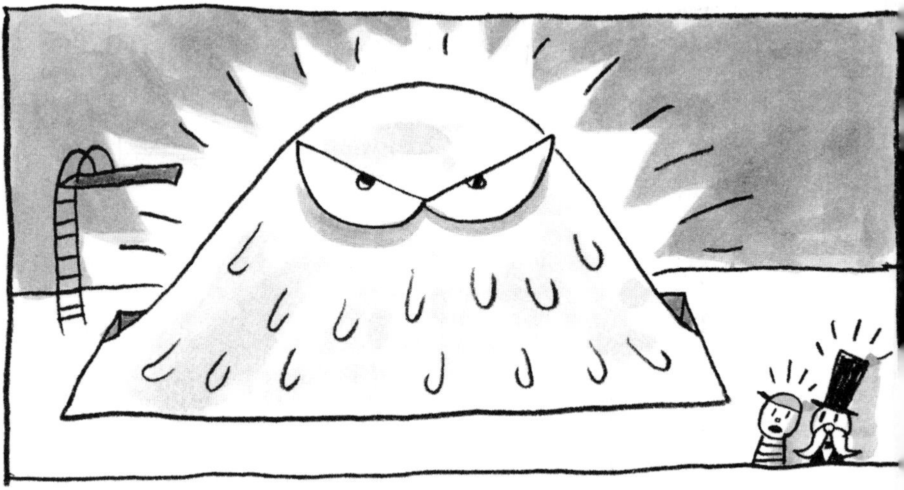

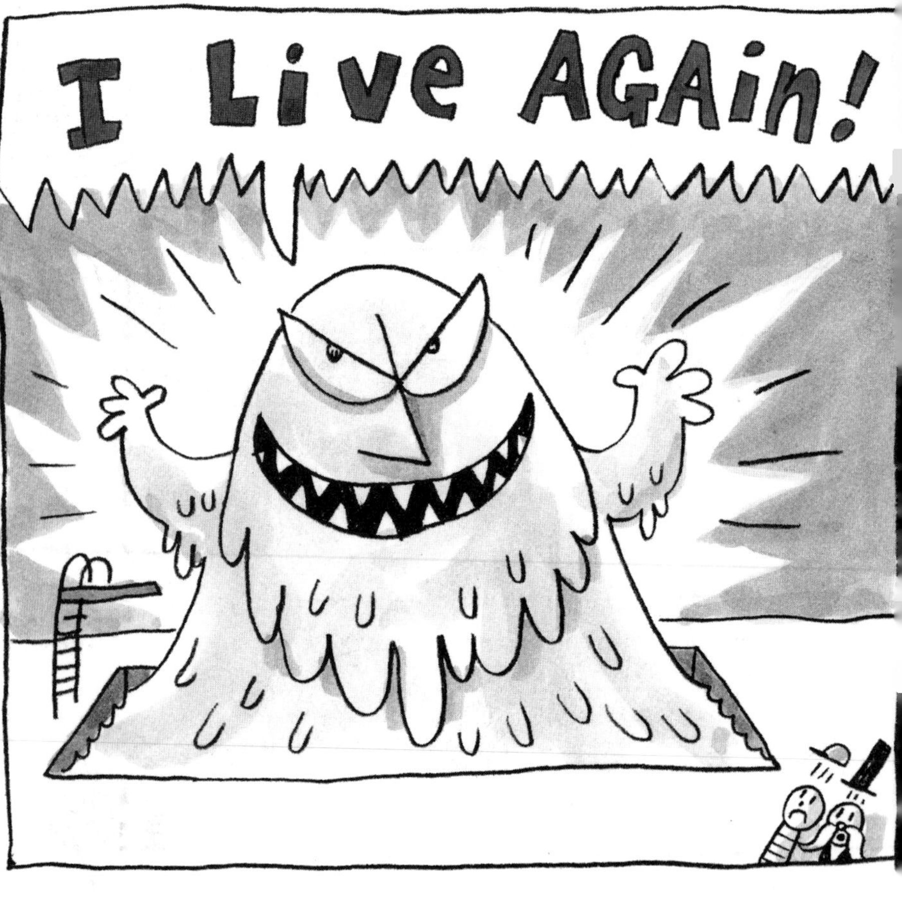
I Live AGAin!

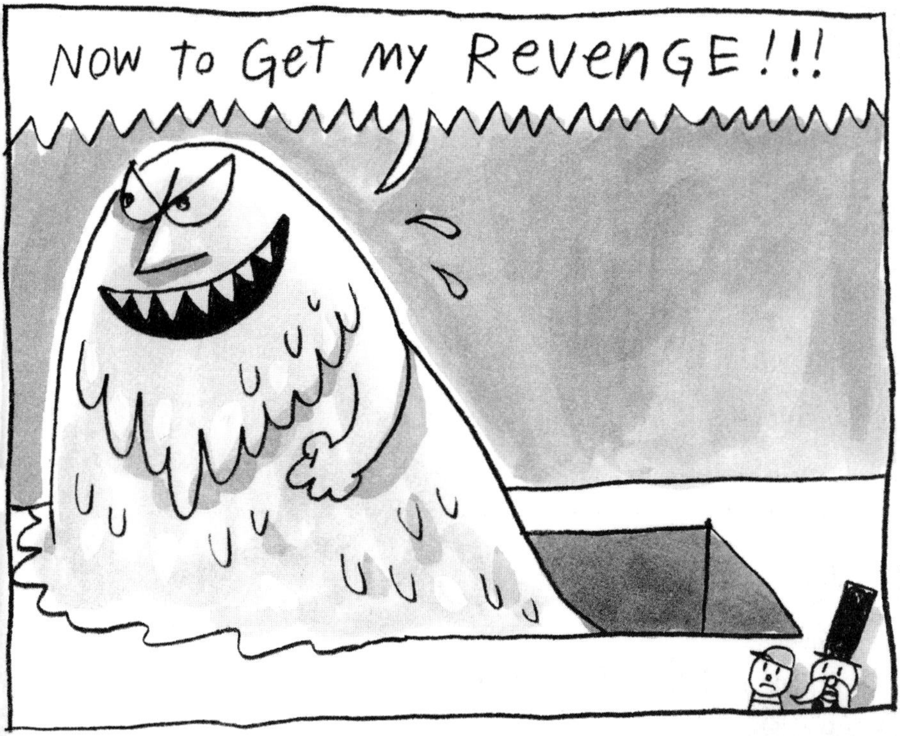
Now to Get my RevenGE!!!

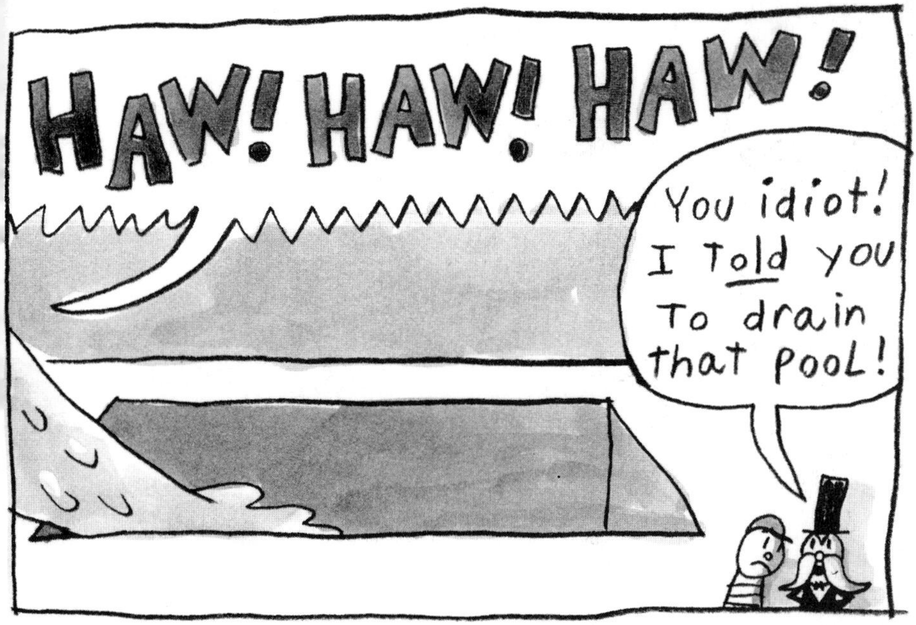
HAW! HAW! HAW!
You idiot! I told you to drain that pool!

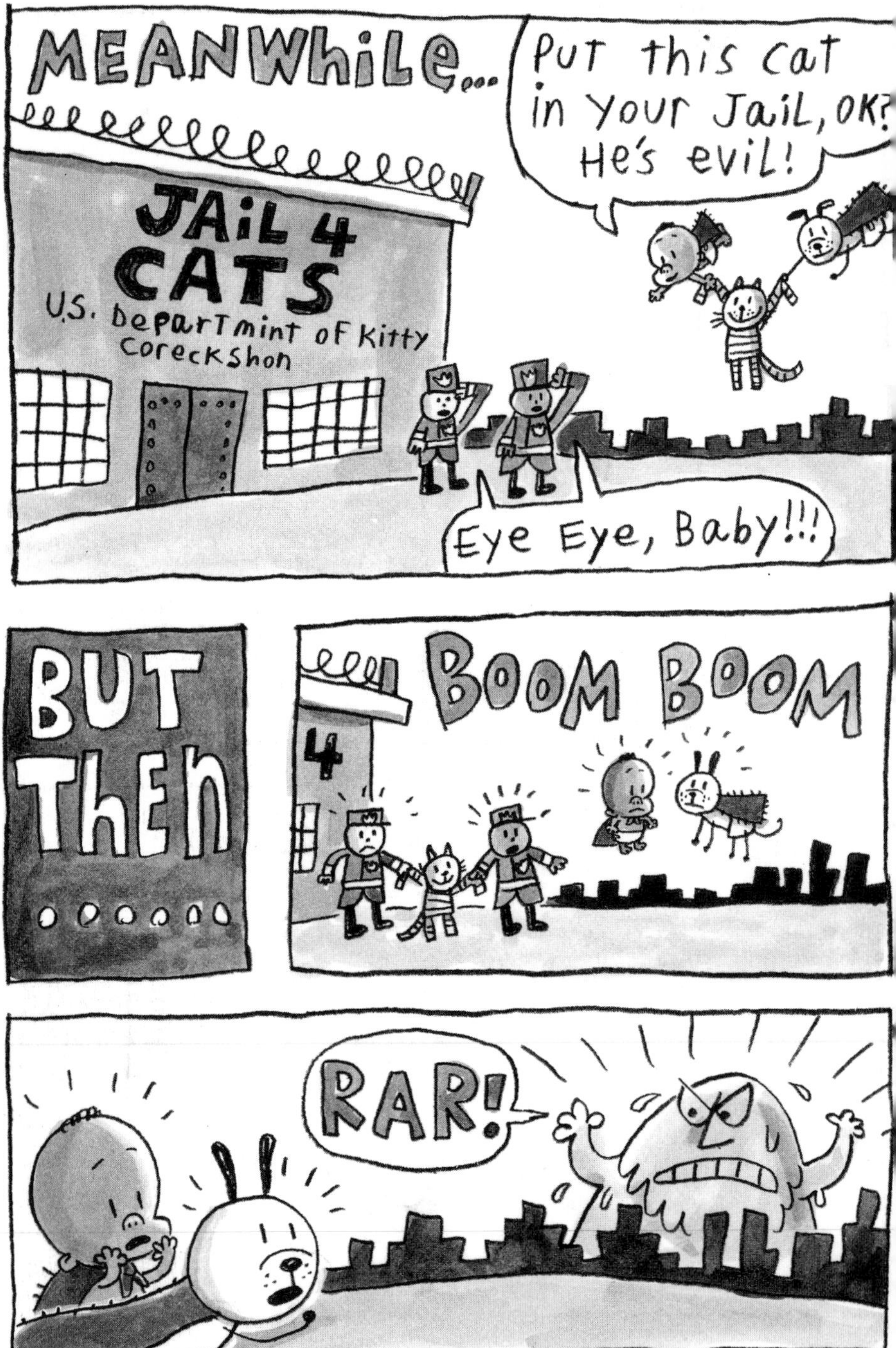
MEANWhiLe...
Put this cat in your JaiL, OK? He's evil!
JAiL 4 CATS
U.S. DeparTmint of Kitty Coreckshon
Eye Eye, Baby!!!
BUT ThEn
BOOM BOOM
4
RAR!

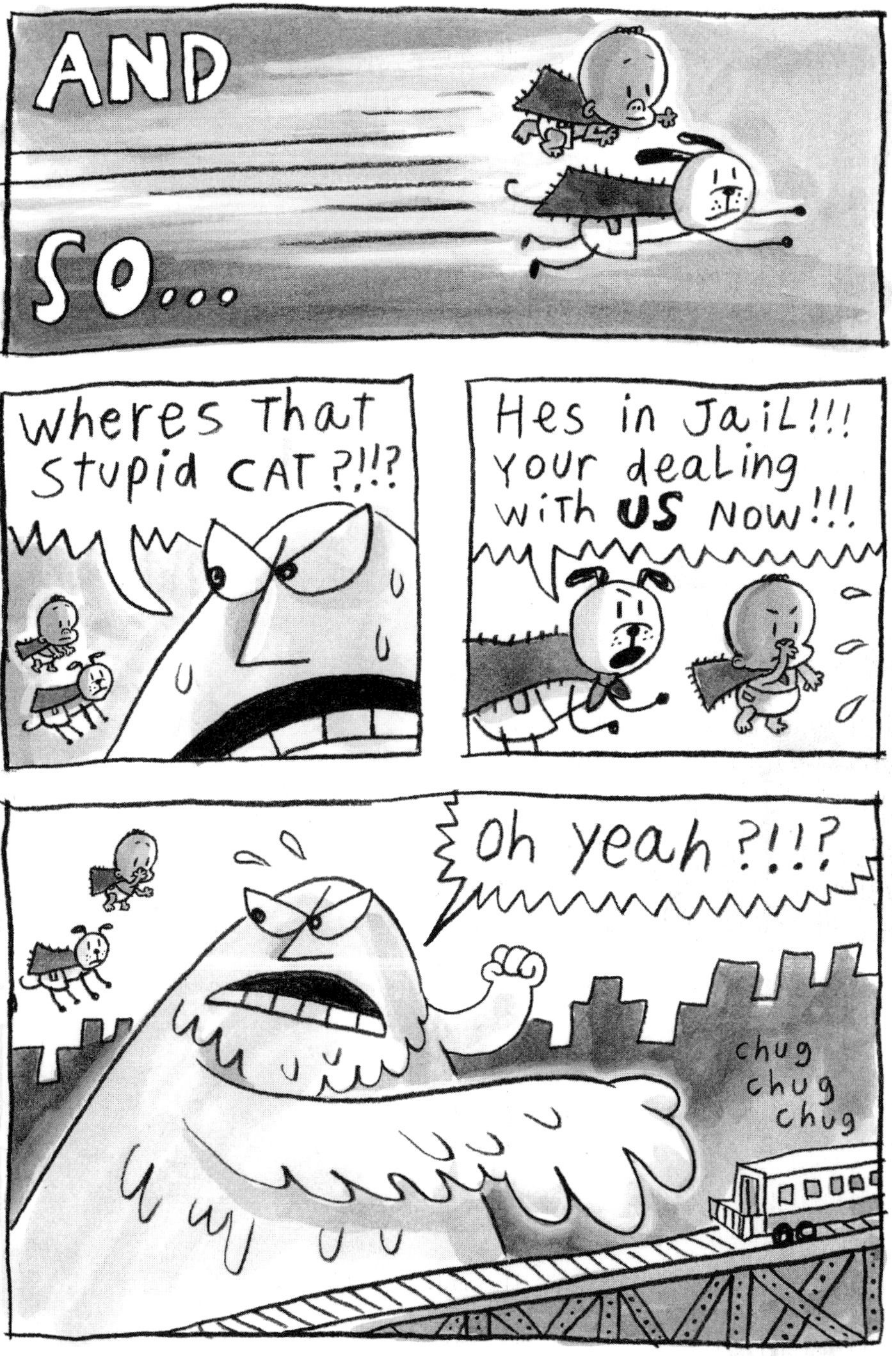
AND SO...
Wheres That Stupid CAT ?!!?
Hes in JaiL!!! Your deaLing with US Now!!!
Oh yeah ?!!?
chug chug chug

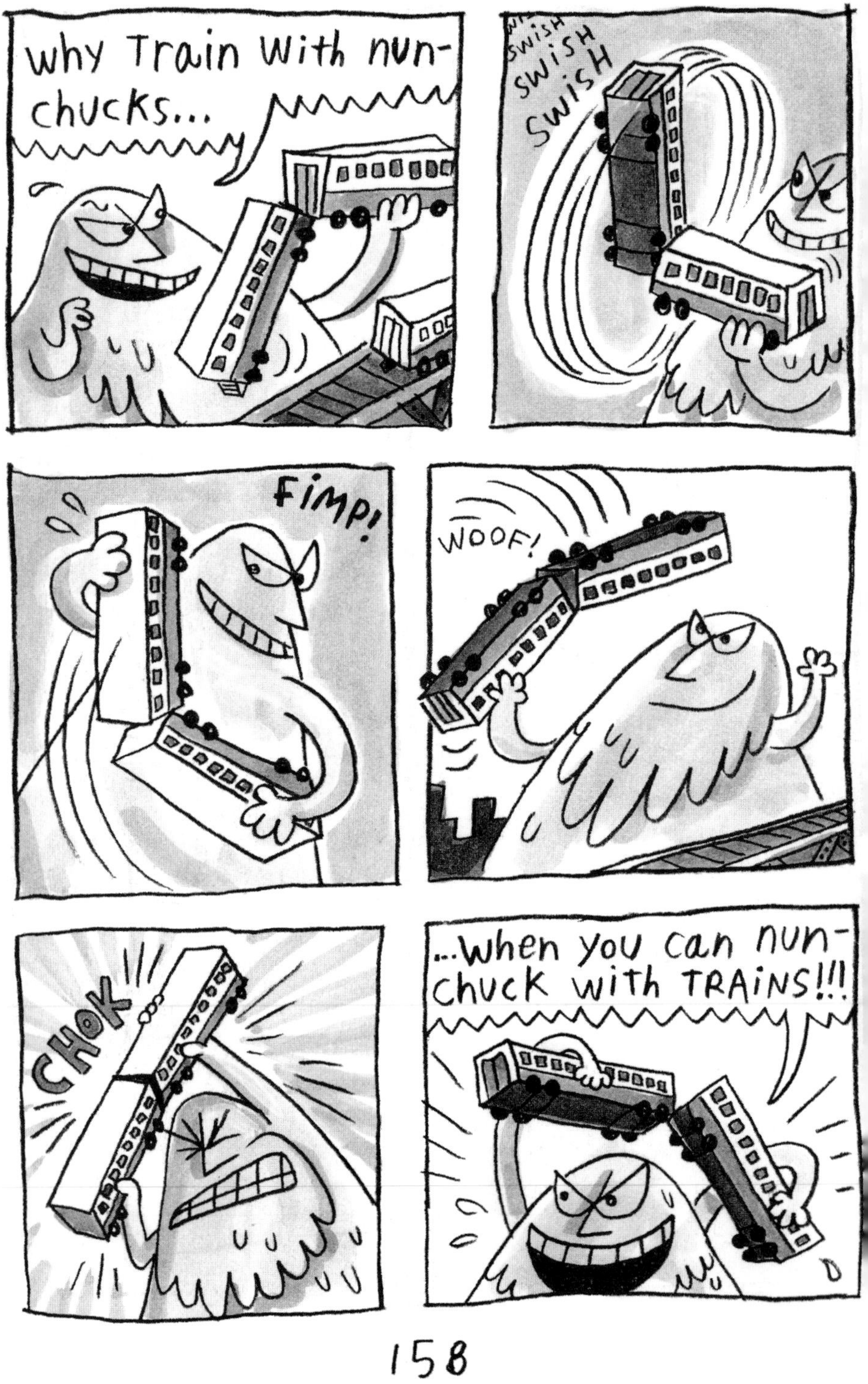
why Train with nun-chucks...
SWISH
SWISH
SWISH
FIMP!
WOOF!
CHOK
...when you can nun-chuck with TRAINS!!!

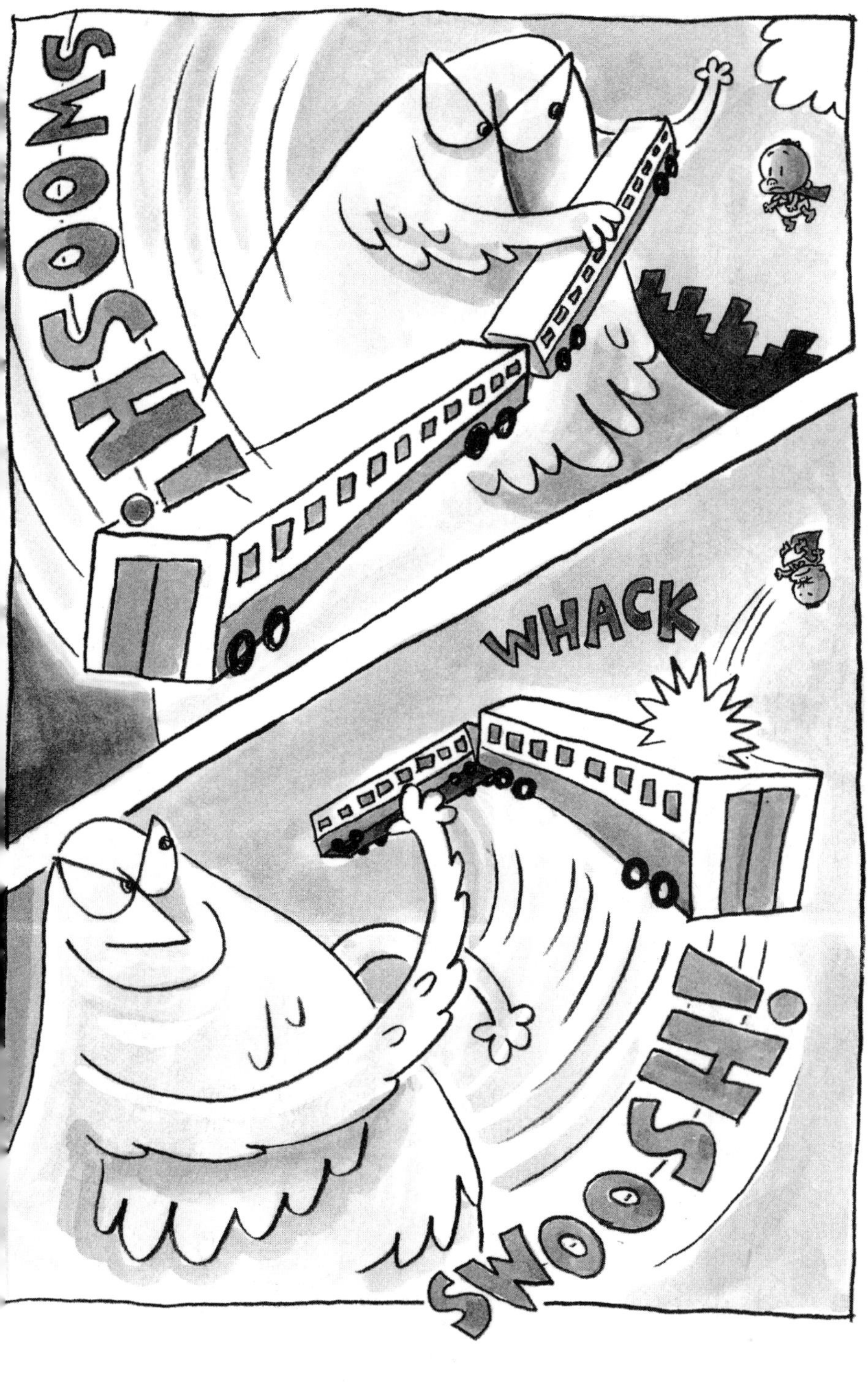
SWOOSH!
WHACK
SWOOSH!

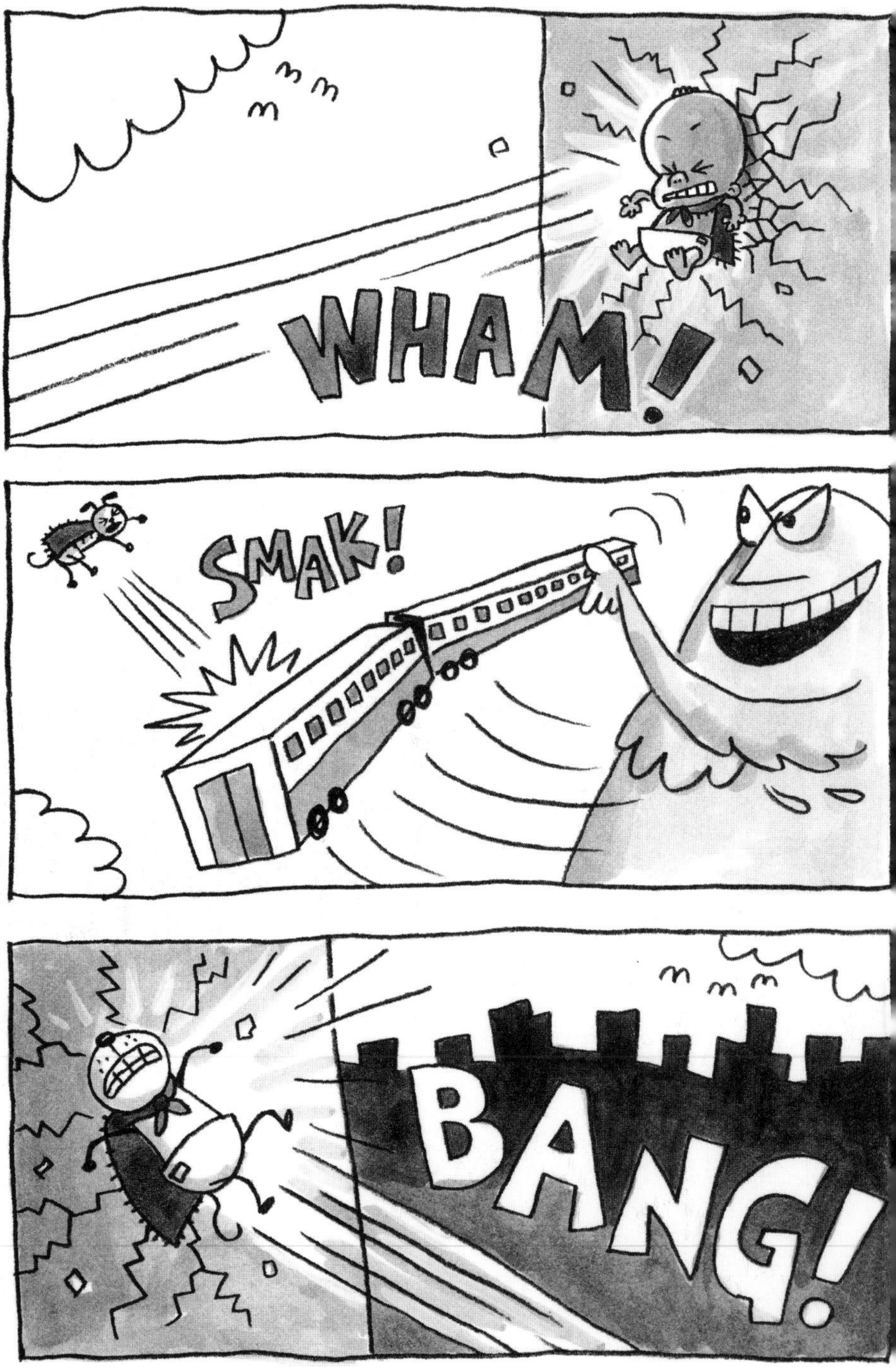
WHAM!
SMAK!
BANG!

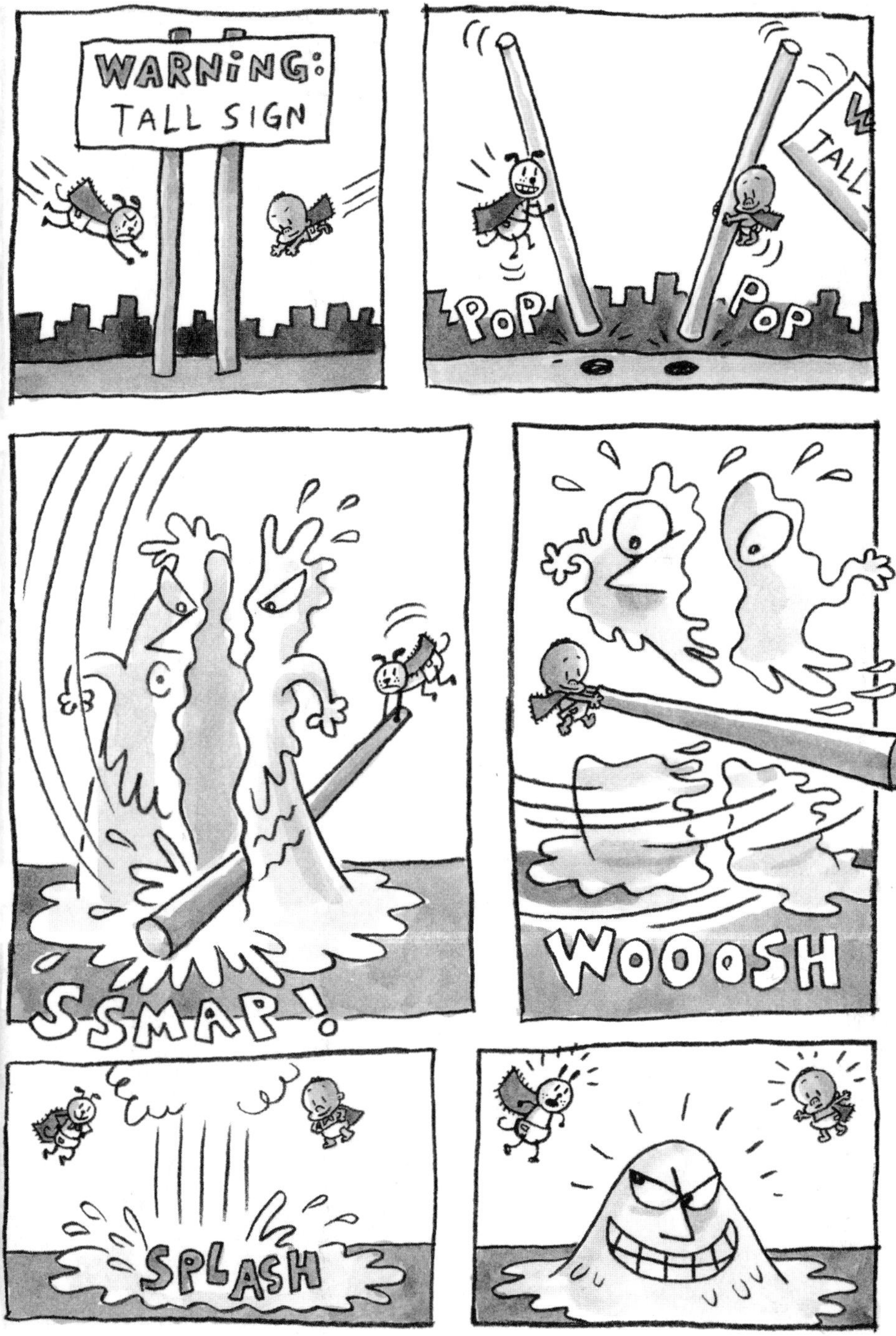
WARNING:
TALL SIGN
POP
POP
SSMAP!
WOOOSH
SPLASH

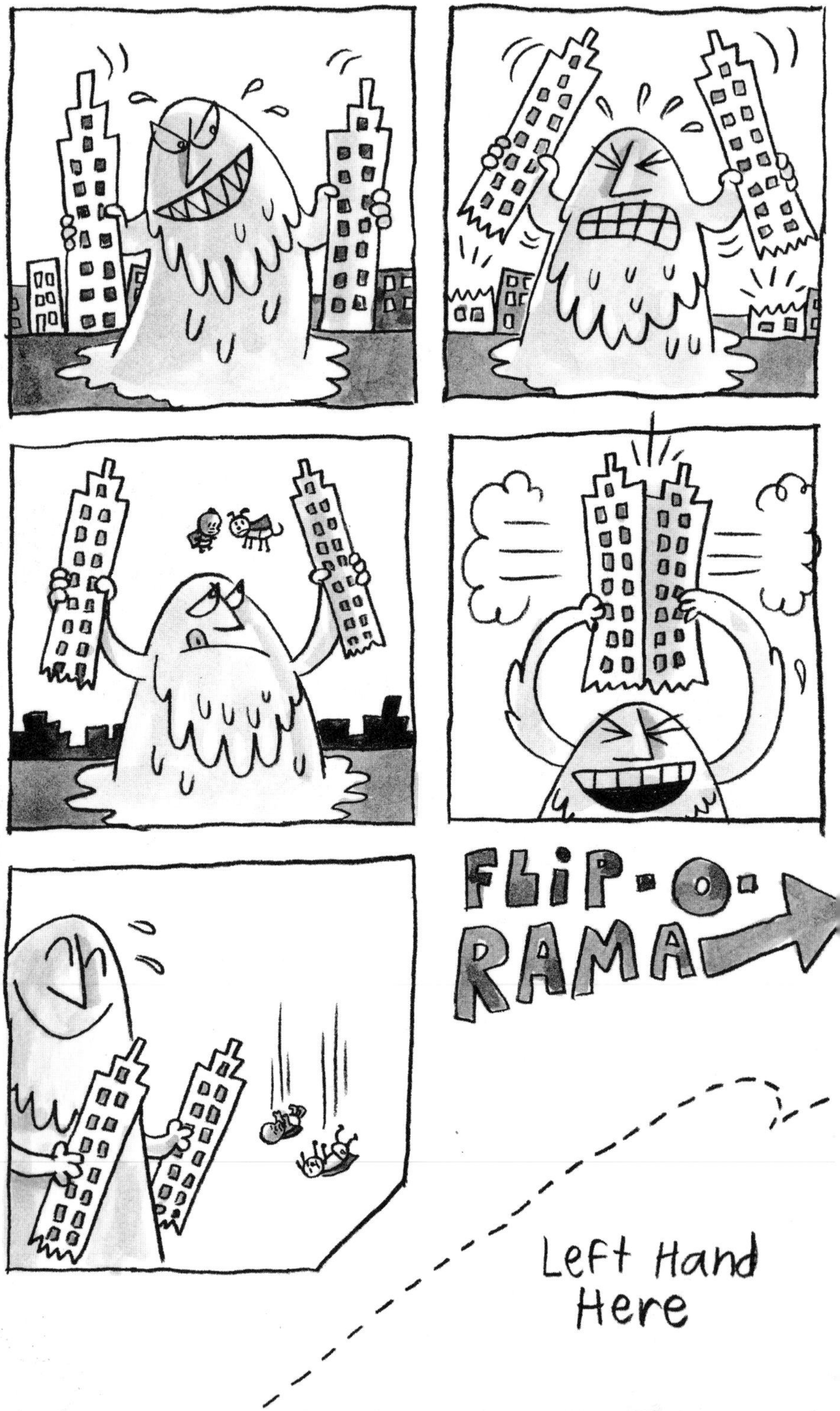
FLIP-O-RAMA
Left Hand Here

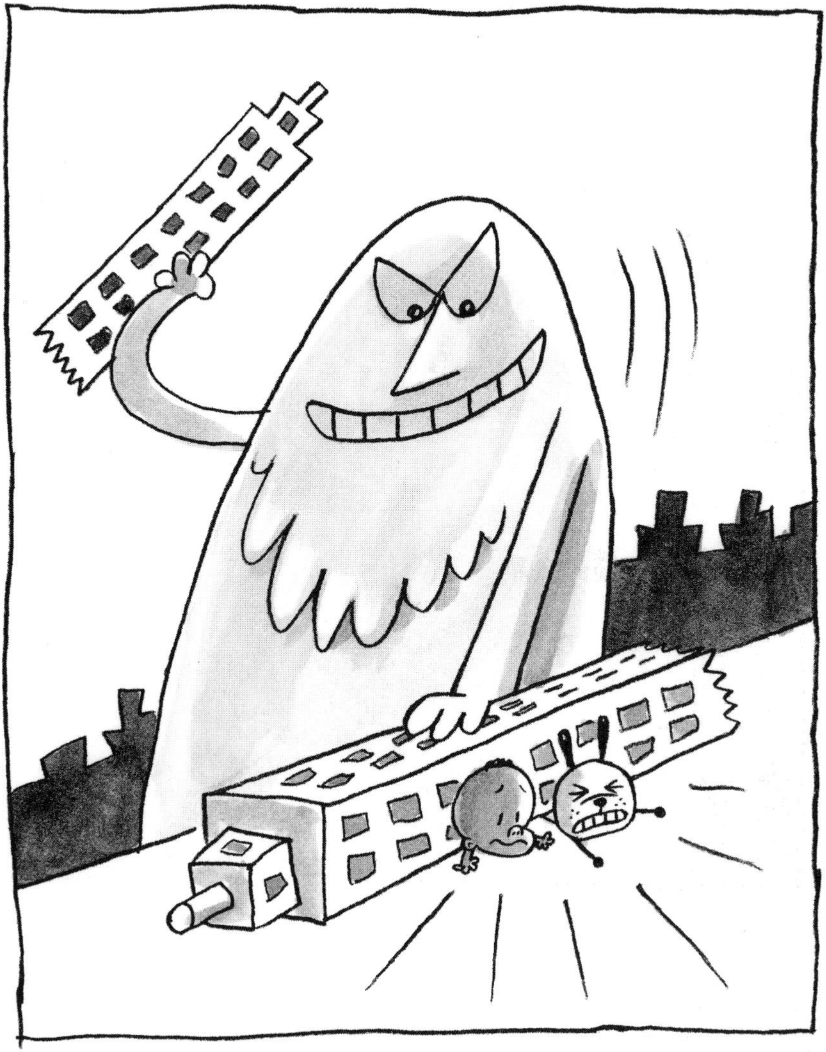

Building Basher

Right thumb Here

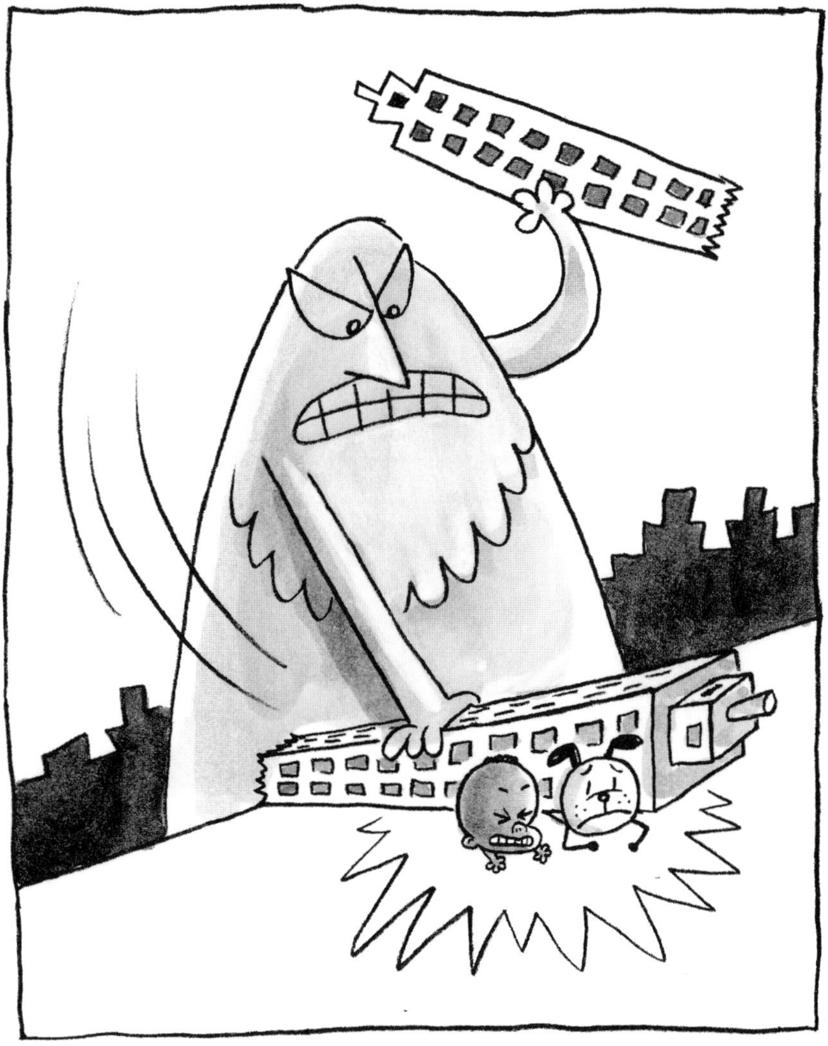

Building Basher

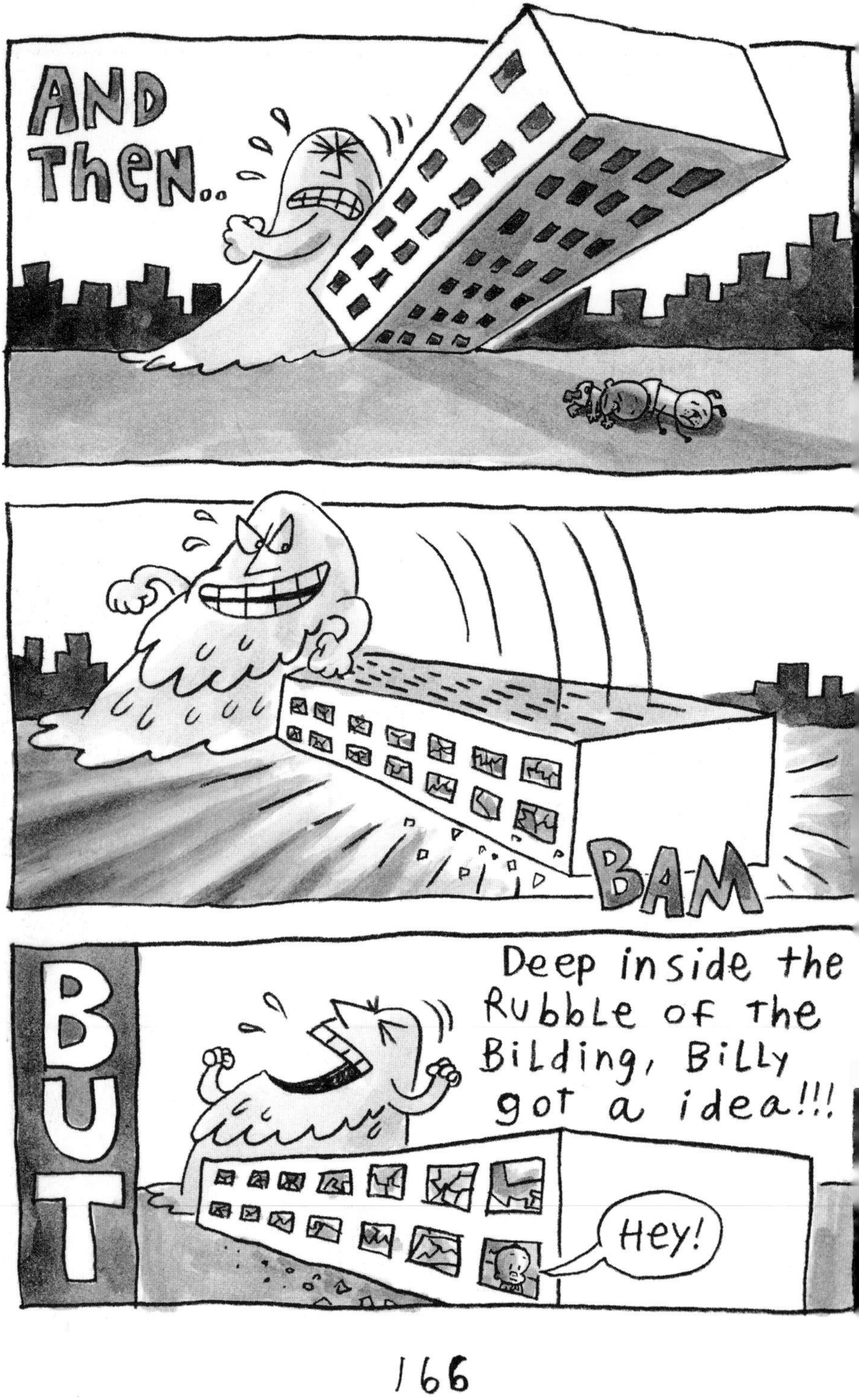
AND
Then..
BAM
BUT
Deep inside the
Rubble of the
Bilding, Billy
got a idea!!!
Hey!

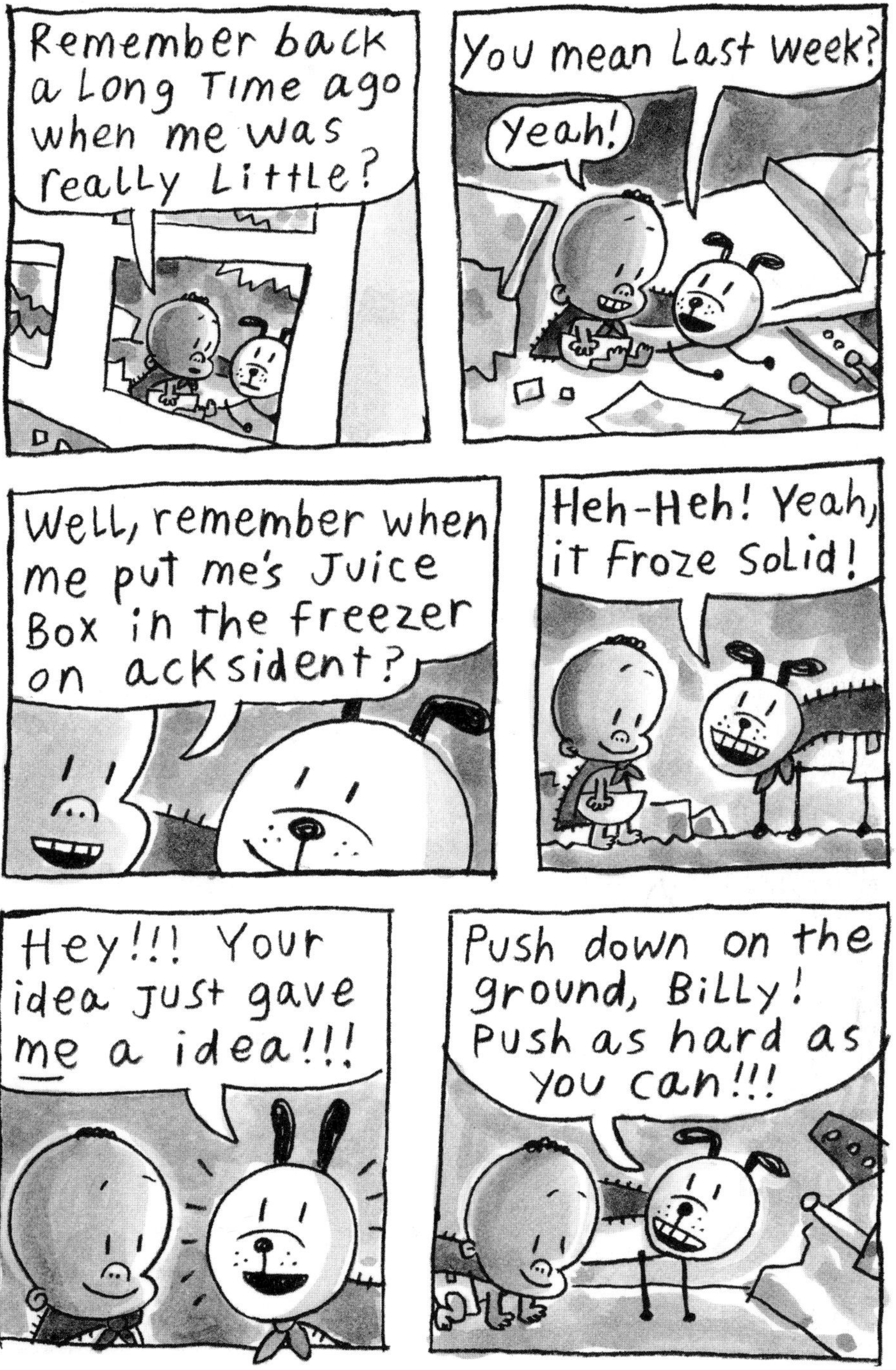
Remember back a Long Time ago when me was really Little?
You mean Last week?
Yeah!
Well, remember when me put me's Juice Box in the freezer on acksident?
Heh-Heh! Yeah, it Froze Solid!
Hey!!! Your idea just gave me a idea!!!
Push down on the ground, Billy! Push as hard as you can!!!

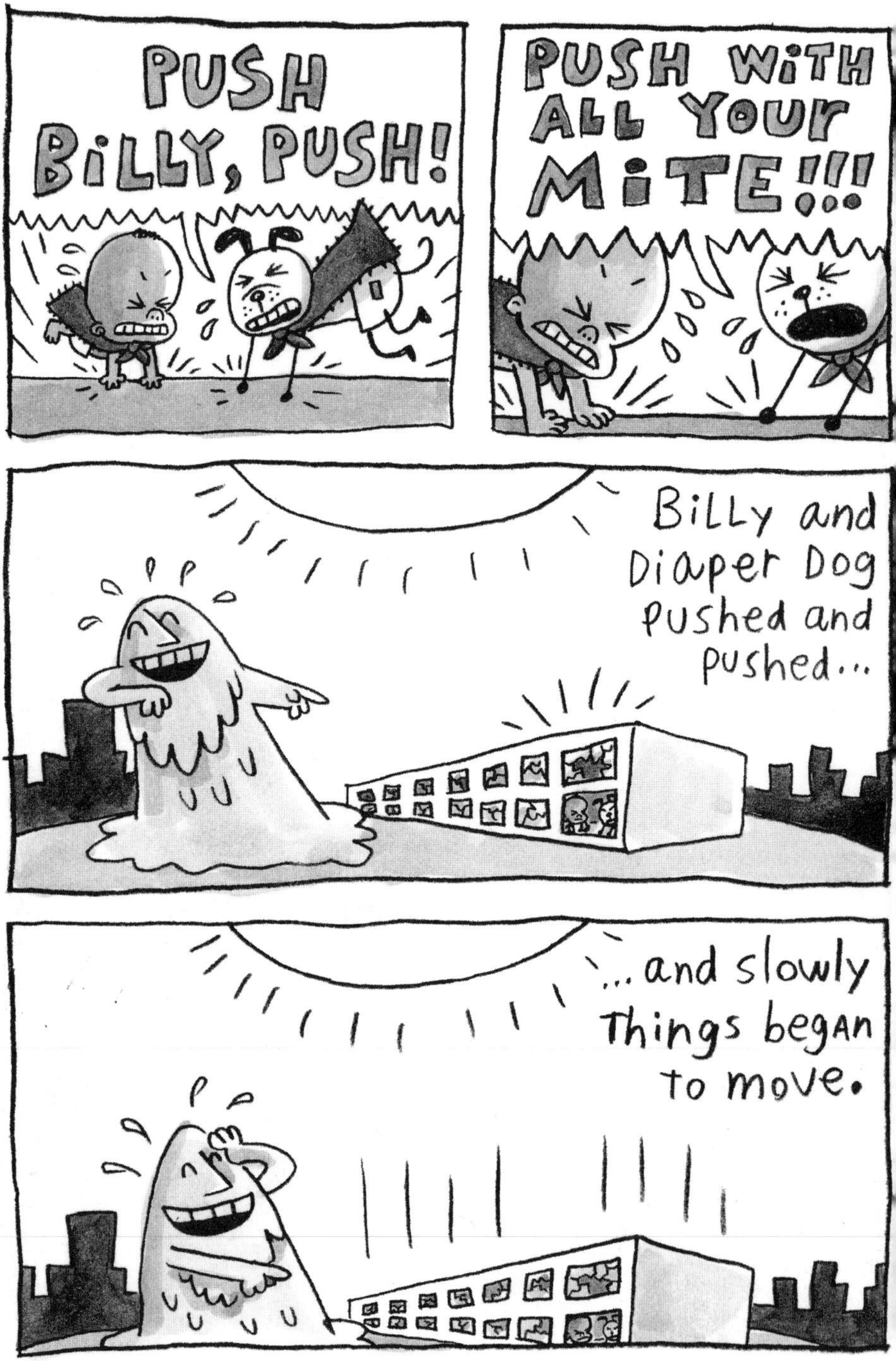
PUSH BILLY, PUSH!
PUSH WITH ALL YOUR MITE!!!
Billy and Diaper Dog pushed and pushed...
...and slowly Things began to move.

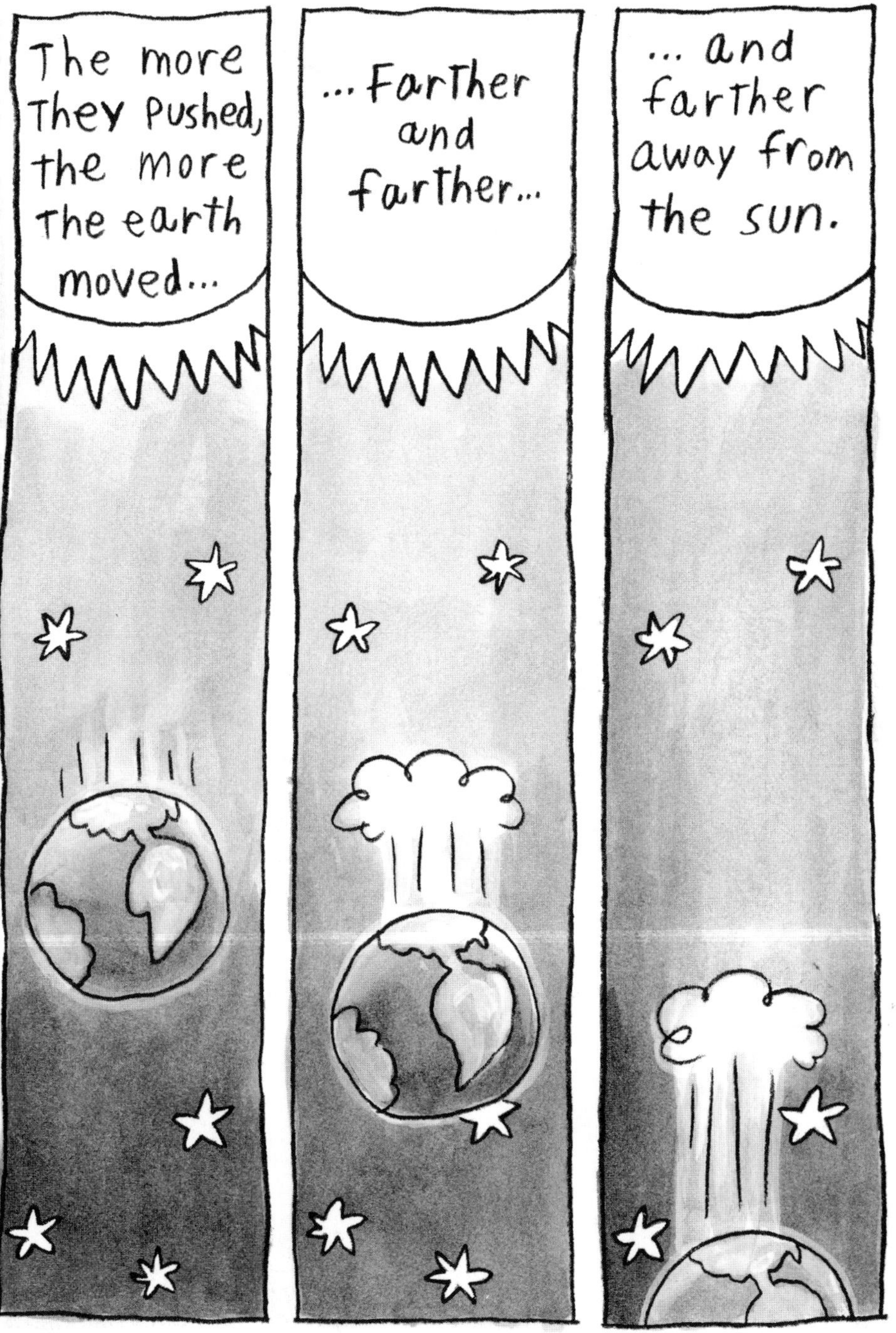
The more they pushed, the more the earth moved...
...farther and farther...
...and farther away from the sun.

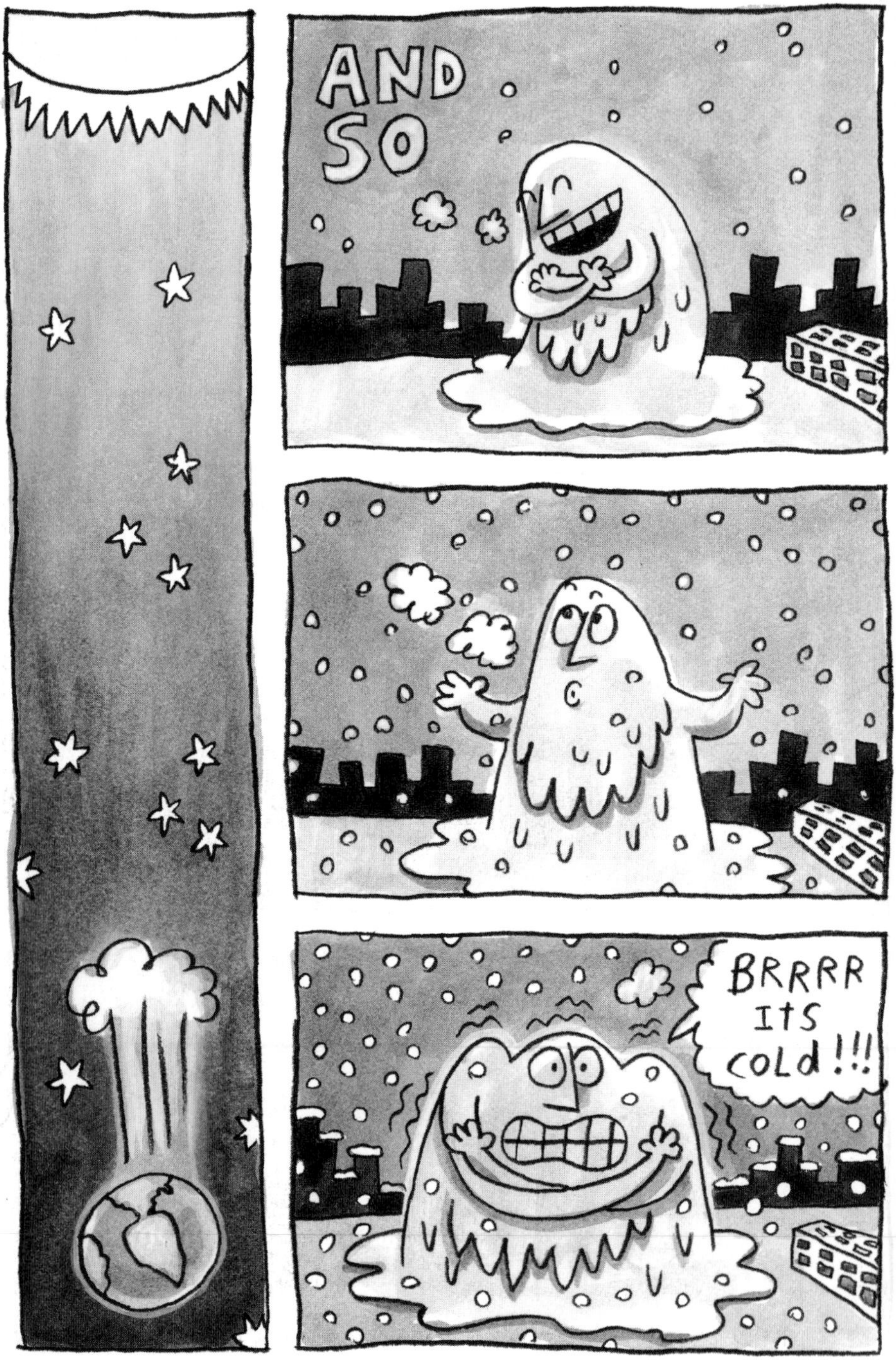
AND SO
BRRRR ITS COLd!!!

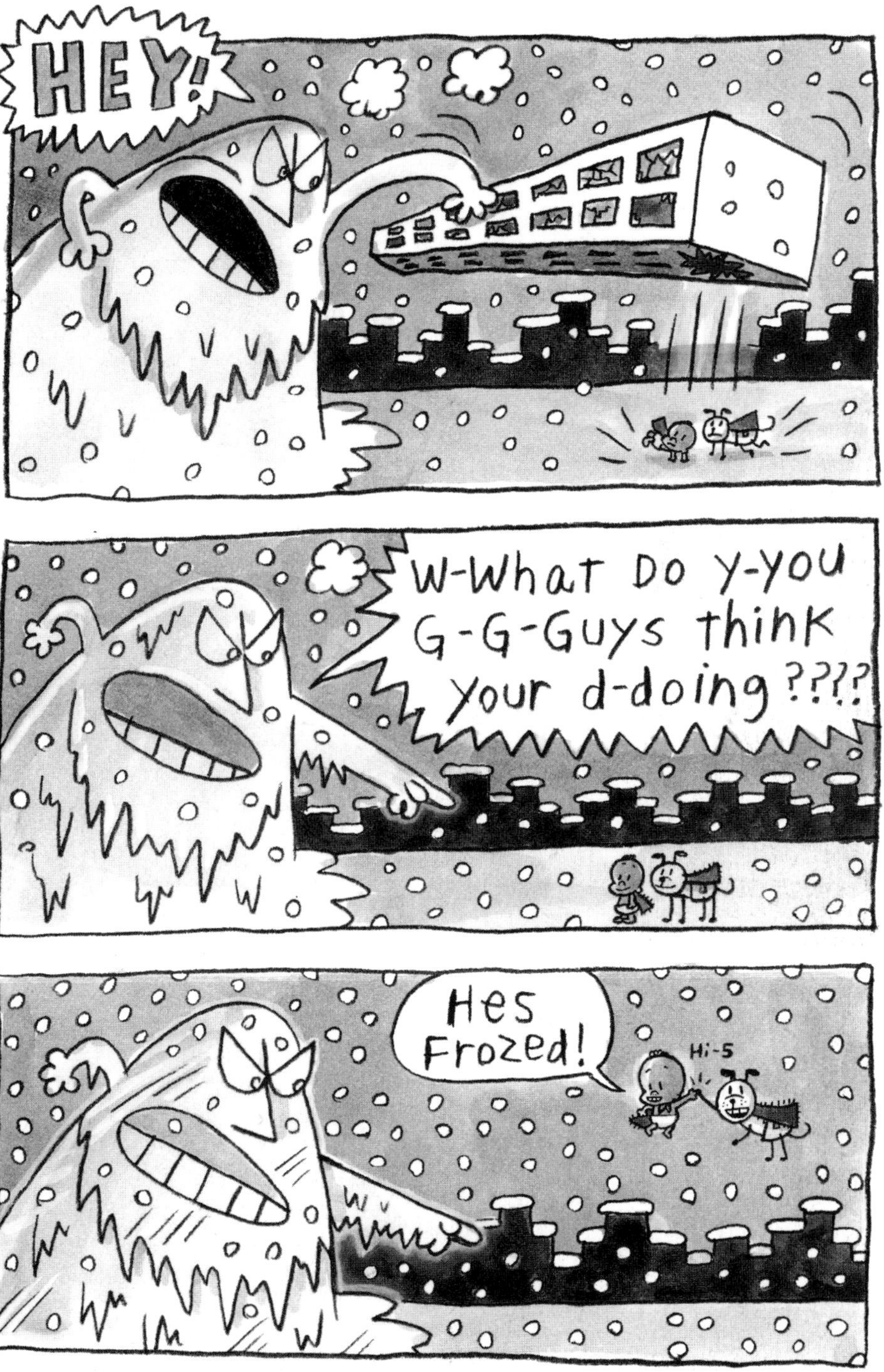
HEY!
W-What Do y-you G-G-Guys think your d-doing????
Hes Frozed!
Hi-5

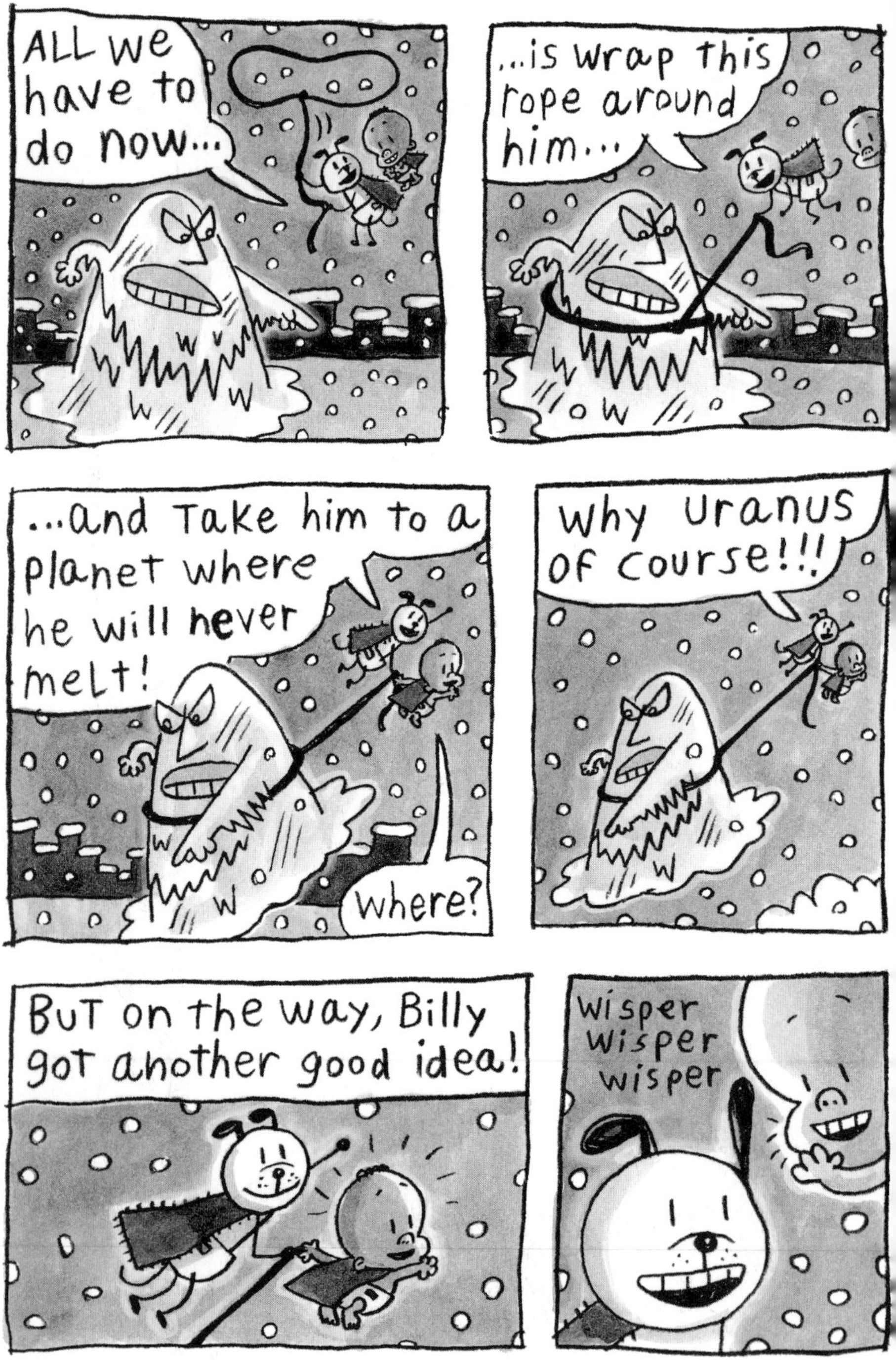
ALL we have to do now...
...is wrap this rope around him...
...and Take him to a planet where he will never melt!
Where?
Why Uranus of course!!!
BuT on the way, Billy got another good idea!
wisper wisper wisper

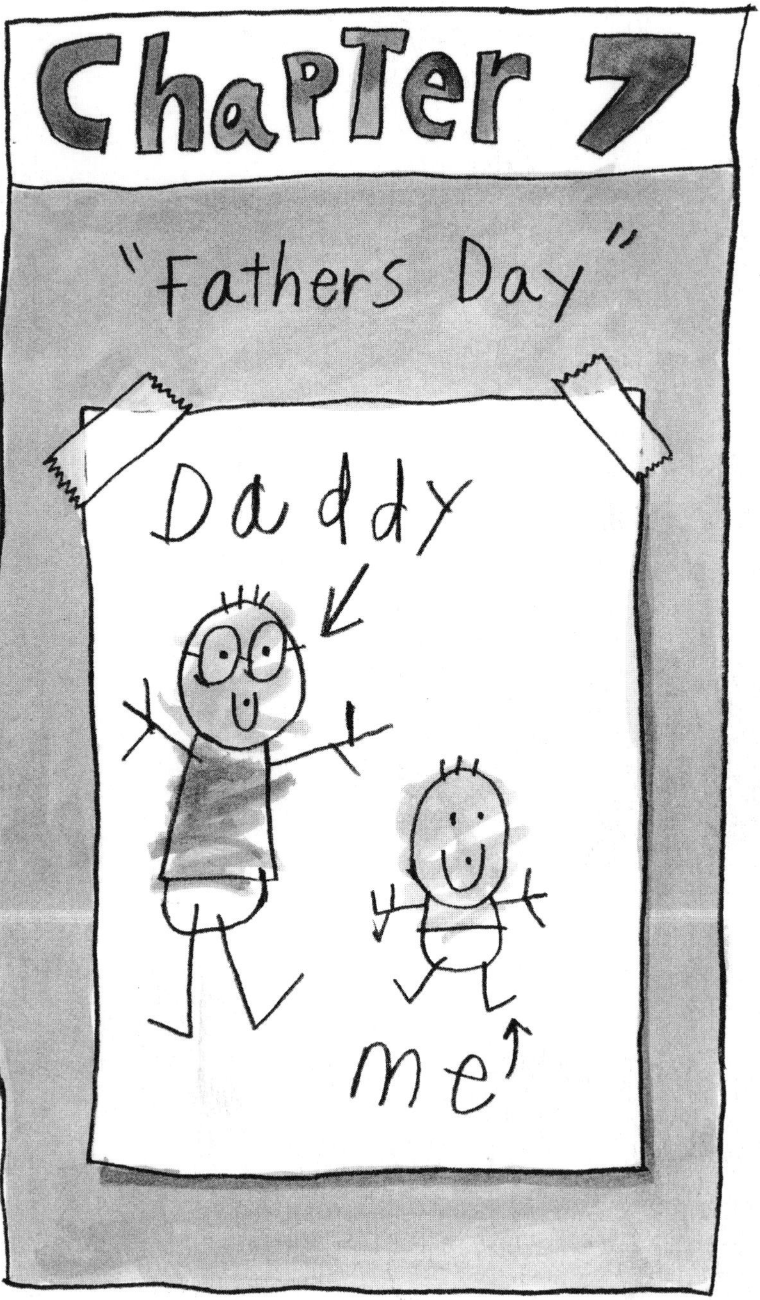
Chapter 7
"Fathers Day"
Daddy
me

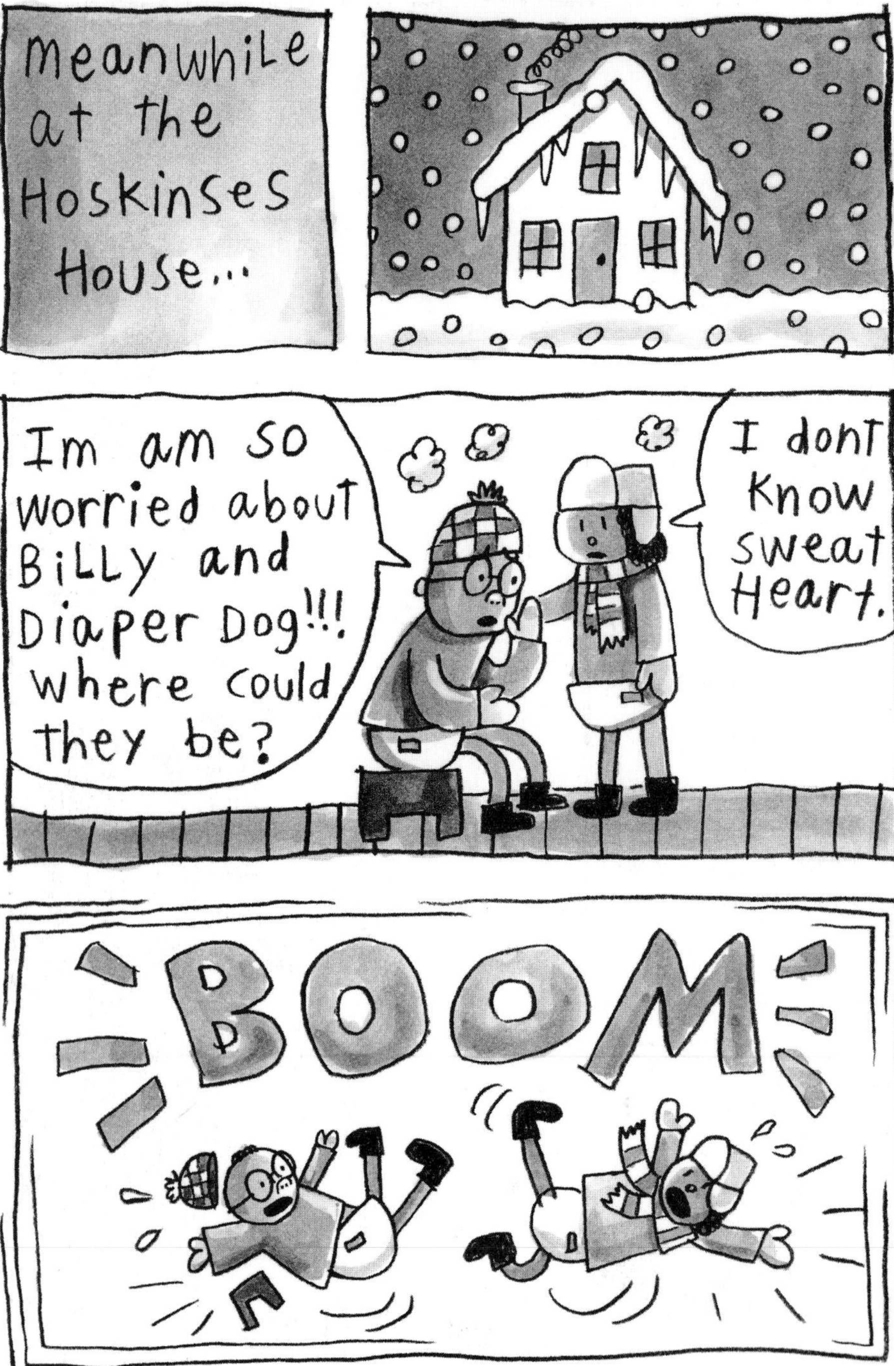
Meanwhile at the Hoskinses House...
Im am so worried about Billy and Diaper Dog!!! where could they be?
I dont know sweat Heart.
BOOM

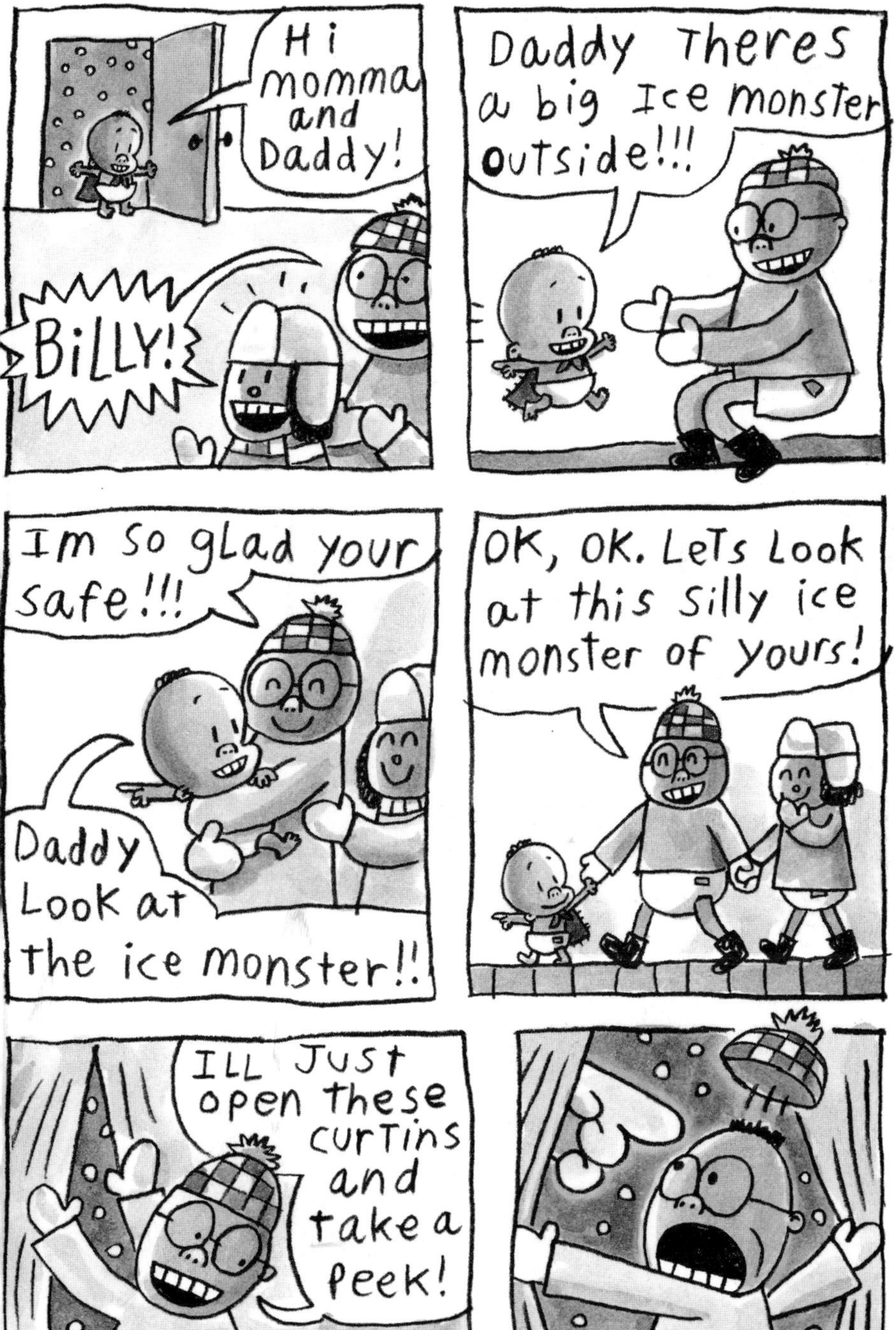
Hi momma and Daddy!
BiLLY!
Daddy Theres a big Ice monster outside!!!
Im so glad your safe!!!
Daddy Look at the ice monster!!
OK, OK. LeTs Look at this silly ice monster of yours!
ILL JusT open these curTins and Take a Peek!

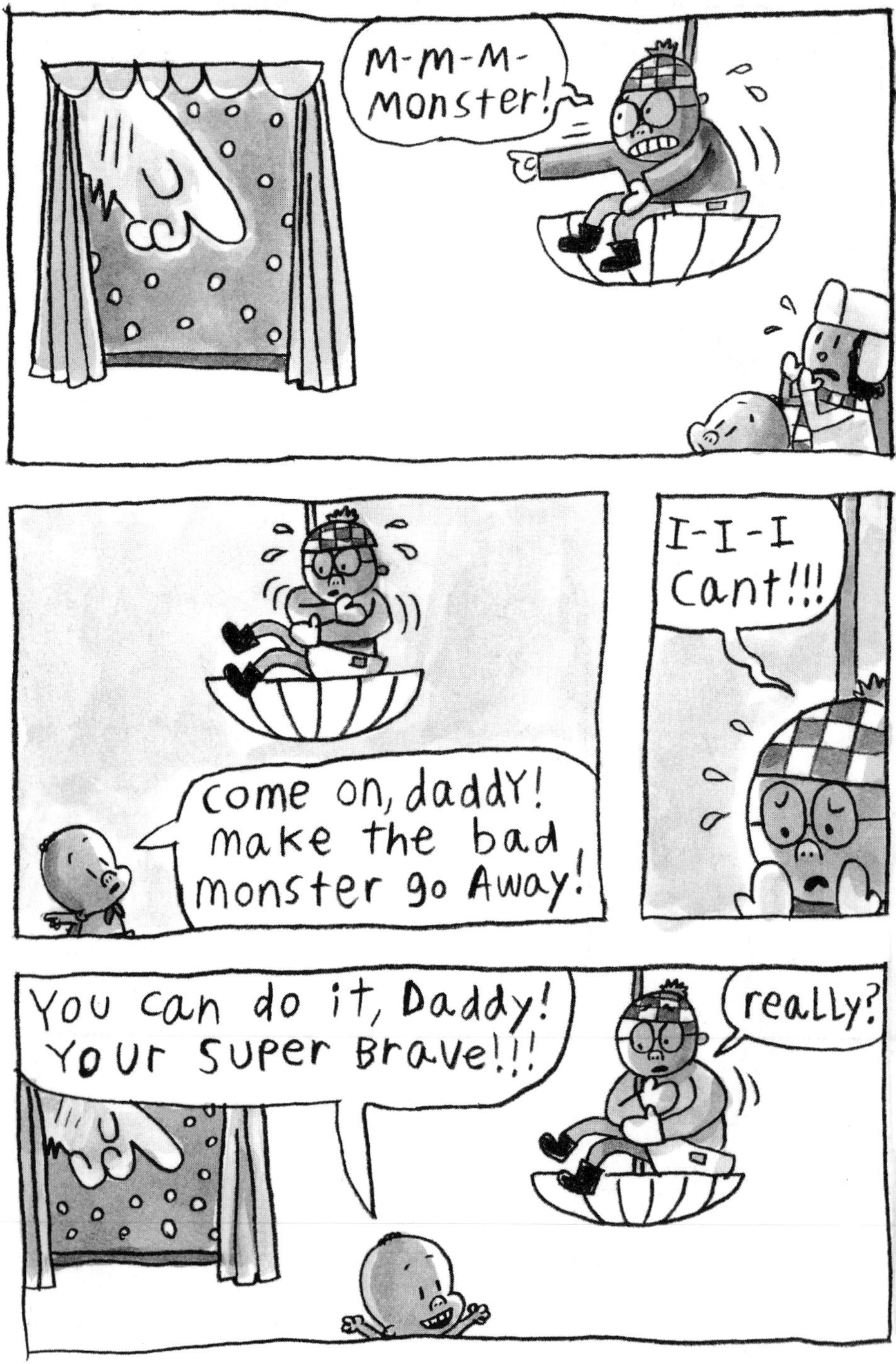
M-M-M-
Monster!
I-I-I
Cant!!!
come on, daddY! make the bad monster go Away!
You can do it, Daddy! Your Super Brave!!!
really?

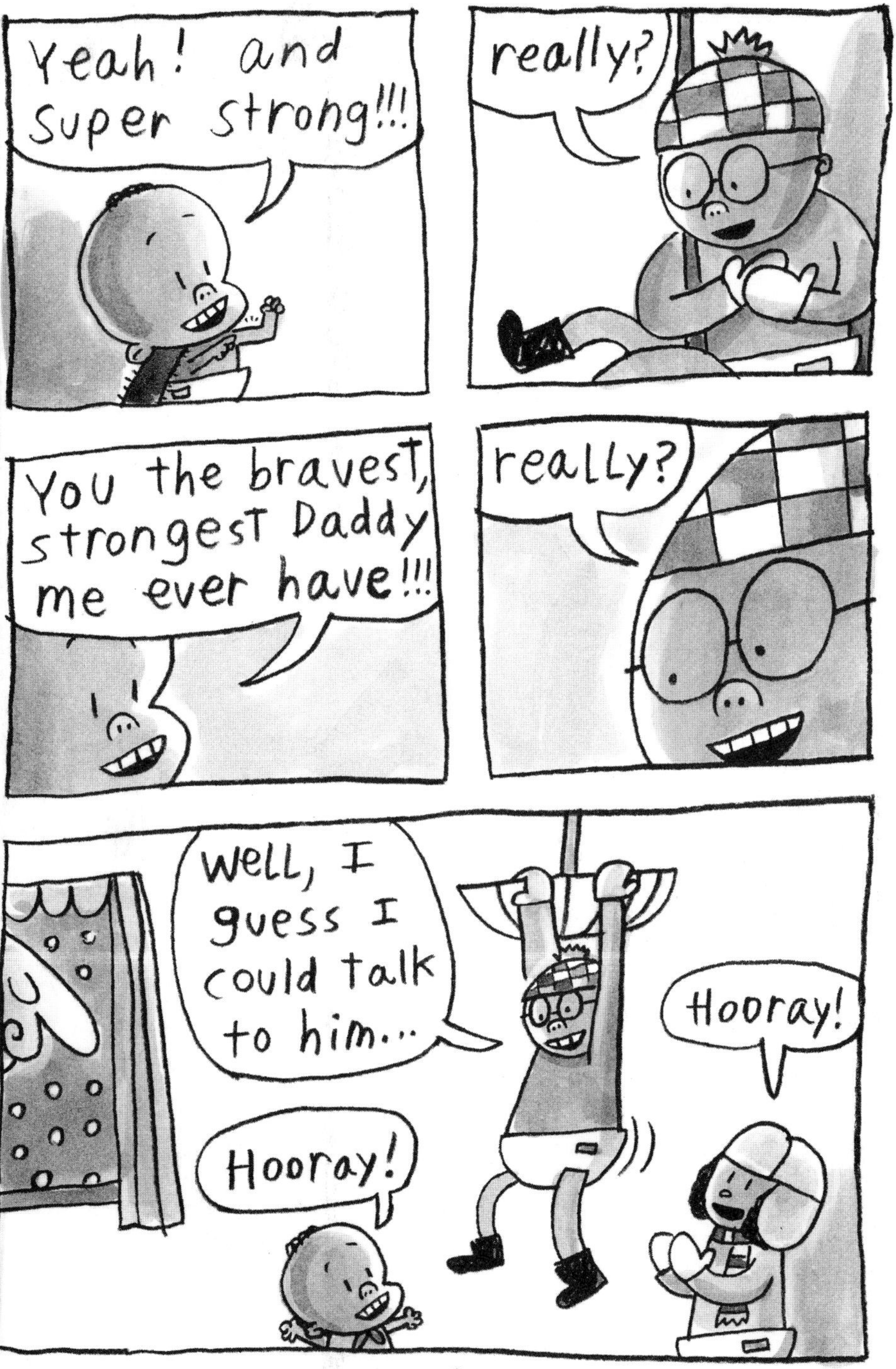
Yeah! and
Super strong!!!
really?
You the bravest,
strongest Daddy
me ever have!!!
really?
Well, I
guess I
could talk
to him...
Hooray!
Hooray!

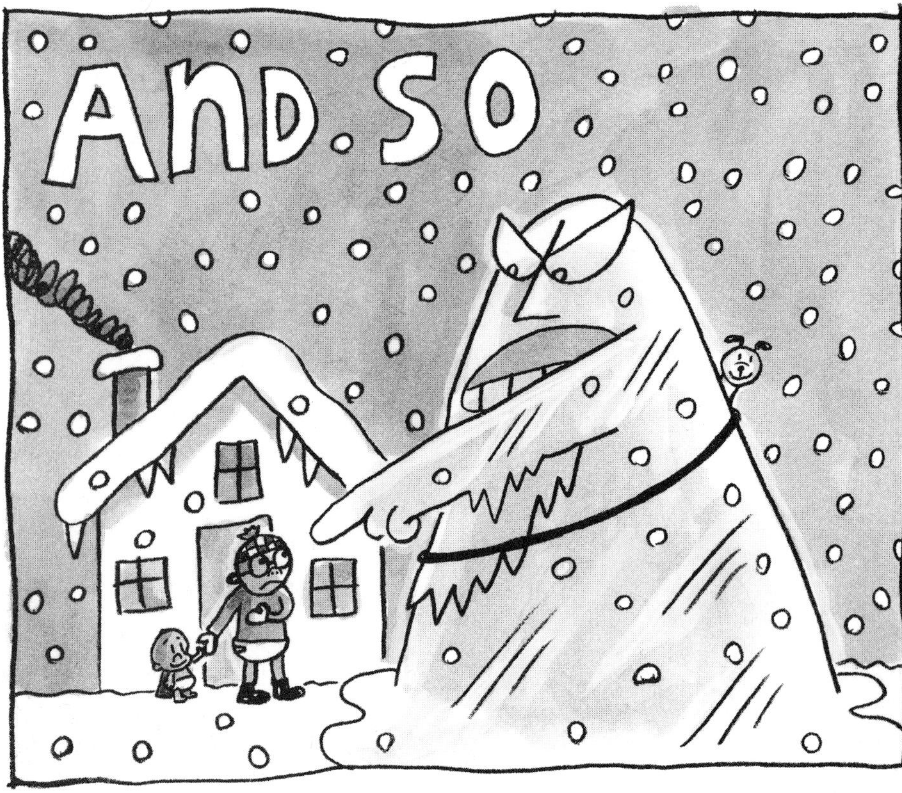
AND SO

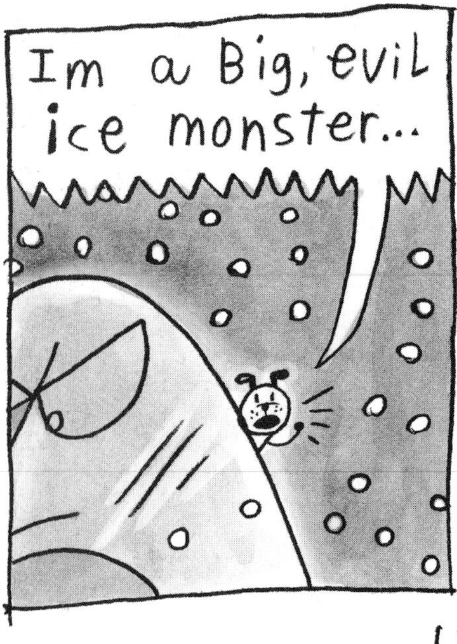
Im a Big, evil ice monster...

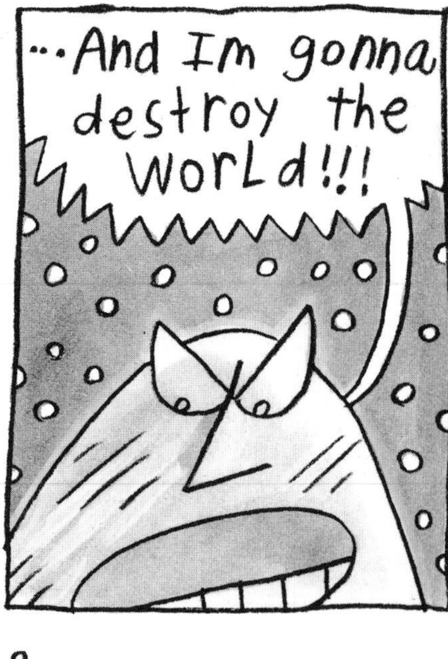
...And Im gonna destroy the WorLd!!!

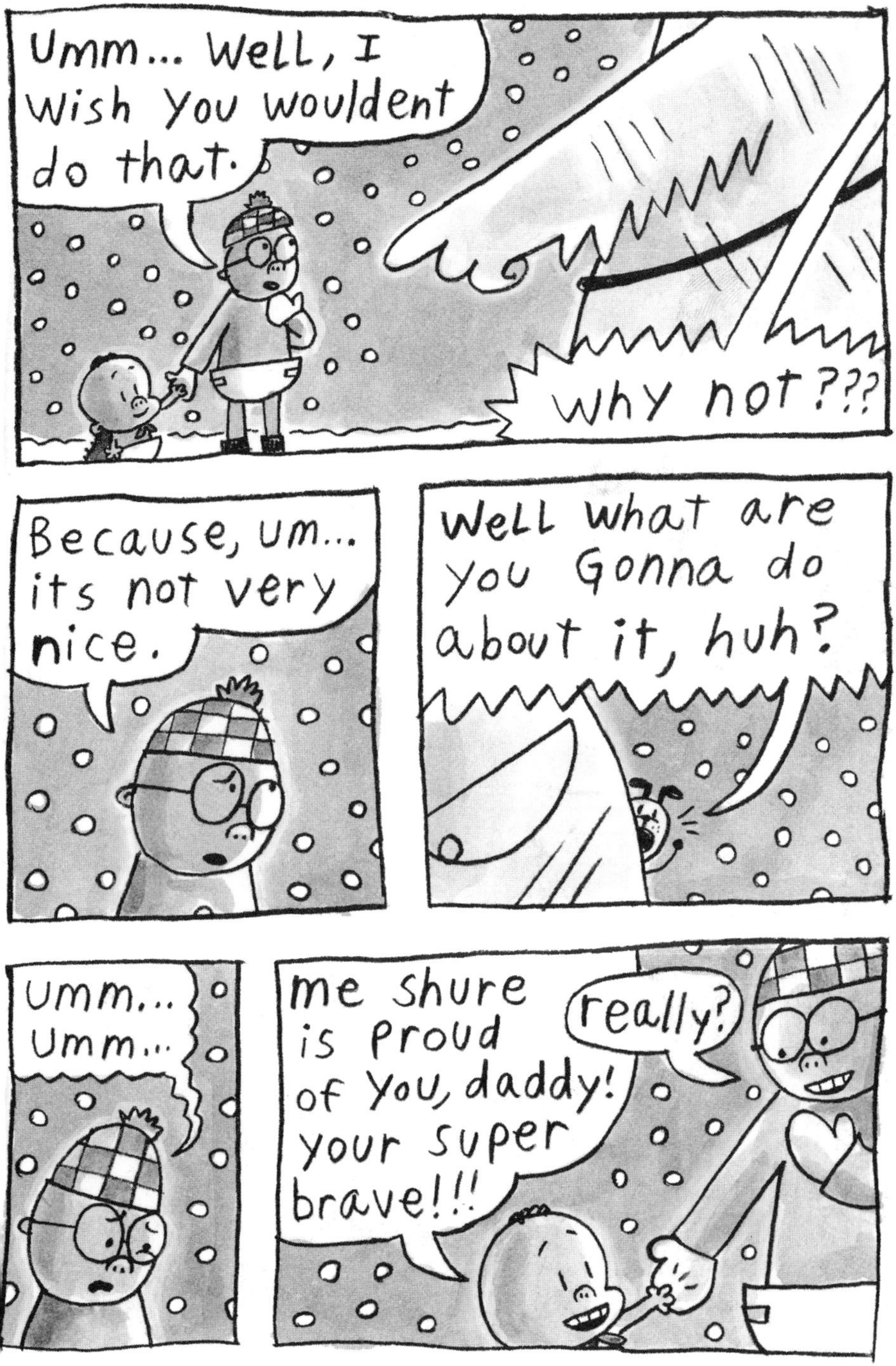
Umm... Well, I wish you wouldent do that.
Why not???
Because, um... its not very nice.
Well what are you Gonna do about it, huh?
Umm... Umm...
me shure is proud of you, daddy! your super brave!!!
really?

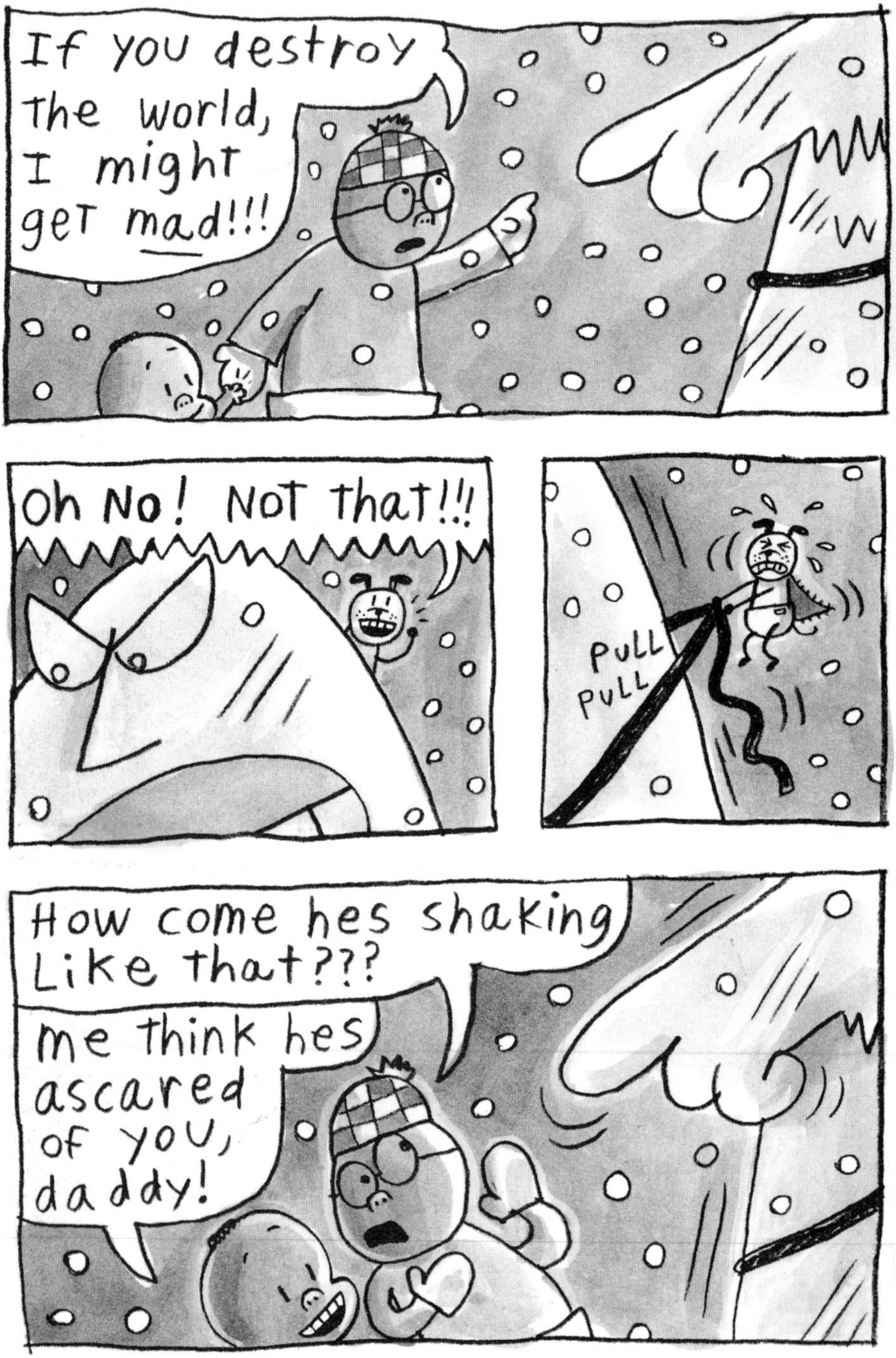
If you destroy the world, I might get mad!!!
Oh No! Not That!!!
PULL
PULL
How come hes shaking Like that???
me think hes ascared of you, daddy!

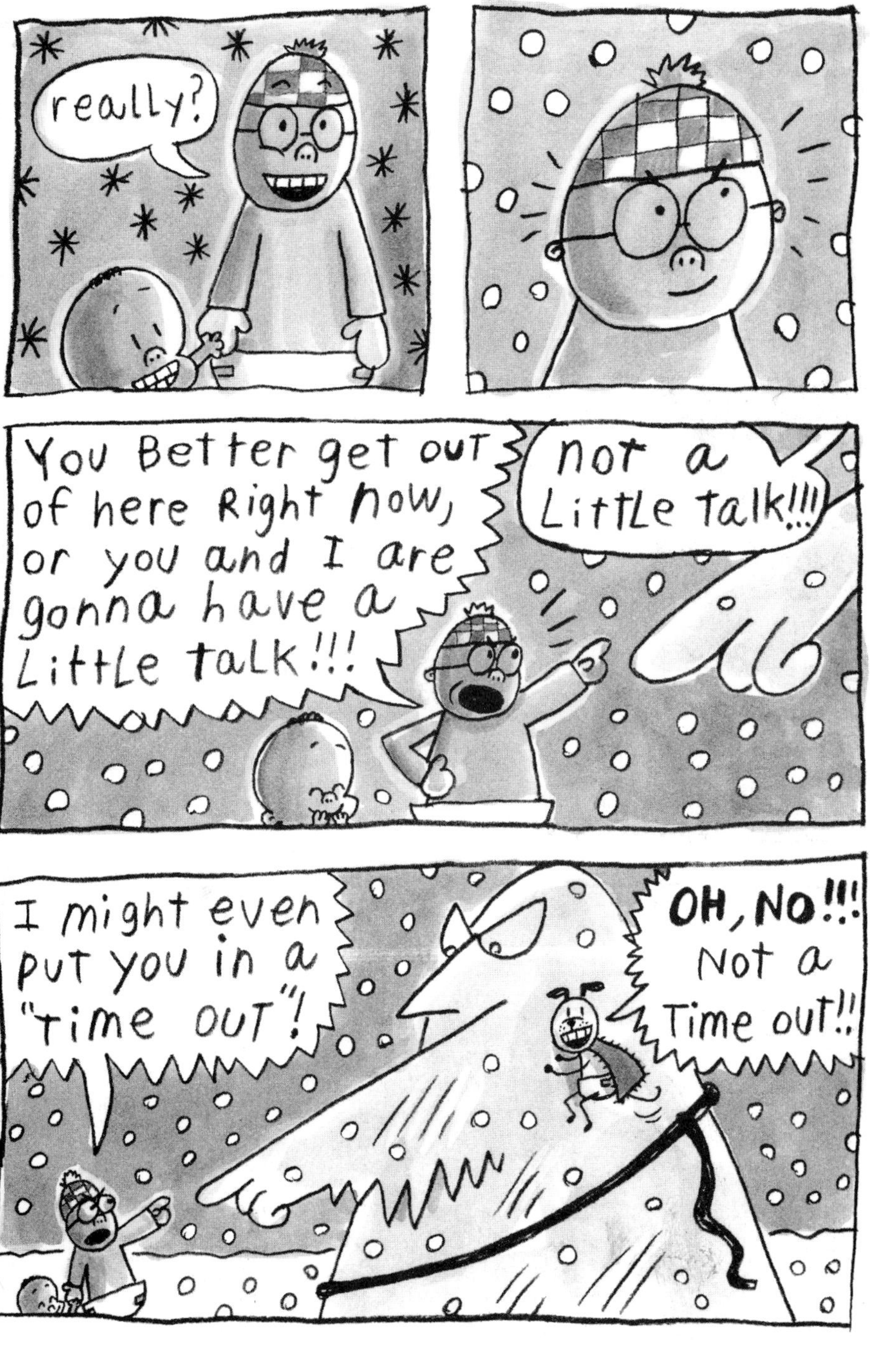
really?
You Better get out of here Right now, or you and I are gonna have a Little talk!!!
not a Little talk!!!
I might even put you in a "time out"!
OH, NO!!! Not a Time out!!

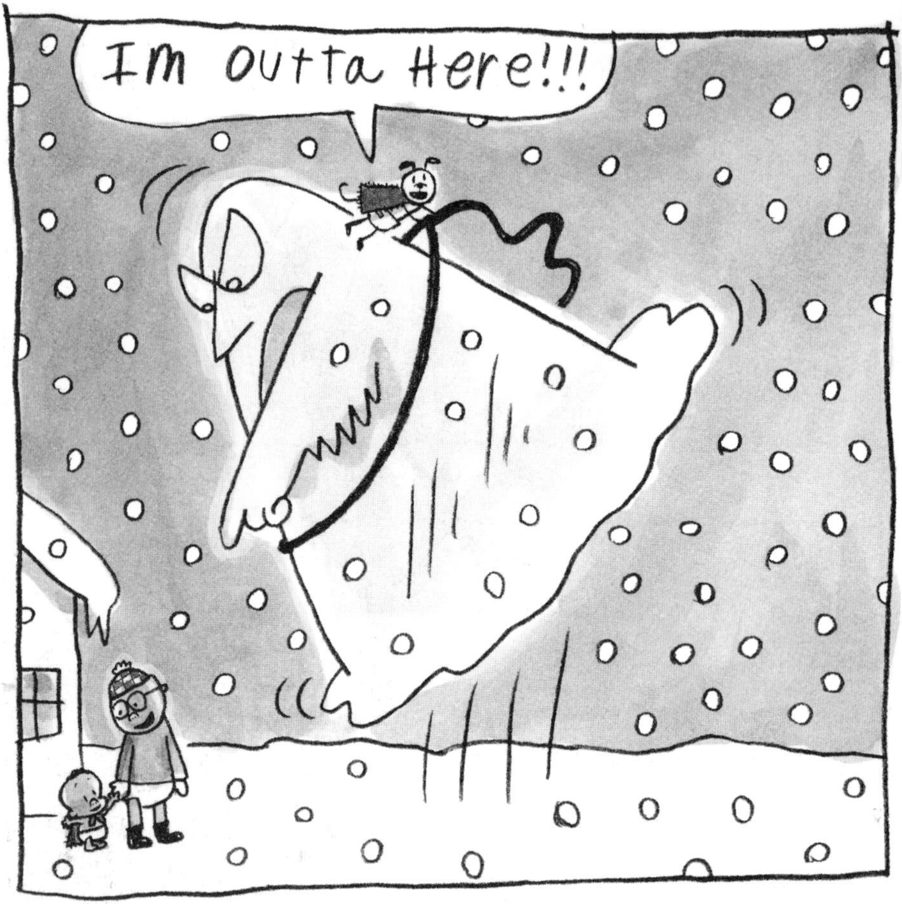
Im outta Here!!!

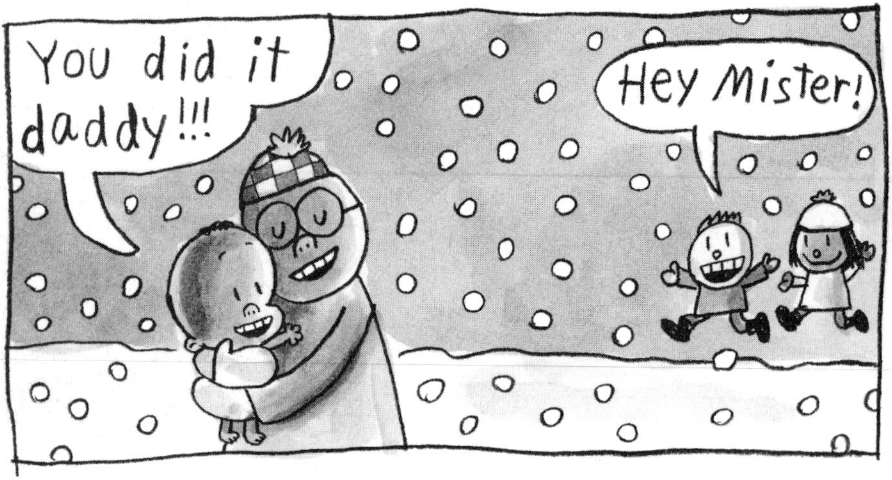
You did it daddy!!!
Hey Mister!

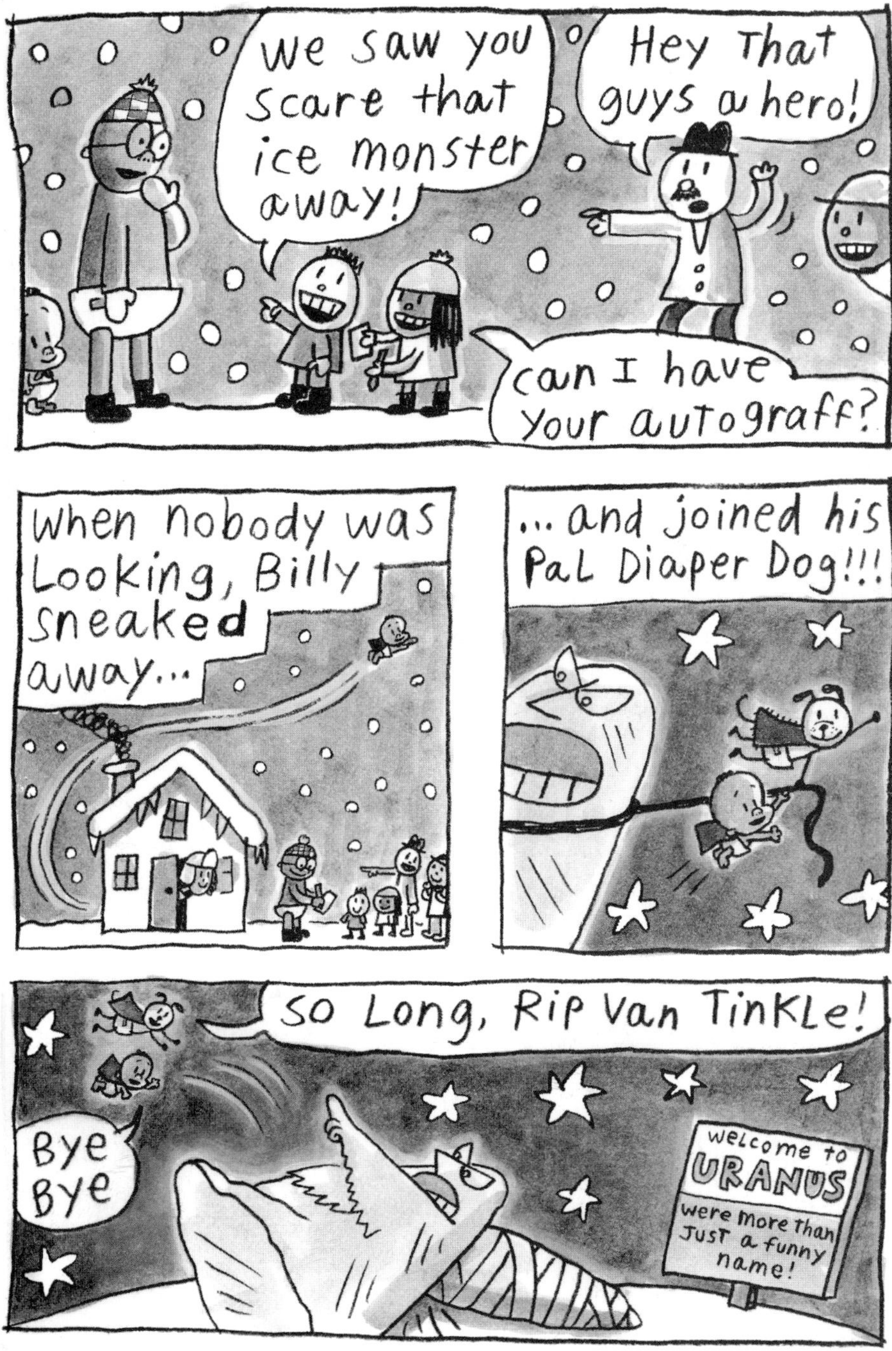
We saw you Scare that ice monster away!
Hey That guys a hero!
can I have your autograff?
When nobody was Looking, Billy sneaked away...
...and joined his PaL Diaper Dog!!!
So Long, Rip Van TinkLe!
Bye Bye
welcome to URANUS
were more than just a funny name!

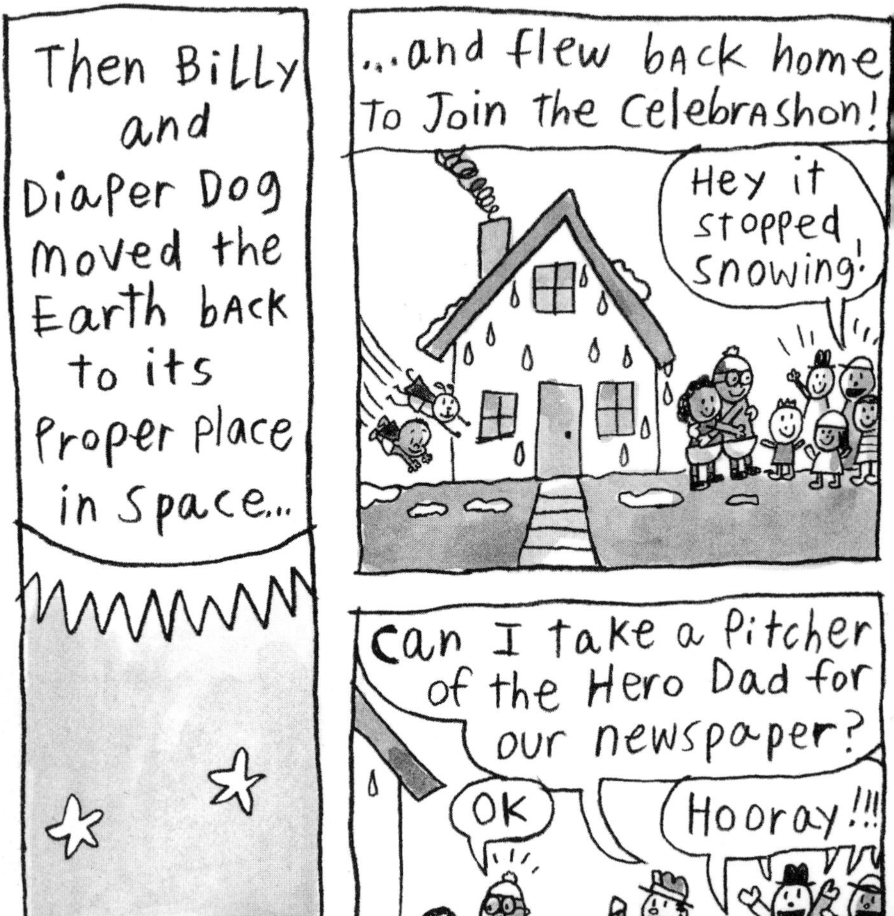

Left Hand Here.

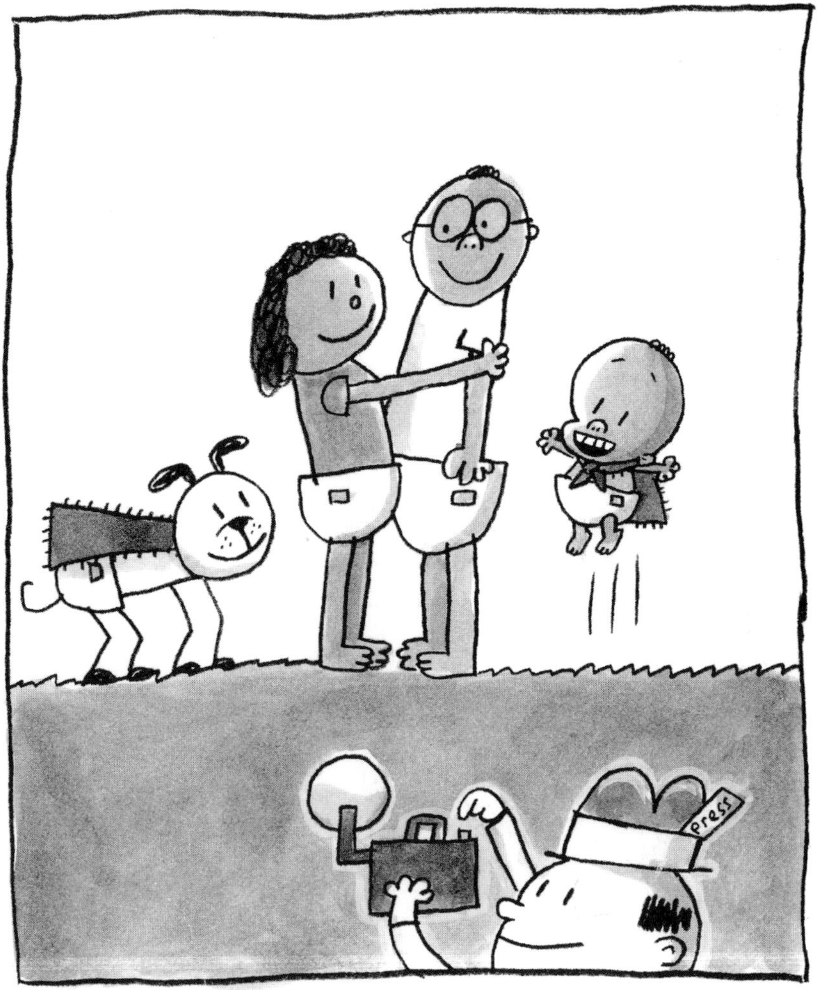
press

say Cheese!!!

Right thumb Here

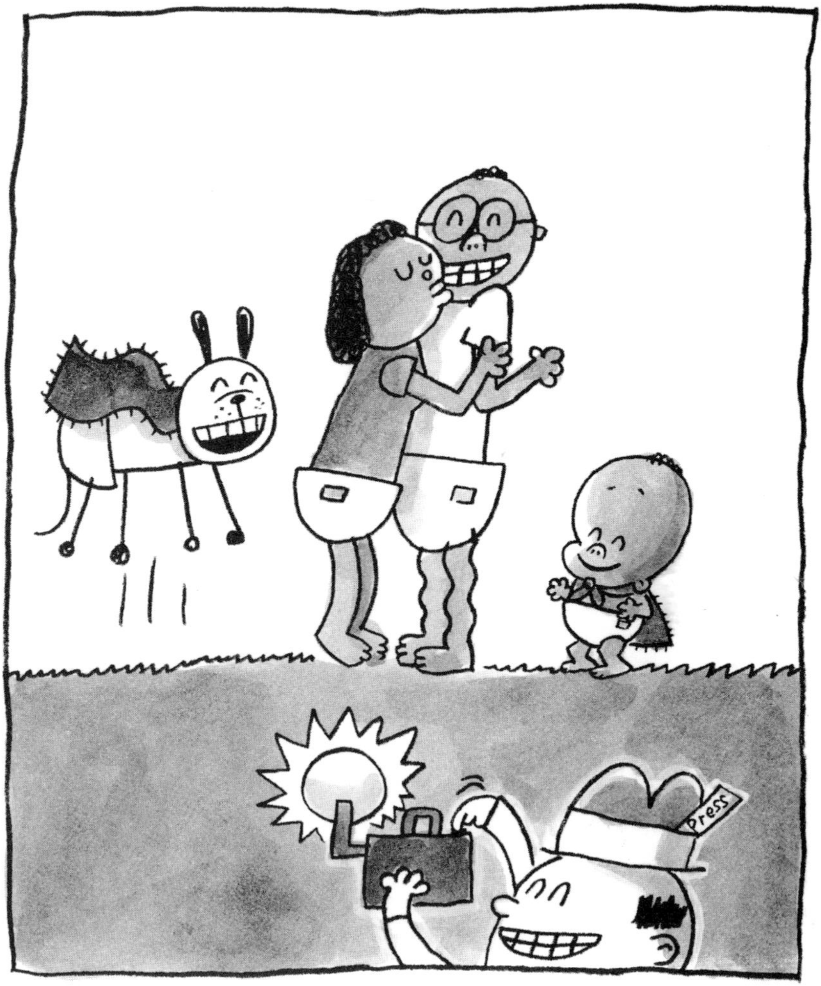
Press

say Cheese!!!

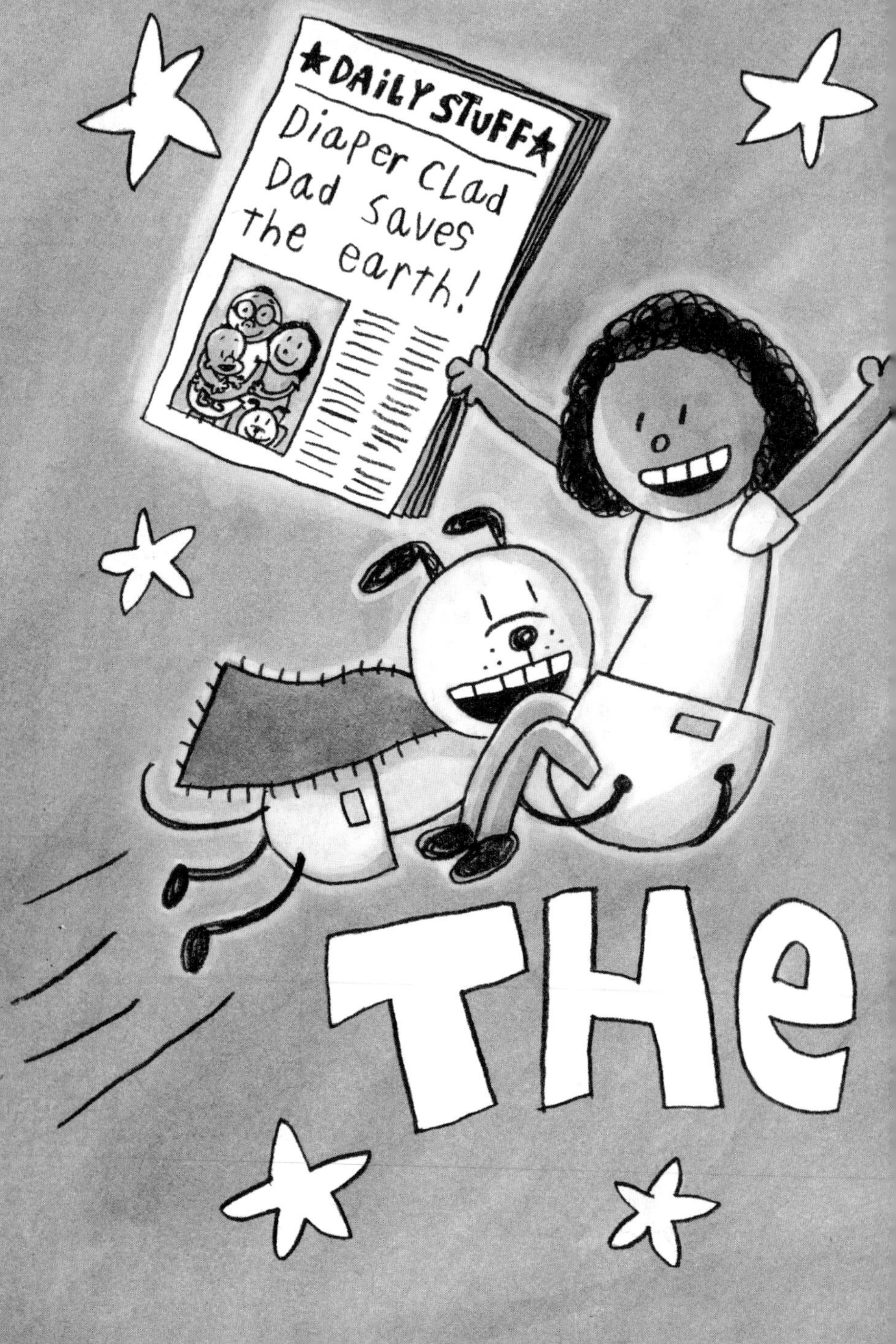
★DAILY STUFF★
Diaper Clad Dad Saves the earth!
THe

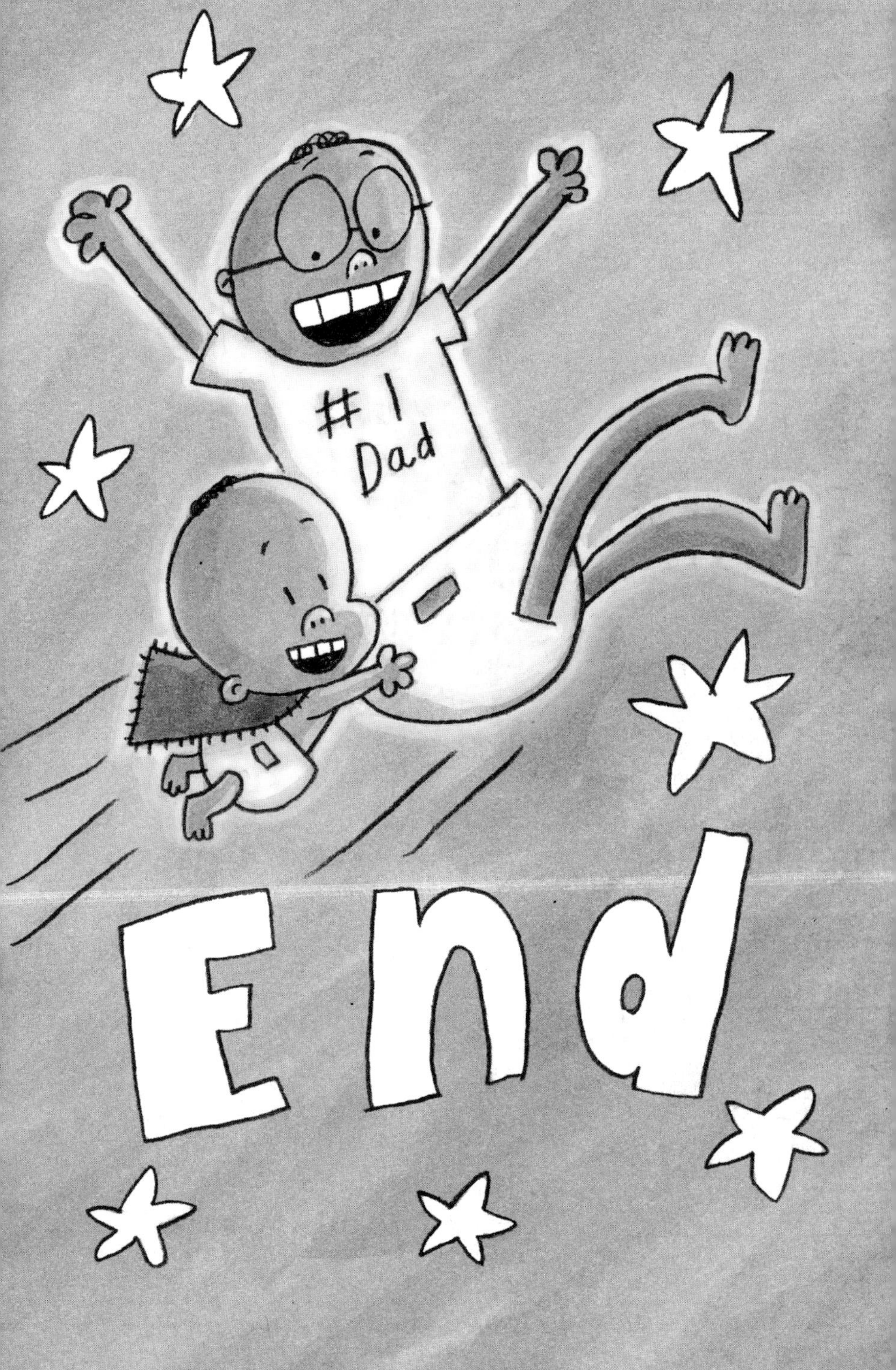
#1 Dad
End

READ GEORGE AND HAROLD'S FIRST TWO EPIC ADVENTURES!

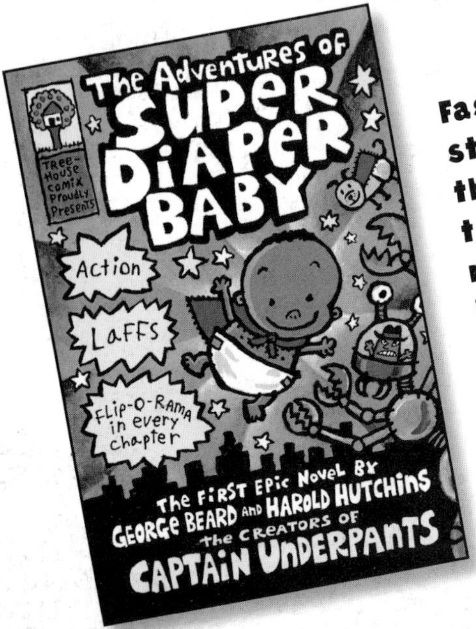

The Adventures of
SUPER DIAPER BABY
Tree-House Comix Proudly Presents
Action
Laffs
Flip-O-Rama in every chapter
The First Epic Novel by
George Beard and Harold Hutchins
the creators of
Captain Underpants

Faster than a speeding stroller, more powerful than diaper rash, and able to leap tall buildings without making poopy-stinkers, it's Super Diaper Baby!

"Readers . . . will revel in the humor." —*Kirkus Reviews*

"All the kid-tickling silliness that fans . . . can't get enough of." —*Publishers Weekly*

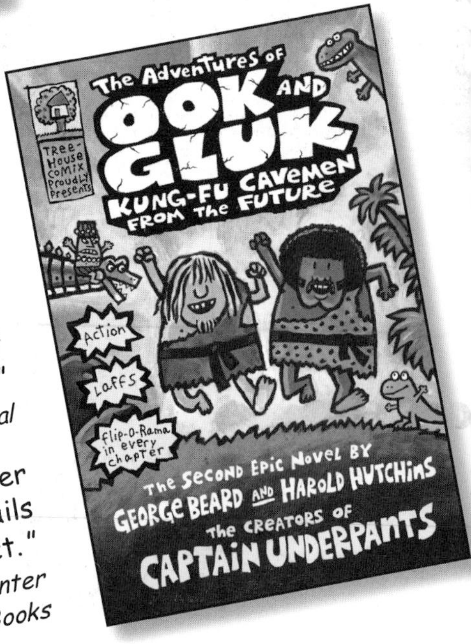

The Adventures of
Ook and Gluk
Kung-Fu Cavemen from the Future
Tree-House Comix Proudly Presents
Action
Laffs
Flip-O-Rama in every chapter
The Second Epic Novel by
George Beard and Harold Hutchins
the creators of
Captain Underpants

Meet Ook and Gluk, the two coolest caveboys to step out of the Stone Age!

"Completely immature . . . completely hilarious. . . . Destined to fly off the shelves."
—*School Library Journal*

"Pilkey continues to offer the exact goofy, quirky details that [readers] will find perfect."
—*The Bulletin of the Center for Children's Books*

What ever happened to Professor Pooypants?!!
Find out in . . .

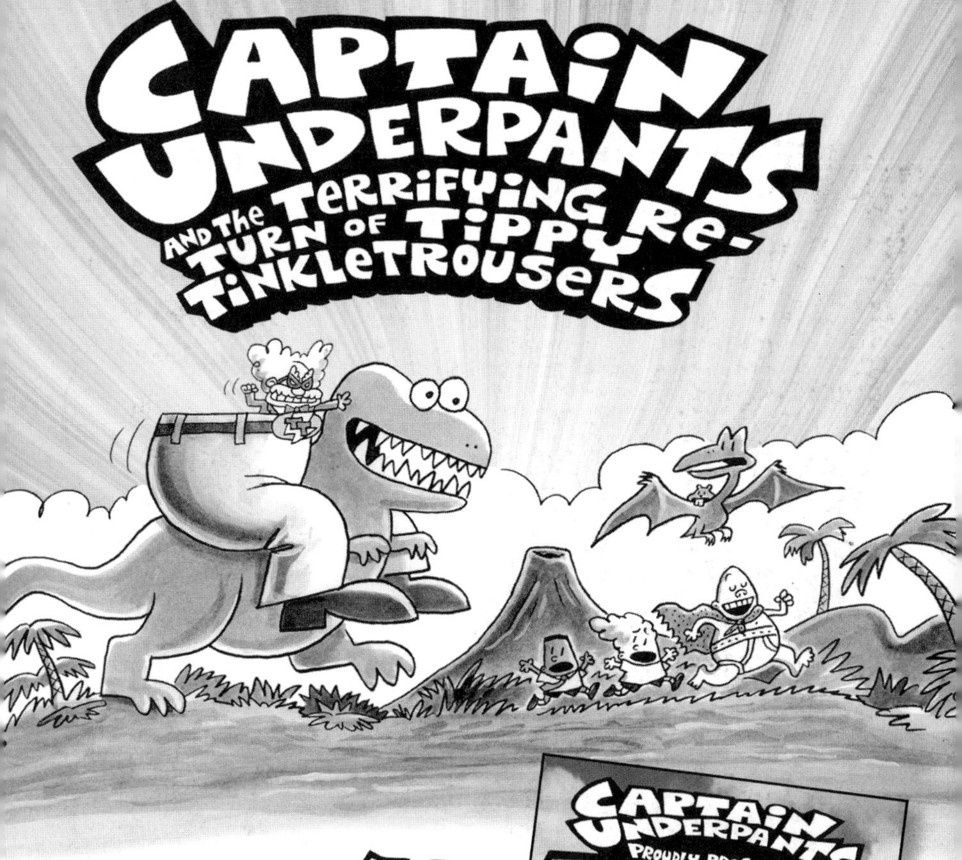
CAPTAIN UNDERPANTS
AND THE TERRIFYING RE-TURN OF TIPPY TINKLETROUSERS

ALSO COMING SOON-ISH

Get ready for a zany new adventure starring the Fantastically Awesome Ranger Team Squad!

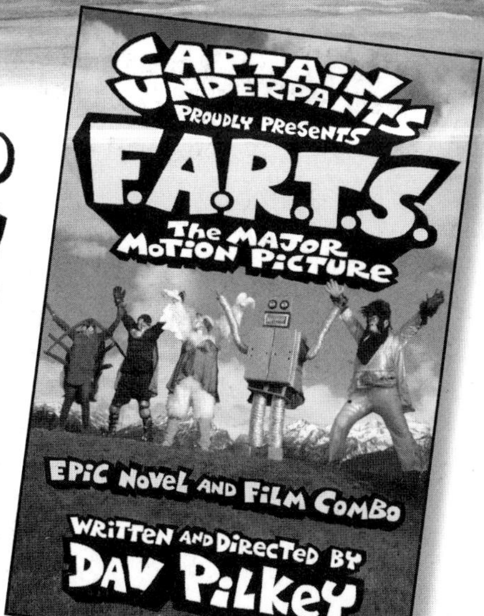
CAPTAIN UNDERPANTS
PROUDLY PRESENTS
F.A.R.T.S.
THE MAJOR MOTION PICTURE
EPIC NOVEL AND FILM COMBO
WRITTEN AND DIRECTED BY
DAV PILKEY

The **SUPER DiaPer BABY** ADVeNTURe CONTiNUeS ONLiNe AT WWW.PiLKeY.COM AND WWW.SCHOLASTiC.COM

COOL!

Free Music, Video Games, Movies, and MORE!

Free!

HoW-2-DRAW Petey (Part 4 of 8)

HoW-2-DRAW Rip Van Tinkle (Part 3 of

HoW-2-DRAW Pee drop (side) (Part 6 of 8)

Learn to draw more than 20 characters from George and Harold's epic novels!

AWeSome!

MAKE YOUR OWN **PeTeY** the world's most evilest Cat!

HAW! HAW!